continued . . .

"Witty with a splash of romance and a dark puzzle to unravel, *Crouching Vampire, Hidden Fang* is a sure-fire hit!"
—Romance Junkies

Zen and the Art of Vampires

"A jocular action-packed tale . . . [a] wonderful zany series."
—*Midwest Book Review*

"Has all of the paranormal action, romance, and humor that fans of the author look for in her books. This is a fast-moving read with sizzling chemistry and a touch of suspense."
—Darque Reviews

"Pia Thomason just might be my favorite heroine ever . . . an entrancing story, and a very good escape."
—*The Romance Reader*

"I completely loved *Zen and the Art of Vampires*! . . . The chemistry between Pia and Kristoff sizzles all the way through the novel. . . . I don't think I can wait for the next Dark Ones installment! Please hurry, Katie!"   —Romance Junkies

"Steamy."   —*Booklist*

The Last of the Red-Hot Vampires

"MacAlister's fast-paced romp is a delight with all its quirky twists and turns, which even include a murder mystery."
—*Booklist*

"A wild zany romantic fantasy. . . . Paranormal romance readers will enjoy this madcap tale of the logical physicist who finds love."   —The Best Reviews

"A fascinating paranormal read that will captivate you."
—Romance Reviews Today

"A pleasurable afternoon of reading."
—The Romance Reader

"The sexy humor, wild secondary characters, and outlandish events make her novels pure escapist pleasure!"
—*Romantic Times*

Also by Katie MacAlister

Paranormal Romances

STEAMED, A Steampunk Romance
ME AND MY SHADOW, A Novel of the Silver Dragons
CROUCHING VAMPIRE, HIDDEN FANG,
A Dark Ones Novel
ZEN AND THE ART OF VAMPIRES, A Dark Ones Novel
UP IN SMOKE, A Novel of the Silver Dragons
PLAYING WITH FIRE, A Novel of the Silver Dragons
HOLY SMOKES, An Aisling Grey, Guardian, Novel
LIGHT MY FIRE, An Aisling Grey, Guardian, Novel
FIRE ME UP, An Aisling Grey, Guardian, Novel
YOU SLAY ME, An Aisling Grey, Guardian, Novel
THE LAST OF THE RED-HOT VAMPIRES
EVEN VAMPIRES GET THE BLUES

Contemporary Romances

BLOW ME DOWN
HARD DAY'S KNIGHT
THE CORSET DIARIES
MEN IN KILTS

Katie MacAlister

Love in the Time of Dragons

A Novel of the  Light Dragons

A SIGNET BOOK

SIGNET
Published by New American Library, a division of
Penguin Group (USA) Inc., 375 Hudson Street,
New York, New York 10014, USA
Penguin Group (Canada), 90 Eglinton Avenue East, Suite 700, Toronto,
Ontario M4P 2Y3, Canada (a division of Pearson Penguin Canada Inc.)
Penguin Books Ltd., 80 Strand, London WC2R 0RL, England
Penguin Ireland, 25 St. Stephen's Green, Dublin 2,
Ireland (a division of Penguin Books Ltd.)
Penguin Group (Australia), 250 Camberwell Road, Camberwell, Victoria 3124,
Australia (a division of Pearson Australia Group Pty. Ltd.)
Penguin Books India Pvt. Ltd., 11 Community Centre, Panchsheel Park,
New Delhi - 110 017, India
Penguin Group (NZ), 67 Apollo Drive, Rosedale, North Shore 0632,
New Zealand (a division of Pearson New Zealand Ltd.)
Penguin Books (South Africa) (Pty.) Ltd., 24 Sturdee Avenue,
Rosebank, Johannesburg 2196, South Africa

Penguin Books Ltd., Registered Offices:
80 Strand, London WC2R 0RL, England

First published by Signet, an imprint of New American Library,
a division of Penguin Group (USA) Inc.

First Printing, May 2010
10 9 8 7 6 5 4 3 2 1

Copyright © Katie MacAlister, 2010
All rights reserved

Shortly after I finished writing this book, my beloved furry girl Jazi died. She was my constant companion for twelve years, and literally at my side for the writing of every book, curled up on a bed next to my desk while I tapped away on the keyboard. She was spoiled, demanding, and obstinate in her desire to have her own way. She also gave me more happiness and love than I could ever have hoped for. This book is dedicated to her memory, which will forever remain bright.

Chapter One

"You're going to be on your knees saying prayers for hours if Lady Alice finds you here."

I jumped at the low, gravelly voice, but my heart stopped beating quite so rapidly when I saw who had discovered me. "By the rood, Ulric! You almost scared the humors right out of my belly!"

"Aye, I've no doubt I did," the old man replied, leaning on a battered hoe. "Due to your guilty conscience, I'm thinking. Aren't you supposed to be in the solar with the other women?"

I patted the earth around the early-blooming rose that I had cleared of weeds, and snorted in a delicate, ladylike way. "I was excused."

"Oh, you were, were you? And for what? Not to leave off your sewing and leeching and all those other things Lady Alice tries to teach you."

I got to my feet, dusting the dirt off my knees and hands, looking down my nose at the smaller man, doing my best to intimidate him even though I knew it wouldn't do any good—Ulric had known me since I was a wee babe puling in her swaddling clothes. "And what business is it of yours, good sir?"

He grinned, his teeth black and broken. "You can come over the lady right enough, when you like. Now, what I'm wanting to know is whether you have your mother's leave to be here in the garden, or if you're supposed to be up learning the proper way to be a lady."

I kicked at a molehill. "I *was* excused . . . to use the privy. You know how bad they are—I needed fresh air to recover from the experience."

"You've had enough, judging by the weeding you've done. Get yourself back to the solar with the other women before your mother has my hide for letting you stay out here."

"I . . . er . . . can't."

"And why can't you?" he asked, obviously suspicious.

I cleared my throat and tried to adopt an expression that did not contain one morsel of guilt. "There was an . . . incident."

"Oh, aye?" The expression of suspicion deepened. "What sort of an incident?"

"Nothing serious. Nothing of importance." I plucked a dead leaf from a rosebush. "Nothing of my doing, which you quite obviously believe, a fact that I find most insulting."

"What sort of an incident?" he repeated, ignoring my protests of innocence and outrage.

I threw away the dried leaf and sighed. "It's Lady Susan."

"What have you done to your mother's cousin now?"

"Nothing! I just happened to make up some spider-wort tea, and mayhap I did leave it in the solar next to her chair, along with a mug and a small pot of honey, but how was I to know she'd drink all of it? Besides, I thought everyone knew that spiderwort root tea un-plugs your bowels something fierce."

Ulric stared at me as if it were my bowels that had run free and wild before him.

"Her screams from the privy were so loud, Mother said I might be excused for a bit while she sought one of Papa's guards to break down the privy door, because her ladies were worried that Lady Susan had fallen in and was stuck in the chute."

The look turned to one of unadulterated horror.

"I just hope she looks on the positive side of the whole experience," I added, tamping down the molehill with the toe of my shoe.

"God's blood, you're an unnatural child. What posi-tive side is there to spewing out your guts while stuck in the privy?"

I gave him a lofty look. "Lady Susan always had hor-rible wind. It was worse than the smell from the jakes! The spiderwort tea should clear her out. By rights, she should thank me."

Ulric cast his gaze skyward and muttered something under his breath.

"Besides, I can't go inside now. Mother said for me to stay out of her way because she is too busy getting ready for whoever it is who's visiting Father."

That wasn't entirely true—my mother had actually snapped at me to get out from underfoot and do some-thing helpful other than offer suggestions on how to break down the privy door, and what could be more helpful than tending the garden? The whole keep was gearing up for a visit from some important guest, and I would not want the garden to shame her.

"Get ye gone," Ulric said, shooing me out of the garden. "Else I'll tell your mother how you've spent the last few hours rather than tending to your proper chores. If you're a good lass, perhaps I'll help you with those roses later."

I smiled, feeling as artless as a girl of seventeen could feel, and dashed out of the haven that was the garden and along the dark overhang that led into the upper bailey. It was a glorious almost-summer morning, and my father's serfs were going about their daily tasks with less complaint than was normal. I stopped by the stable to check on the latest batch of kittens, picking out a pretty black-and-white one that I would beg my mother to let me keep, and was just on the way to the kitchen to see if I couldn't wheedle some bread and cheese from the cooks when the dull thud of several horses' hooves caught my attention.

I stood in the kitchen door and watched as a group of four men rode into the bailey, all armed for battle.

"Ysolde! What are you doing here? Why aren't you up in the solar tending to Lady Susan? Mother was looking for you." Margaret, my older sister, emerged from the depths of the kitchen to scold me.

"Did they get her out of the privy, then?" I asked in all innocence. Or what I hoped passed for it.

"Aye." Her eyes narrowed on me. "It was odd, the door being stuck shut that way. Almost as if someone had done something to it."

I made my eyes as round as they would go, and threw in a few blinks for good measure. "Poor, poor Lady

Susan. Trapped in the privy with her bowels running amok. Think you she's been cursed?"

"Aye, and I know by what. Or rather, who." She was clearly about to shift into a lecture when movement in the bailey caught her eye. She glanced outside the doorway and quickly pulled me backwards, into the dimness of the kitchen. "You know better than to stand about when Father has visitors."

"Who is it?" I asked, looking around her as she peered out at the men.

"An important mage." She held a plucked goose to her chest as she watched the men. "That must be him, in the black."

All of the men were armed, their swords and mail glinting brightly in the sun, but only one did not wear a helm. He dismounted, lifting his hand in greeting as my father hurried down the steps of the keep.

"He doesn't look like any mage I've ever seen," I told her, taking in the man's easy movements under what must be at least fifty pounds of armor. "He looks more like a warlord. Look, he's got braids in his hair, just like that Scot who came to see Father a few years ago. What do you think he wants?"

"Who knows? Father is renowned for his powers; no doubt this mage wants to consult him on arcane matters."

"Hrmph. Arcane matters," I said, aware I sounded grumpy.

Her mouth quirked on one side. "I thought you weren't going to let it bother you anymore."

"I'm not. It doesn't," I said defensively, watching as my father and the warlord greeted each other. "I don't care in the least that I didn't inherit any of Father's abilities. You can have them all."

"Whereas you, little changeling, would rather muck about in the garden than learn how to summon a ball of blue fire." Margaret laughed, pulling a bit of grass from where it had been caught in the laces on my sleeve.

"I'm not a changeling. Mother says I was a gift from God, and that's why my hair is blond when you and she and Papa are redheads. Why would a mage ride with three guards?"

Margaret pulled back from the door, nudging me aside. "Why shouldn't he have guards?"

"If he's as powerful a mage as Father, he shouldn't need anyone to protect him." I watched as my mother curtseyed to the stranger. "He just looks . . . wrong. For a mage."

"It doesn't matter what he looks like—you are to stay out of the way. If you're not going to tend to your duties, you can help me. I've got a million things to do, what with two of the cooks down with some sort of a pox, and Mother busy with the guest. Ysolde? Ysolde!"

I slipped out of the kitchen, wanting a better look at the warlord as he strode after my parents into the tower that held our living quarters. There was something about the way the man moved, a sense of coiled power, like a boar before it charges. He walked with grace despite the heavy mail, and although I couldn't see his face, long ebony hair shone glossy and bright as a raven's wing.

The other men followed after him, and although they, too, moved with the ease that bespoke power, they didn't have the same air of leadership.

I trailed behind them, careful to stay well back lest my father see me, curious to know what this strange warrior-mage wanted. I had just reached the bottom step as all but the last of the mage's party entered the tower, when that guard suddenly spun around.

His nostrils flared, as if he'd smelled something, but it wasn't that which sent a ripple of goose bumps down my arms. His eyes were dark, and as I watched them, the pupils narrowed, like a cat's when brought from the dark stable out into the sun. I gasped and spun around, running in the other direction, the sound of the strange man's laughter following me, mocking me, echoing in my head until I thought I would scream.

"Ah, you're awake."

My eyelids, leaden weights that they were, finally managed to hoist themselves open. I stared directly into the dark brown eyes of a woman whose face was located less than an inch from mine, and screamed in surprise. "Aaagh!"

She leaped backwards as I sat up, my heart beating madly, a faint, lingering pain leaving me with the sensation that my brain itself was bruised.

"Who are you? Are you part of the dream? You are, aren't you? You're just a dream," I said, my voice a croak. I touched my lips. They were dry and cracked. "Except those people were in some sort of medieval clothing, and you're wearing pants. Still, it's incredibly vivid, this dream. It's not as interesting as the last one, but still interesting and vivid. Very vivid. Enough that I'm lying here babbling to myself during it."

"I'm not a dream, actually," the in-my-face dream woman said. "And you're not alone, so if you're babbling, it's to me."

I knew better than to leap off the bed, not with the

sort of headache I had. Slowly, I slid my legs off the edge of the bed, and wondered if I stood up, if I'd stop dreaming and wake up to real life.

As I tried to stand, the dream lady seized my arm, holding on to me as I wobbled on my unsteady feet.

Her grip was anything but dreamlike. "You're real," I said with surprise.

"Yes."

"You're a real person, not part of the dream?"

"I think we've established that fact."

I felt an irritated expression crawl across my face—crawl because my brain hadn't yet woken up with the rest of me. "If you're real, would you mind me asking why you were bent over me, nose-to-nose, in the worst sort of Japanese-horror-movie way, one that guaranteed I'd just about wet myself the minute I woke up?"

"I was checking your breathing. You were moaning and making noises like you were going to wake up."

"I was dreaming," I said, as if that explained everything.

"So you've said. Repeatedly." The woman, her skin the color of oiled mahogany, nodded. "It's good. You are beginning to remember. I wondered if the dragon within would not speak to you in such a manner."

Dim little warning bells went off in my mind, the sort that are set off when you're trapped in a small room with someone who is obviously a few weenies short of a cookout. "Well, isn't this just lovely. I feel like something a cat crapped, and I'm trapped in a room with a crazy lady." I clapped a hand over my mouth, appalled that I spoke the words rather than just thought them. "Did you hear that?" I asked around my fingers.

She nodded.

I let my hand fall. "Sorry. I meant no offense. It's just that . . . well . . . you know. Dragons? That's kind of out there."

A slight frown settled between her brows. "You look a bit confused."

"You get the understatement-of-the-year tiara. Would it be rude to ask who you are?" I gently rubbed my forehead, letting my gaze wander around the room.

"My name is Kaawa. My son is Gabriel Tauhou, the silver wyvern."

"A silver what?"

She was silent, her eyes shrewd as they assessed me. "Do you really think that's necessary?"

"That I ask questions or rub my head? It doesn't matter—both are, yes. I always ask questions because I'm a naturally curious person. Ask anyone; they'll tell you. And I rub my head when it feels like it's been stomped on, which it does."

Another silence followed that statement. "You are not what I expected."

My eyebrows were working well enough to rise at that statement. "You scared the crap out of me by staring at me from an inch away, and I'm not what *you* expected? I don't know what to say to that since I don't have the slightest idea who you are, other than your name is Kaawa and you sound like you're Australian, or where I am, or what I'm doing here beyond napping. How long have I been sleeping?"

She glanced at the clock. "Five weeks."

I gave her a look that told her she should know better than to try to fool me. "Do I look like I just rolled off the gullible wagon? Wait—Gareth put you up to this, didn't he? He's trying to pull my leg."

"I don't know a Gareth," she said, moving toward the end of the bed.

"No . . ." I frowned as my mind, still groggy from the aftereffects of a long sleep, slowly chugged to life. "You're right. Gareth wouldn't do that—he has absolutely no sense of humor."

"You fell into a stupor five weeks and two days ago. You have been asleep ever since."

A chill rolled down my spine as I read the truth in her eyes. "That can't be."

"But it is."

"No." Carefully, very carefully, I shook my head. "It's not time for one; I shouldn't have one for another six months. Oh god, you're not a deranged madwoman from Australia who lies to innocent people, are you? You're telling me the truth! Brom! Where's Brom?"

"Who is Brom?"

Panic had me leaping to my feet when my body knew better. Immediately, I collapsed onto the floor with a loud thud. My legs felt like they were made of rubber, the muscles trembling with strain. I ignored the pain of the fall and clawed at the bed to get back to my feet. "A phone. Is there a phone? I must have a phone."

The door opened as I stood up, still wobbling, the floor tilting and heaving under my feet.

"I heard a—oh. I see she's up. Hello, Ysolde."

"Hello." My stomach lurched along with the floor. I clung to the frame of the bed for a few seconds until the world settled down the way it should be. "Who are you?"

She shot a puzzled look to the other woman. "I'm May. We met before, don't you remember?"

"Not at all. Do you have a phone, May?"

If she was surprised by that question, she didn't let on. She simply pulled a cell phone out of the pocket of her jeans and handed it to me. I took it, staring at her for a moment. There was something about her, something that seemed familiar . . . and yet, I was sure I'd never seen her before.

Mentally, I shook away the fancies and began to punch in a phone number, but paused when I realized I had no idea where I was. "What country is this?"

May and Kaawa exchanged glances. May answered. "England. We're in London. We thought it was better not to move you very far, although we did take you out of Drake's house since he was a bit crazy, what with the twins being born and all."

"London," I said, struggling to peer into the black abyss that was my memory. There was nothing there, but that wasn't uncommon after an episode. Luckily, a few wits remained to me, including the ability to remember my phone number.

The phone buzzed gently against my ear. I held my breath, counting the rings before it was answered.

"Yeah?"

"Brom," I said, wanting to weep with relief at the sound of his placid, unruffled voice. "Are you all right?"

"Yeah. Where are you?"

"London." I slid a glance toward the small, dark-haired woman who looked like she could have stepped straight out of some silent movie. "With . . . uh . . . some people." Crazy people, or sane . . . that was yet to be determined.

"You're still in London? I thought you were only going to be there for three days. You said three days, Sullivan. It's been over a month."

I heard the note of hurt in his voice. I hated that. "I know. I'm sorry. I . . . something happened. Something big."

"What kind of big?" he asked, curious now.

"I don't know. I can't think," I said, being quite literal. My brain felt like it was soaking in molasses. "The people I'm with took care of me while I was sleeping."

"Oh, *that* kind of big. I figured it was something like that. Gareth was pissed when you didn't come back. He called your boss and chewed him out for keeping you so long."

"Oh, no," I said, my shoulders slumping as I thought of the powerful archimage to whom I was an apprentice.

"It was really cool! You should have heard it. Dr. Kostich yelled at Gareth, and told him to stop calling, and that you were all right, but he wouldn't say where you were because Gareth was always using you. And then Gareth said he'd better watch out because he wasn't the only one who could make things happen, and then Kostich said oh yeah, and Gareth said yeah, his sister-in-law was a necromancer, and then Ruth punched him in the arm and bit his ear so hard it bled, and after that, I found a dead fox. Can I have fifty dollars to buy some natron?"

I blinked at the stream of information pouring into my ear, sorting out what must have been a horrible scene with Dr. Kostich, finally ending up on the odd request. "Why do you need natron?"

Brom sighed. " 'Cause I found the dead fox. It's going to need a lot of natron to mummify."

"I really don't think we need the mummy of a fox, Brom."

"It's my hobby," he said, his tone weary. "You said I needed a hobby. I got one."

"When you said you were interested in mummies, I thought you meant the Egyptian ones. I didn't realize you meant you wanted to make your own."

"You didn't ask," he pointed out, and with that, I could not dispute.

"We'll talk about it when I get back. I suppose I should talk to Gareth," I said, not wanting to do any such thing.

"Can't. He's in Barcelona."

"Oh. Is Ruth there?"

"No, she went with him."

Panic gripped me. "You're not alone, are you?"

"Sullivan, I'm not a child," he answered, sounding indignant that I would question the wisdom gained during his lifetime, all nine years of it. "I can stay by myself."

"Not for five weeks you can't—"

"It's OK. When Ruth and Gareth left, and you didn't come back, Penny said I could stay with her until you came home."

I sagged against the bed, unmindful of the two women watching me so closely. "Thank the stars for Penny. I'll be home just as soon as I can get on a plane. Do you have a pen?"

"Sec."

I covered the phone and looked at the woman named May. "Is there a phone number I can give my son in case of an emergency?"

"Your son?" she asked, her eyes widening. "Yes. Here."

I took the card she pulled from her pocket, reading

the number off it to Brom. "You stay with Penny until I can get you, all right?"

"Geez, Sullivan, I'm not a 'tard."

"A what?" I asked.

"A 'tard. You know, a retard."

"I've asked you not to use those sorts of . . . oh, never mind. We'll discuss words that are hurtful and should not be used another time. Just stay with Penny, and if you need me, call me at the number I gave you. Oh, and Brom?"

"What?" he asked in that put-upon voice that nine-year-old boys the world over can assume with such ease.

I turned my back on the two women. "I love you bunches. You remember that, OK?"

"'K." I could almost hear his eyes rolling. "Hey, Sullivan, how come you had your thing now? I thought it wasn't supposed to happen until around Halloween."

"It isn't, and I don't know why it happened now."

"Gareth's going to be pissed he missed it. Did you . . . you know . . . manifest the good stuff?"

My gaze moved slowly around the room. It seemed like a pretty normal bedroom, containing a large bureau, a bed, a couple of chairs and a small table with a ruffly cloth on it, and a white stone fireplace. "I don't know. I'll call you later when I have some information about when I'll be landing in Madrid, all right?"

"Later, French mustachioed waiter," he said, using his favorite childhood rhyme.

I smiled at the sound of it, missing him, wishing there was a way to magically transport myself to the small, overcrowded, noisy apartment where we lived so I could hug him and ruffle his hair, and marvel yet again that such an intelligent, wonderful child was mine.

"Thank you," I said, handing the cell phone back to May. "My son is only nine. I knew he would be worried about what happened to me."

"Nine." May and Kaawa exchanged another glance. "Nine . . . years?"

"Yes, of course." I sidled away, just in case one or both of the women turned out to be crazy after all. "This is very awkward, but I'm afraid I have no memory of either of you. Have we met?"

"Yes," Kaawa said. She wore a pair of loose-fitting black palazzo pants and a beautiful black top embroidered in silver with all sorts of Aboriginal animal designs. Her hair was twisted into several braids, pulled back into a short ponytail. "I met you once before, in Cairo."

"Cairo?" I prodded the solid black mass that was my memory. Nothing moved. "I don't believe I've ever been in Cairo. I live in Spain, not Egypt."

"This was some time ago," the woman said carefully.

Perhaps she was someone I had met while travelling with Dr. Kostich. "Oh? How long ago?"

She looked at me silently for a moment, then said, "About three hundred years."

Chapter Two

"Ysolde is awake again," May said as the door to the study was opened.

I looked up from where I had been staring down into the cup of coffee cradled in my hands. Two men entered the room, both tall and well-built, and curiously enough, both with grey eyes. The first one who entered paused at May's chair, his hand smoothing over her short hair as he looked me over. I returned the look, noting skin the color of milky coffee, a close-cut goatee, and shoulder-length dreadlocks.

"Again?" the man asked.

"She fainted after she woke up the first time."

I eyed him. After the last hour, I'd given up the idea that May and Kaawa were potentially dangerous—they let me have a shower, had promised to feed me, and had given me coffee, and crazy people seldom did any of that.

"Ah. No ill effects from it, I hope?" he asked.

"Not unless you call fifty-two elephants tap-dancing in combat boots while bouncing anvils on my brain an ill effect," I said, gazing longingly at the bottle of ibuprofen.

"No more," May said, moving it out of my reach. "You'll poison yourself if you take any more."

I sipped my coffee with obnoxious noisiness as punishment for her hard-heartedness.

"I'm afraid there is little I can do for a headache." He nodded toward the man with him. "Tipene, when we are done here, e-mail Dr. Kostich and let him know his apprentice has recovered."

The second man was also black, but with much shorter dreadlocks. He nodded. Beneath the light-colored T-shirt he wore, I could see thick black curved lines that indicated he bore rather detailed tribal tattoos across his chest.

"We were just having some coffee while waiting for lunch," May continued, smiling up at the first man. "Ysolde says her brain is a bit fuzzy still."

"Not so fuzzy that I can't correct something that's seriously wrong," I said, setting my cup down. I addressed the man who stood next to May. "I assume you're Gabriel Tao . . . Tow . . ."

"Tauhou," he said, his eyes narrowed as he searched my face.

"Sorry, I have the memory of maple syrup when it comes to people's names. I was trying to tell your . . . er . . ." I waved vaguely toward May.

"Mate," he said.

"Quite." I didn't even blink over the odd word to use for a partner. What people called their significant others in the privacy of their own homes was not one iota my business. "I was just trying to tell her that I think you have me mistaken for someone else. My name isn't Ysolde. It's Tully, Tully Sullivan."

"Indeed," he said politely, taking the seat that May had been using. She perched on the arm of the chair instead, not touching him, but I could sense the electricity between them.

"I'm an apprentice mage," I explained. "You mentioned contacting Dr. Kostich—I'm sure he'd be happy to tell you that you've got me confused with someone else."

"Whether or not you are a mage remains to be seen. That you are Kostich's apprentice, we know. You were introduced to us by him almost two months ago, when you came to the home of the green wyvern to prevent an attack."

"Wyvern?" The word was mentioned earlier, but it took until now to sink in through the fog wrapped around my brain. If it meant what I thought it did, it would go a long way to explaining their odd behavior. "The kind that are . . . oh! That's why you mentioned dragons. You're them, right? Dragons?"

"My father is a dragon, and May is my mate," Gabriel said, taking May's hand. "Tipene is also a silver dragon, as is Maata, whom you will meet shortly. As, I need not say, are you."

I would have laughed, but my brain was still slogging along at a snail's pace. I gave him what I hoped was a jaunty little smile, instead. No wonder they seemed to be so very odd—they were dragons! "You know, in a way this is very exciting. I've never met a dragon before. I've heard about you, of course. Who hasn't? But I can assure you that I am *not* one of you. Not that there's anything wrong with, you know, being an animal. There's nothing wrong with that at all. I'm sure some very nice people are dragons. I just don't happen to know any other than you guys, and I just met you. Oh, hell. I'm babbling again, aren't I?"

"Yes," Kaawa said. "But that is all right. We understand."

"Do you?" I asked hopefully. "Good, because I don't understand anything since I woke up, not the least of which is why you'd think I was the same as you."

"You are Ysolde de Bouchier, silver dragon, and mate to Baltic, who used to be wyvern of the black dragons," Kaawa said, her gaze seeming to strip away all my defenses and leave my soul bare. I squirmed in my chair, uncomfortable with her intense regard.

"I think I would know if I was a fire-breathing shape-shifter with a love of gold," I said gently, not wanting to upset her because she seemed rather nice, if a bit odd. I racked my sluggish brain to remember everything I knew about dragons. "I'm afraid I don't even know much about you folk, although there's been some talk of you lately at the mages' commune, since Dr. Kostich has been forced into dealing with an uncontrollable, irresponsible wyvern's mate who evidently is also a demon lord. But other than that—sorry. I'm afraid you have me mixed up with someone else."

Doubt was evident on May's face as she glanced down at Gabriel. "Could you be wrong?" she asked.

He looked thoughtful as his mother shook her head. "I am not wrong," Kaawa said with determination. "Although I have seen Ysolde de Bouchier only once before, the image of her is burned into my memory for all time. You *are* Ysolde."

I rubbed my forehead, suddenly tired despite my five-week sleep. "I don't know what I can say to prove I am who I am. You can ask Dr. Kostich. You can ask the other apprentices. I'm human. My name is Tully. I live in Spain with my son, husband, and sister-in-law."

"Husband?" Surprise showed in Gabriel's eyes for a few minutes before turning to amusement. "You're married and you have a child?"

"Yes, I do, and I have to say that I don't at all see what's so funny about having a family," I said, frowning a little at the man named Tipene as he chuckled to himself.

"Nothing is funny about it," May said, but even she looked like she was struggling to keep from laughing. "It's just that Baltic is kind of volatile, and when he finds out that his precious Ysolde is alive with a husband and child . . . well, to be honest, he's going to go ballistic."

"That's tough toenails for him, but since I'm not his precious Ysolde, I don't particularly care."

"I think the time will come when you will care very much," Gabriel said, still amused.

"Doubtful. I have this policy about not wasting time on people who are big pains in the ass, and he sounds like a major one. Oh!" I grimaced. "He's not . . . er . . . a friend of yours, is he? If that major pain in the ass comment was out of line, I apologize."

May choked on the sip of coffee she was taking. Gabriel helpfully pounded her on her back while saying, "No, he is no friend to silver dragons."

"Gotcha," I said lightly as I got to my feet. "This has been a really . . . special . . . experience, but I should be on my way. Thank you for the coffee, and for taking care of me while I was out of things. I appreciate it, but my son has been left alone far too long, and I really need to get him from the neighbor who's been taking care of him."

"I don't think it's a very good idea for you to leave just yet," May said slowly as she and Gabriel exchanged yet another of those knowing glances.

"Look, you seem nice and all, but I'm getting tired of saying that I'm not this person you think I am—" I started to say.

"No, I meant that given your physical state, it would be best for you to stay here for a few days," she interrupted.

"My physical state? You mean the fugue?" I asked.

"Is that what you call it?"

"That's how the psychiatrist I saw referred to it. I assure you that although the fugues are inconvenient for everyone, once they are over, I'm fine. A little headachy, but nothing serious."

"You saw a psychiatrist about these…fugues?" Kaawa asked, her dark eyes watching me carefully.

"Well . . . yes. Once. I didn't know what happened to me, and thought…" I sat down again, biting my lip, hesitant to tell them I had thought I was going crazy. "Let's just say I was concerned about what was causing me to have them."

"What was the judgment of the psychiatrist?" Gabriel asked, also making me uncomfortable with his unwavering gaze.

I shrugged. "I only saw him once. Gareth didn't like me going to him."

"Gareth is your husband?" May asked.

"Yes." I tried to make a light little laugh, growing more and more uncomfortable in the situation. "Why do I feel like I'm playing twenty questions?"

"I'm sorry if it appears we're grilling you," May said with a tight little smile of her own. "It's just that you took us all by surprise, and now even more so."

"If you can tolerate another question . . . ," Kaawa said, moving over to sit next to me. I shifted on the couch to give her room, the hairs on my arms pricking at her nearness. There was something about her, some aura that led me to believe she was not a woman who tolerated either fools or lies. "When did you see the psychiatrist?"

I stared at her in surprise. "Er . . . when?"

She nodded, watching me with that same intent gaze.

"Well, let me think . . . it was . . . um . . ." I stared at my fingers, trying to sort through my memories to find the one I wanted, but it wasn't there. "I don't seem to recall."

"A month ago? Two months ago? A year? Five years?" she asked.

"I don't . . . I'm not sure," I said, feeling as lame as I sounded.

"Let me ask you this, then—what is your earliest memory?"

I really stared at her now. "Huh? Why would you want to know something unimportant like that?"

She smiled, and I felt suddenly bathed in a warm, golden glow of caring. "Do my questions disturb you, child?"

"No, not disturb, I just don't see what this has to do with anything. I really have to go. My son—"

"—will be all right for another few minutes." She

waited, and I glanced around the room. The other three dragons sat watching me silently, evidently quite happy to let Kaawa conduct this strange interview. I gave a mental sigh. "Let's see . . . earliest memory. I assume you mean as a child."

"Yes. What is the first thing you remember? Your mother's voice, perhaps? A favorite toy? Something that frightened you?"

Supposing it wouldn't hurt to humor her, I poked again at the black mass that was my memory. Nothing was forthcoming. "I'm afraid I have a really crappy memory. I can't remember anything as a child."

She nodded again, just as if she expected that. "Your son is only nine, you said. You must remember the day you gave birth to him."

"Of course I do—" I stopped when, to my horror, I realized I didn't. I could see his face in my mind's eye, but it was his face now, not his face as an infant. Panic swamped me. "By the rood! I don't remember it!"

"By the rood?" May asked.

I stared at her in confusion, my skin crawling with the realization that something was seriously wrong with me. "What?"

"You said 'by the rood.' That's an archaic term, isn't it?"

"How the hell do I know?" I said, my voice rising. "I'm having a mental breakdown, and you're worried about some silly phrase? Don't you understand?" I leaped to my feet, grabbing the collar of May's shirt and shaking it. "I don't remember Brom's first word. I don't remember the first time he walked, or even what he looked like as a baby. I don't remember any of it!"

"Do you remember marrying your husband?" Kaawa asked as May gently pried my hands from her shirt.

Goose bumps prickled up my arms. I prodded, I poked, I mentally grabbed my memory with both hands and shook it like it was a brainy piñata, but nothing came out. "No," I said, the word a whisper as fear replaced the panic. "What's wrong with me? Why can't I remember anything?"

"It is as I thought," Kaawa said, taking my chin between the tips of her fingers so she could search my eyes. "Your memory has been expunged."

"Why would someone do that?" I asked, the words a near wail as I fought the desire to race out of the house and onto the first plane to Spain. "Did you do this to me?"

"No, child," she said solemnly, releasing my chin. "I suspect you have been conditioned to forget."

"Conditioned to forget my own son? That doesn't make any sense! Who would want me to forget him?"

"It's all right, Ysolde. Er . . . Tully," May said in a soothing voice, gently guiding me back to the couch. "I know you're scared by all this, but you talked to your son earlier, remember? You said he was all right."

I clung to that, fighting the rising fear that threatened to overwhelm me. "Yes, he was all right, although I really need to go home. I'm sorry, but I can't stay here any longer."

I made it all the way to the door before Kaawa's voice reached me.

"And what will you do if you have another fugue while your son is with you?"

I froze at that, turning slowly to face the room of people. "I only have them once a year. I believe I mentioned that."

"You told your son that you didn't know why you had it now. That was what you were referring to, wasn't it?"

I nodded, my shoulders slumping. "I shouldn't have had it until the end of October."

"And yet you had it now."

"But, Kaawa, that was—" May started to say.

The older woman raised her hand, and May stopped.

"I've only ever had them once a year," I told them all. "This was an anomaly. I don't know why it came early, but I'm sure it won't happen again."

"How can you be sure? You can't, not really. There is nothing to stop you from having another one right now, or an hour from now, or a week from now, is there?" Kaawa insisted.

I gritted my teeth in acknowledgment.

"What if you were driving a car with your son and you were suddenly sent into a fugue?"

"That would be very unlikely—"

"But it could happen," she pressed. "Would you risk his life?"

"It's never happened like this before," I said, but the horrible ideas she was presenting couldn't be denied. The fugue shouldn't have happened now, but it did. What if it came again, while I was with Brom? My gut tightened at all the terrifying possibilities of disaster.

"I think what Kaawa is trying to say is that until you know why you're having these . . . er . . . events, you should probably stay with us," May suggested.

"No," I said, shaking my head. "I've left Brom alone long enough. I must go home."

"What if—" She slid a glance toward Gabriel, who nodded. "What if your son joined you here?"

"I don't know," I said slowly. "I think it would probably be better to be with my family. Gareth may not be any great shakes as a husband, but he has looked after me this long."

"How long would that be?" Kaawa said, pouncing on my words.

"A long time," I said finally, not finding any answers in my brain.

"Would he have any reason for wanting you to be without your memory?" Gabriel asked.

I opened my mouth to deny such a thing, but remembered the manifestations. "He might. There is . . . when I have a normal fugue, I manifest . . . that's not the right word, really, but it's how I think of it . . . I make . . ." They all watched me with an avidity that made my skin itch. I took a deep breath and said the word. "Gold."

The two male dragons sat up straighter.

"You *make* gold?" May asked, her expression puzzled.

"Ahh," Kaawa said, sitting back, as if that explained everything.

"Yes. Gareth—my husband—says that I'm a natural alchemist. That's someone who can transmute base metals without a need for apparatus or any special elixirs or potions. Every year, when I have the fugues, he brings me lead. Lots and lots of lead, great huge wads of it, and leaves it in the room with me. When the fugue has passed, the lead has been changed into gold. I don't know how it's done, but he assures me that it's some process that happens when I'm asleep."

"That must be very handy," May said, somewhat skeptically, I felt.

I made a face. Whether or not she believed me wasn't the problem at hand. I was more concerned about this sudden loss of memory. Maybe it was me who was going insane, not them, as I'd first thought. "To be honest, I'd much rather do without the fugues. Especially if they're doing something to my brain."

"I imagine you would."

"I admit that's a curious talent to be given, and one that leaves me wishing I had some lead to place in your room," Gabriel said with a rueful smile, "but I don't follow the reasoning between that and why your memory would be wiped."

I made a noncommittal gesture, and for a second, a scene flashed in my mind's eye—Ruth, lying on a cot in a dimly lit hut, covered in boils, sweating and trembling with an illness while Gareth shook her, telling her I was awake, and demanding that she rise and take care of me. I tried to push the fragment of a memory, tried to see more, but there was nothing there, just a black abyss.

"I don't know," I said finally, sadly aware that I couldn't trust the images my brain suggested. There was no way to know if it was an actual memory, or a fabrication of a mind that more and more I was beginning to fear was not normal.

"I can think of any number of reasons why her husband might prefer her without memories," Kaawa said calmly. "For one, he might not wish for her to know what sept he's from."

"Sept?" I shook my head. "Gareth isn't a dragon. I would know if he was."

"Just as you would know if you were one?" Gabriel asked lightly.

"Yes, exactly." He raised his eyebrow and I hurried on. "Besides, Gareth is an oracle, and I've never heard of a dragon being an oracle."

"Just because no dragon has ever sought the position of oracle does not preclude the possibility of doing so," he pointed out.

"He's not a dragon," I insisted. "I would know. I've been married to him for . . ." I slid a quick glance at Kaawa. "However long it's been, I would know."

"I agree," she said, taking me by surprise again.

"You do?" I asked.

"Yes, child. You would know if your Gareth was a dragon." She laid her hand on mine, the gesture one that would normally leave me recoiling—as a rule, I do not like to be touched other than by Brom—but the gesture was a kind one, and offered an odd sort of comfort. "But there are other reasons he might like you to be without memories of what you do during these fugues of yours."

"What do you mean, what I do? I sleep," I told her.

She raised her eyebrows just as Gabriel did, giving her the same disbelieving expression. "How do you know?"

"I know. I mean, I must sleep. Otherwise, I would not have dreamed—" I stopped, not wanting to go into the oddly vivid dream I was having when I woke up.

The look she gave me was shrewd, but she said nothing about the dream, merely commented, "You wake without a memory. You may think you sleep, but what if you don't? What if your husband has you performing acts that he knows would be repugnant to you? Would he not want your memory wiped of them to protect himself? What if your son knows what he does—"

I bolted for the door, alarmed by the pictures she painted in my mind. "I have to go. *Now*!"

"Calm yourself, Ysolde," Kaawa said soothingly. Tipene had somehow gotten in front of the door before me and stood blocking the exit, his arms crossed over his chest.

"My *name* is Tully," I said through clenched teeth.

"I do not say that your husband is doing anything heinous," she continued. "I merely offered that as a possible reason why he might want you in a perpetual state of unawareness."

"Please let me leave," I said, turning to May. Of all the people in the room, she seemed the most sympathetic, the most familiar. "I must go back to my family."

She looked uncomfortable as Gabriel said, "We are your family, Ysolde. You were born a silver dragon. You need our help. You will stay here while we give you that help."

"I don't want your damned help!" I said, losing my temper, while at the same time I wanted to sob in frustration.

"You need assistance recovering your memory," Kaawa pointed out. "Even if you are not who we believe you to be, you cannot wish to live your life without any memories."

That stopped me, as did a thought that struck me as important. "Why didn't I notice before this that I can't remember things like Brom's birth?"

She was silent for a moment, searching my face before answering. "I suspect that whoever expunged your memory applied a compulsion that would keep you from being troubled by the lack. It is only a guess, of course, but you did not become distraught about it until I drove home just how peculiar your circumstances are."

I slumped down on the chair nearest the door, exhausted, mentally bruised and battered. "I just want my son."

"And you will have him. He will come here as soon as possible," Gabriel said.

Hope flared within the dullness of pain inside. "He's only nine," I said.

"May and I will fetch him ourselves," he answered smoothly. May smiled and twined her fingers through his. "We will let no harm come to him, of that I swear."

I watched him for a minute, not sure whether I should trust him or not. A worried little voice warned that I knew little about these people, but they had taken very good care of me for the last five weeks, and I felt an odd bond with May, almost as if I had known her for a very long time. She seemed comfortable to me, trustworthy, and after giving it some thought, reluctantly I agreed. "All right. If you bring Brom to me today, I will stay. For a little bit. Just until you help me discover my memories, so I can prove to you that I'm not a dragon."

Two dimples showed deep on either cheek as he smiled at me. I was unmoved by them. I didn't actually distrust Gabriel, but he didn't seem as familiar and comfortable to me as May, and the sense of power around him made me wary and left me feeling vaguely unsettled.

Brom, unfortunately, could not be whisked to me at a moment's notice. After a lengthy conversation with Penny, the American friend who had taken Brom and me to her heart, she promised to hand him over to Gabriel and May when they arrived in Spain later that afternoon.

"I've never been to England," Brom said when I told him he was to join me. "Not that I remember. Have I, Sullivan?"

I panicked. "Brom, you remember last Christmas, don't you?"

"Last Christmas? When you got upset because I asked for a dissection kit and you wanted to give me a Game Boy, you mean?"

I relaxed, the sudden fear that my memory issues were hereditary—or that someone had been abusing his mind—fading into nothing. "Er . . . yes. That's right."

"What about it?"

"Just remember that sometimes, you may not understand why things are happening, but they turn out for the best," I said in my "vague but wise" mom manner. "I want you to behave yourself with May and Gabriel when they get there, but if anything happens to them, you call me, all right?"

"Yeah, OK. Penny says I have to go pack now. Bye."

I hung up the phone feeling relieved, but at the same time I was worried. Could I trust Gabriel and May? Where was Gareth, and why had he left Brom for so long? And what was going on with my brain? Was I insane, or just the victim of some horrible plot?

"I need some serious therapy," I said aloud, thinking of the small garden plot that I shared with the other residents of our apartment house. It was my haven against daily trials and tribulations, providing me with boundless peace.

"All silver dragons like plants," Kaawa said from behind me. "May hasn't had time yet to take the garden in hand, but I'm sure she'd be happy if you wanted to tidy things up out there."

I whirled around to pin her back with a look. "How did you know I was talking about a garden?"

She just smiled and gestured toward the French windows. Gabriel's house, although in the middle of London, had a minuscule garden guarded by a tall redbrick wall. My heart lightened at the sight of tangled and overrun flower beds, and before I knew it, I was on my knees, my eyes shut as I sank my hands into the sun-warmed earth.

"I'll leave you here. It will be four hours before Gabriel will reach your son," she said, watching with amusement as I flexed my fingers in the soil, plucking out the weeds that choked a chrysanthemum.

"I know. The garden is as good a place as any to wait," I said, looking about to see how bad it was. There were only three beds. One appeared to have suffered some calamity, since the wild lilac bush in it was crumpled to the ground, and wild grass filled the rest of the bed. The second contained miniature rhododendrons run amok, tangled up with irises and what looked to be phlox. The bed I knelt before contained autumn plants, all of which were threatened by the rampant weeds and wild grass.

Kaawa left, and I spent a pleasant hour clearing out the chrysanthemum, amaryllis, and saffron sprouts, worrying all the while about what had become of my life.

Chapter Three

"Where is she?"

The roar reached me, even hidden from view as I was in the farthest corner of the stable, behind the broken wagon that Dew, the smith, was supposed to have mended months ago.

The doors to the stable slammed shut with a force that I felt in the timbers behind my back. The horses inside with me protested with startled snorts and whinnies. Hastily, I set down the two kittens I had been nuzzling for comfort, returning them to their anxious mother before dusting off my knees and picking my way through the gloom of the stable. The man's voice was deep, and he spoke in French, not the English of the serfs, but there was an accent to his voice that I had never heard.

"Where are you hiding her?"

Anger was rich in that voice, anger and something else, something I couldn't define. I patted Abelard, my mother's gelding, and slipped beside him to peek out through a rotten bit of wood next to his manger, watching as the warrior-mage stomped across the bailey, my father and mother trailing behind him.

"We are not hiding anyone, my lord," Papa said, his tone apologetic.

My mouth dropped open in surprise. Papa never apologized to anyone! He was a famous mage, one of so much renown that other mages travelled for months just to consult with him. And yet here he was, following the warrior around, bleating like a sheep that had lost its dam.

"Kostya saw her," the warrior snarled, spinning around to glare at Papa, the tall guards moving in a semicircle behind him. "Do you call us liars?"

"No, my lord, never that!" Papa wrung his hands, my mother next him looking pale and frightened. "If you will just come back inside the hall, I will explain to you—"

"Explain what? That you are holding a dragon prisoner, a female dragon of tender years?"

"She is not a prisoner—" Papa started to say, but I stopped listening for a moment. A dragon? Here? I had heard tales of such beings, but had never seen one. Margaret told me they did not really exist, that it was just a bit of foolishness spoken by men who had too much wine, but once I had overheard my mother talking to her maid about a female dragon she had befriended in her youth. Perhaps Mama had hidden her here all these years. Who could it be? Leah, the nurse who tended both Margaret and me? One of my mother's serving women? The flatulent Lady Susan?

"I just wager you it's her," I told Abelard. "She is very dragonlike."

"Bring her forth!" the warrior demanded, and I pushed Abelard's head aside in order to get a better view of the bailey, watching with bated breath to see the dragon.

"My lord, there are circumstances that you are not aware of. Ysolde has no knowledge of her ancestry. We have sheltered her as best we could, indeed, raised her as our own daughter—"

My skin crawled. My blood curdled. My brain exploded inside my head. I stared at Papa, my papa, the papa I had known for my entire life, unable to believe my ears.

"—she has been protected from those who would ill use her, as sworn by my lady wife to the dragon who bore her here."

"Me?" I said, touching my throat when my voice came out no more than a feeble squeak. "I'm a dragon?"

"That is none of my concern," the warrior said now, his voice thick with menace. "She is a dragon, and evidently of age. She belongs with her own kind, not with humans."

My own kind? Scaly, long-tailed, fire-breathing monsters? A sob of denial caught in my throat, the noise almost inaudible, and yet as I stood there reeling from the verbal blows my father—the man I thought of as my father—dealt me, the warrior spun around, the gaze of his black eyes so piercing, I could swear he could see straight through the wood of the stable.

Run, my mind told me as the man started forward toward the stable doors, and I knew at that moment that he was one of them. He was a monster the like of which I'd never seen. My brain didn't wait for me to absorb that knowledge. *Flee*, it urged. *Flee!*

I didn't stop to question the wisdom of that command. I spun on my heels, racing down the narrow aisle of the stable to the far corner, where a small window had been cut in order to pass hay through from the fields. I wasn't fast enough, however, not if the roar of fury that followed me was anything to go by.

"Stop!" the warrior bellowed as I leaped through the window, not even pausing as I hit the ground hard before I was off again, racing around the pens holding the animals to be slaughtered, dashing between the small huts housing craftsmen and their families, dodging chickens, dogs, and occasionally serfs as I raced for the postern gate along the west curtain.

"Lady Ysolde," John, the man on guard at the gate, called in surprise as I rounded a cart loaded with wool destined for the market, not even slowing down as I flung myself past him and through the postern gate. "Are you off to the village—hey, now! Who are you, and what right do you have to be chasing Lady Ysol—oof!"

I didn't stop to see how John fared, although I sent up a small prayer that he hadn't been hurt by the warrior. I ran along the rocky outcropping that led down into the village, the moat not coming around to this face of the castle since it would be impossible for anyone to scale the cliffs that hugged the west and south sides. Behind me I heard the noise of pursuit, but I had always been fast on my feet, and I dug deep for speed as I leaped down the last of the rocks and headed for the trees beyond the village. They marked the edge of the thick forest where I had spent many an hour, wandering pathways known to only a few. If I could just make it there, then I could hide from the warrior . . . and then what?

I didn't stop to answer that question. I just knew that

I needed to be by myself, to absorb the strangeness that had suddenly gripped me. And I couldn't do that with the intense, black-haired dragon storming around me.

He was still behind me as I skirted a newly plowed field, ignoring the calls of greeting from the serfs as I raced by, intent on my goal, greeting the dappled shade of the outer fringes of the forest with relief. I'd made it, no doubt due to the extra weight the warrior wore in the form of his armor. I risked a quick look behind me as I sped around an ancient birch tree. The warrior was about thirty feet behind me, but just beyond him, his guards approached on horseback, leading his horse.

"By the rood!" I swore to myself as I leaped over a downed tree trunk, heading for the densest part of the forest.

The sounds of pursuit were muted in the calm of the forest. Birdsong rose high above me as the swallows dipped and spun in the sunlight, making elegant arcs in the air. Patches of sunlight shone here, and I slowed down, trying to control my breathing, picking through the muffled noises of the animals of the forest as they went about their business. Somewhere near, a badger was snuffling along the ground, disturbing earth and fallen leaves. A woodpecker drilled a few yards away, while farther afield, foliage rustled and snapped as a large animal, probably a stag or hind, grazed. In the distance, the jangling of horses' harnesses was audible. I smiled to myself at that, pleased that the growth was too thick for the warrior's men to ride through.

I was just looking around for a suitable tree that I could climb and hide myself in when a man's voice sounded, uncomfortably near. "Where are you, *ché-*

rie? You do not need to be afraid of me. I will not hurt you."

I snorted to myself, trying to pinpoint the origin of the voice. Usually I had very good hearing, but the denseness of the trees and sounds of the forest combined to muffle the warrior's voice, making it hard to judge where he was.

"We want only to help you," he continued. I moved around the tree, clutching the rough trunk as I peered into the depths in the direction I thought the voice came from. A branch moved, but before I had time to react, a wren popped out and gave me a curious look.

"Are you frightened, *chérie*?"

I strained my ears, but it was impossible to pinpoint a direction. Which is the only reason I called out, "No."

Laughter edged his voice. "Then why do you run from me?"

"Why are you chasing me?" I asked boldly, moving to the cover of another tree, peering intently around it for any signs of the man.

"We only just learned of your existence from the mortals."

The scorn he put in the last words irritated me. "Those mortals are my family!" I yelled.

"No, *chérie*. We are your family. We want to bring you home, where you will be taken care of and taught."

I didn't think much of that statement.

"I know you have no knowledge of us," the man continued. Was his voice fainter? Had he been misled into moving away from me? "But we will correct that. We will teach you what it is to be a dragon."

His voice *was* softer. I smiled to myself as I hugged

the tree. "I don't wish to be a dragon, warrior. I wish simply to be myself."

Another man's voice called in the distance. I smiled again and turned around, intent on making my way out of the forest while the intense dragon and his guard stumbled around it searching for me.

The warrior was leaning on the tree behind me, watching me with a half smile that made my blood freeze. "That is all we wish for you, too—that you be yourself."

"How did you do that?" I asked, momentarily too intrigued to be incensed by his trick.

He shrugged and strolled toward me, all long-legged grace and power. "There are many things you will learn." He stopped before me, reaching out to touch my face. I slapped his hand. He laughed. "You have fire. You will learn well."

"And you are impertinent. What makes you think I'm who you think I am?"

"You need proof?" he asked, his eyebrows raised, but there was still amusement in his onyx eyes.

"That I'm a gigantic scaly beast who breathes fire? Yes, I think I'm going to need proof," I said.

"There is a way," he said, taking my arm, and with a quick jerk, he ripped the laces from the wrists of my tunic. He bent over my wrist as if he were going to bite it, paused, and looked up at me, an odd expression on his face. "How old are you, *chérie*?"

"My name is Ysolde," I said, trying to pull my arm free. His fingers tightened around it. "Ysolde de Bouchier, and I am *not* your *chérie*."

"How old are you?" he repeated, a stubborn glint in his eyes.

"I have seen seventeen summers, not that it is any concern of yours," I said primly.

He grimaced, then shrugged, and instead of biting my hand, he pulled me up against his chest, his arms around me in an unbreakable vise. "This is the test, *chérie.*"

His mouth was on mine before I could do more than slap my hands on his chest. I was no stranger to being kissed—Mark, the brewer's son, was always happy to hide behind the ale barrels with me and kiss me as long as I liked—but this was not a kiss as I knew it. Where Mark's kisses had been interesting and vaguely pleasurable, this was a kiss of an entirely different variety. The warrior's mouth was hot on mine, hotter than I had ever experienced, hot and sweet and spicy all at the same time, as if he'd been eating spiced plums. His hands moved down my back, holding my hips, pulling me closer to his body, his tongue teasing the seam of my lips even as his fingers dug into my hips.

With a frustrated snarl, he suddenly pushed me away. I stood shocked to my toes by the kiss, watching with astonishment as he doubled over, sliding his mail hauberk off over his head. He stood back up, pulling off the padding armor, then the leather jerkin beneath it, his eyes glittering like sunlight sparkling off rocks in a stream.

"Now," he said.

"Now?" I asked, not understanding, taking a step back.

He made a noise in his chest that sounded like a growl, his arms around me again as he pressed me up against the tree trunk.

"Now I will prove to you what you are," he said just before his mouth descended again, his body holding me against the tree. Gone was the mail that stood between us; now I was smashed up against his body, aware of the difference between his hard lines and my softer curves. But it was his mouth that captured and held my attention as his tongue swept along my lips again, urging me to open them. I did so, goose bumps prickling down my arms as his tongue swept inside, touching my own, tasting me even as his hands pulled my hips tighter against his, his fingers cupping my bottom in a way that was shockingly intimate and wildly thrilling at the same time.

His tongue twined around mine, and I gave up all thoughts of fighting, tasting him as he tasted me, reveling in the groan of pleasure he gave when I mimicked his action and let my tongue dance into his mouth.

Heat blasted me then, heat of such intensity I swore I was going to go up in flames, the fire of it pouring into me and setting my soul alight. Impossibly, the kiss deepened, the warrior pulling me upward along the tree trunk until my feet dangled a good foot off the ground, my mouth at the same height as his. I wrapped my arms around his back and gave myself up to the heat, to the pleasure he was stirring with just the touch of his mouth. The heat was in me and around me and through me, and with every second it filled me, my heart sang. I was consumed by it, burning just as bright as the biggest bonfire, my soul soaring with the sensation. I didn't want it to stop, never wanted to stop kissing this strange, handsome man.

"That, *chérie*, is the test," he said, his face tight with some emotion as he let me slide down his body.

I blinked at him a couple of times, trying to regain my wits. "Test?" I asked stupidly, my mind clearly too dazzled by that kiss to do anything but parrot what was said to me.

"Only a dragon or a mate can take dragon fire and live," he said, his lips almost touching mine. His eyes were as deep and shiny as the bit of onyx hung in a pearl necklace that my mother sometimes wore.

"Who are you?" I asked, searching his face, memorizing it in order to tuck away the memory of that kiss.

A slow smile curled his lips. "I am the wyvern of the black dragons, Ysolde de Bouchier. I am Baltic."

Baltic. The name resonated within my head like a bell, repeating and echoing until I thought it would deafen me.

Baltic. The word spun around in my brain as I was swept up in a hurricane of thoughts, confused and tangled beyond hope.

Baltic . . .

"Sullivan?"

My eyes shot open at the voice. I was disoriented, my brain feeling muzzy again, but as my eyes focused on the worried face peering down at me, joy leaped within me.

"How come you're out here in the dark by yourself? Are you OK?" Brom asked as I pushed myself up from the ground, where I'd evidently fallen asleep. Immediately I wrapped him in my arms in a bear hug to beat all bear hugs. "Geez, Sullivan, there are people watching."

I finished kissing his adorable face, giving him another hug just to reassure myself that he was really there. "I'm fine. Did you have any trouble at the airport?"

"Nope. Gabriel said there might be some problems, but he bribed a few people, and it ended up being OK after all."

I looked over Brom's head to where Gabriel and May stood, leaning against each other with that ease of longtime lovers. "Trouble with his passport?"

"Not that," Brom said before Gabriel could answer, squirming out of my hold. "With my mummies!"

"Your . . . you didn't bring those horrible things, did you?"

He shot me a look that was oddly adult in its scorn. "It's my work, Sullivan. You didn't think I was going to leave it behind so Gareth or Ruth could take it when I wasn't there? The customs dudes didn't want to let me bring them, but Gabriel gave them some money to look the other way. He says I can use a room in the basement as my lab. It's got a table and sink already, and he said he'll get me a big tub to soak the bodies in."

"How very generous of Gabriel," I said, trying not to grimace at the thought of Brom's current scholarly pursuits.

May laughed. "It actually sounds very interesting, if a little gruesome. Brom says he only works on animals that have died naturally, because he feels too much empathy to kill one for research purposes."

"For which I am truly grateful," I said, ruffling his mousey brown hair.

"That's not all. Gabriel says you get to give me some sort of a tattoo of the silver-dragon sept. He says most members of the sept have them on their backs, but I thought it would be cool to have it on my arm, so I can show it off."

"No tattoo!" I said firmly. "You're far too young for that. And I wouldn't know how to give you one even if you weren't."

"It's not really a tattoo," May said quickly. "It's more of a brand. It's done with dragon fire."

I stared at her for a few seconds. "Is that supposed to make it better?"

Gabriel laughed and pulled his shirt off, turning around. "All members of the silver sept bear the emblem marking them as such on their backs."

High on his shoulder blade was a mark that looked like a hand with a crescent moon on the palm.

"May has one too, although she wouldn't show me hers," Brom said, giving her a disgusted look.

"I don't take my shirt off in public quite as easily as Gabriel does," she told him.

"I don't care what it is," I said. "You're not having it. You're not a member of the silver dragons."

"Gabriel says I am because you're one of them."

"Well, I'm not." A thought occurred to me. "And I can prove it. You said all the silver dragons have that mark—well, I don't."

They all looked at me as if they wanted me to take my shirt off.

"She's right," Brom said after a moment of silence. "I've never seen anything like that on her back."

"You see?" I tried to keep the triumph in my voice to a minimum. "I wish you'd mentioned this emblem or tattoo or whatever it is before—it could have cleared things up instantly. I don't have any such marks on me."

"Well . . . except for that one on your hip," Brom said.

"That is a scar, not a tribal marking," I told him.

"Scar?" Gabriel asked, his gaze dropping to my midsection. "What sort of a scar?"

"Just the remnants of an old injury, nothing more," I said quickly.

"It's shaped kind of like this," my son said, holding his hands up, fingers spread, thumbs touching.

"Oh, it is not. It's just a simple scar!"

"Is it a figure resembling a bird?" Gabriel asked him.

"Of course it's not! And no, before you ask, I'm not going to—Brom!"

The child I had labored to bring into the world—even if I couldn't remember the event—grabbed the bottom of my broomstick skirt and lifted it, squinting at my exposed hip. "I suppose it looks kind of like a bird."

"You are in serious trouble, buster," I told him, trying to wrestle my skirt out of his grasp.

Gabriel started around the back of me, but stopped at a pointed look from May, who gave me a little smile, and said, "I'm sorry, Yso— Tully," as she bent her head to look at the mark that rode high on my hip. I'd never thought much of it, assuming that I must have had a painful fall sometime in my past.

I realized now that Kaawa had been right—something had made me not worry about the fact that I couldn't remember my past.

"I have to say, the part that I can see looks like a . . . well, like a phoenix," May said, examining the scar. "It disappears into your underwear, but it looks like those are outstretched wings."

"I think everyone has seen enough," I said, giving Brom one of my scariest mom looks.

He didn't even flinch, the rat.

"We could see this better if you took your underwear off," he pointed out.

"You did not just say that," I said through clenched teeth.

Confusion flashed across his face. "Yeah, I did. See, that part of it is underneath your underwear—"

I slapped his hand where he was about to yank down the side of my undies. "That is quite enough!"

"I'm sorry, Tully," May said, straightening up. "This isn't a scar. It's not a brand, though, either. I don't quite know what it is—it's like it's an anti-tattoo."

"Mayling," Gabriel said, clearly asking her permission to look at the silly scar.

She narrowed her eyes at him. "You do not need to be looking at strange women's hips."

"I'm a healer! I've seen women's bodies," he protested.

"Ysolde isn't injured!"

"You wouldn't recognize a sept emblem as I would."

"I think I would. I've seen enough of them now."

"You are far from an expert—" he started to say, but I had finally had enough.

"Oh, this is ridiculous." I jerked the material of my skirt out of Brom's hand and spun around, pulling the top side of my underwear down a few inches. "You want to see? Fine, you can see. Why don't we get Kaawa and your big friend in to see as well? Perhaps announce it on the street and bring in a few strangers!"

Gabriel ignored my little hissy fit as he stared at my hip for a few moments before his gaze rose to mine. His grey eyes were somber and considering. "I believe I have been mistaken."

"A voice of sanity at last!" I said, readjusting my underwear and letting the skirt fall back into place. "Thank you! It's nice to know there's someone who recognizes a scar when he sees one."

He shook his head. "That is no scar, Ysolde."

"Tully. My name is Tully."

"Your name is Ysolde," he said firmly, his eyes glittering strangely in the night. I opened my mouth to protest, but he continued. "I was wrong about you being a silver dragon. You do not bear our emblem. You do, however, bear that of the black dragons."

I closed my mouth and, taking Brom's hand, turned on my heel, walking back into the house and up the stairs to the room where I'd woken up.

Brom watched me for a few minutes before saying, "May says I can sleep in the room next to this one 'cause she figures you'll want me close by. I told her you didn't think I was such a baby."

"That was very thoughtful of May. I do indeed want you close by. I've missed you terribly."

He grimaced. "I hope you're not going to go all mom on me in front of everyone. I like them. I like Gabriel and May. They're nice, huh? Did you know May can go invisible?"

I shook my head, my brain numbed by the events of the day. What was happening to me? Was I losing my grip on reality, or was something more profound, infinitely more frightening, controlling my life?

"She said she's made up of shadows, but I think she was just teasing me, because she feels just like a normal person. But she showed me in the car coming here how she can disappear. She said you have to be born that way to do it, that she's something with a long name, and that's why she can become invisible."

A word nudged its way to the front of my mind. "Doppelganger."

"Yeah, that's it." He plopped himself down on the bed next to me. "Gabriel says if Gareth had been a mortal human, I could have been a wyvern, and one day challenged him for the job."

"Gareth *is* human," I said, feeling as if a thousand ants were marching up and down my body.

"Sullivan," he said with an exaggerated eye roll. "Have you seen those pictures of him and Ruth and you in old-time clothes? He's got to be at least a hundred years old. Maybe more."

"Pictures? What pictures?" I roused from my stupor in order to look at him.

"The ones in Ruth's room."

I dug through what remained of my memory. "I don't remember seeing any pictures in her room."

"In a box in the locked drawer in her bureau," he said, looking around the room with casual curiosity.

"How do you know what's in a locked drawer?" I asked, then realized just how stupid a question that was. "I don't care if your father gave you a lock-picking kit for Christmas—you are not going to be a cat burglar when you grow up, and you are not to hone your skills on your aunt's locked bureau."

"She has pictures of you, too," he said with blithe disregard to my chastisement.

"I highly doubt that. Ruth and I aren't the very best of friends."

"Yeah, I know, but she has pictures of you and Gareth and her, and you're all wearing clothes like out of that movie you made me watch."

I racked my brain, or what was left of it. "What movie?"

"The one you like to watch so much. You know, the one with the girls in long dresses and they walk around and talk a lot."

"Pride and Prejudice?"

He nodded. "Yeah, you were wearing stuff like that."

"They didn't have cameras during the Regency period," I told him, distracted by the thought of pictures.

Brom wouldn't lie, but he might have misinterpreted what he had seen.

"Whatever. I think I'll go move my stuff down to the room in the basement Gabriel said I could have."

I eyed him, his round face as dear to me as life itself. Thank god whatever was happening to me hadn't stripped me of memory of him altogether. "You will go to bed. It's well past your bedtime."

"I'm nine, Sullivan, not a baby," he said with exaggerated forbearance.

"Go to bed," I repeated.

He sighed and got to his feet, pausing at the door to send me a martyred look before saying, "Gabriel says he won't kick us out because we're not silver dragons anymore. He said you were born into the silver sept, and that they'd honor that, even though you were married to a black dragon. Did you know Gareth when you were married to the dragon?"

I closed my eyes and bowed my head, wanting to cry, wanting to scream, wanting to tell Brom that I had only been married once in my life, to his father. "Time for bed," was all I said, however, before escorting him to his room. I made sure that he was settled before disgusting him with not one, but three hugs, and two smooches to the head, which he tolerated, but only just barely. Clearly Brom was moving into that stage of life where motherly affection was a thing to be borne with much martyrdom.

"Sleep well. If you need anything, come and get me," I told him as I left the room.

"I'm glad you're OK," he said before the door closed. "Penny said you would be, but I was kind of worried. I didn't know you had May and Gabriel to look after you.

You know what I think? I think you're lucky they found you."

My heart swelled at the fact that he had been concerned. "Lucky?"

"Yeah. What if it had been one of the other dragons who found you? Someone not from your own group? What would have happened then?"

What indeed. "Go to sleep," I said, blowing him a kiss.

Silence filled my little room when I returned to it, but all it did was heighten the desperate confusion of my mind.

Chapter Four

"I don't want to go."

The lid of my traveling basket closed with solid finality, punctuated by the muted sounds of weeping.

"I don't like him. He's arrogant," I added, watching as my mother's tirewoman tightened the straps on the basket so it wouldn't come open during travel. "Although he's a much better kisser than Mark, the brewer's son."

"He kissed you?" My mother moved into view, her face pinched and white as she glanced around my bedchamber. Margaret sat on the bed, weeping into her sleeve.

Sorrow at leaving her filled me, but anger at the sudden upheaval in my life was the emotion that rode me. "Yes. I don't see why I have to go with him."

"Mama, can't she stay?" Margaret begged, looking up with red-rimmed eyes.

I sat next to her on the bed and hugged her. Margaret and I had sometimes had a turbulent relationship, but she was the only sister I had, and I would miss her. Especially since I was being taken from my home against my will.

"I promised your mother—" Mama choked on the word before continuing. "I promised the one who was your mother that I would raise you as my own to ensure your safety. I have done so, but I know she would not have wanted me to keep you from your true family. I would not let you go, but indeed, I have no choice in the matter. And Lord Baltic said that no ill would come to you, not that I told him anything about your past. Still, he swore that you would not be harmed, and that is what we must hold to."

"I don't care what that Baltic says," I murmured, holding tight to Margaret. "I'm not an animal."

"I've explained to you, dear—dragons do not take their bestial form very often. They prefer to be in human form, and live amongst us as a mortal would." She gestured to the maids to carry down my traveling baskets. "Come, Ysolde. It is time. Lord Baltic is waiting, and I do not wish for his anger at a delay to fall upon your father."

"Lord Baltic can go stick his head in the pig's wallow for all I care," I said, stalking out the door after the maids.

Mama made noises of distress, but followed after me, speaking to herself as she ran over the things I was taking with me. "I asked him if he wanted the bed, but he said no, he wanted to travel fast. I have done my best by her, I hope he knows that."

Margaret hurried after me, wiping her face. "Ysolde will be able to visit us, won't she, Mama?"

"Of course I will," I said as our little procession

marched down the stairs to the great hall below. "No one can stop me from seeing you whenever I want."

"Is that so?" a deep male voice asked.

I turned my head as I stepped off the last step, meeting Baltic's ebony gaze with a level look. "Yes, that's so."

He watched me for a moment, then gave a jerky nod of his head. "We will do our best to make you happy, *chérie*."

"Stop calling me that," I hissed through my teeth as I passed him.

His laughter rolled out across the hall in response.

The leave-taking that followed was not something I ever wish to live through again. I clung first to my mother, then my father, unable to keep tears from spreading tracks down my cheeks, their wetness blending with that of Margaret's when she hugged me, her face pressed to mine as she whispered her desire that I not be long in returning.

By the time the imperious Baltic lifted me onto my horse, I wasn't in much better shape than Margaret, although I had enough presence of mind to glare at him when he gripped my leg as he adjusted the stirrups.

"I am not a strumpet to be handled such," I snapped, my emotions frayed and irritated, placing my boot in the middle of his chest and pushing him backwards.

One of his guards, the one he called Kostya, a black-eyed devil if ever there was one, laughed and said something in a language I did not know.

Baltic shot me a look filled with ire, but said nothing. Before I knew it, we were riding across the bridge over the moat, the only home I'd ever known slowly slipping away behind me.

I didn't speak to any of the dragon men for three days.

On the fourth, I was sick of my own thoughts, tired of grieving for my lost family, and bored almost to the point of insensibility.

"Where are we going?" I asked that evening, when we passed through the gates of a small town.

Baltic, who was riding next to me, shot me an amused glance. "You're speaking to us?"

"Since I have no other alternative," I said in my most haughty manner. "I would like to know where these other parents of mine are."

We stopped in front of a small inn. The three guards dismounted; one of the men, a short, stocky man named Pavel, disappeared into the low opening of the inn. Baltic tossed the reins of his horse to a stableboy before helping me off my mount. "I am not taking you to your parents."

I stared at him in surprise. "Why not?"

He put his hand on my back and gave me a little shove toward the inn. Since it looked like it was about to rain, I went inside, ducking at the low beam at the doorway. The inn was of modest size, smoky and dark inside, but there were no foul odors as you will sometimes find in such places. To the right was a rough staircase leading to a floor above, while to the left was a common room filled with benches and rough-hewn plank tables.

"We do not yet know who your parents are. The mortal woman would not tell us the name of the dragons who left you with her, and although it would have been possible to get that information from her, such methods can take time, and I wished to be on my way. We will go to my home in Riga, and from there begin the search for your true parents."

I felt like a dog hackling up at his arrogant tone. "I suppose you expect me to be grateful you decided not to torture my mother!"

"No." He looked nonplussed. "She was not your mother. She was merely a mortal who had sworn her fealty to a dragon."

"Did you even talk to her?" I demanded, grabbing his arm when he was about to walk away from me. "Did you even ask her why I was left with her? You didn't, did you? You couldn't be bothered to find out what really happened!"

His eyes glittered dangerously, but I was never one to take heed when I should, and I saw no reason to start now. He leaned close, his fingers biting hard into my arm, his breath fanning my face as he growled, "You will not address me in such an insolent tone. I am a wyvern. You will show me respect at all times."

"I will respect you when you prove worthy of such an honor!" I snapped back.

His jaw worked as if he wanted to shout at me, but all he did was release me with a muttered oath. He started off toward the innkeeper, but I wasn't through with him. "Finding out the truth may have been beneath your concern, but it wasn't beneath mine! My mother told about the woman she knew from her youth, a woman who was gravely injured, and whom she healed. She told me about how they had remained friends until one day, the woman arrived covered in blood, bearing a baby—me—and begged her to hide the child away lest it be discovered by her enemies. She told my mother the name of that enemy."

Baltic froze and turned slowly around to face me, his expression blank.

I squared my shoulders and met his gaze without flinching. "Baltic. The woman said the one who would destroy her and the child was named Baltic."

With a snarl, he lunged at me, moving so fast I could barely follow him. I didn't even have time to scream before he spun me around, ripping off my cloak and shredding my surcoat. I ran forward, sobbing, intent on escaping the suddenly mad warrior, but he caught me, pressing me into the wall as he tore the cotte until only my chemise hid my skin from his view.

Even that wasn't enough. As I clutched the wall, terrified that in his animal frenzy he would tear the flesh from my bones, he jerked down my chemise until my back was exposed.

"Silver!" he snarled, releasing me suddenly. I half collapsed on the stairs, clutching my clothing to my chest, trying to understand what brought on this brainstorm.

"What is silver?" I asked, flinching when he kicked tables and chairs out of his way as he stormed across the room.

"The mark you bear."

"On my back?" I snatched up the cloak that lay on the ground, wrapping it around myself.

At the sound of wood being smashed, Kostya burst into the room, his sword in hand. "What is it?"

Pavel stood at the top of the stairs, silently watching as his master literally destroyed the meager furnishings in the common room.

Kostya frowned, looking from Pavel, to me, and finally to Baltic. "What's wrong?"

Baltic swore, profanely and with a fluency that I

couldn't help but admire. He slammed a chair into the wall. It exploded in a thousand little splinters. "Ask her!" he snarled, kicking debris out of the way. The innkeeper had run into the back room the second Baltic had become enraged. He peeked out of the door, quickly hiding when Baltic pulled out his sword and started hacking away at a barrel of ale.

"What have you done?" Kostya asked me, sheathing his sword.

"Nothing. Baltic is upset over a birthmark on my back."

"That is no birthmark!" Baltic yelled, his face red with fury as he started toward me, his sword still in hand. I backed up, stumbling over a broken chair, wanting nothing more than to get out of the way of the madman. He stalked forward, menace rolling off him, his eyes narrowed and focused on me.

I thought briefly of running, but knew I wouldn't make it more than two steps before he would be on me.

"I've done nothing to anger you," I said, putting on a brave front.

His lips curled. "You bear the mark of a silver dragon."

Behind him, Kostya looked shocked.

"Silver, not black! You are the spawn of a traitor, one who has betrayed us! I should kill you where you stand!" He raised the sword until the tip of it was pressed into my throat.

I stood still, confused why he should be so angry with me, but aware that if I showed the least sign of weakness, he would kill me.

"Baltic—" Kostya approached, stopping just short of us. His expression was wary, but I did not see in him the unwholesome fury that was in his master. "She is innocent of wrongdoing."

"No silver dragon is innocent," Baltic said in a low growl. Pain pricked my neck as the sword tip pierced my skin. I lifted my chin, keeping my gaze steady on his. "They will either rejoin us, or they will die."

"But this one knows nothing of our ways. She has not even accepted that she is a dragon," Kostya argued, gesturing toward me. "What purpose is there in killing her?"

Baltic opened his mouth to answer, but I was through being tolerant.

"His purpose is to bully and frighten," I said loudly. "He is a coward, nothing more."

His breath hissed in as he leaned forward. "No man has ever spoken those words to me and lived."

"I am not a man," I said, gritting my teeth against the burn of the sword as it slid deeper into my flesh.

"You would be dead if you were," he snarled, lowering the sword and stepping back.

"You wish to challenge me?" I asked, shoving him hard in the chest.

He looked so surprised by the action, I had to bite back the urge to laugh. Kostya's mouth dropped open into an O as I took two steps forward until I stood toe-to-toe with Baltic. "I will meet your challenge, warrior, but on my terms."

An odd look crossed his face. "What terms?"

"No weapons," I said, lifting my chin. "If you wish to challenge me, I will meet you body to body, but with no weapons, no armor. Just your fists against mine."

Pavel gave a short bark of laughter. Kostya's frown relaxed into a smug smile. Baltic's face remained expres-

sionless, nothing but his eyes giving away any indication
of what he was thinking.

"Very well," he said after a minute's silence. "But you
must make it worth the ridicule I will suffer for such an
indignity."

"Indignity!" He actually had the nerve to smile when
I hit him on the chest. "Because I am a woman, you
mean?"

"Because I am the wyvern, and you are merely a
young female who has not yet learned her place." He
handed Kostya his sword. "I will be happy to teach it to
you, but I must have payment."

I eyed him as Pavel came down the stairs to help di-
vest him of his mail and armor. Both guards were smiling. "What form of payment do you seek?"

"When I win the challenge, you will disavow your
fealty to the traitorous bastard who rules your sept."

"I don't know any bastards other than Jack, the cart-
er's brother, and he is simpleminded and hardly could
be called traitorous."

"I refer to Constantine of Norka," Baltic said, all but
spitting the words out.

"Well, I don't know him either, and I certainly haven't
sworn fealty to him."

"Your parents must have, else you would not bear the
brand of the silver dragons on your back." Baltic peeled
off his leather armor and stood before me wearing nothing but boots, braies, and jerkin.

It struck me for the first time that he was quite comely
for a man. The high, sharp cheekbones gave his face a
measure of strength. His nose was thin and sharp, sitting
below a broad forehead from which dark hair swept back.
Twin slashes of straight black eyebrows drew attention

to his deep, dark eyes beneath. His jaw was angular, but blunted at the chin, as if God had decided that he had too many angles in his face and wanted to soften the sharpness a little. But it was his mouth that seemed to hold an unholy attraction for me. His lips were full, the lower creating a down-turned crescent, while the upper had a gentle curve that belied the anger held within him.

"Do you agree to the terms?" he asked, and I realized I'd been staring at his mouth.

I cleared my throat. "You have neglected to state the full terms. I must have a boon if I defeat you."

All three men laughed loud enough that the remaining guard came in from where he had been tending to the horses.

"Lady Ysolde has accepted Baltic's challenge," Kostya told him when he entered casting curious glances around the now-destroyed common room.

"What challenge?" the guard asked. His name was Matheo, I remembered from the brief introduction Baltic had made when he took me from my home. Kostya leaned over and whispered to him. Matheo smiled broadly.

"You will not defeat me," Baltic said, and once again, I was possessed with the desire to slap him. "But let us live in the world of the impossible, and say that you do. What boon would you like of me?"

"I wish to go home," I said, my gaze steadfast.

He was silent for a moment, then made me a bow. "I accept the terms of the challenge. When would you like to begin?"

I looked around the room. It was only four warrior dragons and myself, the innkeeper wisely keeping himself out of sight.

"Is there anything wrong with now?" I asked, pinning my cloak so my hands were free.

"No." He waved a hand around the room. "Would you like to fight here, or would you prefer we go out—"

I moved swiftly. He dropped like a sack full of bulls, his body curling into a circle as he clutched at his privates, unable to speak except to gasp for air.

"You should never have taken off your codpiece," I said, gesturing toward that piece of armor that lay half hidden by the leather cuirass that had been discarded a few minutes before. "And I believe this qualifies as a win."

His guards, all three of them, stared with open-mouthed surprise as Baltic stopped writhing on the ground, his eyes open and glaring at me with promised retribution. He uncurled himself, his face beautiful and deadly.

"You . . . will . . . pay . . ." he finally managed to get out.

"No, I think you will pay—you will take me home." I kept my ground as he got painfully to his feet, his body hunched as if . . . well, as if he'd just taken a very hard kick to the privates. "Do you deny that I won the challenge?"

His face worked again, and I was certain that he was going to either spit at me or strike me, but he did neither; he simply turned and slowly made his way up the stairs to where the bedchamber was located.

The guard Matheo, after a long look at me, followed him. Pavel shook his head and gathered up Baltic's armor before doing the same.

Only Kostya was left with me, and he watched me with an expression that I found difficult to read.

"You do not approve of my method of winning?" I asked him.

He was silent for the count of six, then shook his head. "You are a woman. He is a wyvern. I would expect you to use whatever method you could to disable him. It is not how you struck the blow that you will regret."

"Then what?" I asked, feeling more than a little ashamed at the way I'd taken Baltic off guard.

Slowly, Kostya smiled. "There may come a day when you wish to enjoy those parts you have this day so grievously injured."

Heat flooded into my cheeks as he, too, made a bow, then went outside.

Had he seen me staring at Baltic's mouth, and assumed I was a woman of no virtue? I couldn't blame him if he did. I didn't feel particularly virtuous around Baltic, not with my mind reliving over and over again that kiss in the forest.

"By the rood," I swore to myself. "Kostya's right. But the saints help me, Baltic is driving me insane."

Guilt ate at me later, as I sat alone in a cramped bedchamber, nothing more than a closet, really, with a pallet crammed up against the eaves, a three-legged stool, and a cracked chamber pot.

The inn boasted two rooms—this one, and the larger room that took up the remainder of the upper floor—but as it was a communal room, one containing several pallets upon which Baltic and his guards would sleep, I had been given the closet. I walked the two paces that was the available free space, turned, and paced back, listening with half an ear to the sounds coming up through the floorboards.

Kostya had evidently made things right with the innkeeper, because earlier, when I had come in from using the privy, two lads and a frightened-looking woman were clearing away the debris left by Baltic's fit, and shortly after that, three new benches appeared. Two hours later the locals slowly arrived, no doubt reassured that the mad lord was safely asleep upstairs. The soft murmur of conversation drifted upward, livened now and again by a hearty laugh that was stifled quickly, as if the patrons feared causing too much noise.

"This is silly. He challenged me. He held a sword to my neck. I shouldn't feel the least bit sorry for what I did," I told myself, touching the spot on my neck where the sword had pierced my flesh.

The wound wasn't there. It had healed almost immediately, and if a thin trickle of blood hadn't seeped into my chemise, I might have thought I imagined it. I had changed my torn clothing once Pavel brought my traveling basket, but my chemise lay on top of it, the rusty stain a glaring accusation. I rubbed at the dried blood and tried to ignore the feeling of guilt and shame.

"It's no good," I said finally, and straightening my shoulders, opened the door and entered the main chamber.

There was no light but the moonlight that came in through the shutters. I held high the candle from my closet, scanning the pallets to locate the one Baltic had chosen. To my surprise, they were all empty, all but one.

I approached the dark shape cautiously. I couldn't tell which man it was—a fur was thrown over him, leaving only the tip of his head showing, and all the guards had varying shades of dark hair.

Setting the candle down on the ground next to the pallet, I reached out to pull back the fur just far enough to see who lay there, but before I could touch it, a hand shot out and grabbed my wrist in a grip that came close to grinding my bones. I cried out, and the man sat up, releasing my wrist when he saw it was me.

"What are you doing?" he snarled.

It was Baltic, and he didn't look any too pleased to see me.

"I came to see if you were hurt," I said, suddenly feeling very awkward. I gestured toward his legs. "In your ... place."

He stared at me a moment just as if two carrots suddenly sprouted from my ears. "You came to see if I was hurt?"

"Yes. I know men are sensitive there. Well, you would have to be, wouldn't you? I mean, it's all just hanging there, right out in the open, not tucked away nicely like women. And I knew it would disable you, but I was thinking about it, and I realize that perhaps I took you by surprise, and that even though I said we'd start right then, you weren't ready for my attack. So I thought I would see if you were hurt. Seriously hurt, that is, because I know you were hurt, or else you wouldn't have rolled around on the ground as you did."

He sat through that entire speech without saying anything, but when I was finished he shook his head, and said in a quite reasonable tone of voice, "Yes, you hurt me. You damn near kicked my stones up into my belly. But you didn't permanently damage me, if that's what you're having this attack of conscience about."

"Are you sure?" I asked, kneeling down next to him. I wanted to check his parts, but couldn't think how to suggest that without sounding like I just wanted to ogle him. Which, sadly, I had to admit I wouldn't mind. "Perhaps I should make sure. My mother—Lady Alice—taught me much about tending ailments. I'm known throughout the keep for my healing skills."

He muttered something that sounded like a blasphemy against healers, then suddenly sat up straight. "You want to look at my cock?"

"I think it would be best if I examined your man parts for signs of injury, yes," I said, trying my best to look knowledgeable in the area of genitals. "After all, I caused the injury. If anyone should look at your ... er ... area, then I should."

He scooted back until he was leaning against the wall. "Go ahead," he said, crossing his arms.

I licked my lips nervously, biting my lower lip as I pushed the fur down his legs. He was dressed in a thin tunic and braies, and unless he had donned his armor, he would have no codpiece on under the tunic. Carefully I lifted the edge of his tunic. "Oh. My. Um. I was expecting ... hmm."

"What were you expecting?" he asked, pulling up his tunic in order to stare down at himself. "What are you hmming about?"

"Oh, it's nothing, really," I said, frowning just a little at his man parts.

"Like hell it is!" he said, sounding quite incensed.

I looked at him in confusion.

He sighed, closed his eyes for a minute, then opened them back up, and with a tight jaw, asked, "Are you going to examine my cock or not?"

I eyed the part in question. "I don't want to touch it if it's bruised."

"It's not bruised," he snapped.

"It looks ... angry."

"For god's sake, woman, it doesn't have emotions of its own!"

"Of course not. All right then. I will just check to make sure everything is as it should be." I put one hand on his shaft. He didn't move, the expression on his face suspicious.

"Well?" he demanded.

There was nothing for it. I put my other hand on his parts, lifting them to look for signs of damage.

A noise at the door had Baltic jerking up the fur, my hands trapped beneath it.

Kostya stood at the top of the stairs, giving us a puzzled look. "I heard loud voices. Is everything all right?" he asked.

"Yes!" Baltic answered through gritted teeth.

Kostya looked pointedly at me.

"Baltic's man parts are angry, and I was seeing if there was something I could do to ease the pain," I explained, not wanting him to think me wanton.

Kostya's expression went absolutely blank. Baltic ran a hand over his face, clearly trying to maintain a grip on his formidable temper. "It's not like that. She wanted to see if she had seriously hurt me. I told her she could look for herself to see that I wasn't."

"I see," Kostya said in a voice that sounded as if he were choking. "I'll just leave you to that, then."

He disappeared. A roar of laughter came up from below that had Baltic swearing under his breath as he shoved the fur down again. "For the love of the saints— get on with it, woman!"

"Very well." I lifted his shaft, looking for signs of injury, but saw nothing. Despite the knowledge that I was renowned in the village and by folk of the keep as a healer, I couldn't help but feel wicked as I touched him. I was no stranger to the sight of man parts—the male villagers frequently wore short tunics that left little to the imagination when the wind was high, but my mother had kept Margaret and me from bathing visitors, as was the common custom. Baltic's parts were . . . interesting. "You don't appear to have any injury," I added, suddenly feeling a bit breathless. I let his stones slide slowly from my fingers, and was surprised by both the sudden hitch in his breath and the fact that his shaft began to harden.

"You are becoming aroused," I said, looking at it.

"I'd have to be dead not to. Are you stopping?"

I trailed my fingers down the length of his shaft. It was gaining in stature, the skin of it sliding like the softest silk over a piece of polished ivory my mother kept in her sewing box. "Do you want me to stop?"

"Hell, no."

I continued to lightly run my fingers down it. "How much bigger will it grow?"

A short, pained-sounding bark of laughter escaped him. "I've never measured it. Why do you ask?"

"Idle curiosity. That part is pushing back. Is it supposed to do that, or did I damage it?"

"It's supposed to do that."

I slid one hand underneath the shaft, stroking it like I would a cat. Baltic groaned and closed his eyes, his hips rocking forward. "I'm enjoying this," I told him, feeling a sense of pride in the fact that I could arouse him with my hands.

Eyes of purest black regarded me, shimmering with something I couldn't put a name to. His lips quirked. "So am I."

"It seems rather monotonous, however," I said after a few minutes of repeated stroking. His shaft was fully aroused now, and I marveled to myself that he ever fit it into his codpiece.

"There are . . . variations . . . you can do," he said in a choked voice.

"Oh?" I looked down at the shaft. "Changes in pressure and speed?"

"No. Instead of your hands, you could use your mouth."

"You're jesting," I said, staring at him in disbelief.

His lips quirked even more. "I thought that would shock you."

I eyed his shaft again. "I'm not shocked. I'm just a little taken aback. If I were to use my mouth, that would give you pleasure, too?"

"*Chérie*, if you were to use your mouth, I would probably spill my seed within two seconds of your tongue wrapping around me."

"It's a sin to spill your seed outside of a woman," I said, parroting Father David, the priest at our keep.

"That is a human belief. Dragons do not hold with such foolish dogma. If you weren't a silver dragon, I would be happy to do as you suggest."

I touched the very tip of him with one finger. A bead of moisture had formed there, a tear that glistened as I spread it about the head of his shaft. "I don't wish for you to bed me, if that's what you are implying."

"Why not? You seem to enjoy touching me."

I met his black-eyed gaze with calm assurance. "One day I will marry, and I must save my maidenhead for my husband."

"Marriage is also a human tradition, one dragons seldom follow. Ysolde?"

"Hmm?" I spread the moisture around a little more, enjoying the sensation of it, wondering what he tasted like, and whether it would be a sin to find out.

His jaw tightened. "Nothing. Go back to your bed. I'm not injured, as you can—"

I bent over him and took the tip of his shaft into my mouth. He stopped speaking. In fact, for a few seconds, he stopped breathing. He just sat there stiff as a plank, staring with wide eyes as I tasted him.

It was . . . different. Different, but pleasant. He tasted hot, somewhat salty, but it was the feeling of his silken flesh against my tongue that gave me boldness. I slid my tongue around the head of it, and Baltic groaned loudly, clutching with both hands the linen covering the pallet.

"Stop!" he cried, his voice sounding as if he had a mouthful of stones.

I released him from my mouth, worried I had done something to harm him. "Did I hurt you?"

"No. You just have to stop, or else I'm going to—"

I took his shaft in my hand again, sliding my fingers around the flesh now made slick by my mouth. He groaned again, his hips thrusting forward as he growled, "Too late."

"I don't see how that's not going to count as a sin," I said, my hand full of his seed. "You'll have to do penance for that."

"I already am," he muttered, jerking up one edge of the pallet linen to clean my hand. He rose when he had done so, pulling me up and swinging me into his arms.

"What are you doing?" I asked, panicking slightly as he marched tense-jawed toward my closet.

"Taking you to bed."

"I told you that I don't wish for you to bed me."

"I heard you the first time," he said, his voice sounding rough and harsh.

He shoved open the flimsy door and dropped me onto the pallet.

"I'm serious. I don't want to hurt you again, but I will defend myself if you make me."

He dropped down onto his knees. "I don't bed silver dragons."

"Then what—"

"I'm just going to reciprocate."

I frowned as he pushed my feet apart in order to move between them. "Reciprocate what?"

His face lost its tense look as he suddenly grinned at me. "Bliss."

Chapter Five

Bliss. What a lovely word it was. I lay on the bed and stared up at the shimmers from a streetlight dappling the ceiling of my room, listening to the faint sounds of London traffic, sounds that were muted by the fact that the house had exceptionally good windows, and by the time of night. It was two in the morning—deep night, someone had once called it.

I frowned. "Now where did I hear that?"

A sliver of light pierced the darkness of the room as the door opened a tiny bit. "Are you awake?"

"Unfortunately, yes."

Kaawa opened the door wider and gave me an inquisitive look. "I was passing your room a short while ago and heard you call out. I thought perhaps you were having a nightmare. Would you like some company?"

"So long as you don't mind being shut up with a nutcase, sure," I answered, pulling myself up to a sitting position. I clicked on the bedside lamp and watched as she hauled an armchair a little closer to the bed.

"That's a lovely caftan," I said, admiring the black and silver African batik animals on it.

"Thank you. My daughter sent it to me. She lives in Kenya, on an animal preserve. Why do you think you are a nutcase?"

I looked back up at the ceiling for a minute, debating whether or not I wanted to talk about the fear that was eating away at me. Kaawa seemed nice and motherly, but I didn't really know her.

Then again, there weren't too many people I *did* remember knowing.

"I think I might be mentally unstable," I said at last, watching her to see if she looked at all frightened of me.

She didn't look anything but mildly interested. "Because of the memory loss?"

"No. I think I might be schizophrenic. Or suffering from multiple personalities. Or some other mental disorder like that."

"You are having dreams," she said, nodding just as if she understood. "Dreams of your past."

"I'm having dreams, yes, but it can't be my past. I'm not a dragon. I'm human. Evidently mentally unstable, but human."

She was silent for a moment. "Struggling against yourself is not making the situation any easier, you know."

"I'm not struggling against myself. I'm trying to hold on to my sanity. Look, I know what you think, what everyone thinks. But if you were in my place, wouldn't you know if you weren't human?"

"Do you think humans have dreams of their past life as a dragon?" she asked with maddening calm.

"The only reason I'm having those dreams is because you people put it in my mind!" I said, my voice tinged with desperation.

She shook her head slowly. "It was a dream that brought you out of the month-long sleep, was it not?"

I looked at my hands lying clenched tight on the bed cover. "Yes."

"Child." She laid her hand on my arm. "The dragon inside of you wishes to be woken, whether you desire that or not. I will admit that you appear human to me, and I do not know how it can be that you have changed thusly, but deny it though you may, you are Ysolde de Bouchier, and you will not be calm in your mind until you accept that."

"Calm in my mind? At this point, I can't even conceive of what that's like." I took a deep breath, trying to keep from going stark raving mad. "I'm sorry. I don't mean to be the biggest drama queen there ever was, but you have to admit that this whole situation is enough to drive a girl bonkers."

"It is a test, yes," she agreed in that same soothing voice.

I just wanted to shriek. Instead, I took another deep breath. "OK, let's go into the land of totally bizarre, and say you're right. I'm a dragon magically reincarnated—"

"Not reincarnated—resurrected," she corrected me.

"What's the difference?"

"I am reincarnated—when my physical form has run its appointed time, I retreat into the dreaming and await a new form. I am born again, remembering all that has passed before, but with a new body. That is reincarnated. Resurrection is the bringing back to life of that which was dead."

I took a third deep breath. It's a wonder there was any air left in the room. "That's cool. You're reincarnated. I'm resurrected. We'll just move past that and get to the meat of my argument—if I'm a dragon, why don't I like gold? Why can't I breathe fire? Why can't I turn into great big scary animal shapes?"

"Because the dragon in you has not woken yet. I think . . ." She paused, her gaze turned inward. "I think it is waiting."

"Waiting for what?"

"I don't know. That is something you will find out when the time is appropriate. Until then, you must stop fighting the dragon inside you. The dreams you have, they are about your past, are they not?"

I looked away, feeling my cheeks grow hot as I remembered the highly erotic dream I'd just had. "They concern someone named Ysolde, and a man named Baltic."

"As I expected. The dragon part of you wants you to remember," she said, patting my hand as she rose. "It wants you to accept your past in order to deal with the present."

"Well, the dragon part can just go take a flying leap off the side of a mountain, because I want my life to go back to what it was."

"I don't think that's possible. It has stirred. It wishes for you to remember. It is time, Ysolde."

"Cow cookies!" I snapped. "No one tells me what to do. Well, Dr. Kostich does, but that's fully within the bounds of my apprenticeship. And he doesn't give me erotic dreams!"

"Erotic dreams?" Kaawa asked, a little smile on her lips.

I blushed again, damning my mouth for speaking inappropriately again. "I don't really think the type of dream matters as much as the fact that my mind is cracking."

"Your mind is doing nothing of the sort. Allow the dragon side to speak to you, and I think you will find your way through this trying time," she said from the door. She hesitated a few seconds, then added, "This is truly none of my business, but I have prided myself on my knowledge of history of dragonkin, and I admit to being very curious about this. . . . When you and Baltic met—did he offer to make you his mate right away, or did that come after Constantine Norka claimed you?"

I blinked in surprise, then gave a rueful chuckle. "Assuming the dreams are not a figment of my warped mind, then no, Baltic did not ask me to be his mate when we met. Quite the contrary. He came very close to killing me, and later told me he would never bed a silver dragon."

"Fascinating," she said, looking thoughtful. "Absolutely fascinating. I had no idea. Sleep well, Ysolde."

"Tully," I said sadly, but it was said to the door as she closed it.

"You look horrible," the fruit of my loins told me six hours later as I found the dining room. Brom was seated behind a bowl of oatmeal, a plate heaped high with eggs, potatoes, and three pieces of jam-covered toast waiting next to him.

"Thank you," I said, dropping a kiss on his head before taking a cup off the sideboard. "And I hope you're planning on eating all of that. You know how I feel about wasting food."

"That's just 'cause Gareth makes such a big fuss over money," Brom said, turning to May, who sat at the end of the table with a cup of coffee in front of her. "He's a tightwad."

"Quite possibly the fact that you eat like a horse has influenced his lectures regarding economy," I said, giving him a meaningful look. I lifted the lid to a silver carafe and peered in. It held coffee.

"If you prefer tea, we can get you some," May said, watching me.

"Actually, I'm really big on chocolate," I said with an apologetic smile. "I'm afraid the term 'chocoholic' applies to me far too well."

"I'm sure we can rustle up some hot chocolate," she said, rising.

"Don't go to any bother for me—"

"It's no bother. I'll just go tell Renata."

May disappeared, leaving me with Brom. I sat across from him, trying to make a decision.

"Gabriel says there's a museum here that has human mummies. Can we go see them?" Brom asked.

"Possibly. I have to see Dr. Kostich today, though. I was told he's in town, and I will need to see what work he has for me."

Brom's expression was made strangely horrible by the mouthful of toast and eggs he stuffed in. "Gabriel said Tipene or Maata would take me 'cause you're going to be busy with dragon stuff."

"Dragon stuff?" I frowned, idly rubbing my finger

along the beaded edge of the table. "What sort of dragon stuff?"

Brom thought for a few seconds, his cheeks bulging as he chewed. "It had some foreign word, like sarcophagus."

"*Sárkány,*" May said, entering the room with a tall, athletic woman who towered over her. Like Tipene, she appeared to be of Aboriginal descent, with lovely dark skin that gave emphasis to her grey eyes. "This is Maata, by the way. She's the second of Gabriel's elite guards."

We exchanged greetings. Maata moved to the sideboard, loading up a plate almost as full as Brom's.

"Before you ask," May continued, retaking her seat, "a *sárkány* is basically a meeting where the wyverns discuss weyr business. Kostya called one for today."

"Kostya?" I sat frozen for a second as a face rose in my mind's eye.

"Yes." Both May and Maata watched me. "Do you know him?"

I blinked away the image, saying slowly, "He was in a dream I had."

"Kaawa mentioned you were dreaming of your past. It must be very confusing to you to see yourself but not be able to relate to it."

"Yes," I answered, falling silent as a young woman bustled into the room with a pot of hot chocolate for me. I thanked her, breathing deeply of the lovely chocolatey smell.

"The *sárkány* is called for three this afternoon," May continued, sipping her coffee.

"I'm sure we can stay out of your way while you have your meeting."

"That's actually not what I meant," May said with a

little smile. "The *sárkány* has been called so the wyverns can be introduced to you."

I sighed. "I'm getting very tired of telling people I'm not a dragon."

"I know. But I do think it would be good for you to meet them. If nothing else, they will be able to see for themselves that you're human."

"There is that. . . ." I chewed my lip for a moment. "All right. I will come to your meeting."

"Excellent!" May said, looking pleased. "Brom would probably find it pretty dull stuff, so Maata volunteered to take him to the British Museum to see the mummies."

I assessed Maata. She looked sturdy enough to take on a semitruck, and since she was one of Gabriel's elite guard, I assumed she was beyond trustworthy. "That's very kind of you, but I wouldn't want to impose," I told her.

She waved away the objection with a fork loaded with herbed eggs. "It's no imposition at all. I happen to like mummies, and am very interested in Brom's experiments with mummifying animals. Before I knew I was to be part of Gabriel's guard, I thought I might be a veterinarian."

"That's what Sullivan wants me to do," Brom said around another mouthful of food.

I frowned at him, and he made a huge effort to swallow.

"You are not a python," I told him. "Chew before you swallow."

"This is none of my business, but why do you call your mother Sullivan?" May asked.

Brom shrugged. "It's what Gareth calls her."

May's gaze transferred to me. "Your husband calls you by your last name?"

"Gareth is a little bit . . . *special*," I said, pouring out more hot chocolate. It was excellent, very hot, just as I liked it, and made with Belgian cocoa.

She murmured something noncommittal.

"I've decided after talking with your . . . er . . . what do you call Kaawa?" I asked May.

"Call her?"

"Yes. I mean, you're not married to Gabriel, are you? Not that I'm judging! Lots of people shack up without getting married. I just wondered what you call his mother."

She blinked at me twice. "I call her Kaawa."

"I see."

She smiled, and I realized again that there was something about her that struck a familiar chord. "Marriage is a human convention. I've never been human, so I don't feel the need to formalize the relationship I have with Gabriel in that way. The bond between a wyvern and a mate is much more binding than a mortal marriage ceremony, Ysolde. There is no such thing as divorce in the dragon world."

Brom's eyes grew round as he watched her.

"Dragons never make bad choices so far as their significant others go, then?" I couldn't help but ask, trying hard to keep the acid tone from my voice.

"I'm sure some do," she said, glancing at Maata. "I've never met any, though. Have you?"

"Yes, although it is rare," Maata told me. "It is not common, but it can happen that two people are mated who should not be."

"So what do they do? Live out their lives in quiet misery, trying to make the best of what they have despite the fact that they have no hope, no hope whatsoever of any sort of a satisfying or happy connubial and romantic life?" I couldn't help but ask.

"What's connubial?" Brom asked around another mouthful of eggs.

"Married."

May hid her smile, but Maata openly laughed. "I would like to see the dragon that is content to live in quiet misery. No, if a mated pair is not compatible, they take the only solution."

I waited for her to continue, but she didn't. I had to know, though. My curiosity would not be satisfied until I asked. "And what's that?"

"One of them kills the other," she said, shrugging slightly. "Death is the only way to break the bond. Of course, usually the one who remains does not survive long, but that is the way of dragons. They mate for life, and when one mate is gone, the other often chooses to end his or her suffering."

"Cool," Brom said, looking far too fascinated for my ease of mind. "Do you know of a dragon who's died? I wonder if I could mummify something that big. Do they die in dragon form or people form? What happens to them when they're dead? Do you bury them like mortals, or do you burn them up or something else?"

"Enough of the 'like mortals' comment, young man," I told him. "You are a mortal. I don't care what anyone tells you—you are a perfectly normal little boy, albeit one with a bizarre mummy fascination."

"Sullivan is all over denial," he told Maata, who nodded her head in agreement.

"We are going to move on, because if we don't, someone will find himself confined to his room rather than going to a museum," I said with a dark look at my child.

"Are you going to kill Gareth?" he asked me, completely ignoring the look.

"What?" I gawked at him.

"Gabriel said you're married to a dragon named Baltic, but you're also married to Gareth. That means you have to get rid of one of them, and you don't like Gareth, so you should get rid of him." He frowned. "Although I don't want you to if you'll do what Maata said, and end your suffering."

"I assure you that I have no intentions to kill either myself or your father. Shall we move on? Excellent. I really need to see Dr. Kostich today. What time were you thinking of going to the museum?" I asked Maata.

"We can leave right after breakfast, if you like. There's enough to see there to keep us busy all day."

"I'd better take my field notebook and camera," Brom said, starting to rise from his chair.

"Sit," I ordered. "Finish that food or you won't go anywhere today."

He slumped back into his chair, grumbling under his breath about not wanting to waste valuable time.

"Tipene called Dr. Kostich yesterday to tell him you were awake, in case you were worried he didn't know," May told me.

"It's not that. I'm his apprentice. I have no doubt there's a huge mountain of work that's been waiting for me."

"What sort of work does an apprentice do?" May asked.

"Lots and lots of transcribing," I said, sighing. "We're

expected to copy out vast compendiums of arcanery, most of which are bizarre things that no one in their right mind cares about anymore. There are some useful things to be learned, like how to wield arcane destructive spells, but those come to more advanced apprentices. Ones at my level spend their days perfecting their wart removal spells, and ways to make a person's ears unstop. Last week—or rather, the last week I remember—I ran across the mention of a really rocking spell to make a person's eyebrows spontaneously combust."

"Wow," May said, an odd expression on her face.

"I know. Underwhelming, right?" I sighed and glanced at my watch. "Someday I'll get to the good stuff, but until then . . . I should be going now. Brom, I expect you to behave yourself with Maata, and not give her any trouble."

He made a face as I grabbed my purse, but his eyes lit up when I tucked a few bills into his shirt pocket.

"Don't forget, the *sárkány* is at three," May said as I ruffled his hair.

There was a slight undertone of warning to that, a fact I acknowledged with a nod as I left the dining room.

I'm not quite sure what sort of a reception I was expecting from Dr. Kostich, but I assumed he would express some sort of pleasure that I was once again amongst the cognizant.

"Oh. It's you," was the greeting I received, however. He looked over a pair of reading glasses at me, a frown pulling his eyebrows together, his pale blue eyes as cold as an iceberg.

"Good morning, sir. Good morning, Jack."

"Hi, Tully. Glad to see you're up and about again. You scared the crap out of us when you just keeled over a month ago." My fellow apprentice Jack, a young man in his mid-twenties, with a freckled, open face, wild red hair, and a friendly nature that reminded me of a puppy, grinned for a few seconds before some of the chill seeped off of our boss.

As Dr. Kostich's gimlet eye turned upon him, Jack lowered his gaze back to a medieval grimoire from which he was making notes.

"Thanks. I have no idea why the fugue struck me just then and not in October, as it should have, but I am very sorry for any inconvenience it's caused you," I told Kostich.

He tapped a few keys on the laptop before him and pushed his chair back, giving me a thorough once-over. I had to restrain myself from fidgeting under the examination, avoiding his eye, glancing around the living room of the suite he always booked when he was in London. Everything looked the same as when I had left it some five weeks before, everything appeared normal, but something was clearly wrong.

"I have been in contact with the silver wyvern, whom I believe you are currently staying with," he said finally, gesturing abruptly toward a cream and rose Louis XIV chair. I sat on the edge of it, feeling as if I had been sent to the principal's office. "He informed me of a number of facts that I have found infinitely distressing."

"I'm sorry to hear that. I hope that perhaps I can explain some of the circumstances and relieve you of that distress," I said, wishing I didn't sound so stilted.

"I have little hope that will happen," Kostich said, steepling his fingers. "The wyvern informed me that you are not, in fact, a simple apprentice as you represented yourself."

I glanced over at Jack. His head was bent over the grimoire, but he watched me, his gaze serious. "You know, Gabriel is a nice guy and everything, but he and May have some really wild ideas. I don't hold with them at all," I said quickly, just in case he thought to wonder about my mental status. Lord knows I was doing enough of that for both of us.

"In fact, the wyvern tells me that you are a dragon, and were once a member of his sept," Kostich continued just like I hadn't said a word.

I flinched inwardly at the grim look on his face. I knew from the rants he'd made over the past year that Kostich did not like dragons very much. "Like I said, wild ideas. He's wrong, of course. Everyone can see I'm human!"

"No," he said, taking me by surprise. "That you are not. You appear human, yes, but you are not one. I knew that when you applied for apprenticeship."

"You did?" I had a feeling my eyes were bugging out in surprise. I blinked a few times to try to get the stupefied expression off my face. "Why didn't you say something to me?"

He shrugged. "It is not uncommon to find those of mixed heritage in the L'au-dela."

"I'm not . . . mixed heritage."

"I assumed that you had one human parent, and one immortal, as does your husband."

I gawked at him. "You're kidding, right? Gareth? My Gareth? He has an immortal parent?"

"Your husband is of little concern, except when he interrupts me with demands and foolish threats," he answered, shooting me a look that had me frozen in my chair. "You are aware, are you not, of the Magister's Code by which we live our lives?"

"Yes, sir," I said miserably, sure of where he was going.

"You will then be in no surprise to find that due to the violation of statute number one hundred and eighty-seven, you have been removed from the rolls as an apprentice."

A little zap of electricity ran through me as his words sank in. "You're kicking me out?" I asked, unable to believe it. "I know you're pissed about my unexpected absence, but to kick me out because of it? That hardly seems fair!"

"I do not get 'pissed,' as you say." His pale blue eyes looked bored. "That is a useless emotion. You have been stripped of your apprenticeship. Furthermore, as of this moment you are under an interdict prohibiting you from using any of the knowledge you have gained during your time as my aide."

He sketched a couple of symbols in the air. They glowed white-blue for a moment before dissolving into me. "But, sir—"

"Strictly speaking, an interdict is not necessary, since you have limited powers." He peered at me in a way that left me shivering with unease. "You haven't been using your powers lately, have you?"

"No. You know I'm not comfortable doing so without a good deal of preparation." I squirmed in the chair.

His lips tightened. "I am well aware of that fact. That you wasted my time and resources trying to teach you, a dragon, one who has no ability to handle arcane power, is something I shall not forget for a long time."

"But I have power," I protested. "It may not be a lot, and I may not be terribly comfortable with it, but I've learned tons of things from my time as your apprentice! I can take off even the most stubborn of warts. Eyebrows live in fear of me! My neighbor had a case of prickly heat, and I had that sucker gone and her toes back to normal in nothing flat!"

His lips thinned even more until they all but disappeared into each other. "You have been my apprentice for seven years, and yet you still struggle with the most elemental of skills. Jack has been with me for six months, and already he has surpassed your skill tenfold!"

I glanced at Jack, wanting to protest that it wasn't my fault, that magic didn't come easy to me. But the words rang in my head that dragons could not wield arcane power.

"Now that I know the truth about you, there is little wonder that you failed to progress in your studies as you should have. I don't know how I could have been so blind, so foolish as to believe your stories that you simply needed more time to learn the ways of the magi, but I assure you that I will not make the same mistake a second time. You are released from your duties, Tully Sullivan."

Pain lashed me at the invocation of my name. I stood up, not knowing what I could say or do to make him change his mind. "I was making progress," I said sadly. "I almost have that spell down to clear out a plugged ear."

"A child of four could deal with the earwax spell better than you after four months' study at it," he snapped.

"I've tried," I said simply, my spirits leaden.

"Foolishly, yes. I have not doubted your devotion; it is your ability for which I've made allowances, and now that I know the reason for your lack, my path is clear."

"I'm sorry," I said, ridiculously wanting to cry. "I never intended any deception or insult to you, and if there was some way I could make it up to you, if there was some epic sort of task I could undertake, or some hugely intricate bit of magic I could perform to show you how serious I am about my career as a mage, I would do so."

He was silent for a moment, and I was convinced he was going to turn me into a toad, or worse. But to my surprise, he said slowly, "There is, perhaps, a way you could serve me. It will in no way influence my decision to remove you as apprentice, but if you truly wished to be of service to the L'au-dela, then perhaps we can come to an understanding."

I bit the inside of my lip, wanting to tell him that if I was going to do him a favor, I expected to be reinstated to my position, but I had been acquainted with him long enough to know that he couldn't be pressured into any act. But perhaps I could sway him with my devotion and dedication.

"What would that be?" I asked.

"There is a dragon that you have no doubt heard of," he said, his voice deep and persuasive. "He is known as Baltic, and he possesses most alarming skills and abilities, one of which is to enter and leave the beyond at his whim."

I sat somewhat numb, wondering if the whole world revolved around the ebony-eyed Baltic.

"I wish to know how he has come by the arcane skills he has shown on numerous occasions. His companion, whom we captured the day you collapsed, refuses to talk despite being threatened with banishment to the

Akasha. I also wish to know how he obtained Antonia von Endres' light sword, and remove it from him."

"Baltic has a light sword?" I asked, confused. "But that's made up of arcane magic. No one but an archimage could wield it."

"And yet he does, and quite proficiently, I will say," he answered, rubbing his arm as if it hurt.

"You want me, an apprentice of little power and skill—"

"You are no longer an apprentice," he interrupted quickly, his eyebrows making elegant arches above his long nose. "Nor can you wield any power with the interdict upon you."

"You want me, with no power and skills, completely unable to work any sort of magic, to take a priceless sword away from a dragon mage-warrior?" I shook my head. Even to me it sounded like the sheerest folly. "I wouldn't have the slightest clue how to do something like that, even assuming I could."

"Your inability to see all the possibilities is your failing, not mine," he answered, his attention returning to his laptop.

"But I don't even know how to find this Baltic—"

"When you have something to report to me, you may contact me. Until then, good day."

"Perhaps if we were able to talk this over—"

He looked up, power crackling off him. I was at the door before I realized he had compelled me to move. "Good *day*."

A few minutes later, I stood outside the hotel, buffeted by happy tourists and visitors, numbly aware of people and traffic passing by me, but unable to sort through my thoughts. They all seemed to whirl around in a horrible jumble that I doubted I could ever unravel.

The silver dragons thought I was mated to Baltic. The dreams I had focused on Baltic. Dr. Kostich wanted me to retrieve something from Baltic. "I'm beginning to hate that name," I muttered to myself.

The doorman shot me a curious glance. I moved a few feet away, not sure where I was going to go. "Can I help yóu?" the doorman asked.

"I ... I have some time to kill. Is there a park nearby?" I asked, falling back on an old standby that never failed to leave me comforted.

"Six blocks to the north, ma'am. Straight up the street."

I thanked him and walked quickly, needing the calming influence of green, growing things to restore order to my tortured mind. I felt better almost the instant my feet hit the grass, the scent of sun-warmed earth and grass and leaves from the trees that ringed the park fence filling me with a sense of well-being.

There were a great many people out in the park that day, no doubt enjoying the late summer day before the fall gloom set in. Groups of children raced after Frisbees and remote-controlled helicopters, couples lay in languid embraces, harried mothers and fathers herded their respective broods, and great giggling groups of schoolgirls clustered together to fawn over a musical group that was setting up on an entertainment stage in the corner of the park.

I headed in the opposite direction, breathing deeply to fill my soul with the smell and sensations of green life, eventually settling on one of two benches that sat back-to-back next to a boarded-up refreshment stand. No sooner had I slumped onto my claimed bench than two young women who appeared to be in their late teens hurried over and grabbed the one behind me, shooting me brief, curious glances.

I smiled and closed my eyes, turning my face up to the sun, hoping they wouldn't stay long in such an out-of-the-way place, not when a band was going to be playing elsewhere.

The girls evidently decided I was harmless, because they started chatting in voices that I couldn't help but overhear.

"I can't believe that he had the balls, the steel balls, to tell me he'd rather go visit his parents in Malta than go with me to Rome, but he did, and that was it, that was just it as far as I'm concerned. I mean, Rome versus Malta? Rome absolutely wins."

"Absolutely," the second girl said. "You are so right to dump him. Besides, that leaves you free for doing a little shopping in Italy, if you know what I mean. Italian men are so lickable, don't you think?"

"Some of them," the first girl allowed. "Not the really hairy ones. They are just . . . ugh." She shuddered and I started glancing around to find another spot. "I mean, my god, the things they stuff into their Speedos! It's positively obscene!"

My phone burbled at me just at that moment, causing me to send up a prayer of thanks as I flipped it open, expecting to hear Brom asking if he could have another advance on his allowance for some horrible instrument of mummification. "Hello?"

It wasn't his voice that greeted me, however. "Sullivan? What the hell are you doing still in England?

Brom said you were staying there! Is this some sort of a joke?"

"Gareth." The two girls glanced over their shoulders at me. I half turned away and lowered my voice. "I wondered when you would think to call me."

"Think to call you? Are you daft? I've been trying to get hold of you for weeks. What is Kostich making you do?"

"It's a bit complicated," I said, mindful of the girls, although they seemed to have moved on to judging the qualities of every male who wandered past. "I'm still here because I had an episode."

"What?" His shriek almost deafened me. "When? How? What the hell are you thinking?"

"I wasn't—I was asleep. And I don't know how or why, it just happened. I've been staying at the house of some people Kostich was working with. They took me and Brom in."

"Did you manifest?" he asked quietly, but I could hear the eagerness in his voice.

"No. But that brings up a very good question—how long have I been doing that?"

"What?" His voice was wary.

"How long have I been making gold for you? Dr. Kostich says you're immortal. How long have we been married?"

"You know how long we've been married—ten years. You've seen the license."

I had? "I don't remember any of that. Have you been doing something to my memory?"

"What the hell are you talking about?" He sounded furious now, speaking in a low, ugly voice that sent goose bumps up my arms. "If you're trying to distract me because you manifested for some bastard who took you in—"

"I just told you I didn't. Fortunately, no one had large chunks of lead lying around."

"Fortunately? You stupid bitch. Do you have any idea how much that's going to cost us by missing it? How the hell am I going to tell Ruth?"

"I don't know, and I don't appreciate being called names. Look, Gareth, things are a bit confused right now. Dr. Kostich kicked me out of the magister's guild, and I—"

"He *what*?" Profound swearing followed, for a good two minutes. "What did you do?"

"Nothing, I swear."

"Then why did he kick you out?"

"It's because of these"—I cast a glance over my shoulder, but the girls had their heads together, watching as three young men in soccer outfits strolled past—"because of some dragons."

"Dragons?" he repeated, his voice suddenly very small.

"Yes. The people I'm staying with are dragons. They've asked Brom and me to stay with them for a bit while I try to figure things out."

Silence filled my ear for a good minute. "Get out," he finally said.

"What?"

"You heard me—get out. Get away from the dragons."

"Don't you think that would be rude? They've given me a lot, Gareth. The wyvern's mother herself tended me while I was in the fugue—"

"Get out, you stupid woman! Do I make myself clear? Get out before they kill you!"

"You are watching way too much TV, Gareth, you really are." I kept my voice low, but allowed anger to sound in it. "If these people wanted to kill me, all they would have had to do was to dump me in the Thames while I was asleep."

"Listen carefully to me, Sullivan," he said, breathing heavily. "You may think they're your friends, but they aren't. You have to get away from them, today, right now."

"That's not going to be quite so easy," I said, hesitating. I really didn't want to talk to Gareth about Gabriel and May. Somehow, it seemed that it would taint the relationship if I were to try to explain them to him. "I told them I'd stay for a while. I'm having . . . well, they're kind of dreams, and they're—"

"I don't want to hear about your goddamned dreams!" he thundered, breathing like a bulldog for a few minutes before continuing. "I can't leave just yet. Ruth and I are . . . we're following up a potential client. But I'll send someone to help you."

"Will you please stop doing the Darth Vader impression and listen to me?" I lost all remnants of patience with him. "Brom and I are fine. The dragons aren't going to hurt us. We don't need anyone to help us, because we're fine, just fine!"

"Be prepared to leave tonight," Gareth said. I clenched my teeth against screaming in frustration. "Don't tell anyone. Stay in your room."

"By the rood, Gareth! If I wasn't already going insane, you'd be enough to push me right over the edge, do you know that?"

"Wait a minute—did you say Brom was there?"

"Yes! Yes, I did! Hallelujah and let fly the doves! You actually listened to something I said!"

He cursed again, but under his breath this time. "Well, it's of no matter. They can't want him. You'll just have to tell him to stay there until Ruth or someone can get him."

"You're nuts," I said flatly, so flabbergasted that he actually expected I would leave my own child, my brain couldn't come up with anything more than that.

"They won't harm him," he said testily. "Just make sure you're ready to leave."

The very idea that Gareth was willing to abandon Brom, his own child, to people he considered dangerous was so obscene, I sat staring at the grass in utter disbelief. At that moment, I knew the marriage was over. I could not remain married to a man who cared absolutely nothing for his son.

Gareth, obviously taking my silence for compliance, warned me again to have nothing to do with the dragons until I could be rescued.

"What do you expect me to do even if I were to leave the dragons?" my curiosity forced me to ask. "I'm not an apprentice anymore, and I've had an interdict placed on me. I can't practice arcane magic at all."

"You'll get your job back," he said grimly.

"How?"

"That's your problem," he said, echoing Dr. Kostich. With one last word of warning he hung up, leaving me to shake my head. It was all so much to take in—first the dragons, then the dreams, and now the scales falling from my eyes where Gareth was concerned. How had I lived with such a monster for all those years?

"Holy Mary, mother of god," one of the girls behind me said as I tucked my phone away in my purse. "Get a look at those two. Mmrowr! I call the back one."

"Oh! I was going to call him. I suppose I'll have to take the tall one in front, then. What do you think— seven? Seven and a half?"

"Are you kidding? He's too intense. He probably has OCD or something. Five at the most. Now, the one behind him, he's a definite eight point nine."

I glanced between them to see who they were talking about. Two men were walking parallel to the bench, some thirty feet away. I couldn't see much of the far man, although glimpses indicated he was in his late thirties, with short dark hair and a slight goatee. An intricate Celtic tattoo wrapped around his biceps was made visible by a black sleeveless shirt. His companion, nearest me, was taller, and of a similar coloring. He also wore black, unremarkable except for the way the wind rippled the man's shirt against his chest. He moved swiftly, his long legs making nothing of the expanse of the park, his body moving with an almost feline grace.

Something about him struck me as familiar. I turned a little more to get a better look as they continued past. The nearest man, the one with the graceful walk, had shoulder-length dark chocolate brown hair that was pulled back from a pronounced widow's peak into a short ponytail. He was clean-shaven, although a faint hint of darkness around his jaw hinted at stubble.

"Maybe I should go for the tall one. I love me some manly stubble," one of the girls said, as if she'd read my mind. "He's just one hundred percent delicious. Hey! Why don't we see where they're going, and if they'd, you know, like us to go with them?"

The second girl looked hesitant as she watched the ponytailed man. "I don't know. Mine looks kind of intimidating, doesn't he?"

I agreed. He did look intimidating. He also looked sexy as hell. I wished I could indulge in a little illicit daydreaming about him, but I had enough on my plate without dwelling on the lamentable state of my personal life.

My gaze slid to him again, and once more I was struck with a sense of the familiar. It was as if something inside of me recognized something inside of him—a foolish notion if ever I'd had one, and of late, I'd had nothing *but* foolish notions.

To my surprise, the first man stumbled and came to a stop, turning full circle as he scanned the area. He hesitated when he faced us, and the first girl squealed and nudged her friend as she rose to her feet, blocking my view.

"Look! They've seen us! Let's go over to them. Come on, Dee!"

Her friend was slower in getting up. "I don't know that they're looking at us, Sybil."

"Don't be stupid," the first girl said, grabbing her purse. "It's as clear as day! Let's go say hello."

The two women headed toward the men. I tried to watch them but my vision started to fog, as if I were suddenly enveloped in a cocoon of cotton wool. I clutched the back of the bench to keep from pitching forward, but it was no use. I fell.

Pain burst to life in my head in waves of red that pounded and pulsed stronger and stronger until I thought it would explode from me.

"Stop!" I yelled, and miraculously, it did.

I opened my eyes and glared at the two men who faced each other over the altar of the cathedral, the echoes of their shouting disturbing the dust motes that danced in the thin sunlight streaming through the lovely stained-glass rose window. I turned to the man on my right. Slightly taller than me, of a thick, muscular stature, with golden brown hair and almost identically colored eyes, he reminded me of one of my father's prized bulls. "Baltic has done nothing to harm me, *nothing*."

"He has sworn to destroy all silver dragons who do not submit to his obscene demands," Constantine Norka said, glaring at Baltic. "Why would he bring you to me unless you were damaged?"

I held up a hand to stop Baltic's retort, which I knew would be loud and vicious. "He didn't harm me because he is a man of honor. He swore to take me home, and he did, although"—I shifted my gaze to give him a reproachful look—"I meant my father's keep, not to be delivered into the hands of dragons."

"You belong to my sept," Constantine said, his hands fisted.

"Your *sept* belongs to me!" Baltic snarled.

"For the love of the saints, please don't go through that again!" I said, rubbing my forehead. The remnants of a headache, caused by listening to the two wyverns circle each other snapping and snarling for the last hour, still lingered. "The fact is that he did as he said."

"Including spending the nights in your bed?" Constantine asked, his gaze tight on Baltic.

I raised my eyebrows and considered whether I should respond with maidenly indignation, or a more worldly approach. I decided for indignation. "My maidenhead is intact, if that is what you are desirous of knowing. Baltic did not bed me."

"No? Then why do his men say he was in your cabin every night?"

I thought of the weeklong journey from England to the southern coast of France. It was true Baltic had visited me each night—I had been unable to refuse him, and had, in fact, learned much about what pleased him, and what drove him to the point of losing control.

"I was afraid of the journey," I said truthfully. The sea was a foreign thing, and I did not trust or like it.

The corners of Baltic's mouth curved upward.

"It's true that when we were on the ship he came into my cabin at night, but it was to comfort me."

That also was true, although more of a half-truth. I would have to seek a confessor in my new home.

Constantine made a noise of disbelief, but I raised my chin and said calmly, "I say again that my maidenhead is intact. If you insist on an examination, I will submit to one."

"No," he said, never taking his eyes off Baltic, who was still smiling faintly, an amused look in his obsidian eyes, as glossy and shiny as polished stone. "I will accept what you say."

"Thank the heavens. And now, I would greatly appreciate it if someone would tell me where my family is. My dragon family. So long as I have been ripped from the only parents I have known, I would like to meet the ones who gave me up."

Constantine's hands flexed, but at last he stepped away from the altar, finally turning his gaze to me. In the distance, the song of the monks could be heard as they prayed in a smaller chapel. "It grieves me to tell you this, but your parents are dead, Ysolde."

"No," I said, stopping when he tried to take my arm and lead me out of the cathedral. "They can't be. I came all this way to find them."

"I'm sorry. Your father died in battle with your *savior*." His words and expression were bitter as he nodded toward Baltic. "Your mother did not long survive him. They were a very devoted pair. I did not know you survived—your mother told us you had drowned. I don't know why she placed you with mortals rather than her own kin, but we rejoice that you have been returned to us."

A deep sense of sadness leached into my heart, filling me with a black despair. I lifted my gaze to meet that of Baltic. He was waiting for me, his eyes guarded, his face devoid of emotion. "You killed my father?"

"We are at war," he said. "Lives are lost during wars, Ysolde."

I nodded, tears filling my eyes, my heart so heavy I couldn't speak.

"Come. I will take you to your mother's family. They will welcome you," Constantine said, one hand on my back as he escorted me down the aisle of the cathedral, his guard falling in behind him.

I paused at the great double doors and looked back. Kostya and Pavel had joined Baltic at the altar. All three watched me. I wanted to thank Baltic for honoring his word to me, even when it meant he had to meet with his most hated enemy. I wanted to tell him how much pleasure he had given me in our nights together. I wanted to tell him that I was no longer angry that he took me away from the only family I'd known.

I said nothing. I simply looked at him, then turned and accompanied Constantine out of the cathedral and into my new life.

"You will be cherished now, Ysolde," Constantine reassured me. "We have much to teach you, but you will learn that by-and-by."

Chapter Six

By-and-by, I thought, my heart filled with so much sadness I knew it must shatter into a hundred little pieces. *By-and-by*.

By-and-by? No, that wasn't right.

"I said hi. Hello? Howdy? Hidy ho? Hi hi hi?"

I blinked, the fog evaporating into nothing, the back of the bench once more solid under my hand. In front of me sat a large shaggy black dog, panting in the sunlight, long streamers of drool dribbling from his slobbery lips. I looked around for the dog's owner, but no one was there.

"There you are. Ysolde, right?"

My eyebrows raised, I looked down at the dog. The voice was coming from him.

He tipped his head to the side and I swear he winked at me. "Wow, you look like hell. How ya doing after that header you took into Ash's marble coffee table?"

"Er . . ." My jaw sagged slightly. "Do I know you?"

"Yeah. We met at Aisling and Drake's house during the big birthing hullabaloo. I'm Jim. Effrijim, really, but that's way too girly for a butch guy like me. You look kind of funny. You didn't see me when May ordered me into human form, did you? Because that would explain why you look like you're seeing a three-headed alien dance *A Chorus Line*."

"Human form," I repeated stupidly. "No, I was . . ."

I was dreaming. In the middle of the day? Panic gripped my stomach with clammy fingers. Now the dreams were coming to me while I was wide awake? "Dear god, the shock treatments are going to be just around the corner if my brain keeps going at this rate!"

"Ya think?"

I stared at the dog; my thoughts panicked.

"Ouch. You look like you're gonna pass out or hurl. If you're going to do the latter, can you aim away from me? This magnificent coat takes forever to dry after a bath."

"I'm all right," I said, managing to get a grip on my errant emotions. "You're a dog, but you can use human form?"

"I'm a demon. Sixth class, so it's OK. I'm not going to rip your entrails out and drape them over a tree or anything like that. Besides, Aisling would lop off my package if I did that. She's always threatening to lop off my package. I think she's got a secret genitalia fetish, if you want to know the truth, but she's a nice enough demon lord otherwise, so I don't make a big deal about it. You sure you're OK? Hey, put your head between your knees or something—you're as white as Cecile's underbelly fur."

I did as the dog—demon—suggested, wondering where I knew him from. Before I could even complete that mental sentence, I corrected myself. Demons, I remembered hearing one of my mage instructors say, were always referred to by means of gender-neutral pronouns. Why, I had no idea; it just was. "You said I know you?" I asked after a couple of minutes of trying to get a little blood back into my brain.

"Now you're all red," it said, giving its shoulder a lick. "You don't remember me?"

"I don't remember anything," I said with more honesty than I liked.

"Yeah?" Its eyes narrowed on me. "That looks like an interdiction on you. Kostich kick you out of mage's camp?"

I looked down to my chest where a faint blue swirly pattern glowed. "I'm not even going to ask how you know that, because frankly, if I have to listen to one more bizarre thing today, I'm just going to curl up in a little ball and pretend I'm a hedgehog, and then where would Brom be?"

"Who's Brom?"

"My son."

"Oh, man! You have a son? Does Baltic know about it? If he doesn't, promise me I can be there when you tell him, because he's going to go totally psycho dragon. Well, more psycho dragon than he already is, which I gotta tell you is pretty wacked out."

I took a deep, cleansing breath of the grass-scented air. "For the sake of my sanity and my son, I shall now pretend you aren't saying anything. In fact, you're not even here. I'm all alone. And now I'm going home."

"Where's home?" the demon asked, getting up as I gathered up my purse and started off toward what I hoped was the street. It didn't seem to take the slightest offense to my comments, but on the other hand, it also didn't seem inclined to leave me alone.

"Barcelona."

"That's gonna be a hell of a walk."

"I'm staying with some people in town."

"May and Gabriel, yeah, I heard Ash dumped you off on them because you're Baltic's long-lost love. What's it like doing the humpy-jump with a crazy dragon?"

I glanced down at it as I walked. "You are the single most strangest demon I have ever met."

"Face it, babe—I'm the best, aren't I?" it asked, cocking a furry eyebrow at me. Catching sight of someone, it yelled, "Hey, Suzanne! Look who I found!"

A small blond woman hurried over, a leash and a plastic bag in her hand. "Jim! There you are! I thought I'd lost you. Oh, you're Ysolde, aren't you? Hello."

"My name is Tully," I said. "Although to be honest, I'm about ready to give up and change my name because no one listens to me."

"Ysolde's feeling crappy," Jim told her. "I think we should take her home. Wouldn't want her to turn into road pizza because no one was here to watch her."

Suzanne glanced at her watch, but agreed.

"That's not necessary. I'm quite fine on my own. I'm just a little insane, not bad enough I would do something crazy like take off all my clothes and dance on Nelson's Column."

"Damn," Jim said, looking disappointed.

"I think perhaps we should accompany you," Suzanne said, giving me an astute look. "You seem somewhat distraught."

"Distraught . . . insane . . . it's really a moot point by now."

They came with me as I strolled toward Gabriel's house, my thoughts a jumbled mess that I didn't want to examine. Jim chatted nonstop all the way, insisting on accompanying me inside.

"If you want to pay back my chivalry with belly scratches, go right ahead," it said, rolling over onto its back at my feet when I collapsed bonelessly onto a leather couch in a green-and-brown-toned study.

I complied silently, my thoughts still tangled around the vision, Gareth's cruelty, and my newly granted membership in the Club of the Mentally Bewildered.

"Suzanne says you're not feeling well?" May said, coming into the library with Gabriel on her heels. "Jim, really! Do we need to see that?"

"Can't have belly scritches without barin' Jupiter, Mars, and the really Big Dipper," Jim answered, its back leg kicking slightly in the air as my fingers found a particularly itchy spot on its stomach. "Oh, yeah, baby. I really dig chicks with long nails."

"Time to go," May said, prodding the demon with the toe of her shoe. "Thanks for bringing Ysolde back, Suzanne. We'll take it from here."

"But I want to stay!" Jim complained as it followed Suzanne out of the room. "I never get any excitement anymore, what with Drake not letting anyone in the house unless he has five references and a comprehensive background check...."

The door closed on the demon's voice. Gabriel knelt next to me, tipping my chin up to look into my eyes. I let him look, feeling mentally battered. "What has happened to you?"

I hesitated for a moment, remembering Gareth's words. "They will kill you," he had warned, but that didn't make sense, not on an intellectual or an emotional level. The only vibe I was getting from May and Gabriel was one of sympathy and concern.

"Baltic," I said, licking my lips, my thoughts finally stopping their endless spinning to coalesce into one solid thought. My voice was rough, my lips dry, as if I'd been exposed to the elements for a very long time.

May murmured something and moved over to pour me a drink. It was spicy, very spicy, redolent of cloves and ginger and cinnamon, and it burned as it went down my throat, but it was a good burn. It filled me with energy as it pooled in my belly, allowing me to focus my thoughts.

"What about him?" Gabriel asked.

I took another sip, enjoying the burn. "Is Baltic here? In London?"

Gabriel and May exchanged glances. He said, "He was here the day you collapsed. After that, we believe he returned to Russia."

"To lick his wounds, most likely," May added. "He was soundly defeated by Gabriel, Kostya, and Drake. Three of his guards died, and we captured his lieutenant, a woman named Thala."

"Well, unless I really am going insane, I think he's returned. I believe I saw him in Green Park." I explained about seeing the two men, and the vision that followed, although I left out specific details. "There's just one thing that confuses me—the man I saw in the park does not look like the man I've seen in my dreams. If it's Baltic I've really been dreaming about, then he couldn't be the man in the park."

"Yes, he could," Gabriel said slowly, getting to his feet. "I think something happened when Baltic was reborn. I think it changed his appearance, both dragon and human."

"He was reborn?" I asked.

"Of course—you don't know. Or rather, you don't remember," Gabriel said. "Baltic was killed three hundred years ago."

Well, that was a bit of a kicker. "Who killed him?"

"His right-hand man. Kostya Fekete."

"Kostya?" I gaped at him, truly gaped. "Tall, black hair and eyes, little cleft in his chin, square jaw—that Kostya?"

"Yes. You've seen him?"

"In my dreams, yes, but he is Baltic's friend."

"Was. He *was* Baltic's friend," Gabriel said. "The day came when Kostya realized that Baltic's mad plan to rule the septs was destroying the black dragons, and he put an end to it by killing Baltic, but not before the damage was done. The black dragons were all but exterminated."

"By who?" I asked, my voice a whisper.

"Constantine Norka, the wyvern of the silver dragons."

I slumped back, my brain reeling. It was just too much to take in, especially since I realized with a shock that, cling as I might to the idea that I was insane, I was beginning to believe that they could all be right, and I really was a freak of nature, a dragon trapped in a human body.

How sad is it that insanity was preferable to that?

Three hours later I sat surrounded by dragons. Evidently a *sárkány* was a big deal, being held in a large conference room of a very chic hotel, and attended by a number of people who looked perfectly ordinary. A long center table that would seat about twenty dominated the room, while chairs lined the walls. A podium stood at one end of the room, and at the other end a huge white screen was lowered, indicating there was going to be some sort of visual display.

I let my gaze wander around the clumps of approximately thirty people standing and chatting. Without exception, the expressions turned toward me were hostile. Tired of that, I looked at my neighbor to the right. "How long do these things usually last?"

"Depends," Jim said.

"On what?"

"Whether or not your boyfriend starts mowing everyone down like he did in Paris."

I shook my head, not sure if I should goggle at him, blink my eyes in surprise, or do the "water on a duck's back" thing and let it all roll off me. "I think I'll go with 'roll off me,'" I told Jim.

"Really? Like roll in the hay? With someone else, or with Baltic?"

"Baltic tried to kill people at a *sárkány*?" I asked, taking a firm grip on myself. I had decided that I would not go insane. Brom needed me, especially now that I knew what a bastard his father really was, and I couldn't take care of him if I was locked away, drawing pictures on the padded walls using only my own drool.

"Yeah, a while back. I wasn't there because Aisling was about to pop with the spawns, but I heard it was a real Wild West shoot-out. Until May exploded the dragon shard and blew up the top floor of the hotel."

I let that, too, roll off. In fact, I would have just sat back and closed my eyes in an attempt to let everything and everyone roll off my back, but a woman was approaching us with a glint in her eye.

"Jim, so help me, if you're bothering poor Ysolde—"

the woman said as she stopped in front of us, her hands on her hips.

"Hey, I'm just sittin' here partaking in polite chitchat, being my usual Mr. Helpful self. Right, Soldy?"

"The name is Ysolde," I said stiffly, then realized what I'd said. "No, it's Tully! Tully! My name is Tully, not Ysolde. Oh dear god, now you people have me doing it!"

"This is Aisling, my demon lord. She had twin spawns the day you keeled over in her house," Jim told me as Aisling clucked her tongue sympathetically at my outburst.

"You're a demon lord?" I asked, finding it hard to reconcile the image of the pretty woman with curly brown hair and hazel eyes, and a being who commanded demons.

"Yup. May says you don't remember anything, not that we met, but still, that has to be a serious pain in the butt. I'm married to Drake. He's the wyvern of the green dragons. That's him, over there, the good-looking one."

I looked to where she was pointing. Several men were clustered together at the far end of the room. I hated to say anything because they all looked pretty darn good to me, but a vague sense of recognition twinged in the back of my head when my gaze reached a tall man with dark hair. "And are you a dragon, too?" I asked Aisling.

May entered the room just as she laughed. "Oh, lord no. I was as human as they come before I met Drake. I was a courier, and we met when he stole the aquamanile I was taking to Paris. It was very romantic."

Jim choked, coughing and hacking as if he'd swallowed a hairball. "Romantic!" it finally said. "Man, if you knew what sort of hell she put us through while she was deciding to hook up with Drake—"

"Silence, furry demon." She smiled at May as she joined us. "It was almost as romantic as May and Gabriel's courtship."

May rolled her eyes. "What courtship? One minute I was myself, the next Gabriel was there demanding I be his mate. Not that I minded, but still. Oh, there's Cy. That means Kostya won't be very far away. Excuse me a minute."

"I forgot for a minute she was a doppelganger," I said as May crossed the room to join the woman who'd just entered. Although they were dressed differently, and the other woman's hair was longer, it was clear they were identical twins.

"Cyrene is more or less the mate to Kostya," Aisling said. "It's kind of confusing, really, but basically, he's accepted her as his mate, but she isn't technically a wyvern's mate, if you get my drift."

"I don't think I do, no."

"Well, as I understand it, it means that she is his mate in the eyes of the weyr, but can't be taken by another wyvern."

"Kidnapped, you mean?" I asked, confused how that could have bearing on anything.

"No, taken as in challenged for. Say if Bastian—he's the handsome blond on the right—if he wanted Cy as his mate, he couldn't challenge Kostya for her, because she's not technically a wyvern's mate. Whereas he could challenge Drake for me, or Gabriel for May, because we are mates. Does that make sense?"

"Only if it means that there is some bizarre rule to

this world that says one man can steal someone else's wife. Er . . . mate."

"Archaic, huh?" Aisling asked with a little shrug. "That's the dragons for you—they look hip and modern and may have lusts for all things technological, like Drake, but deep down, they're still in the fourteenth century."

"You mates should unionize," Jim suggested, wiping a tendril of drool on the empty chair next to it. "Mates Local 51. Make a new rule prohibiting mate swapping, and go on a sex strike if they refuse to negotiate."

Aisling looked at her demon with a startled expression. "That's not a bad idea," she said.

"Really?" Jim sat up a little straighter. "Can I watch when you tell Drake that you're not going to let him chase you naked through the house anymore?"

"You were supposed to be asleep!" Aisling said, leaning across me to pinch the demon on its shoulder. "You did not see us! You couldn't have!"

"Let me tell you, the sight of nursing boobies flopping all around while you tear through the house isn't something I'm going to forget anytime soon," Jim added, leaning away from me so Aisling couldn't reach it again.

"That's it! From now on, I'm locking you into the bathroom at night!"

"You're just lucky Drake didn't put an eye out with his gigantic—"

"Silence!" Aisling roared, and all of the occupants of the room turned to look.

She smiled at everyone before turning a look on Jim that would have scared a couple of years off my life. "Ignore Jim, please," she added. "It has moments of derangement. Oh, look, there's Chuan Ren and Jian. Chuan Ren is the red wyvern. Those are her bodyguards with her, although I don't see her mate, Li. Jian is her adopted son. I'll take you over and introduce you. She hates me, so it's always fun to say hi."

Aisling spoke cheerfully enough as we strolled over to the newest arrivals, a group of four people, all Asian, three men and one woman. The woman had long, straight black hair, and a figure that belonged on a runway. Two of the men were rather short but powerfully built; the third was tall and also would have been perfectly at home as a model.

"Hello, Chuan Ren. Hi, Jian, nice to see you again. Hi, Sying and Shing. This is—"

"Ysolde de Bouchier," the woman named Chuan Ren said, her gaze locked onto mine. "So, you are not dead as they said you were. Too bad."

She turned on her heel and marched off, her two guards in tow.

"She's in a good mood today, I see," Aisling said to the remaining red dragon.

He made a face. "Chuan Ren has had a trying time the last few weeks. Her mate, Li, has disappeared."

"Oh no! I'm sorry to hear that, although he obviously can't be dead or we'd know it," Aisling said, glancing at Chuan Ren.

"How would you know?" I asked.

"Wyverns can't survive the loss of their mates," she said simply before waving at the blond she'd called Bastian. "I'd better see what the latest gossip is about Fiat before things start. Ysolde, it was a pleasure to meet you at last. If you need any help with things, let me know. I know how hard it is trying to come to grips with some of the dragon lore."

She left us, and after another moment of polite chat with Jian, I was about to return to my chair when I turned and saw a man standing in the doorway staring at me, his eyes burning with black heat.

"Kostya," I said, the word a whisper on my lips.

He nodded slowly, stalking toward me. "It's true. They said it was, but I didn't see how it could be possible. I saw your body. I saw your severed head."

I touched my neck, horror crawling up my skin at his words.

"I . . . I really don't know what to say to someone who tells me he saw my severed head," I admitted. "'Hi' seems a little bit of an anticlimax."

I swore he was going to bare his teeth at me, but he managed to stop. "A miracle has happened, Ysolde de Bouchier."

"Tully Sullivan. I'm thinking of having it tattooed on my forehead."

"A miracle has happened, and now the time has come for you to pay in like coin for all the deaths, for all the suffering."

"Punky! There you are!" May's twin appeared at Kostya's side, alternating glances between me and him. "Hi, I'm Cyrene. You must be Ysolde. May's told me all about you. I don't blame you one bit for losing your memory. I would have, too, if I'd had to be mated to Baltic."

"Pleasure to meet you," I said, unable to break Kostya's gaze.

He leaned forward, his voice low. "If there is any

justice in the world, you will suffer as long as the black dragons have suffered."

"Kostya, I thought Drake said you weren't supposed to scare Ysolde," Cyrene scolded, taking his arm and tugging him toward the big table. "Ignore him. He's a bit grumpy because we ran out of his favorite cereal for breakfast."

He stopped glaring at me and transferred his glare to her. "You did not just tell her that! For the love of the saints, woman, I am a wyvern! You do not tell people I'm grumpy over breakfast foods!"

"If someone makes a fuss about not having Cap'n Crunch, then that someone is just going to have to take his lumps," she said, blithely unaware of his furious gaze. "Come on, I think they're waiting for us."

Kostya turned without another word and stomped over to the table, Cyrene at his side. I returned to my chair and watched with interest as the wyverns gathered around the table. There were only five chairs there, and before they sat, Gabriel, Drake, and Kostya all made a point of retrieving a chair and placing it next to theirs. The guards and the other dragons in attendance all took up spots on the chairs lining the wall.

Jim gave me a poignant look, but bound to silence as it was, it said nothing. I was grateful for that, since it meant I could try to sort through my mental turmoil while the dragons went through the formalities of their meeting.

"Kostya Fekete," the blue wyvern named Bastian said. "You have called this *sárkány* on behalf of the black dragons. State your business."

I looked up from where I'd been sightlessly staring at my hands.

Kostya stood at the foot of the table and looked at all the wyverns present. "I am here to seek reparation. The mate of Baltic has revealed herself, and the black dragons demand that she be held liable for the crimes he committed against the weyr."

"What?" I asked, standing up, so stunned by Kostya's demand I forgot that May warned me not to speak before I was called upon. "That's ridiculous!"

Bastian frowned at me. "You have not yet been recognized by the weyr. Please remain—"

"I will not remain silent!" I stormed over to the table, suddenly furious. "Certainly not while you people accuse me of something I didn't do."

"You are the mate of Baltic," Kostya snarled. "By the laws that govern the weyr, you are just as responsible for his actions as he is."

"I am not his mate. I am not even a dragon! I'm human! You all must be able to tell that!"

The wyverns exchanged glances.

"You see? No one is denying it, because it's true. I'm human."

"You appear human, yes," Drake said in a voice that held an Eastern European accent. "But Gabriel's mother assures us that your dragon self resides within you, simply waiting for you to waken it."

"Even if that's true, that doesn't give you people the right to try me for a crime I didn't commit! Don't you watch *CSI*? That's totally illegal!"

Kostya's scowl darkened. "You are a mate, *his* mate. And unless you'd like to bring him before us, then it is you who will pay the price for his crimes."

"What crimes, exactly? The war with the silver dragons that Gabriel said wiped out your sept?" I made a disgusted sound. "If the dreams I had were actually echoes of the past, then you were a part of that sept, too, which means you were a part of the war. How many silver dragons did *you* kill, Kostya?"

He snarled something extremely rude under his breath. "We are not discussing my actions. I have made my peace with the weyr."

"Oh, did you really?" Furious, I did something I never do—I made a scene. I leaped onto the conference table and stomped down its length to stand in front of Kostya. "You supported Baltic in everything he did! Everything! He couldn't pass gas without you telling him how fabulous he was!"

Kostya growled, positively growled as he leaped to his feet, his chair flying backwards several feet. "That is not true!"

"Do your friends here know just how much of a yes-man you really were? Do they know how you followed him around like a puppy, doing anything he demanded?"

"My past has nothing to do—"

"Do they know how you let Baltic hold a sword to my throat and threaten to kill me just because I was born a silver dragon?" My voice rang out loudly.

The entire room was silent.

"Er . . ." I cleared my throat as I realized what I'd just declared. "That's assuming that I am what everyone says I am, which I still maintain is very unlikely."

Kostya, goaded into a fury, yelled at me. "I am not to blame for Baltic's actions! I kept him in check until he rescued you. He was unbalanced then, but he became uncontrollable after you sided with Constantine Norka against him."

"I what?" I asked, feeling at a loss.

"I might have been able to reason with him if it wasn't for you!" Kostya accused me. "He wanted you. He was willing to take you despite the fact that you were a silver dragon."

"Should we be offended by Kostya's implication?" May asked Gabriel. "I have my dagger. I could poke him with it a few times."

Cyrene shot her twin an outraged look.

"Perhaps later," Gabriel told May.

"But you spurned him, and bound yourself to Constantine Norka instead!" Kostya's face was dark with anger. "Baltic was furious! His madness knew no bounds after that."

"I really don't know what you're talking about," I said, my anger starting to cool. I looked around at the dragons gathered at the table, embarrassed by my show of temper. "Sorry, can I just . . . thank you," I said as Bastian stood and held out a hand to assist me off the table.

"You cannot deny what happened in the past," Kostya said, his voice and face sullen.

"I wouldn't dream of trying. But I don't think I've gotten to this betrayal in my visions. I assume it will come at some point, but I have to say that I find it difficult to believe."

"Kostya, this is old history," Drake said, one eyebrow raised at the black dragon. "The blame for the Endless War has long since been settled. You cannot try Ysolde for that crime."

"There wouldn't have been an Endless War but for her!" Kostya declared.

"I thought Chuan Ren started that war?" Aisling leaned close and asked her husband.

Chuan Ren narrowed her eyes at Aisling, her mouth moving silently as if she was speaking a curse.

Aisling quickly drew protection wards over herself and Drake.

"Kaawa said Ysolde tried to stop the war by bringing the dragon shards together to re-form the dragon heart," May said. "She would hardly do that if she was responsible for the whole thing."

"That was later, after she realized what she had started," Kostya said stubbornly.

"You know, not even I think that makes any sense," Cyrene said, looking at him. "Seriously, punky, I think we're going to have to go to some anger management classes. You need to learn how to let go and move on."

"The black dragons—" he started to say.

"Are not the reason Ysolde has been called before the *sárkány*," Drake interrupted in a forceful voice.

"Exactly what crime did Baltic commit that you're all so intent on punishing me for?" I asked, suddenly tired and emotionally drained.

Drake looked at me with eyes that held infinite sadness. "The deaths of sixty-eight blue dragons, killed by Baltic almost two months ago."

Chapter Seven

Silence filled the conference room as every person—every dragon—looked at me. I shivered, rubbing my arms against a sudden chill.

"Lucky me. I'm out of it for five weeks, lose my job, learn my husband is a rat to beat all rats, and now I find out that evidently I'm the girlfriend of a homicidal maniac. Is that it? Is that all you guys have to hit me with? Because I'm not quite over the edge yet."

"There is the matter of who held Kostya prisoner in his aerie for seven years," Cyrene said thoughtfully. "No one seems to know for sure who captured him there, but I think it was your mate, so by rights, you should be charged with that, too."

"Thank you," I told her. "That did the job."

Before anyone could react, I spun around and started for the nearest exit. I didn't make it, naturally, but I knew I wouldn't.

Kostya was there at the door. "You will not escape justice again, Ysolde de Bouchier."

I slapped him. It felt so good, I slapped him again, then stepped back, my hand over my mouth because I'd never struck another person in my life.

That I could remember.

Well, there was nailing Baltic in the groin, but that was just a dream.

"I'm sorry," I stammered, horrified. "I don't know what came over me. Not that you didn't deserve it, because if anyone deserved to be slapped, you did, but still, I'm shocked that I actually struck you. Did I hurt you?"

Cyrene screamed and ran toward us, clearly about to launch herself at me, but Kostya caught her before she could attack.

I just stared at them as she struggled to get free, cursing me roundly as she fought him, my eyes filling with tears. I'd never felt so alien, so alone, so completely out of my depth. I just wanted to sink into oblivion.

"Sit down," Kostya told Cyrene when she had worked out the worst of her swearing.

"She struck you! Twice! No one hits my dragon and lives to tell about it!"

"Go sit down," he commanded.

"No!"

"Cy, it was an open-handed slap," May said as she took her twin's arm and forcibly steered her toward the table. "I'm sure Kostya will survive it."

"I'm very sorry," I told him again.

To my surprise, rather than look angrier with me, he rubbed his abused cheek and looked thoughtful.

"Ysolde?" Gabriel indicated the table. "I believe since the subject of the blue dragons' deaths has been broached, you would be welcome at the *sárkány* table. Perhaps we can discuss the issue more calmly."

"I'm not at all a violent person," I told him, allowing him to escort me to a chair he placed on his other side. "I can't even spank my son."

He said nothing, just held out a chair for me.

"You must understand that the weyr does not seek to punish an innocent person," Bastian said, taking charge of the meeting again. "But there are laws that govern us, and as Kostya said, one of those laws holds that wyverns' mates are held accountable for the actions of their wyverns."

"What about other dragons?" I asked, too weary to be incensed.

Bastian looked confused. "What other dragons?"

"What about a normal dragon's mate, a non-wyvern. Are they held accountable, too?"

"No," he said, frowning.

"Why not?"

Silence fell on the table. Drake cleared his throat and answered, "Wyverns' mates are unique in dragonkin. They have power of their own, and are accorded a place of honor in the sept second only to the wyvern himself. Mates always support the wyverns' decisions, and thus the law was set into place recognizing that position and power."

"Let me make sure I have this straight. You all think that because I was alive two months ago, unaware of any of you, unaware of Baltic, unaware of anything but doing my job as an apprentice for Dr. Kostich, and being a wife and mother, you seriously expect me to believe that I am guilty of the deaths of sixty—"

"Sixty-eight," Bastian interrupted.

"My apologies. I didn't mean to make light of that tragedy. Where was I? Oh, you want to hold me responsible for the deaths of dragons I didn't even know existed in the first place? Is that what you're saying?"

Drake's gaze dropped. Gabriel and May exchanged uncomfortable glances. Kostya coughed softly and scowled at the table. Bastian looked into the distance. Chuan Ren smiled at me, showing far more teeth than was called for.

"Do I want to know what the punishment is for killing sixty-eight blue dragons?" I asked.

No one looked at me. "The punishment for a crime of such a heinous nature outside of a declared war is death," Bastian said at last.

"Lovely. You want to kill me for someone else's crime. That certainly sounds like justice to me."

No one said anything to that bit of sarcasm, either.

I thought of fighting, thought of running away, thought of damning them all and just letting them make me a scapegoat, but something inside me finally reached a breaking point.

"There is something going on with me," I said slowly, looking again at my fingers spread on the table. "Much as I want to deny it, I am willing to admit that I have some sort of a connection to this person named Baltic. Despite that, no one can deny that I *am* human, and it is for that reason that I do not, cannot, *will not* admit that I am the dragon named Ysolde. However, if any of you can prove to me that I am, if you can show me that what I'm experiencing is due to a dragon hiding inside of me, then I will acknowledge the laws of this weyr, and will accept the punishment for the deaths of those dragons."

That got their attention. They didn't look happy, though.

"That seems reasonable to me," Aisling said, nudging her husband with her elbow. "Of course you want proof that you're really Ysolde. We'll just have to show you that it's so. I'm not sure how we'll go about doing that other than giving you time to find yourself, so to speak. That's only right and fair, especially since the weyr is asking you to give up your life. Doesn't it seem fair to you, Drake?"

His frown cleared. "It would seem that such a demand is not unreasonable given the circumstances. What say the other wyverns?"

"I agree wholeheartedly," Gabriel said quickly. "Ysolde must have proof. She must be easy in her mind that she is who we know her to be. It would be a gross misinterpretation of the weyr laws to condemn her without her acknowledging her dragon self."

"I agree," Bastian said, a bit to my surprise since it was his sept members who had been killed. I thought if anyone would have wanted to see me condemned, it would be him. But he actually looked relieved, and turned to Kostya. "What do the black dragons say?"

Kostya pursed his lips as he looked at me.

"I think she needs to be smacked upside the head," Cyrene muttered. Kostya shot her a glare, then said, "I am influenced by the memories of what Baltic did to the black dragons because of Ysolde. Long have I sought to see her pay for the pain and suffering she caused us for her treachery with Constantine Norka—"

"She was a silver dragon," Gabriel said abruptly. "She agreed to be his mate. That can hardly be said to be treachery!"

Kostya leaped to his feet, his face red with anger. "Baltic wanted her for *his* mate!"

"Then he should never have handed her over to Constantine, saying he didn't want her!" Gabriel shot back, jumping up as well.

"Oh, *that* makes me feel good," I said softly.

"That discussion is not pertinent at this time," Bastian said, pounding on the table with his fist until the two dragons retook their seats. "Kostya, how say you?"

He sat down with a huff, his arms crossed, his expression black. "I will agree to a temporary stay so long as it's for a reasonable amount of time."

I was taken aback by his agreement. That left one wyvern.

"Chuan Ren?" Bastian asked her.

"The red dragons don't care what happens to the woman," she answered. "Kill her, or do not kill her, it is of no concern to us. We are only interested in the whereabouts of Baltic."

"Why do you care where he is?" May asked.

Chuan Ren just smiled again. It wasn't a pleasant smile.

"We are agreed, then, that Ysolde should have time to ... what?" Bastian asked, looking puzzled. "How does one find oneself?"

"My mother says the dragon inside her is waiting to be woken," Gabriel said. "That is what must be done."

"But how do you go about doing that?" Bastian shook his head. "I've never before met a dragon who didn't know he was a dragon, who wasn't able to *be* a dragon."

"I think I may know of a way to do that," May said thoughtfully. She sat up a little straighter when she realized all eyes were on her. "There is a house in the country that belongs to Baltic."

"It is mine now," Kostya interrupted. "I have claimed it on behalf of the black dragons."

"That's right, we have," Cyrene said. "It's a bit too big as houses go, and needs a lot of redecorating, but it has a nice pond. Kostie says we can dig up the garden to enlarge the pond into a small lake."

Kostya gave his mate a thin-lipped look that she ignored.

"When I bore the dragon shard, it caused me to react quite strongly to the house." May's gaze turned to me. "It actually had me feeling things that I believe you felt while you bore the shard."

"I bore a shard?" I asked, refusing to cope with one more bizarre thing. "A shard of what?"

"A dragon shard, one of the five pieces of the dragon heart."

I closed my eyes for a minute. "Is the dragon heart something that's going to make me completely lose the tiny shred of sanity I'm holding on to? Because I have to tell you, if it is, I think I'd rather just not know about it."

May laughed. "It's not that bad, honest."

"The dragon heart is made up of five shards. Each of the wyverns here possesses a shard," Gabriel told me. "For a while, May bore the same shard that you bore.

Just as she did, you successfully re-formed the dragon heart—imbued with the power of the First Dragon—and allowed it to reshatter into five pieces."

"That sounds very clever of May and me, and I'm thrilled to bits to hear it despite the fact that I don't have the slightest idea of the significance of any of that, but so long as it has no bearing on whether or not there is a dragon curled up inside me, I'm willing to move on."

"Brava," Aisling said, applauding until her husband scowled at her.

"I take it you think that if I were to go to Baltic's home—"

"My home! It belongs to me now!" Kostya said.

"Pardon me, Baltic's former home, that it would somehow prove I'm a dragon? Will I start setting things on fire? Burst into scaly lizard form? Suddenly become fascinated with gold?" I asked, too tired to mind my manners as I should.

"Judging by what I felt when I was there, yes, I think you'll have some sort of a definitive experience," May said.

"But Ysolde doesn't bear the Avignon Phylactery anymore," Kostya said.

May slid an unreadable smile toward her wyvern. "No, but I can attest to the fact that once you've borne a shard, it changes you. I'm sure it changed Ysolde, too."

"It sounds like a good idea to me," Aisling said.

"With Kostya's permission, we will take you to the house in question tomorrow," Gabriel said. "You will not, I hope, mind if May and I accompany you?"

"I will be there as well," Kostya said.

"Oooh. That sounds interesting. Can we go?" Aisling asked Drake.

He raised his eyebrows and looked at Gabriel. "We have no reason to, but if Gabriel—and Ysolde—have no objection, I admit that I am curious to see if the house does have some effect on her."

Gabriel stated a time, and everyone agreed to meet at the house. I sat back in my chair, drained by the emotions I'd been through in the last few days, wanting nothing more than . . . I sighed to myself. I didn't even know what I wanted anymore, other than peace of mind.

I expected to dream that night, and I did. I closed the door to Brom's room after seeing him settled for the night, wished May a pleasant evening, and stepped into my room, and straight into a maelstrom of testosterone.

"You are too late, Baltic," the man who stood in front of me taunted. "Ysolde has spoken the words. She has sworn fealty to me. She is now my mate."

I stepped to the side to look around Constantine. Baltic and about ten men emerged from the trees that formed a gentle curve around the cliff top where we stood, Kostya and Pavel immediately to his rear.

Instantly the silver dragons pulled their swords, surrounding Constantine and me.

"Is that true?" Baltic asked me, his expression as stormy as the sea that raged behind us.

I took a step forward, but Constantine put his hand out to stop me. "You will address me, and not my mate. Ysolde is mine. You will never have her."

"Why are you here?" I asked Baltic, shrugging off Constantine's hand and pushing past his guards. They made a move to stop me, but fell back when I glared at them.

"Why do you think I'm here? I came to claim my mate," Baltic answered, his eyes glittering darkly.

"Your mate? You said you didn't want me. You said you would never have anything to do with a silver dragon," I cried.

"I said I would never bed a silver dragon," he corrected. "I have since changed my mind. You are my mate. I sent a messenger telling you I would come to claim you as such."

"I know of no messenger!" I said, shocked and horrified.

His expression darkened. "I should have known that Constantine would claim you for himself rather than let you be mine."

"Ysolde, my dove, let me deal with this," Constantine said, his voice warm and rumbly and comfortable just as it had been for the three months while I had been with him in the south of France.

I spun around to face him, suddenly filled with knowledge that left me furious. "You knew he was coming for me, didn't you? You knew my heart was breaking, and still you kept his message from reaching me. By the rood! That's why you pressed me to make the oath to you! You deceived me!"

"You are my responsibility," Constantine said, taking my hands in his.

Baltic positively growled. Kostya, his eyes on the silver guards, held him back.

"I promised to care for you that first day when you were given to me," Constantine continued. "I could not help but love you, my precious dove. Can you blame me for wanting you as my mate?"

How stupid I'd been. How stupid and naïve, falling for the honeyed words and the promise of a lifetime of being loved, when in reality, I was being used as an instrument in a war that had raged for two hundred years. I pulled my hands from his and backed up, sickened by the way he'd fooled me. The guards looked to Constantine, but he lifted his hand to stop them. "You told me I was the one meant to be your mate, but all the while you knew Baltic was coming for me. You watched as I pined for him, pined for the love I would give my soul to have, and yet you bound me to you? Why?"

"I love you," he said, his eyes glowing with a strange golden light. "How could I let the one thing I love more than life itself go to a madman, a monster who would destroy our sept rather than let us live in peace?"

I couldn't look at him any longer. "You say you love me, and yet you ensured that I would spend the remainder of my days a shadow of what I could have been."

Constantine reached out for me, but let his hand drop before he could touch me. "You are merely confused, Ysolde, not truly in love."

"How do you know?" I lifted my head to glare at him. "How do you presume to know what's in my heart? You won't even listen to me! I told you that I loved him, Constantine, and you just told me he would rather see me dead than alive."

"You—" he started to say.

"No," I said, cutting him off with a sharp gesture. "I know my own mind and heart. I love Baltic. If he had asked me to be his mate, I would have accepted."

Baltic smiled, a slow, smug smile.

"That doesn't mean I'm not furious with your high-handed dealings," I told him over my shoulder.

His smile slipped a notch.

"Even knowing what he is, knowing what he's done

to our people, to your own family, you would bind your-self to him?" Constantine asked, his voice reflecting the anger now in his eyes. "You would let him use your body, taint your soul?"

I met his gaze, my own steady. "I would do what I could to bring calm to this troubled time."

"You swore fealty to me," he answered.

"What choice did I have?" I countered. "You deceived me!"

He was silent for a moment, pain flickering across his face.

"If only you had told me the truth," I said softly, putting my hand on his arm. "I have great respect and affection for you, Constantine. You are a wonderful wyvern, and a generous, loving man. But much as I honor you as such, I would never have pledged myself to you if I had known the truth. You tricked me into becoming your mate simply to spite the man who holds my heart. How can I find happiness with you knowing that?"

Baltic stepped forward. "Constantine Norka, by the laws governing the weyr, I challenge you by *lusus naturalae* for your mate, Ysolde de Bouchier."

Constantine and I both stared at him.

"*Lusus* what?" I asked.

"*Naturalae*. It has many meanings, but to dragonkin, it applies only to one thing—the ability to steal a mate," Constantine answered, eyeing Baltic with palpable hostility.

"It is not stealing if I win the challenge," Baltic said, striding forward. At a gesture, all of his men but Kostya remained standing where they were. Likewise, Constantine nodded at his guard, who gestured the others back.

The dragons spread out until they formed a loose circle, in the center of which the five of us stood. "Do you accept the challenge?"

"I do," Constantine said, his stance aggressive. "Ysolde is young and confused. She has not yet had time to adjust to our ways. I am convinced that with time, she will realize what a tragedy her life would have been if she spent it with you."

"I dislike being spoken of as if I weren't standing an arm's length from you," I told him somewhat acidly. "I am not invisible, nor am I witless. This is *my* life you're talking about, and I demand the right to have a say in it."

"You are female," Constantine said abruptly. "You are young and inexperienced with the ways of dragons. You will allow me to decide what is best for you."

"I am the one who found her," Baltic said arrogantly, swaggering forward until he stood a foot away from us. "I will decide what is best for her, and that is to become my mate."

"Does no one think it is a good idea for me to decide what's best for me?" I asked.

"No!" both wyverns said.

I crossed my arms and looked daggers at both of them. "I think you're both obnoxious. I've changed my mind. I don't want either of you. I'll take Kostya instead."

Kostya's eyes widened in surprise and something that looked very much like dismay. "Er . . ."

"Are you trying to make me jealous?" Baltic asked, irritation pulling at his lips.

"No. If I were, I would do this." I walked toward Kostya, but he evidently read the intention in my eyes because he backed away from me. I stopped, stomped my foot in irritation, and demanded, "Stop running away from me and let me kiss you!"

"I'd really rather you didn't," he said with a wary glance at his wyvern.

"Ysolde," Baltic said in an even, almost disinterested tone of voice.

I marched over to him, narrowing my glare until it could have sharpened the edge of his sword. "What?"

"You don't have to attack Kostya to make me jealous, *chérie*," he said, the irritation in his face replaced with wry amusement. He gestured toward Constantine. "I'm ready to fight him to the death for his audacity in claiming you. I don't think I could get much more jealous than that."

"Oh." I thought about that for a moment, then took a step closer to him, not quite touching, but close enough I could feel the heat of his body. I looked deep into his eyes, searching there for the answers I so desperately sought. "You really want me for your mate even though I'm a silver dragon?"

"Yes." A muscle in his neck twitched.

"Why?"

His eyes took on the same wary look Kostya's had just borne. "Why?"

I prodded his arm. "Yes, why? Why do you want me for your mate?"

"Eh . . ." He looked from me to Constantine, who was standing watching us with a black scowl. Baltic squared his shoulders and leveled a haughty look at me. "That is unimportant. Only the fact that I have claimed you should matter."

"It matters to me," I said, and put my hand on his chest, over his heart.

Behind me, Constantine took a step toward us.

"You are female. You do not know what you're saying."

"By the rood, I don't. Tell me, Baltic. Why me?"

"Because," he said, his eyes glittering darkly. "Just . . . because."

"Do you love me?" I asked.

His jaw tightened. "That is none of your business."

I laughed; I couldn't help but laugh at him. Love in marriage was only a dream, my mother had once told me, and yet I knew she loved my father. She had also said that some men have difficulty admitting to such tender emotions, and clearly Baltic was one of them.

"I think it is my business. It's important to me, Baltic. I would like to know—do you love me?"

He stepped closer until his chest was pressed against my arms. "This is hardly the place to discuss such a thing."

"I think it's the perfect place," I said, gesturing at all the dragons, hesitating a moment when I noticed that every single one of them wore expressions of pain identical to the one on Baltic's face. "I must know. I will not bind myself to a man if he doesn't love me."

"That's foolishness," Baltic scoffed, and the dragons scoffed with him, murmurs of agreement rippling around us.

"Nevertheless, I must know. So I ask you a third time—do you love me?"

He looked around wildly before leaning in. "There are others here, woman!"

"I know."

"You expect me to say it right out in front of them?"

"Constantine did," I said, nodding toward him. Constantine straightened up and looked noble. "He didn't have any problem saying it."

Baltic growled deep in his chest, rolling his eyes heavenward for a moment before he said in a low and ugly voice, "Fine! I love you. Now get the hell out of my way so I can kill your mate."

I don't know what I would have done had Constantine not attacked Baltic at that moment—probably tried to reason with them, although hindsight tells me they wouldn't have listened. It is moot speculation, regardless, because the second the words left Baltic's lips, Constantine's body shifted, stretching and growing and elongating into the form of a silver-scaled dragon with scarlet claws. He flung himself at Baltic with a snarl that left my blood cold.

Baltic shifted as well, but his form, slightly smaller and less bulky, was ebony colored, with curving translucent white claws that flashed in the air as he lunged at Constantine.

Teodore, one of Constantine's guards, tried to restrain me, but I shook him off and stalked forward to where the two dragons were rolling around on the ground, blood arcing in the air as one of them struck true.

"Stop it!" I yelled, my hands fisted in impotence. I wanted to strike both of them back into their senses. "I will not have th—"

Constantine's tail lashed out as he threw himself forward onto Baltic, who just barely rolled out of the way in time. I screamed as I was knocked backwards several yards. Instantly Constantine was there, in human form, leaning over me and cradling my head. "Ysolde! My dove, my cherished one—have I harmed you?"

Baltic shifted back into human form as well, jerking

Constantine off me and onto his back, the glittering silver point of a sword digging into his neck.

"You have lost your mate, your sept," Baltic said, panting, "and now your life."

"No!" I yelled, leaping up as he raised his sword overhead, clearly about to cleave Constantine's head from his body. I threw myself forward over him, looking up at Baltic. "Do not kill him."

Baltic's eyes narrowed on me. "You have a change of heart?"

"No. I will be your mate. My life is bound to yours from this moment forward. But only if you spare Constantine."

His jaw worked, and for a moment, I thought he would refuse. But slowly he lowered his sword, grabbing my arm and pulling me to my feet. "By the grace of my mate, I will let you live," he told Constantine. "But only because she desires it."

The sight of Constantine's face haunted me as Baltic led me away.

Chapter Eight

"After it's dehydrated, I take out the natron that is in the inside, and put cloth soaked in resin and more natron inside the body. Then I get to paint the whole thing with resin. That takes, like, three weeks to dry, so I want to get started right away. I think I have enough resin to do the whole fox."

"Whether or not you do is moot. I think you've spent enough time with your unnatural hobby. I'd like you to make yourself sociable today so May and Gabriel don't think you're a ghoulish little boy who is obsessed with dead things."

"Dead things are interesting," he protested.

"Regardless, I think you can leave your experiments alone for one day and socialize instead. How much?"

I paid off the taxi driver when he stopped in front of Gabriel's house. A strange man was at the front door, about to ring the buzzer as Brom and I got out.

"Hullo," the man said.

"Hello." I gathered up the bags of shopping from the floor of the taxi, eyeing the man as I did so. He had a long face that I thought of as typically English—not too long, but sort of ruggedly handsome—with dark blond hair and bluish grey eyes.

He examined me just as obviously. "You wouldn't happen to be Ysolde de Bouchier, would you?"

I took a deep breath. "My name is Tully Sullivan."

"That was going to be my other guess," he said, laughing. It was a nice laugh. He looked like a nice man, with a bit of a roguish twinkle to his eye, but still, nice.

"Your husband sent me," he said, taking me completely by surprise. "Name's Savian Bartholomew."

Nice? He was the devil incarnate!

"Gareth sent you?" Brom asked. "How come?"

"You must be Brom. It seems he wants you and your mother kept safe from some very bad dragons until he can come and get you," Savian said.

"Eek! Go away!" I said, shoving him toward the taxi.

"Eh?" he asked, looking confused as he clutched the side of the taxi in order to keep from being pushed inside.

"The gent want to go somewhere?" the taxi driver asked.

"Yes! He wants to go far, far away," I said.

"I do not! Stop shoving me, or I will be forced to subdue you!" Savian said, struggling when I tried to force his head down so I could push him into the cab.

"Sullivan, I don't think that man wants to go anywhere," Brom commented from his location on the sidewalk.

"Yes, yes, what the lad said!" Savian squawked as

I grabbed his ear and managed to get his head inside. "Help! I'm being kidnapped!"

"Just the opposite, actually," I grumbled, grunting as I gave a mighty heave that forced his shoulders in. "Just go already!"

"Never! Why are you doing this?" he yelled, somewhat muffled since I blocked most of the door with my body in an attempt to get rid of him.

"Can't you take a hint, you annoying man? Shoo! I don't want you!"

"But your husband—"

"Is a complete idiot! Now go away before I lose my temper and turn your eyebrows into warts!"

"The lady is crazy," I heard him tell the cabdriver in response to his inquiry about what was going on. "I think she fancies me."

"I'm a great and . . . urgh . . . powerful mage . . . unph! . . . and I will . . . dammit, let go of the door! . . . I will smite you with all sorts of unpleasant spells."

"Help!" Savian said to the taxi driver.

The man watched him impassively. "I would, mate, but I don't like the sound of that smiting."

"She's not a mage!" Savian said, yelping when, desperate to release his hold on the car door, I bit his arm. "Where's your male empathy? Go pull her off me! I'd do it for you!"

"Stop inciting innocent people to help you, or I'll turn your testicles into turnips!" I yelled, head butting Savian's back. "Now get the hell into the cab!"

"I will die before I submit to your brutal ways!"

"Argh!" I bellowed, and was just mentally thumbing through the list of spells I knew that might possibly help me, when the front door opened.

"I thought I heard voices—Ysolde! Who is that you're trying to bend in half . . . *agathos daimon*! Savian? What are you doing here? Don't tell me you've come to work for Gabriel again. I thought that, after the last time, you swore you'd never take another job from a dragon."

"Er . . ." I paused, suddenly wary as May rushed out onto the sidewalk.

"Save me, May! This madwoman is trying to bend me into all sorts of unnatural positions! I think she's already broken my liver and quite possibly one or both intestines," Savian called from the cab.

"You big baby," I said, releasing him as I gave May a feeble smile. "I barely laid a finger on him, honest."

"She didn't even turn his testicles to turnips, like she said she might," Brom offered helpfully. "I would have liked to have seen that."

I narrowed my eyes at him. He grinned back.

"Turnips?" May asked, looking from me to Savian as he unfolded himself from the car, clutching his sides.

"It was all just a little bit of fun," I said, putting my arm around Savian. "Wasn't it, old friend?"

He whimpered and clutched his sides. "My liver! Don't hurt my liver again!"

"You know Savian, too?" May asked.

"Ow! My neck!"

"Too? You . . . uh . . . know him?" I countered, releasing the pincer hold I had on the back of his neck.

"May and I are old friends. She's never tried to hurt me," he said, shooting me a belligerent glare as he shuffled away from me and over to her.

"Oh. Uh . . ." I coughed and tried to think of an excuse to get the man alone for a few minutes. "Isn't that a coincidence. We've known each other for . . . oh, forever."

"I've never seen her before in my life," Savian told May. "Don't leave me alone with her. She's vicious. I think she was trying the Vulcan neck pinch on me."

"Hmm," May said. "Why don't we all go into the house?"

I trailed behind them as they entered the house, thinking furiously.

"So what are you doing here?" May asked Savian as I closed the door behind me.

"Savian!" I said, interrupting the man as he was about to answer. I smiled brightly and took his arm, dragging him toward the room I knew to be a small, unused study. "We have so much to talk about! Why don't we go in here and have a cozy little chat, just the two of us, all nice and private-like."

"Help! She's going to smite my testicles!" Savian shrieked.

"You can bet I will if you keep up all that whining," I said through gritted teeth as he fought me. "Stop struggling and you won't get hurt."

"Famous last words!" he said, trying to pry my fingers off his arm. "Damn, lady, you have a grip like a . . . like a . . ."

"Dragon?" May asked.

"Yeah, like a . . ." He stopped struggling and gave me a long look, squinting at me slightly. "Hey. She doesn't look like a dragon."

"That's because I'm not one," I said, flinging open the door. "Now let's have a little chat about this business."

"What business? Have you hired Savian to do something?" May asked, standing in the doorway.

"Not Sullivan, Gareth," Brom piped up from the hall, unloading the books he had purchased from the bookshop where we'd spent the last hour. "He's trying to save us from some bad dragons."

"Go and play with your mummies!" I ordered, pointing toward the back of the house.

"You said I couldn't!"

"Don't do as I said—do as I say!"

He rolled his eyes and mumbled something about people not making any sense, but he duly trotted away toward the depths of the basement.

"Maybe we'd all better have a little chat," May said, giving me a long look as she entered the room. "I'd like to hear about the bad dragons."

"Who is bad?" Gabriel asked, following her in. "Savian! What brings you to our humble abode?"

I sighed and slumped into a heavy leather chair. "Well, I tried."

"Yes, you did. Despite your best attempts at mutilation, my liver will live another day," Savian said, groaning pitifully as he eased himself onto a long, low leather couch.

Gabriel looked at May. "What's wrong with him?"

"Evidently Ysolde was trying to turn his testicles into warts."

"Eyebrows to warts, testicles to turnips," I corrected wearily. I lifted a languid hand toward Savian. "Go ahead. Tell them. Ruin what remains of my life."

He ignored me, speaking to Gabriel. "I was sent to rescue a fair maiden and her small bundle of boyish joy from the clutches of a gang of murderous dragons. No one told me that the maiden had the strength of a dragon, and an unnatural interest in my balls."

"I have no interest in your balls. I never had an interest in your balls, other than wanting them to go away, preferably with you attached."

"Our clutches?" May said, looking appalled.

"It's not like it sounds," I said hurriedly, before she and Gabriel were insulted.

"Who hired you?" May asked Savian.

"Man by the name of Gareth Hunt."

I glared at him, and his hand moved protectively over his crotch.

"Why would your husband feel you needed rescuing?" Gabriel asked in a soft, completely misleading voice. The air positively crackled with anger.

"You see what you've done? Are you happy now? Everyone is mad at me," I told Savian.

"When you go around threatening to smite people's balls, I don't blame them!"

"Ysolde?" Gabriel asked, clearly expecting some sort of an explanation.

"I'm going to remember you," I told Savian before I turned to Gabriel. "Gareth called me a few days ago, and warned me that I was in danger if I continued to stay with you. I told him that you had been nothing but generous and attentive in your care of me while I was asleep, and even brought Brom to me, but he . . . well, Gareth is very single-minded. Once he gets an idea, he clings to it with the tenacity of a terrier with lockjaw. I assure you that I have absolutely no complaints about your hospitality, and I do not intend to be stolen away. That's what I was doing when May found us. I was trying to get rid of this annoying man."

"I am roguishly charming, and not at all annoying!" Savian protested.

May and Gabriel exchanged a loaded glance.

"Fine, you're the most charming man I've ever met. Now please consider yourself unemployed. You can keep whatever my husband paid you—he deserves to lose the money for doing something like this against my wishes."

"Since you are at a loose end," Gabriel said to him, opening the door and gesturing, "perhaps I could speak to you about doing a little job for us. Ysolde believes she's seen Baltic in town, and I'd like for you to find him."

"I'm not going to get my head bashed in again, am I?" Savian asked, grunting as he rolled off the couch and onto his feet. He slid me a glance as he followed Gabriel out of the room. "Or my liver ruptured?"

The door closed quietly behind him.

I looked at May. "You think he can find Baltic?"

"He works as a thief taker for the L'au-dela," she answered with a wry little twist to her lips. "That's how I met him. But sometimes he freelances, and he's a very good tracker. If anyone can find Baltic, Savian can. Are you going to be ready to go in an hour?"

I nodded.

"Good. We'll all go down together. It should prove to be interesting, eh?"

She left me with a little smile that made me wonder what she knew.

"Oh," I said three hours later as the car rounded one last gentle curve and cleared the willow and lime trees that formed a half circle in front of a magnificent house. "Oh, my. It's . . ." Words simply failed me.

"I know," May said, sighing as she gazed upon the redbricked front of the Tudor mansion. "Isn't it just? I would try to get it away from Kostya, but I suppose if anyone has a right to it, you do."

"It's perfect," I said, my face pressed to the window as I tried to take it all in. The house itself was perched on a gentle hill, a typical example of Tudor architecture, with a center square tower that rose with stately grace over the rest of the house, mullioned windows, stone quoins, and parapets that seemed to sweep upward to the sky. "Just . . ."

"Perfect," May finished the sentence, nodding her head. "The very words I said when I first saw it. But Ysolde, there's more. There's a maze. And gardens."

"Gardens?" I craned my neck to look around Gabriel, who was sitting in the seat opposite May and me. "Where?"

"Over there. You can just see a little splash of color."

"Ooh," I breathed in a heady sigh.

"Sullivan likes plants," Brom told May with a tolerant look at me.

"She was born a silver dragon. All silver dragons like plants," Gabriel said, opening the door as the car stopped. He held out his hand first for May, then for me. I stepped out and my heart was suddenly lightened.

"I feel like I should be singing," I said, turning slowly in a circle to take in the lovely soft velvety lawns that spread out endlessly before us.

"I know just how you feel. I was the same way," May said.

A yew maze was at the right, casting coolly intriguing shadows in its pathway. To the left of the house was a formal garden, and I took three steps toward it before I remembered I wasn't here to see it.

"Sorry," I said, turning back to the others.

May laughed and said, "Don't worry. We understand."

A second car pulled up behind ours, a sleek antique Rolls-Royce that disgorged Aisling, Drake, and Jim, along with Drake's two redheaded guards.

"Wow!" Aisling said, leaning back to look to the top of the tower. "This is a heck of a house! No wonder you like it so much, May. It's absolutely gorgeous! Is that a maze? Jim! Don't do that right there!"

"When you gotta go, you gotta go," the demon complained, but lowered its leg and wandered off to a less central shrub, saying as it went, "Don't let Ysolde turn into a dragon and go all psycho, or blow up the house, or whatever it is she's going to do, until I'm back."

"You're going to blow up this house?" Brom asked, looking around him with curiosity, but nothing else. "With what?"

"Nothing. Ignore Jim—it's deranged. Your mom isn't going to blow up anything, least of all this house," Aisling said as she started up the low front stairs. The double doors opened and Kostya and Cyrene came out, very much the lord and lady of the manor.

I wanted to shove them both in the pond I'd seen a hint of as we stopped in front of the house.

"You made it, I see," Kostya said somewhat sourly, his gaze flickering between Drake—who I had learned that morning was his brother—and me.

"Shall we go inside?" Gabriel asked, taking May's hand and leading her up the stairs.

I sent one last poignant glance toward the flower garden, my heart crying at the thought of it in the hands of Cyrene. "It wants someone who understands it, someone who will love it and nurture it," I murmured as I slowly climbed the five stairs to the door.

"You OK, Sullivan?" Brom asked, waiting for me at the top. "You look kind of funny."

I smiled and gave his shoulder a squeeze as we entered the door. "I just really like this pl—"

The world went black the second my foot crossed the threshold. I heard voices exclaiming, and someone calling my name, but it seemed to come from a long distance away. I turned away from the blackness, moving back out into the sunshine.

Another vision, I thought to myself as I went to the garden without consciously making the decision to do so. *I hope this one doesn't last too long. I'd like to see the garden for real before we have to leave.*

As I reached the area where the garden had been, I realized that something was different this time. For one, the flowers and shrubs seemed to shimmer in and out of focus, and nothing like that had happened in the previous visions or dreams. For another, two people stood in the center of a tangle of greenery. As I moved past a young willow tree, I caught sight of a third person standing to my left, a dark shadow unmoving against a tree. A gardener or workman of some sort, I thought, and dismissed him as I turned back to the couple.

It was me . . . or rather, it looked like me, and I realized with a shock that it was the me of the visions, the person whose experiences I had felt and lived. She was smiling up at a man whose back was to me, but I could tell by the love shining in her eyes that it was Baltic.

I moved around to the other side of the willow, wanting to hear what they said, but not wishing to disturb the vision.

"That's too many," Baltic said, frowning at the me-Ysolde. She poked him in the arm, and his frown melted into a smile. "You'll leave me no room for the house. We'll have nothing but garden."

I looked behind me. The house was there, but like the flowers and shrubs of the garden, it seemed to shimmer and fade in and out of view.

I was seeing a memory of the land as it was before the house and gardens had been built.

"And here, Madonna lilies and pinks, heartsease and leopard's-bane. Campion over there, against the wall, and daffodils and violets down by the pond. On that side, we'll have beds of wallflowers and lavender, marjoram and roses, great long beds of roses of every hue. And we'll have an orchard, Baltic, with apple trees, pears, plums, and cherries, and on the long summer days, we will sit beneath one and I will love you until you fall asleep in my arms. We will be happy here. At least . . ."

A shadow fell over her face. She looked into the distance for a few seconds.

"*Chérie*, do not do this to yourself."

"I can't help it. What if it was true, Baltic? What if I was his mate?"

"Constantine wanted you as all males want you," Baltic said, taking her loosely in his arms. "But you were not meant to be his mate."

"How do you know?" She looked troubled, and I understood the worry and guilt she felt at causing pain in another.

"I just know. If you were to die, I would cease living. That tells me you are my true mate, and no one else's."

"But you don't *know*—"

"I know," he said, catching up her hands and kissing her fingers.

She hesitated, and Baltic smiled and brushed a strand of hair off her face before pulling her past me, toward the place where the house now stood. "Enough of these dismal thoughts. I have something that will please you. I have designed the house. If you approve of it, it will be done by Michaelmas."

"I will get started on the gardens right away," she answered, smiling up at him again. My throat ached at the joy in her face, at the love that shone so brightly in her eyes. "And there I will pledge my fealty to you, surrounded by the sweet-smelling flowers."

He growled something in her ear I couldn't hear, and she ran off ahead of him, laughing, her long hair fluttering in the wind as he chased her out of my sight.

I held on to the tree for a moment, my fingers clutching painfully at the bark, possessed with a sorrow so great it seemed to leach up out of the ground.

A noise caused me to look up, and I noticed the third figure as he took a step away from the tree against which he'd been leaning. He dropped suddenly to his knees, his head bowed, his shoulders shaking as if he'd given in to the most devastating anguish, the grief that racked his body so profound, waves of suffering rolled off him, choking me with his despair and hopelessness. Mindlessly I stepped forward, driven to comfort him by the bond of one living being to another, even knowing as I did that this shadow figure was beyond my reach.

Gravel crunched beneath my foot and the figure looked up, getting clumsily to his feet. He stepped out of the shadows of the trees and my breath caught in my throat, my heart pounding so loudly I thought it would burst out of my chest.

"Ysolde?" His voice was ragged and raw, as if he'd swallowed acid. He stared at me in stark, utter disbelief.

"You're . . . Baltic?" I asked.

My voice seemed to bring him from his stupor. He took a step toward me, stumbling, his head shaking all the while his eyes were searching me, searching my face, trying to tell if I was real or not. "It cannot be."

"I saw you in the park. You *are* Baltic, aren't you?"

"You . . . live?"

"Yes," I said, chills running down my arms. He looked nothing like the man in the visions—except for his eyes. Those were the same onyx, glittering like sunlight on a still pond. "My name is Tully now."

He stopped a few feet from me, reaching out tentatively, as if he wanted to touch me, but was afraid to do so.

"Ysolde?"

A woman's voice called my name. Baltic froze, then whirled about.

"That sounds like May," I said, frowning as I gazed back at the house. "I wonder how she got here?"

"Silver mate!" Baltic spat, running a few yards away from me as if he sought something.

May emerged from behind the tree, smiling as she saw me. "There you are. We've been looking all over for you. We thought something might have happened to—*agathos daimon*! It's Baltic."

"Yes, he is sharing the vision with me," I said. "How is it that you're seeing it, too?"

"Run!" May said, grabbing my arm and pulling me after her as she took to her heels.

"You don't understand. I need to talk to him—"

"Not here in the shadow world," she yelled, her grip like steel on my wrist.

"Ysolde!" Baltic's roar was filled with fury like nothing I'd ever heard.

"This way!" May jerked me brutally as I tried to stop, pulling me so hard I slammed into the side of the car, seeing stars for a few seconds.

"Whoa!" Brom said, hurrying over to me, concern written all over his face. "You just appeared, like, right out of the air! Sullivan?"

"I'm all right. Just a little dazed."

"Baltic is here," May gasped, throwing herself on Gabriel. "In the shadow world. He almost had her. We barely escaped."

"Then he will be"—as Gabriel spoke, the air gathered and twisted upon itself, stretching to form the figure of a man who leaped forward out of nothing—"soon upon us."

"Don't hurt him!" I cried as Gabriel and Kostya both jumped on Baltic. "Let me talk to him—"

"Hold him!" Drake ordered, coming around the far side of the car.

"Oh, man, I can't believe I almost missed this," Jim said, running down the stairs with Aisling right behind it.

"I'll put a binding ward on him," she called as she started to sketch a shape in the air.

"No!" I yelled, catching her hand to stop her. "Why are you people doing this? Stop, all of you! This has to stop!"

Baltic screamed an oath in a Slavic language, shaking off both Kostya and Gabriel. For a moment, for the time it took to pass from one second to another, his gaze met mine. Anger and hope and pain were in it, but before I could blink, he was gone.

"Holy cow," Brom said, his eyes huge as he waved his hands around the spot where Baltic had stood. "I need to learn how to do that!"

"He's gone," I said, inexplicably feeling as if a part of me had just died.

"He's run back into the beyond," Kostya snarled as he wiped blood from his nose. "He is nothing but a base coward. He has escaped us by that means before because he knows only May can follow him."

"Aargh!" I screamed, suddenly filled with the same fury that I knew must have possessed Baltic. I grabbed Kostya by the shirt and shoved him backwards, slamming him up against the car.

"Sullivan?" Brom asked, his voice full of wonder.

"Why did you do it?" I yelled at Kostya, grabbing his hair and banging his head into the car. "You were his friend! He trusted you! And you betrayed him just as all the others did!"

A wildcat landed on my back, biting and clawing and pulling at my own hair.

"Make her stop, make her stop!" Brom yelled, dancing around us as all three of us—Kostya and Cyrene and I—fell to the ground.

It took a moment for them to separate us—Cyrene refused to let go of me until May pried her hands out of my hair—but by the time they did, the strange sense of anger had passed, leaving me shaking and panting with the aftereffects.

Aisling handed me a tissue to mop up the blood from the scratches that Cyrene had left on my face. Brom leaned into me, wordlessly needing reassurance. I hugged him, resting my cheek on the top of his head, fighting the sobs that threatened to shake me apart.

"Well, we wanted some proof that she was Ysolde," Aisling said as Cyrene cooed over Kostya while he gently felt the back of his head. "I guess you could say that was pretty definitive, huh?"

Chapter Nine

"Do I have to call you de Bouchier now?" Brom asked as I tucked the journal in which he kept his science experiment notes into his backpack.

"No, of course not." I stood up, wanting to hug him again, but I'd already done that, and he had placed a firm "one hug per leave-taking" moratorium on me twenty minutes earlier.

"But that's your name now, right? That guy who appeared used to be your husband before you married Gareth?"

I sighed. There wasn't any way I could deny what life insisted on beating me over the head with. "Yes, I think he was."

Brom leaned in close, his eyes on May and Gabriel as they held a brief confab with Maata and Tipene. "So why is everyone trying to hurt him?"

"It's kind of a complicated story," I whispered back.

"But I'm going to do my best to stop them so that we can talk to Baltic."

"Is he my stepdad now?"

"I . . . we'll talk about that later."

"What's Gareth going to say when he finds out your first husband is still alive?"

I sighed again. "We'll talk about that later, too." I looked up to where Maata and Tipene approached. "I'm not really happy about this."

"We won't let anything happen to him," Maata said, giving Brom a little punch in the arm. He grinned and punched her back. She pretended to flinch, which made him grin all that much harder.

"We were just reunited. I don't like being separated again."

"It is just a precaution, and will not be but for a day or two. Aisling and Drake will take very good care of Brom," Gabriel said in a soothing voice that did nothing but make my jangled nerves more jumpy. "Drake takes his security very seriously now that his children have been born, and I would not be honest if I didn't admit that your son will be safer with them than he would be here should Baltic attack."

I waited until Brom and the two silver bodyguards left, waving with as cheerful a smile on my face as I could put there, but the second the car drove off, I turned on Gabriel. "Why do you persist in the belief that Baltic is going to attack your house?"

He took my arm and escorted me back inside, making sure the elaborate security system that monitored the doors was set. "He's done it before. He blew up our previous house, and destroyed much of the entryway of Drake's. You were there that day—that is how your head was injured."

I touched a little scar in my hairline. I'd wondered how I'd come to get that.

"Now that he knows you are alive, he will put two and two together and arrive at the conclusion that we have taken you in for protection, and he will do everything in his power to steal you from us."

"But that's just the point," I said tiredly, rubbing the headache that throbbed in my temples. "There's no need for him to steal me, as you put it. I want to speak with him. No, I need to—I need to talk to him in order to clear up all the things I don't understand."

"I don't think that would be terribly smart right now," May said softly. "Baltic is . . . I hate the use the word 'insane,' but he's not mentally balanced, Ysolde. You don't remember the things he's done to the silver dragons, to his own people, but Gabriel was there two months ago when they discovered the corpses that Baltic had left when he cut a deadly swath through the blue dragon population."

"No sane being, dragon or otherwise, could have done the things that were done to them," Gabriel said grimly.

His normally bright gaze was dark with remembered pain.

I looked down at my fingers, unable to justify that I was bound to a man who was homicidal.

"You said he looked surprised to see you," May said. "That means he didn't know you were alive, so he's probably frantic to find you now. And you can take it from us that an emotionally upset Baltic does not make for a pleasant companion."

"All I know is that I must have some time to talk to

him. I realize you want to capture him so he can face the charges that are now hanging over my head, but isn't there some neutral ground where we can meet him and talk to him, find out if he really is deranged?"

They were silent for a minute before Gabriel finally said, "I will present that suggestion to the weyr."

What he didn't say was that it would do no good.

I nodded, still rubbing my temples.

"You are fatigued," Gabriel said. "You should rest now. You may have a disturbed night if Baltic chooses to attack tonight."

"Would you like me to send some supper up to you?" May asked.

"Actually, I'm famished. I'd love some food."

"You go upstairs and get into bed, and I'll have Renata whip something up for you."

An hour later I was full of ginger chicken, fresh snow peas, and an intention that I prayed Gabriel and May would never find out. Dressed in jeans and a sweatshirt, I slung my bag over my back, pressed a red button that blinked slowly in a tiny little panel set into the corner of the windowsill, and cautiously opened the window, bracing myself for a siren.

Silence greeted me. I sighed in relief that the switch deactivated the alarm on the window, and peered out. I was three stories up, with no convenient drainpipe, balcony, ivy stuck to the building, or ladder casually leaning against the side of the house. There was literally no way out but to jump to the ground.

"Talk about your leap of faith," I muttered as I sat on the windowsill and swung both legs over the edge. "I just hope to heaven that this works or I'm immortal, because if I'm not, I'm going to be in very bad shape."

I took a deep breath, closed my eyes, and held out my hands as I whispered the light invocation, a spell used to temporarily guard mages from harm. A faint golden glow rippled up my body, skimming the surfaces, leaving me with a familiar tingly feeling that told me I was surrounded by arcane power. "So much for an interdiction, Dr. Kostich," I said somewhat smugly, and jumped off the windowsill.

"Ow." I spat out the bit of dried lawn and dirt and a very startled beetle. "Ow. Dear god in heaven, ow."

The light spell didn't work. That became apparent to me about half a second after I left the windowsill, and just before I hit the ground of the tiny garden spread-eagled and facedown.

I touched my nose, wondering if I'd broken it. "Ow." It wobbled back and forth just fine, so I gathered that it wasn't shattered, as it felt. I sat up slowly, gingerly moving my arms and legs. Everything on me hurt, but nothing seemed to be more than bruised. Either the spell did work after all, or I was immortal.

"Wish I . . . ow . . . knew which it was," I muttered to myself as I got painfully to my feet and limped off around the side of the house. By the time I took a few steps, I was moving a bit easier.

"Now to find Savian," I said as I glanced up and down the street. There was little traffic at this time of night, just a few cars passing. As I started off toward a busy intersection where I hoped to find a taxi stand, a car passing me suddenly slammed on its brakes with a squeal of tires on wet pavement that was painful to the ears.

To my amazement, the car backed up, and a door to the backseat was flung open.

"Get in!" the man who emerged said.

I stared at him in amazement. "How did you—"

"Get in!" Baltic didn't wait for me to comply; he simply picked me up and tossed me into the car, following me with a growl to the driver. Before I could pick myself off the floor, I was flung backwards when the car shot off like a rocket.

"Hey!" I struggled to sit upright, allowing the man next to me to pull me upward onto the seat. "That was totally uncalled-for! I am not a sack of potatoes you can just toss around!"

"Under no circumstances do I regard you as a sack of potatoes."

"Good." I gave him the meanest look I had. "If you intend on blowing up Gabriel's house, you can just think again!"

To my surprise, a little smile flickered over his lips. "I see that the centuries have not diminished your desire to tell me what to do, mate."

"I'm not your mate," I said primly, untwisting the sweatshirt that had been whipped around my torso when he'd thrown me into the car. "I may have been in the past, but now my name is Tully, and I would appreciate it if you would call me that."

"Your name is Ysolde de Bouchier, and you are my mate. Why have you sought refuge with the silver dragons?"

I glanced at the driver.

Baltic followed the path of my gaze, and said something in a language I didn't understand.

"I'm sorry. I don't speak Russian."

"That was Zilant, not Russian," he said.

"Well, I don't speak that, either."

"Yes, you do."

"No, I don't."

"You do. I taught it to you myself."

"I'm happy to argue with you about this all night, but honestly, there are approximately a thousand questions I have for you, and we aren't going to get to any of them if we spend all our time on whether or not I know a language."

"I have a solution to that—don't argue with me."

"You are just as bossy as you used to be, do you know that?" I told him, poking him in the chest.

He grabbed both my arms and pulled me over until his nose was a fraction of an inch from mine. "And you are just as argumentative and lacking in respect as you used to be."

We stared at each other for a minute. He narrowed his eyes. He sniffed the air. "Why do you not smell as you should?"

I pushed myself out of his grip, straightening my sweat-shirt a second time. "Well, I am sorry I offend you, but you have no one but yourself to blame for that, Mr. Disappear into the Beyond. Rather than take a bath, I opted to go find Savian in order to force him to find you so I could talk to you, which, I would like to point out, I wouldn't have had to do if you hadn't disappeared like you did."

"You might think it's an afternoon's frolic to face three wyverns bent on your destruction, but I have other ways I'd prefer to spend my time," he said dryly.

I smiled to myself. I didn't remember the Baltic from my dreams having a sense of humor. "All right, I will grant you the right to make a timely escape—they were unfairly ganging up on you. But that doesn't give you the right to make insulting personal comments by telling me I stink."

"I didn't—for the love of the saints, mate! I did not say you stink!"

"You did, too! You said—"

"I said you do not smell as you should, and you do not." He held up a hand when I was about to protest. "You do not smell like a dragon."

"Oh. Well. That's probably because I'm not—hey!"

Baltic lunged at me, burying his face in the crook of my neck. "You smell . . . human."

"I *am* human," I said, my body suddenly coming to life in a way that almost stripped the breath from me. It was as if his touch electrified me, sending little zaps of pleasure down my skin. His hair brushed my cheek, and it was all I could do to keep from grabbing his head and kissing him until he was insensible.

"You are not. You are a dragon."

"No, I'm human. My name is Tully, and I'm human now. I've only just decided to accept the fact that in the past I was a dragon named Ysolde, but now I'm human, and are you *licking* me?"

I couldn't stand it. The feel of him against me, the scent of him, something almost indefinable, like the smell of a rain-washed sky, pushed me close to the edge of my control. When his tongue licked a flaming path along my collarbone, I knew I had to stop him. I heaved him away from me with all my strength.

He licked his lips, an indescribable look on his face. "You taste the same. How is it that you smell differently but you taste the same?"

"How do I know?" I said, shakily trying to regain my wits and keep from flinging myself on him. "I'm still trying to get over the fact that you were dead and now you're not. Where are we going, by the way?"

"I am stealing you from the silver wyvern," he said with great satisfaction.

"You can hardly be said to be stealing me if I come with you of my own accord, not to mention escaping the house to go find you."

"I would expect nothing less from my mate," he said with that same satisfaction.

I sighed, probably for the fifteenth time that day. "I seem to be sighing a lot lately," I commented.

"That is because you were pining for me. Why did you not tell me you were alive?" he demanded.

"Have you always been this arrogant and egotistical?" I asked, then continued quickly before he could answer. "No, don't bother to tell me. The few visions I've had answer that question. I will tell you what I know, but I warn you that it's just going to raise more questions than answers."

It took the whole of the ride to a large house about an hour outside of London for me to tell Baltic what had happened since I woke up in Gabriel's house.

"You knew I was alive but you did not seek me out immediately?" he asked as we stopped outside a gate, the driver punching in a security code.

"People mentioned you, yes, but most of the time, I figured I was nuts and made you up," I answered, watching the driver in order to memorize the code, just in case I ever needed to make a fast escape.

"You are not insane."

"No, I gather that, but if you woke up remembering hardly anything, and having the most vivid dreams of your life about a bossy man who threatened to kill you at one point, what would you think?"

I turned to him, a stab of pain piercing my heart at

the pain visible in his eyes. "Oh, Baltic!" Without thinking I took his hand in mine, pressing it against my cheek. "I wasn't avoiding you. I truly didn't believe you were real until I saw you in the park, and then I knew I had to find you, to talk to you. You have to understand that it's been very difficult to accept that what I was reliving weren't just imaginings, but shadows of the past."

His fingers curled around mine, and he leaned forward to kiss my fingers as we drove up a paved driveway to a rather squat, blocky white Regency-era house covered with ivy on the front. "When I saw you this afternoon—I thought for a moment that I, too, had gone mad."

I smiled and rubbed his knuckles against my cheek. "I had no idea you were real. You were watching the past?"

"Yes. I do sometimes. Usually, it's too painful."

Anguish appeared to rise within him at the memory, and once again, I was helpless against it. I wrapped my arms around him, holding him against the pain, wanting to bring only light to his darkness. "It saddened me, too, seeing them—us—so happy, knowing how things ended."

"Nothing has ended," he said, his mouth moving across my temple with gentle little kisses that almost left me weeping. "You are here now. Life has begun again."

I turned my face into his neck, kissing his pulse point, but saying nothing.

The car stopped in front of the house, and I took a minute to gaze around before allowing Baltic to escort me inside. The grounds were pleasant, if a bit bare of anything but a tennis court and a hint of a swimming pool in the back.

Baltic led me inside, turning back for a moment to speak with the driver. I looked around, curious as to whether this home would be as soul-satisfying as the other. The entry hall was done in shades of white and egg cream, with white tile on the floor, an elegant staircase in white to the right, and a magnificent crystal chandelier. It was very pretty . . . and completely barren of warmth or soul or heart.

"Come," Baltic said holding out his hand, having finished with the driver. I noticed that he, too, set the security alarms before escorting me to a room that opened onto the entryway.

I ignored his hand, needing a little distance to keep my mind—not to mention libido—under control. "So, this is—ack!"

He leaped on me, positively leaped on me, pulling me down onto the couch, his mouth hot on my skin.

"Baltic!" I shrieked, trying to push him off me.

"We will now mate," he announced, just like that was the end of the story.

"Like hell we will!"

He kissed me then, kissed me with enough fire that my feet were burning by the time he was done.

"Whoa," I said, gathering my wits together enough to push him back. "I can't do this. You have to give me some time. Besides, there's something I haven't told you about—"

"There is no time," he interrupted, sliding his hands beneath my sweatshirt. "I must claim you as my mate now, before another can do so."

"Now hold on here a minute!" I seized his wrists and stopped his hands from moving farther. "I agree that we

have a lot to talk about, and I'm ashamed to say that I
enjoyed that kiss more than I should have."

"There is no shame in what we do," he interrupted
again. "We are mated."

"We are not mated. We may have been mated in the
past, but that was before you died. I don't know for sure
what happened to me, but—"

"You died, as well."

I stopped and stared at him. "You knew that?"

"You died right before me." Pain filled his eyes and
he closed them for a moment, his face twisted with remembered agony. Without thinking, I moved closer,
putting my hand on his chest. "I was in the tunnel beneath Dauva. Kostya had turned traitor and was trying
to kill me. I was just about to disembowel him when my
heart stopped, and I knew you had been killed, knew
that bastard Constantine had finally made good his
threat and destroyed you rather than let me have you."

"Constantine killed me?" I asked, goose bumps rippling up my arms and legs. "But . . . he said he loved
me."

"He swore that if he could not have you, I should not.
And without you, I would have no life." His eyes opened
and tears filled mine at the depths of pain so visible on
his face. I pressed myself against his body, wanting to
comfort him, wanting to ease the agony that time did
not lessen. "My heart died with you at that moment, and
I knew I would not survive. So I let Kostya kill me. It was
easier than surviving the few remaining hours I had."

"I'm sorry," I said, blinking back tears.

His mouth brushed mine in a gentle acknowledgment
of what I offered. "It wasn't your fault. I know now that

you were only trying to stop the war. But you were once my mate, and you will be so again, now, this minute. I must claim you, Ysolde. We must mate as dragons mate, so that all will know you are truly mine once again."

I slipped out of his arms, my stomach sick and cold. "If things were different, if my life had not turned out as it had, I would accept your offer. But there is something you don't know, and aren't going to like."

"What?" he asked, gripping my arms tightly.

"I have a husband. He is an oracle."

Anger flared in his ebony eyes. "You have taken a lover?"

"No, I have taken a husband. Had taken. I don't remember marrying him, and for that matter, don't particularly like him. In fact, I'm planning on divorcing him, because he's a bastard. But I must have had nicer feelings for him at some point, because why else would I marry him?"

A muscle in his neck twitched. "You said your memory has been destroyed. You are not to blame for taking a husband."

"I'm glad you think so, but he is my husband, regardless, and I'm sorry, Baltic. It may not be much of a marriage, but I would be less of a person if I were to be unfaithful. I can't sleep with you until I am separated from him."

"You are my mate," he repeated stubbornly.

"Yes, I think I would be, but I have some moral values, and one of those is to not commit adultery."

The muscle twitched again. "This is not an issue. I will kill this husband who dares claim what is mine, and then you will be able to give yourself to me freely."

I laughed; I just couldn't help myself. He was so earnest, and it tickled my funny bone. "I appreciate the fact that you have absolutely no qualms about killing an innocent man, but that would be even less tolerable to me than straying. No. You will not kill my husband."

"Stop saying that word," he snapped, releasing me to pace the width of the room.

"I'm sorry. I will endeavor not to talk about him." It was an effort, but I managed to keep from smiling.

"I realize that you feel some mortal emotions toward this . . . person . . . but you are a dragon. You are my mate. You must be claimed. It would be dangerous for you to remain as you are."

"Dangerous," I said, skeptical to my toes. I managed to keep from throwing myself on him, knowing if I did, I wouldn't be able to resist him a second time.

"You are a wyvern's mate. If other wyverns were to see you and know you for what you are, they could steal you from me," he said, and I realized that he was deadly serious.

"I hate to break this to you, but unless there are some septs that I don't know about, I've seen all the wyverns. I met them all at the *sárkány*. No one even looked twice at me, at least not in the way you're implying."

"Nonetheless, you could be claimed by another." He paced past me, his hands behind his back. "I can't tolerate that. Once, I let you slip away from me—I have learned from that mistake, and will not do so again."

My heart warmed. I couldn't help it. Oh, he was being arrogant and pushy and domineering, but none of that really mattered, not when I could see the insecurity and fear that he tried so hard to keep from me. "I appreciate the fact that you want to protect me, but it's not necessary."

"Even now they are plotting to take you!" he said stubbornly.

"Who?" I asked, confused.

"The unattached wyverns, Bastian and Kostya. They have seen you, and they want you."

"Oh, for the love of all that's good and glorious! It's flattering that you think every wyvern out there is panting after me, but you're way off the scale here, Baltic. No one gives a damn about me, at least not in that sense. You really do take the cake, do you know that?"

"I have no cake!" he said, deliberately misinterpreting me.

I slapped my hand down on the table, frustrated, amused, and wildly aroused, all at the same time. "Well, that's a shame, because I could sure go for a piece right now."

"If you are hungry, I will feed you," he said somewhat grumpily

"Maybe later," I said with a smile. I looked around the room, examining the few objets d'art scattered around. "This is a very pretty house."

The sitting room was also done in white and egg cream, with beige and white striped overstuffed armchairs, less substantial black and gold Regency chairs, and a honey oak parquet floor.

"It's abominable, but it has an excellent view of the surrounding area, so I will be able to see attackers before they can strike."

I stopped in front of the long fireplace, tipping my head as I examined him. He looked the same as he had earlier—chocolate hair pulled back in a short ponytail, the widow's peak drawing attention to his high brow, his eyes just as piercing as they had been in my dreams. I sensed power about him that I realized with a shock was his dragon fire, carefully leashed, but present nonetheless. "Is that how you think? In terms of people attacking you?"

"Dragons, not people."

"Well, perhaps if you didn't run around slaughtering other dragons, you wouldn't have to protect yourself from them when they seek revenge."

A frown pulled his eyebrows close. "If you are referring to the wars—"

"Actually, I'm not," I said, heedlessly interrupting him. "I'm talking about the sixty-eight blue dragons you killed a couple of months ago."

He said nothing for a moment, pulling a long cream and gold curtain across a floor-to-ceiling window before turning to consider me. "What would you think if I told you that I was not responsible for those deaths?"

"I'd say . . ." I thought for a moment, my lips pursing. "I'd say that everyone believes you are."

He shook his head. "That is not what I wanted to know."

"It's what you asked," I pointed out.

"But it is not what I wanted to know, a fact of which you are well aware." To my surprise, he smiled. "If you had any doubt that you are a dragon, Ysolde, the fact that you avoid answering a direct question should be proof positive."

"You should do that more often."

"Point out reasons why you should recognize the fact that you're a dragon?"

"No, smile."

His smile faded. "I have had no reason to do so."

"Maybe not, but a sense of humor is right at the top of traits I find sexy in a man."

"You already think I'm sexy," he said with arrogant ease, strolling toward me with the same sense of a panther gliding silently down a jungle path that I remembered from the other Ysolde's life.

"In the past? No doubt. But there are a whole lot of sexy men around today." I kept my voice light, striving not to let him hear the smile in it.

He paused, a moment of uncertainty in his face. "You find this other man, this husband, sexy?"

"Gareth? Lord, no." I frowned, wondering about that.

"Then why did you mate with him?"

"Physically, you mean?"

He nodded, watching me with the intensity of a panther, too.

"I don't really know. I must have slept with him at some time. That's what married people do. But . . ." I sat and tried to examine the still impenetrable mass that was my memories. "No. There's nothing there. I can see his face, and I know he's a bastard, and I don't wish to be married to him anymore, but beyond that, it's pretty much a void."

"That is a small comfort," Baltic said with a wry twist to his lips. "What man is it you find sexy, then? Is it Gabriel? You find him arousing?"

I couldn't help but smile at the sudden look of sheer outrage that passed over his face. "Why on earth would you think that?"

"You are a wyvern's mate," he snorted. "He is a wyvern, and you were staying in his house. Did he touch you?"

"Even if he wanted to—and I assure you, he views me as nothing more than a big pain in the ass—May would kill him. And quite probably me, although perhaps she'd let me live because if she killed me, she'd feel obligated to take in Brom."

"Who is Brom?" he asked, his frown back. "Is he yet another man who arouses you?"

"I think lots of men are sexy, but that doesn't mean squat," I said, trying not to laugh again.

"It does to me."

"Pfft. Like you haven't ever seen a woman and thought she was attractive?"

"No," he said in complete seriousness.

I gawked at him, just a little gawk. "Oh, come on, Baltic."

"You doubt my word?" he said, bristling at the implication that I thought he was lying.

"I think you're trying to make me feel bad, yes."

He sighed a very exaggerated sigh, pulling me to my feet. I stepped away immediately, knowing that just being close to him would leave me indulging my carnal desires. "Ysolde, you are my mate. I desire no other woman than you. I would not try to make you feel bad. I would not lie to you, a fact you should know."

"All right, I apologize for doubting your word," I said humbly, moving over to the window. Although my body screamed to be near him, my mind knew it was wiser to put a little distance between us.

"Good. Now tell me where this Brom is so that I might geld him."

I laughed again, amused by the flash of ire in his eyes.

"You laugh at me, woman?" he said, stalking toward me.

I laughed even harder, holding him back with a hand on his chest. "Please do not geld my son."

He blinked at me. "Your son?"

"Yes. Brom is my son. He's nine. I think you will like him. He's a little odd, but very clever, and has an amazing range of interests, including a love of history. I'm sure he'd love to talk to you about the things you've lived through."

A muscle in his neck twitched. "You had my son with another man?"

"No, I had *my* son with another man."

His hands fisted, his face a veritable storm cloud of anger. "By rights he should be mine! You are *my* mate! Any child you bear should be mine!"

"Oh, grow up," I said, tired and suddenly annoyed.

I thought he might explode at that.

"I had Brom nine years ago. Nine years ago! So you can just deal with it, or not, but I warn you, I love Brom with all my heart, and I will not tolerate you treating him as if there is something inferior about him."

"You love *me* with all your heart," he yelled.

"Do you always yell?" I shouted back.

"Yes!" he snarled.

"Fine!" I bellowed.

He was so angry I swear his eyebrows were bristling, and before I could finish my sentence, he was on me again, his arms as hard as the oak floor beneath us, his mouth hot and demanding and just as exciting as it had been in my dreams. His tongue was everywhere, twirling around my tongue, tasting me, firing my blood with little touches that seemed both gentle and demanding at the same time. He filled my senses, overwhelming me with the scent and taste and feel of him pressed up against me.

And then the fire came. Actual fire, the kind that burns things down. One minute I was kissing him, feeling as if I were on fire, and the next I really was. For a second I panicked, sure I was going to be horribly burned, but just as I was about to fling myself away from Baltic's fire, an amazing thing happened—something inside me shifted. It was as if the entire world seemed to go slightly out of focus for a moment, then snapped back to its normal clarity.

The fire that threatened to char my skin suddenly danced along it instead, leaving me with a sensation of warmth, but nothing more. Well, nothing more that was harmful—it also fired up the burn inside me to new levels, until I wiggled against Baltic, doing a seductive little dance that I'd never done before. He groaned into my mouth as his fingers dug into my behind, pulling me tighter against him as his lips and mouth and dragon fire consumed my every thought.

"You love *me* with all your heart," he growled, his control very close to snapping.

As I told myself that I really needed to stop before things went too far, the words he had spoken sank in through the miasma of lust and love that raged in my brain, settling into a righteous annoyance.

"You know, I really hate people telling me what I do," I answered, biting his lower lip, and not gently, either. I didn't break the skin, because I didn't wish to cause pain, but it was the sort of a nip that would make him take notice.

And take notice he did. "You dare bite me?" He

reared back, shock evident on his face as he touched his lower lip.

"Yes—yes, I do." With my hands on my hips, I took a menacing step forward. "I don't like being told what to do! So you can just stop this Mr. Demanding bit and kiss me properly, or not kiss me at all!"

"Now you are telling *me* what to do!" he stormed, taking a step forward until his chest rubbed against mine. "I don't like it, either. And as for the kiss, Madame Bossy, I will kiss you any way I see fit. I am the wyvern here, not you!"

"Madame Bossy!" I gasped.

Nose-to-nose, we glared at each other until I couldn't help it, and laughed. To my surprise, Baltic's lips twitched; then a rusty chuckled emerged, which cascaded into an outright guffaw.

My heart sang as I watched him laugh until tears wetted the corners of his eyes.

"Ah, *chérie*," he said, putting his arms around me again. "Thus it has always been between us, eh?"

I brushed the hair out of his eyes, my fingers tracing the satiny length of his eyebrow. "I don't remember."

"You are the only one who has ever made me laugh," he said, kissing the corner of my mouth. "You used to say outrageous things, things I would not tolerate from any other dragon. Then when I was ready to throttle you, you'd tickle me, or perform some other silly act to lighten my mood, and make me think that life could not be any better."

His confession touched me, making my eyes burn as I dabbed away the remnants of laughing tears on his lashes. "Many things have changed about me, Baltic, but

I'm afraid I'm still prone to saying outrageous things. Did I hurt you when I bit you?"

"No." His hands slid down to pinch my behind. "But do not do it again."

I giggled.

"You *do* love me with all your heart."

That was a statement, but there was a shadow in his eyes that had me answering quickly, "Yes, I do. I've just met you, and yet I've loved you for centuries. I love both you and Brom."

"Equally?" he asked, pinching me again.

"Yes," I said, keeping my smile to myself.

"You should love me more." His voice had a faintly disgruntled hint to it.

"That, my little periwinkle, is about a toe and a half over the line." I slid out of his arms. It took more than a little effort to do that, since my body badly wanted to stay smooshed up to his, but the way my insides were humming, it was that or give in to him.

"Why do you push me away?" he asked, his eyes hot with desire.

"I . . . you overwhelm me."

"Good."

"No, it's not good. At least, not until things are straightened out with my husband. Now . . . what were we talking about? I've lost track."

"We were discussing your refusal to mate with me," he said, his eyes still smoldering with heat.

I held my tongue, not wanting to make another pass on that particular verbal merry-go-round. "You said you wanted to claim me in order to protect me. That claiming business is just an oath of fealty, isn't it?"

"That is part of it, yes."

"Can we do the swearing without the sex?"

"It is possible, but unheard of."

"Well, you'd better start hearing it, because I will agree to accept you as a wyvern, but I won't have sex with you. Not until I can resolve the issue of my husband. I fully intend to get a divorce from him, but until I have a chance to tell him I want one, to tell him that we are officially separated, there will be no sleeping together."

He dismissed the entire issue with a little wave of his hand. "I will take care of any concerns you have about the mortal."

"I'm not so sure he is mortal," I murmured, thinking back to what Dr. Kostich had said.

"It matters not. He will cease to be a problem." Baltic stood in front of me, a handsome, vital man who had suffered untold centuries of anguish. I touched his cheek, touched the hard planes of his face, tracing my finger along his high cheekbones and around his eyes, those beautiful black eyes that had a slight upward tilt, giving him a faintly Slavic look.

I brushed a strand of hair off his cheek. "How did we both come to be alive again?"

He captured my hand, kissing the tips of my fingers, his eyes never leaving mine. "I don't know how you came to be resurrected. But I will find out, *chérie*. I will find out."

"What do I need to say to swear fealty to you?"

"Whatever is in your heart."

I laughed. "My heart is confused at this point, so I wouldn't look to it for any help. But I ought to be able to come up with something. Let's see . . . I am Tully Sullivan, and I—"

"You are Ysolde de Bouchier. This other name, this mortal name, has no bearing on us," he insisted.

"I happen to like the name Tully—*fine.* I am Ysolde de Bouchier, also known as Tully Sullivan, and I hereby pledge my fealty to you, Baltic . . . um . . . is Baltic your first name or last name?"

"It is my only name. I have no other."

"Oh. All right. That's very movie star, but that's fine. I hereby pledge my fealty to you, Baltic, wyvern of the black dragons. No, wait, that can't be right. Kostya is the wyvern of the black dragons. He was at the *sárkány.*"

Baltic swore. "His traitorous hide deserves only to be split on the end of my sword."

"Please tell me you're not going to fight him for control of the black dragons," I said, unable to handle the thought of what I knew would be a huge battle between Baltic and everyone in the weyr.

"By rights I should, but I will not. I am no longer a black dragon."

"You're not?" I looked him over as if that would tell me anything. "What sept do you belong to? Not the silver dragons?"

He shifted into dragon form, his body covered with glittering white scales.

"You're a white dragon?"

"Not white—light," he said as he shifted back, holding out his hand. Light formed there, stretching out to form a white and blue sword. "When I was reborn, I became something new, something not seen before—we are light dragons, you and I, Ysolde. Our dragon form reflects the fact that we encompass all colors, just as light does. We wield arcane magic, which other dragons cannot do. Ours is a new sept, with only the two of us as members."

I digested that. "That sword belonged to Antonia von Endres, didn't it?"

"Yes." He glanced at it. "She gave it to me long ago."

"Why would she give you something like that?" I asked. "That sword is famous in magedom, and although you're not a slacker at arcane abilities, you're not a mage."

He tossed the blade up, catching it on the tip of one finger. It balanced perfectly. "Antonia gave it to me because she said I gave her great pleasure."

"What sort of great pleasure?" I asked, a sudden roar of anger whipping through me so great that it drove off my intention to tell him that Dr. Kostich had asked me to take the sword from him. "Great pleasure as in, oh, I don't know, sex?"

"She was my lover, yes." He frowned, shaking his hand so that the sword dissolved into nothing.

"You screwed her for a sword?" I asked, my fingernails digging into my palms with the effort to keep from shaking him. I knew my anger was unreasonable, but I was powerless to stop it.

"Why are you so angry?" he asked, looking thoughtful all of a sudden. "Are you jealous?"

"Of course I'm not jealous! What do I have to be jealous of? I mean, it's not like the man I just told I loved beyond all reason informed me he's been out bonking anyone who has mage toys, is it? It's not like he just admitted infidelity, oh no! It's not like you're standing right there with your penis all bulgy and poking me"—I gestured at the fly of his pants, which was looking rather strained after our steamy kiss—"and telling me that it's been visiting other women, not because you are seeking another lover, but so you can have a fancy mage sword! It's not like that at all, is it, Baltic?"

He looked delighted, the bastard. "You *are* jealous!"

"You are the most obnoxious, reprehensible, despicable man I've ever met."

"I am a dragon, not a man."

"Gah!" I yelled, and slapped both hands on his chest.

He covered them with his own, doing that lovely rusty chuckle that made my knees go all weak despite the fact that I wanted to knock his block off. "*Chérie*, I remember many times you threatened to emasculate or decapitate me when you believed I was looking at other females, but I had thought the centuries we spent together had eased your suspicions."

"Just tell me this," I said, grabbing a fistful of his shirt. "How many times did you betray me?"

Anger followed surprise in his eyes. "What cause have I ever given you to believe I would do such a thing?"

A horrible silence followed, one that was filled with my brain suddenly pointing out that time actually existed before I met Baltic. "Er . . . you knew her before you met me?"

He sighed, unclenching my fingers from his shirt. "Yes."

"But you never told me she'd given you a mage sword."

"I had no cause to use it," he said, shrugging. "I did not have the skills at that time to wield it. It was only after I was reborn that I was able to do so."

"So you didn't sleep with her after you met me," I said, wanting to make absolutely certain of that point.

"I took no females after I met you." He started to smile, but suddenly looked away.

I pounced on that. "Oh, really?"

He made a vague gesture, a flicker of embarrassment in his eyes. "There was a barmaid in Bordeaux, but I did not rut with her. I tried, but I could not."

"What a goddamned shame," I growled, wanting to punch him all over again.

"She was not my mate. I thought I would ease my lust on her, but I could not. I knew then that I must have you and no one else." He took my clenched fists in his hands, stroking his thumb across the top. "That is when I sent to Constantine to let him know I was claiming you."

The fury inside me melted away into a dull throb. "It's very hard to be angry at someone when he's just told you he can't have sex with another woman because he wants you instead."

"You have no need to be angry. I have not given myself to another, as you have." His voice was etched with acid.

"I can't help it if I lost my memory and got married. And wait a minute, are you saying that you haven't had sex in"—I did some quick calculations—"over three hundred years?"

"I have not had a female since I met you, no."

I blinked, unable to keep from asking, "Have you had a male?"

He looked outraged. "No! I do not lust after males, as Pavel does. I have been mated, and to a dragon, that bond exists for all time."

"Pavel your guard? He was gay?" I asked.

"That is the mortal term for it, yes. He enjoys both males and females equally."

I picked up on the present tense of that sentence. "Whoa! He's still alive?"

"Yes. He has been in London, but I expect him back shortly. Are you going to accept me as your mate, or not?"

"Er . . . yes. I'm sorry, I was just distracted by the thought of . . . never mind."

He gave me the oddest look. "You were distracted by the thought of Pavel with another male? Do you lust after him?"

"No, of course not! I don't even know the guy. It's just that, sometimes . . . well, you know, sometimes guys with other guys . . . it's just kind of . . . er . . . hot."

I thought his eyeballs might pop right out of his head.

"Hot? You are aroused by males making love to each other?"

"No! Not normally! Just once in a very rare while. It's kind of . . . titillating."

"I see." He didn't look like he saw at all, what with his lips pursed and his arms crossed over his chest.

"You don't ever think that once in a blue moon, it can be sexy?" I asked.

"No." He thought for a moment. "Two females together, yes. That is always arousing. Especially if they are oiled. But males? No."

"Well, see, I don't get the two girls together thing. It just doesn't ring my chimes at all. Does Pavel bring his dates here often?"

He stared at me for a minute. I cleared my throat. "Sorry. None of my business. What were we talking about?"

"You were saying the words of fealty." He paused. "You really are aroused by the thought of two males?"

"Only very rarely! Sheesh! I'm sorry I mentioned it! Let's move on."

He nodded, then asked suspiciously, "You do not wish for me to engage in sexual acts with another man—"

"No! God almighty, Baltic! That's the last time I'm ever going to share a sexual fantasy with you!"

"It's a fantasy of yours, seeing two men together?" he asked.

I walked over to the wall and banged my head against it a couple of times.

"I do not understand you," he said, a thread of puzzlement in his voice. "You have changed since you were resurrected. My Ysolde would never have wanted to see—"

"Enough!" I yelled, storming over to him and punching him in the chest. Hard. "Move past it or I'm walking out of here right now!"

His lips thinned, but he said nothing.

"Thank you. Now, I suppose I should start over, shouldn't I?" I stopped, pursing my lips as I looked at him. "You're still thinking about it, aren't you?"

"No." Five seconds passed. "Is it the thought of the men engaged in the sexual act itself, or some other facet—"

"Argh!" I yelled, and ran out of the room, out of the hall, and out of the house.

Chapter Ten

Eventually I made the oath, outside under the stars, with the light breeze wafting around us.

"Are you sure you do not wish to mate?" Baltic asked politely as soon as he confirmed the oath, swearing to honor and protect me above all others. "I know how you like to be outside. We could do it out here, if you like."

I chuckled to myself. "Thank you, but until I have a chance to talk to my husband, sex will be out."

A sly look came into his eyes as he slowly pulled me over to his body. "There was another time when you refused to let me bed you, and yet we still managed to bring exquisite pleasure to each other."

"Yes," I said, unable to keep my mouth from moving toward his. My lips brushed his with a wanton display of need. "I very much enjoyed that dream."

"It was not a dream, *chérie*," he murmured against my mouth, his hips moving with persuasive sweeps against mine. "It happened. It can happen again."

"Except this time, I'm not a naïve seventeen-year-old who doesn't know what she's doing," I said, moaning softly when his mouth moved over to my neck, his lips burning my flesh, but it was a good burn, a heat that set my entire body alight.

He pulled back for a moment, his lips curling at the edges. "You knew what you were doing by the time we reached France."

I shared the smile until I felt his hands on the waistband of my jeans. I covered them with mine. "Baltic . . . I'm sorry. I can't. It's . . . there's too much up in the air. I'm not comfortable doing this with you until I talk to—"

He covered my mouth with his, stopping the words. "I won't do anything you do not desire, *chérie*. But you have spoken the words of fealty, and you are now my mate. You must bear the mark of my sept."

I held on to his shoulders as he unzipped my jeans, sliding his hands over to my hips, pushing the material down. "Just where exactly do you intend to put this mark?"

He grinned as he cupped me intimately, his thumb rubbing on my pubic bone. "I thought here."

"Well, you can bloody well think again!" I said, squirming against him nonetheless.

"Here?" He touched the crease of my thigh.

"That would hurt like hell. No."

"How about here?" He pulled me to him, his hands on my butt, giving my cheeks a little squeeze.

"I'm thinking that's fairly disrespectful, don't you?"

He gave a mock sigh, then whipped off my sweatshirt before I could protest, nuzzling my breasts. "Then it will have to be here."

"Over my heart?" I thought about that for a moment. It pleased me. "All right. Wait—don't you have one?"

"I was the only member of the sept until you accepted me. You will have to give me the mark."

I was about to tell him I hadn't the slightest clue how to go about doing that when he opened his mouth and breathed fire on me. It hurt like the dickens for about two seconds; then the heat soaked into me, swirling around until it settled in my groin, pooling in places that hadn't been pooled in for centuries. I looked down to see my bra gone, and Baltic licking my left breast, a strange swirly symbol burned into the flesh. As I watched, the redness of it faded until it was the same color as the mark on my hip—a sort of dark tan.

"Now you have been marked as my mate, although I would appreciate it if you didn't show people," he said, kissing my breast. "Your form, although apparently human, pleases me, and I do not wish for others to ogle you."

I thought seriously of throwing everything to the wind—Gareth, my moral values, decency—and just letting Baltic make love to me until the sun rose high above us. "I wish I could make love to you," I said, gasping when he took my nipple in his mouth. My fingers dug into his shoulders.

"I will if you desire it," he murmured, rubbing his cheek against my breast.

"I can't," I said, pulling his face up to mine. "I shouldn't even be kissing you. That's wrong, too."

"Nothing is wrong between us. But if you do not wish for me to do that, then I will not," he said, sucking my bottom lip.

"I think that would be best," I said, my fingers caressing the long sweeps of muscles in his shoulders. "Until things are worked out."

"Then I will not pay homage to your magnificent breasts, either," he mumbled, his mouth kissing a wet, steamy trail down to my chest.

"That would definitely be over the line," I said, my back arching of its own accord as he swirled his tongue around my nipple, the latter so tight and hard it positively ached with the need for his touch. I groaned again, gripping his shoulders as he tormented first one breast, then the other with long, hot strokes of his tongue.

"Were you to give yourself to me, I would bathe your sublime belly with fire," he said, pulling me down to the ground.

"But I haven't, so you won't," I said, threading my fingers through the cool silk of his hair.

"Of course not." Baltic lifted his head from where he was kissing the curve of my hip, and breathed fire on my stomach. It shimmered along my skin until it was absorbed back into his mouth as he laved a path to the other hip.

"The memory of your scent and taste has driven me almost mad with desire," he murmured into my pelvic bone, his hands gently pushing my underwear down over my hips. "The idea of experiencing it again fills my thoughts."

"That would be far too wrong to do now," I said, my eyes almost rolling back into my head when his tongue flicked across secret, intimate parts of me, parts that tingled with awareness and a need that I couldn't allow.

"I will not taste you, then," he said just before his mouth possessed me in a way that had me clutching the grass, my hips thrusting up against him.

"Thank you for not doing that," I gasped, almost coming off the ground when he sank a finger into me.

"You are so hot, *chérie*. Tell me you burn only for me."

"Only for you," I repeated, mindless with passion and desire now, wanting him like I'd never wanted anything, tears leaking from the corners of my eyes as I struggled with my conscience.

He moved over me, his clothing gone, the hard lines of his body pressing me down, into the earth. I felt him rub against my inner thigh, a hot brand that my body wept for. He framed my face in his hands, kissing me with a long, slow stroke of his tongue against mine.

"Let me love you, Ysolde. Let this happen. Since I was reborn, I have lived every moment in despair because I lost you. Let me worship you now as I've longed to do all those years."

I held on to him, sobbing now. "It's wrong, Baltic. I'm married to another man."

"You don't even remember marrying him. Perhaps you were forced. Will you remain faithful to a man who would so abuse your trust?"

"I don't know," I sobbed, wanting to shift my hips and allow him entrance into my body. I wanted him with a fever that threatened to consume me. "I don't know."

He rolled off me, and I curled up into a ball on the grass, crying for my lost memory, crying for the years that Baltic spent alone. Warmth covered me as he curled himself around me, keeping the cool night air from my naked flesh, comforting me despite his own pain.

"Thank you," I said when I had managed to bring my emotions back under control. I turned to face him and gently pushed the hair from his cheek. "Thank you for protecting my honor, even when I was willing to forgo it."

"You are my mate. I could never force you to do anything you did not want."

I stroked my hand on his chest, the sensation of the soft black hairs making my fingertips tingle. "When I give myself to you, Baltic, I want it to be all of me. I don't want my ties to another man to be there between us, tainting it, tainting the beauty of what we will have."

He looked down at me, the light of an almost full moon bathing the planes of his face in harsh shadows, but his eyes glowed with an obsidian inner light. Slowly he nodded, and touched my lower lip with his thumb. "You were always thus. You never did anything halfway—it was with your whole heart, or not at all."

"I sound like I was very annoying," I said with a little self-conscious grimace as I sat up to retrieve my clothing.

"Not annoying—honorable." He watched me dress, arrogantly naked, still aroused. "It irritated me at the time, but I learned to live with it."

I couldn't help but laugh at that as I finished dressing. I eyed him, guilt pricking away at my scruples. "I feel guilty about that," I said, waving at his penis, which was in no way returning to a more quiescent state.

He pursed his lips as he looked at it. "Why?"

"I more or less led you on. There's a term for that, and I'm appalled that it is applicable to me. Would you . . . I feel ridiculous even saying this after the big scene I just made, but would you like me to take care of it?"

"Yes," he said so fast I laughed again. I sank to my knees next to him, laying a hand on his thigh. "You would do this for me? It would not violate your sense of duty and honor?"

"It does, but not as much as the guilt of what I allowed to happen."

He shook his head, rising up on one elbow and catching my hand as I reached for him. "You did not *allow* me to touch you, Ysolde; I wished to seduce you. I did everything I could to sway you to that goal."

"And I enjoyed every minute of it," I said, slipping my hand from his. "Deep down, I knew if I told you to stop and really meant it, you would. And you did. So we are both to blame for how far things got carried, and although I would never do this for another man, although I feel I am still bound to my husband until I can tell him otherwise, you are the man I would choose to be with. For that reason, I wish to repay your kindness to me with a little kindness of my own."

"It is not kindness," he said as I bent over him, swirling my tongue around the very tip of him. He fell back, his eyes crossing as his hips thrust upward. "It is ecstasy."

"I have to get back to Gabriel's house."

"No."

My shirt went flying.

"They're going to be wondering what happened to me. I don't want them to worry. I have to go back."

"No."

My pants joined my shirt. I stood with hands on hips as I glared at Baltic, who was still naked, and quickly returning me to that state. "I can see where this is going, and it's not going to happen. I will sleep alone tonight."

"No."

My bra arced through the air, landing with a whisper on my shoes.

"Why on earth did I ever think you were a reasonable man?" I cried, slapping my hands on my legs.

He looked up from where he was about to remove my panties, honestly surprised. "I don't know. I'm not reasonable."

"I'm glad you admit that. Baltic, I'm not going to sleep with you."

"You are my mate," he said, yanking the last of my clothing off, and scooping me up in his arms at the same time. He carried me over to a large bed, covered in a quilt of white and gold. "I will not make love to you, but you will sleep with me from this night forward."

"That's going to be a little bit difficult to explain to Brom," I said, sliding beneath the cool linen sheets. For tonight, I saw no purpose in demanding he return me to Gabriel's house. Everything would come out in the morning, since I couldn't hide from either Gabriel or May the fact that I'd found Baltic. Besides, the reconciliation between Baltic and the weyr had to start at some point, and I'd much rather that it began sooner than later.

"Where is this child who should be mine, but who is not?"

"He's with Aisling and Drake because Gabriel insisted that you were going to attack his house. And just so you know—love me, love my son."

He snorted. "I was going to rescue you from Gabriel until I saw you outside."

"Nice change of subject," I said, amused. "But it's not going to change anything. Besides, Brom is a good kid. You'll like him."

"I will not," Baltic said grumpily, and lay down with his arms crossed.

I leaned over him and raised an eyebrow.

"I will tolerate him because he is of your blood, but no more," he conceded.

I slapped a hand down on his chest, and tapped my fingers. "I would hope that once we are free, you will take an active role in his life as a loving, supportive stepfather."

His expression was mutinous. "You ask me to raise this child of another man as if he were my own?"

"Yes. I expect you to love and cherish him. Brom deserves that. His own father doesn't give a damn about him."

He gritted his teeth. I narrowed my eyes. We made quite a pair.

"Very well," he finally snapped, rolling over onto his side so all I saw was his back. "I will do so, but that is the last concession I will make to you! I am the wyvern. You are the mate. It is you who must yield to me from this moment on."

I smiled and snuggled into his back, feeling a weight lift from me that I hadn't been aware of. Things were going to work out all right despite the overwhelming odds. I could just feel that they were.

Fire raged in and around and through me.

"This has got to end!"

"There is only one way it will end—my way!" A shadow flickered through the flames, a black shadow of the man I loved so dearly, and who was destroying not just his beloved sept, but my heart as well.

"Baltic, you will not win! You have decimated your own ranks trying to beat Constantine into submission, but it is for naught! And now that the green dragons have sworn to aid them against you, it is doubly foolish to pursue what is nothing more than a stupid rivalry!"

"Rivalry!" Baltic snarled and stalked across the room of our bedchamber, grabbing my arms in a painful grip. "He has tried to steal you from me. Three times he has tried! He is out there now, rallying yet another force to try to bring down Dauva so that he might take you. Is your love for me so fleeting that you would wish to see both Dauva and me destroyed?"

"You are being overly dramatic once again."

He spun away from me as I spoke, staring out of the narrow window to watch the countryside as if he expected to see a wave of silver dragons at the foot of the castle.

I looked at him, this man I loved, and knew that something would have to be done to stop him. The course he was taking was one of madness, one that could have no good end.

"My love, you know I have chosen you above all others," I said, sliding my arms around his waist and leaning into his back, pressing my cheek against it to hear his heart beating so strong and true. "You are my life, Baltic. I do not want to be Constantine's mate any more than I want this endless war to continue. You must find a way to end it, to make peace amongst the weyr. You are the only wyvern strong enough to do it."

"There can be no peace for me so long as Constantine lives."

"The war between you and Constantine is private, but the results of it are going to tear apart the entire weyr. This war did not begin with me, and I will not have it end with me!"

He turned, the muscles in his jaw tight, his eyes blazing with black fury. "What would you have me do? Go to Constantine with my tail between my legs and beg him to spare the black dragons? Would you have him absorb our sept into his without so much as a whimper? Would you have him strip everything from me?"

"The silver dragons have been autonomous for over a century now," I argued. "You never sought to force them to rejoin this sept until Munich!"

Baltic snarled an invective. "That was the day I knew the true depths of his treachery. To steal you two days after you had been brought to bed—"

Pain laced through my insides at the reminder. I looked down, tears welling in my eyes at the memory of that time. My poor little babe who did not live through the birth. Baltic grieved the loss as much as I did, but he did not see the truth behind the tragedy. I knew it was a sign that I should not bring life into a world that was filled with so much hate, while he went almost mad with rage and an intense need for revenge.

He stopped speaking, taking me in his arms and holding me so I could weep silently into his chest. "There will be other children, *chérie*. I swear to you there will."

"There won't be if there is nothing left for them," I said, looking into his eyes "You are using the war as an excuse to hurt Constantine. It has to stop, Baltic, or there will be nothing left for us."

"Do you have so little faith in your own sept?" he asked, his arms tightening around me.

"I have only faith in the black dragons, but you are not being honest with them."

He pulled back, strapping a leather scabbard around his waist. "We are at war. They know that."

"But you are allowing them and everyone else to believe you have some grandiose plan for domination over all the septs. You should ask yourself why you are so hesitant to tell them what your true purpose is."

Fire flashed in his eyes, manifesting itself in tangible form as it twisted up my body. "I will do anything to keep you safe. Anything!"

"Including sacrifice innocent lives? It isn't right, Baltic! If I didn't know better, I'd say you were mad!"

A slight noise heralded the arrival of Pavel, who stood in the open doorway, his eyes watchful. "My pardon for interrupting. All is ready. Do we ride?"

"Yes." Baltic bent down to kiss me, his lips sweet, but my heart broke nonetheless. "You will be safe here, *chérie*. No one has ever breached Dauva, and no one ever will. I will send word to you as soon as I can."

"Don't go," I said, knowing it would do no good.

"Constantine approaches Warsaw. I can't let him cross the Vistula."

I bowed my head for a moment while he slid his sword into its scabbard. "If you will not stop this war, then I will," I warned as he strode across the room to the door.

He paused and looked back at me, a question in his eyes.

"I will bring together the five shards of the dragon heart, and I will use them to end this battle between you and Constantine."

"The rumors about the dragon heart are grossly exaggerated," he said simply, and left. Pavel gave me a thoughtful look before turning to follow him.

"Stay safe, my heart," I whispered even as my own was shattering.

It took me two weeks to travel to Paris from Riga. The city was still in a shambles; the plague that had been triggered by the dragon war a century before continued killing mortals without prejudice. Rotting corpses of nobility and serfs alike festered in the streets, the stench almost unbearable. Outside of the city proper, the air was a bit cleaner, although carts laden with the dead rumbled by with a frequency that was unnerving.

From the safety of a clump of birch trees in Montfaucon, I watched the small group of people gathered, three men and a woman. One man I recognized. The other two—one blond, one dark-haired—were strangers, as was the woman, who was clinging to the dark-haired man in a manner that bespoke of intimacy. The dragons spoke together for a moment. I stepped out, wary lest the plea Kostya had made was some sort of a trap.

"We were not sure you would come," he called to me as I made my way through the boggy ground to where they stood on a small hillock. The woman squawked when one of the men disengaged her from his person and tried to shoo her away.

I accepted the hand Kostya held out to help me over the remains of an uprooted tree. "You knew I was in Paris. Why wouldn't I meet with you?"

"Come back to the inn with me," the woman cooed to the tall, dark-haired man. She was all but falling out of her bodice, and the look she gave him would be clear to a blind man.

"Go away, woman. I told you that I have business to attend to," the man answered, trying once again to shoo her away.

"With her?" the woman asked, glaring at me.

"Yes, but not the sort you understand. Leave me now or you will make me angry."

"What will you do if I don't?" she asked coyly, trailing her fingers up his arm. "Will you paddle my bottom?"

"No."

"Then what?" Her hand moved around to the front of his breeches.

He turned and breathed fire on her.

She ran screaming from the field, the hem of her skirts smoking.

"Mortals," the dark-haired man said in a disgusted tone, and proceeded to turn his attention to me. Both he and the second man eyed me with frank curiosity. I returned the compliment.

"This is Allesander de Crovani," Kostya said. "He is the younger brother of Mercadante Blu, the wyvern of the blue dragons."

Allesander made a bow, his light blue eyes watching me with amusement. He was slightly taller than me, had hair almost as pale as my own, and was slight of figure, but I sensed strength in him that I would not underestimate.

I murmured the polite responses and was introduced to the third man, the fire-breather. "This is *my* brother, Drake Fekete. He is heir to Fodor Vireo."

I looked at the man in surprise. "You are not a black dragon?"

"No." He had a different sort of accent, one that reminded me of Eastern Europe. He shared Kostya's height and general coloring, but his eyes were a pure, brilliant green. "Our grandmother was a reeve. She mated twice."

"I see. And Kostya is Baltic's heir . . . how unique it

will be to someday have wyverns of two different septs in the same family. Does it cause competition between you and Kostya?"

"Only with women," Kostya said, shooting his brother an irritated look.

"There is no competition," the latter said with blithe indifference.

"True words." Allesander laughed, giving Kostya a little nudge. "The women all go for Drake and give your scowls a wide berth, eh?"

I had no doubt of that. Drake seemed like the ultimate lady's man, if the tavern wench was anything to go by. "Do your wyverns know you are here?"

Both men nodded. "Merca wishes for an end to this battle between septs," Allesander said stiffly. "If you can bring it about, you will have the gratitude of the blue dragons."

"And green," Drake said quickly. "We, too, are tired of fighting our brother septs. We wish for peace in the weyr once again."

"I'm surprised the war continues if everyone is so desirous of its end. Certainly the mortals must be praying peace will return to the dragons," I said softly.

"It would end but for your mate and Constantine," Allesander said with an edge to his voice. "If they would settle their differences, we could band together and force Chuan Ren into an accord. But divided as we are ..." He shrugged and looked away.

"Then we shall have to pray that the dragon heart can do what the dragons themselves cannot," I said, glancing at Kostya. "Baltic does not know I am here, but he is suspicious of your absence. I fear that he may discover I have come to Paris."

His eyes held mine with a fervor that made me uncomfortable. "We will have to risk that. Do you have the Modana Phylactery?"

"Yes." I touched a spot on my cloak. Beneath it, the phylactery hung between my breasts. "I have it with me. Were you successful with Chuan Ren?"

"I was." He reached into his doublet and removed a small box. "This is the Song Phylactery."

"I shudder to ask what it cost you to borrow it."

He grimaced. "It's better if you don't know."

I turned my attention to the other two men. "I take it that you have your respective septs' shards, as well?"

Both men nodded.

I raised my eyebrows as I glanced at Kostya. "Then all we are missing is the shard belonging to the First Dragon. Do you know where the Choate Phylactery is?"

"Yes. I have it, as well."

"How did you get that?" I asked, amazed. From what Baltic had mentioned over the last two centuries, the Choate Phylactery's whereabouts had been unknown since the weyr had formed.

He looked away. "That is another thing you don't want to know."

On the contrary, I very much wanted to know, but now was not the time to pursue such an intriguing subject. "Then nothing is stopping us from doing it now," I said, my palms suddenly damp at the thought.

"No." Kostya turned to a small satchel on the ground. He pulled out a wool cloth and spread it out, gesturing toward it. I knelt on one corner and removed my cloak, shivering a little in the cool morning air as I pulled the gold-chased vial housing the dragon shard from beneath my chemise.

One by one, the other dragons knelt at the remaining three corners of the blanket, each removing from their safekeeping the phylacteries that bore the precious shards.

"Baltic never told me much about the shards," I said nervously, rubbing my palms on my skirt before placing the shards in a line before me. "All he said is that there are five of them, and that together, they make up the dragon heart, the most powerful relic known to dragonkin. What exactly is the dragon heart? And why does it have so much power? It can't really be the actual heart of the First Dragon, can it?"

Kostya shrugged.

"I know less than you do about it," Allesander said. "All I have been told is that it is too powerful to remain whole, and thus it was broken into shards and placed with each sept for safekeeping. Except the silver dragons, but that is only because your sept was not formed when the heart was first sharded."

"So I gathered. Drake, do you know anything about it?"

Drake glared over my head to a point in the distance. I turned to look. Three women were clustered together at the edge of the bog. All three waved and giggled when they noticed he looked their way.

"I take it you're not mated," I said, unable to keep from smiling despite my nerves.

He snorted. "Nor will I be, if I have a choice. Women are good for one thing only, and I don't need a mate to get that."

"Evidently not." The women clutched each other and giggled more, waving and calling to him, trying to tempt him over to them. I looked again at the shards, touching each one of them, hoping against hope that I would be able to do what needed to be done. "Well. Shall we get started? Do you have the words, Kostya?"

"I have them," Allesander said, pulling out a piece of battered parchment. He handed it to me, grimacing at the large blots on it. "I'm not very good at writing, but I took it down just as I heard it from Merca."

"It's in Zilant," I said, deciphering with some difficulty the handwriting on the parchment.

"Yes. You speak that, don't you?"

"I've picked up a little over the last century." I read silently for a moment. "All right, shall we try?"

"I would prefer that you succeed rather than merely try," Kostya said, his face grim. "There will be no black dragons left if we do not stop your mate."

Guilt weighed heavily on me. "I've tried to stop him, I truly have."

"This war is not your doing," Drake said, his arms crossed over his chest as he knelt across from me. His eyes were almost like a cat's, so brilliant were they.

"I did not start it, no, but it continues because . . ." I hesitated, wanting them to know the truth, but wary lest they use that information against Baltic somehow. Drake and Allesander said their respective septs desired peace, but could I trust that? The dragons had been warring for over a hundred years, and I was no longer sure whom I could trust.

"It continues because Constantine, Baltic, and Chuan Ren will not be happy until there are no dragons left but their own," Kostya said bitterly, making a sharp gesture.

"That's not true. Baltic does not desire the elimination of other septs. . . ." Their expressions told me it was useless to continue. I sighed and placed the shards before me. "The sooner we do this, the sooner we can have peace. Let us begin."

The Zilant words were unfamiliar on my tongue as I spoke them, awkward and jarring to the ear as I made an invocation to the dragon heart. The air grew thick and heavy over the shards as they started to vibrate, a hum coming from them that grew louder as I spoke. I watched them with some wariness, not sure what would happen when the heart re-formed, and wanting to be ready to wield it.

As the last word fell heavily from my lips, the hum from the shards ceased, and all was silent for two beats of my heart. We held our respective breaths as the shards seemed to emit a light that twirled and spun around itself, taking the phylacteries with it. It grew brighter and brighter until it blinded me. I turned my head to avoid looking at it, but was compelled to turn back when a face began to form in it, the face of a dragon, one who was as brilliant as the light itself. The dragon's eyes were filled with the knowledge of all times, as old as the earth itself, the past, present, and future all mingling together in their depths. I knew without a doubt in my mind that I was looking at the First Dragon, he who formed the septs and weyr, the creator, the father of every dragon who lived, and who would ever live.

The First Dragon looked at me, searing a path straight down to my soul, his eyes closing slowly, but not before I saw a profound sadness in them that made me want to fling myself forward and weep until I had no more tears.

The spinning mass of shards exploded in a nova of blue-white light that seemed to pierce us, passing through our bodies and minds and souls until it was the only thing that existed, and we were no more.

Two hours later I stood at the inn and watched as the small band of five black dragons I had brought as guards saddled our horses. Kostya stood next to me, watching silently.

Female squeals of delight came from the inn. I glanced over my shoulder. Drake had his arms around the three women who had waited so patiently for him at the bog, escorting them upstairs to a room where he would no doubt partake of their wares. I had already bid him farewell, as I had Allesander.

"What would you like me to tell Baltic?" I asked Kostya, returning my gaze to the yard.

"About the shard?" He glanced at my chest.

I touched the spot about two inches below my breastbone where a small diamond mark now resided. Inside me, the shard that had once belonged to the First Dragon thrummed with a life of its own, the shard mourning with me for the future that I feared would come to pass. "No, although I don't understand how you can be so sure that the shard's rightful owner will not be distressed that I am now the phylactery for it. I would be happy to explain to whoever it is, if you give me the name—"

"I told you the responsibility was mine," he said, a flicker of something in his eyes causing me to wonder. "I will deal with the owner. You have no need to fear that she—"

"She?" I asked as he bit off the word and looked suddenly furious. "By the rood! This shard belongs to Chuan Ren?"

"Belonged," he said, shooting me an annoyed glance before turning his glare onto the courtyard.

"Why would she give you both shards?" I asked, shaking my head.

His jaw worked for a few seconds; then he said, "She didn't."

"The green dragons are renowned thieves," I said, as a few facts slid into place. "Your brother is a green dragon. You had Drake steal the shards from Chuan Ren, didn't you?"

His shoulder twitched. "The Song Phylactery will be returned to her."

"But not the Choate Phylactery," I pointed out, amused despite the situation. Chuan Ren would be livid when she found out. I would have to warn Baltic that she would likely wish to reclaim the shard.

"That can't be helped." Kostya took a deep breath and turned to me, his face hard and unyielding. "I wish things were different, Ysolde, but you must realize that I cannot stand alongside Baltic any longer. You must see that."

Sadness gripped me at his words. "You of all people know why he is continuing the war. You are his oldest friend, his most trusted guard. If we could reason with him together, if we could make him see that Constantine is not really a threat—"

"But he is," Kostya interrupted. "In that I wholeheartedly agree with Baltic. The silver dragons are a threat to every black dragon. They must return to us, or we will face an eternity of destruction."

"You said earlier today that Baltic was unduly perpetuating the war, and now you insist that he continue to do so? You don't make any sense, Kostya."

"There is a difference between trying to retake what is ours, and attempting to control the entire weyr."

"You know full well that Baltic has no desire to take over all the septs," I said, disgusted with his stubborn refusal to admit the truth.

"No?" He gave me a long look. "Ask yourself why he does not simply kill Constantine and bring the silver dragons back into the weyr."

"I will not argue about this anymore; we've both said everything there is to say." I sighed. "My concern is for the immediate future. Are you sure you don't wish to return with me? Surely peace would be worth trying to reason with Baltic again."

"He is past the point of listening to reason, and I will not have the last few black dragons slaughtered for no purpose. Ysolde—" He bit off what he was going to say, hesitating before finally saying, "You must be aware of what is in my heart. I loved Baltic as a brother, but I cannot let him destroy our world. Either he will stop, or I must stop him, by whatever means possible."

Fear gripped my stomach at the deadness in his eyes.

"You would destroy us," I said simply.

"If that's what it takes to stop him, yes." Kostya took my hand and bowed over it. "You will be well enough to travel?"

"Yes," I said, the world suddenly bleak and lifeless.

"What will you tell Baltic?"

"The truth." I met his gaze and carefully pulled my fingers from his. "I will tell him the truth."

Chapter Eleven

"Good morning. Suzanne, isn't it? I don't know if you remember me, but I'm Tully Sullivan. I've come to fetch my son, Brom."

"I could not easily forget you, Ysolde," the green dragon said as she smiled and stood aside so I could enter Drake's house.

I glanced down the street to where a sleek black BMW sat. It had been all I could do to keep Baltic in the car, having to swear to him that I wouldn't go into the house by myself.

"My car is double-parked, so I think I'll just stay out here in case the police come," I said, waving a vague hand toward Baltic's car. "If you could just tell Brom to get his things together, I'll take him out of your hair."

"He's been no problem," she said. "I'm sorry, but I must shut the door. Drake would have my hide if I were to leave the door open. He's a bit crazy over security just now. Are you sure you don't want to come inside?"

"No, it's no problem. I'll just wait out here for Brom," I said, leaning against the white stone railing.

She gave me an odd look, but closed the door. Two minutes later, when I was trying to think how to broach a difficult subject with Baltic, the door opened. I straightened up, expecting to see my son, but instead a furry black demon in dog form marched out. "Heya, Solders! Oooh, sexy top, babe, very sexy top. I like how your boobies are kind of smooshed up over the neckline."

I looked down at the black stretch corset-style lace-up top I'd bought an hour earlier. My boobs did seem to be a bit more pronounced than was normal, but Baltic had expressed nothing but approval for my choice, going so far as snake his tongue down into the valley between my breasts. I put a stop to that, naturally . . . after an appropriate amount of time. "I just bought it at a small boutique this morning. It was on sale. Do you think it's too risqué?"

"No," Jim said, eyeing my boobs with glee. "If you bend over, will you pop out?"

I gave it a dirty look. "You are a demon. You aren't supposed to even notice things like uplifted breasts."

It rolled its eyes. "I may be a demon, but I'm a boy demon, and I'd have to be stuck in the deepest, darkest, most heinous of all of Bael's dungeon cells, suffering the worst torture imaginable, not to notice a fine pair of ta-tas when they passed by, and even then, I'd be thinking about them the whole time."

I mumbled something rude, turned to face the door, and did an experimental bow to make sure nothing untoward happened. "It's fine; you can suck your tongue back in," I told the demon when I turned around to face it.

"You take all the fun out of ogling. Hey, what's that on your left boob?"

I glanced down and edged the neckline over to better cover the sept mark. "None of your business. Where's Brom?"

"Packing his things. You're taking him away? Aisling said he was going to stay a couple of days because your crazy boyfriend was going to blow up Gabriel again."

"My crazy boyfriend will do nothing of the—" I stopped myself, getting a grip on my temper. "I don't have a crazy boyfriend, and no one that I know of is going to blow up Gabriel's house. Thus, yes, I am here to get my son. I hope to heaven you haven't been filling Brom's head with all sorts of inappropriate breast and Baltic talk. He is only nine."

"Naw, he's a good kid, and besides, Aisling told me if I showed him my collection of *Breasticles Monthly*, she'd have my noogies nailed to the wall. We've been good. Well, we did sit up until two in the morning watching old Hammer horror films because Ash and Drake took the spawns out to the country for a couple of days, but I promised to help watch Brom. And what's sitting up until two in the morning if not watching, eh?"

"I shall be sure to speak to him about staying up so late," I said with a mom frown.

The demon grinned. "You gotta let him have some fun. That's why I let him see pictures of my girlfriend, Cecile."

My jaw sagged just a smidgen. "You have a girlfriend?"

"Yeah. Black Welsh corgi with a fluffy white belly, and ears that beg to be sucked on. She's the cutest thing on four legs. She's getting up there in years, but that's OK;

I'm over three thousand years old, myself. Who's that in the car?" it asked, peering around me toward Baltic.

"Just a friend giving me a ride." I moved to block its view. I was about to distract the demon with something, anything, when the door opened again, this time disgorging Brom and his backpack.

"Sullivan, can we go to the British Museum again?"

"Good morning to you, too," I said, hugging him.

"Morning. Can we? Maata said she'd take me again if Gabriel and you said it was OK."

"Er . . ." I glanced back toward the car. Baltic's silhouette could be seen in it, moving in an impatient manner. I'd agreed to stay with him in his house, but I didn't want to break that bit of news to Brom with Jim standing right there, ready to carry the information straight back to Drake.

Momentarily distracted, I gave a little mental chuckle, realizing why Drake had seemed vaguely familiar to me when I saw him at the *sárkány*. The memory of Drake with the three women draped around him at the tavern in Paris left me wondering if he'd really changed from the womanizing tomcat he had once been.

"Sullivan?" Brom nudged me.

"We'll talk about it later, OK? Right now I want to get going. Nice to see you again, Jim."

"Kid's got mummies on the brain," Jim said to me, suddenly lunging to the side, hurrying past me toward the car. "Hey, is that who I think it is?"

"By the rood!" I swore, dashing after him, Brom on my heels. "Jim! Come back here! Heel!"

"That only works if you're my demon lord or duly appointed representative thereof, neither of which you are," it said as it came to a stop by the car. "Holy cheese and tiny little crackers! That's—"

I clamped my hand around its muzzle with one hand, glancing back to the house. The door opened, and Suzanne stepped out, obviously looking for Jim.

"Of all the ..." I jerked open the car's back door, telling Brom, "Get in the front!"

"What are you doing to Jim?" he asked, standing there frowning at me as I heaved the demon halfway into the car.

"Why is it all I seem to do lately is shove people into cars? Just get in, Brom! Jim, so help me god, if you bite me, I'll bite you back!"

The demon's eyes widened as I grasped it firmly around the rib cage and shoved the last bit of it into the car, more or less tumbling in after it. We fell in a tangle of arms and furry legs onto the floor of the car.

"Get going!" I yelled to Baltic, struggling to get free of dog legs.

"What is this?" Baltic said, glaring over the seat at us. "Why are you bringing a demon with you? We have no need of a demon, mate. Release it."

"Heeel!" Jim wailed, its teeth clenched shut due to my grip around its muzzle.

"Wow, you're the guy who came after Sullivan," Brom said, getting into the front seat. He and Baltic regarded each other for a moment.

"Som-un heeell ee!"

"You should have been my son," Baltic told Brom.

Jim kicked with both its back legs, loosening my hold on its mouth.

"I'm being demon-napped!"

"OK," Brom said to Baltic after a moment's thought. The two nodded, just as if that settled the matter.

"Aisliiiing!"

"Be quiet, you pestilent little furball!" I yelled, wrestling it to the floor of the car as Baltic, finally noticing Suzanne, who now stood with her hands on her hips calling for Jim, put his foot on the gas and shot out into traffic, pulling a U-turn that narrowly missed sideswiping a Harrods van. "You brought this on yourself! If you hadn't been so nosy, I wouldn't have had to do this!"

"Aisling is going to go nutso-cuckoo on your butt when she finds out what you're doing!" Jim said, deliberately wiping its slobbery lips on me as I got onto the seat, leaving long, slimy tendrils of drool on my arm.

"You think so? Well, maybe your precious Aisling just needs to watch out, because I'm not some pushover, you know. I'm a mage, and mated to the baddest ass in the dragon world," I said as I looked around for something to wipe off the slobber.

Brom looked speculatively at Baltic. "That's you?"

"Yes. If you were my son, as you should have been, you, too, would have a badass."

"Hmm," Brom said, still thoughtful.

There was nothing in the back of the car, no tissue, no towel, no napkin. Nothing. I eyed the demon's fur.

"You wouldn't!" it gasped.

"If you give me any more grief, I'll do a whole lot more than smear you with your own saliva!" I threatened, bending down to wipe my hand on the floor mat.

It sucked in its breath. "Geez, and I thought Ash was mean! You ever want a job as a demon lord, you'd fit right in. Hey, is that your nipple?"

I eeped and jerked upright, tucking my breast back

into my shirt. Evidently it did not pass the bending-over test after all.

"Keep your eyes to yourself, and—Baltic!" I screamed and pointed at the side of a building we were about to hit because he had turned to look back at Jim's comment about my nipple. "Eyes on the road, mister!"

"I specifically asked you not to bare your breasts to others," he said gruffly, casting angry little glances at me in the rearview mirror.

"Jim isn't a person, and I didn't exactly bare myself—oh, it doesn't matter. Just keep your eyes on the road."

"It is difficult. These people do not drive properly," he said, transferring his glare to a young man on a scooter who flipped him off as he zoomed past us.

"City traffic is always bad . . . wait a minute. What do you mean they don't know how to drive properly? You *do* know how to drive, don't you?"

"Of course I know how to drive. I am doing it now, am I not?"

"Oh, man," Jim said, covering its eyes with its paw. "We're all gonna die."

"Yes, you are driving," I said, "but since I'm the one who drove us into town this mor—red light!"

Baltic slammed on the brakes, sending us fishtailing into the middle of the intersection. Luckily, the light had just changed, so the cross traffic had time to avoid hitting us.

"Will you stop distracting me with irrelevant things?" Baltic said, irritation dripping off each syllable.

"A red light is not irrelevant. Do you have a driver's license?" I demanded.

"I am eleven hundred years old," he snarled, jerking hard on the steering wheel as he sent us spinning out of the intersection. "I don't need a mundane license to drive!"

"We're doomed, I tell you, doomed!" Jim wailed.

"That is a pedestrian crossing!" I yelped as Baltic came close to mowing down two elderly ladies and their little wheely baskets of shopping.

"I did not strike them," Baltic said, his tone injured. "You make too much of a few near misses, Ysolde."

I looked back. One of the little old ladies was staggering to the zebra crossing barrier, her hand to her chest, while the other was making an extremely rude hand gesture at us. "Right, that's it. Pull over."

"Why?"

"When my fabulous form is crushed and burned into an unrecognizable blob of goo, would you please tell Aisling so she can summon me back?" Jim asked.

"Oh, be quiet. We're not going to d—*Baltic*!"

"What now?" he snarled, his teeth gritted and his knuckles white on the steering wheel as he drove in a serpentine fashion down the road, ignoring the blaring horns, anatomically impossible suggestions, and shrieks of horror.

"This is a one-way street!" I bellowed, leaning forward over the seat to try and wrap my arms around Brom in a desperate attempt to protect him from imminent death.

"I'm only going one way!"

"Yes, the wrong waiiiiiiiiiieee!"

"Wow." Brom's voice came from the depths of where I had him smashed against my chest. "That really is your nipple. What's that mark near it?"

"Stop looking at my boobs!" I roared as Baltic, in blatant disregard of the fact that he was driving against traffic, and indeed was now up on the sidewalk scattering pedestrians hither and yon, turned to see just how badly I was popping out of the corset top.

"You will not be purchasing garments from that shop again," he said sternly. "I do not approve of this belief you cherish that exhibition games will arouse me. They do not."

"Pull over!" I screamed, pointing to a parking lot.

He pulled over, the sounds of horns, crumpling metal as cars avoided him but ran into parked vehicles, and breaking glass following us to the car park.

The second we stopped I was out of the car, marching around to the driver's side. I yanked open the door and pointed at the backseat. "I will drive!" I said, daring Baltic to defy me.

He glared, his eyes narrow slits of obsidian. "You are impugning my ability to drive a vehicle, mate. You will cease doing so, and get back into the machine."

"Please," Jim whimpered from the back. "Let her drive. I don't know how many more magnificent forms I can find."

My glare turned into a thing of fulminating beauty.

"Very well," Baltic said with haughty graciousness as he got out of the car. He stared pointedly at my chest. "But you must stop showing everyone your breasts. I realize that your rebirth has caused you to develop odd sexual preferences, but I will not tolerate my mate exposing herself to all and sundry. If you wish to display them, I and I alone will be your audience. You must resign yourself to this, mate."

"Oooh," Jim said, sitting up straight. "What sorts of odd sexual kinks other than flashing nip do you have, Soldie?"

"I am not exposing myself to anyone!" I said, then looked down and saw I was doing just that. I tucked my right breast back into the shirt, saying, "Well, dammit! I don't normally do that! And I don't have odd sexual preferences, so you can just stop whatever suggestive comment you were about to make, Jim."

"I was just going to ask if it involved sticks of butter or cloven-hooved animals," it answered.

"You cannot deny the overriding desire you harbor to watch Pavel with—"

"Gah!" I yelled, wanting to tear out my hair. I slapped my hand over Baltic's mouth, instead.

"Who's Pavel? And what does she want to watch him do?" Jim asked, leaning forward over the front seat.

I glared at it for a second as I slid behind the steering wheel. "Get in," I told Baltic.

He crossed his arms. "I will not share a seat with a demon."

"Hey! I can hear you!"

"I'll sit with Jim," Brom said, giving me a considering look as he scrambled into the backseat.

"There, you see? My son is kindly allowing you to ride shotgun."

"*My* son," Baltic said, giving me another of his patented annoyed looks.

"What?"

"He is *my* son. By rights he should be, and you said you wanted me to treat him as such, so I am doing that. I claim him as my son. You, Bram—"

"Brom," my child corrected him.

"You will cease being the offspring of the usurper who stole Ysolde from me. You are now my son."

"OK," Brom said, not the least bit ruffled by that idea.

"There, you see? I have fixed things," Baltic told me.

"Lovely. Great. Wonderful. I'll get you a Dad of the Year T-shirt later. Can we get going now? I hear police sirens, and if we don't get out of here now, we're going to have a whole lot of explaining to do."

"Yeah. Demon-napping is a federal offense now, I hear," Jim said as Baltic got into the passenger seat.

It was a *very* long ride back to Baltic's house.

"What are we doing here?" Brom asked as I stopped an hour later. He peered out the window at the white house.

"We're going to be staying here with Baltic."

"For how long?"

"Until I can rebuild Dauva," Baltic replied as he got out of the car. The door to the house opened, and a man emerged. "Ah. Pavel is back. Good."

I looked over the roof of the car to the man I recognized from my dreams. He started down the steps toward us, stumbled when he saw me, and stared with huge eyes. "Is that . . . it cannot be . . . is it?"

"Yes," Baltic said, marching over to me in order to wrap his arm around my waist and pull me into his side. "My mate lives."

"So do I, no thanks to Baltic's driving," Jim said as it peed on the back tire. "Nice place. Can I go home now?"

"No," I said, digging my elbow into Baltic's ribs. Brom was watching us with fascinated eyes.

"Aisling's going to open a serious can of whoop-ass on you when she finds out what you did, you know," Jim told me. "And bodacious boobies or not, I'm not going to stop her. I was supposed to go to Paris today to see my beauteous Cecile, and now I won't be able to suck her ears or snuffle her butt or lick her belly or any of the things I wanted to do."

Brom transferred his gaze to Jim, equally fascinated.

"You bared your breasts to the demon, too?" Baltic asked with outraged eyebrows.

"No, of course I didn't! I've told you several times now that I have no desire, fantasy, or other urge to bare anything to anyone, least of all my breasts. I have never, *ever* deliberately showed my breasts. So please stop insisting that's all I can think of. It just doesn't happen, OK?"

Pavel, Jim, and Baltic all eyed my cleavage.

I looked down, swore, and hiked up the neckline yet again. "Gah!"

"We are going to have a long discussion regarding these sexual fantasies of yours," Baltic told me, tugging me toward the house.

"I do not have an exhibitionist fantasy!" I yelled.

"What's an exhibitionist?" I heard Brom ask Jim.

I spun around and sent the demon a look that had it grinning. "It means someone who likes shopping at small boutiques," it said.

"One step out of line, demon, and I'll ... I'll ..."

"Or you'll what?" it asked, tipping its head to the side.

Before I could answer, Baltic paused and shot laser beams from his eyeballs. Well, all right, not really, but the effect was the same. Fire blossomed in a circle around the demon, causing it to dance and yelp.

"Cool," Brom said, looking with speculation at Baltic.

"All right, all right! Call off your wacko boyfriend! I'll behave!" Jim tried to blow out flames that licked up its tail. "Not the package! Anything but the package!"

"See that you do behave," Baltic said, extinguishing the fire with a flick of his eyes. He turned to Pavel and spoke in a low tone of voice, the latter casting periodic glances my way.

I sighed to myself and pulled out my cell phone as we all entered the hall. "I suppose I should tell Aisling that you're with me, Jim, and all right. It wouldn't be fair to make her worry you'd been kidnapped by someone who meant to destroy you."

Jim made a face. "Yeah, well, about that . . ."

"What?" I asked when its voice trailed to a stop.

"Normally I wouldn't worry, because as soon as Ash realized I'd been demon-napped, she could summon me back to her, but she's not going to realize I'm gone. Well, she is, but not. If you get my drift."

"Not in the least. What are you babbling about?"

Jim sighed. "My ride to the airport was due when you showed up. Suzanne probably thought that's where I went. I told you I was supposed to go to Paris."

"Ah, well," I said, not too worried about Jim's missed trip. "I'm sure you can go another time."

"I don't want to stay here," Brom suddenly said, giving the hall a good long look.

"Why not?" I asked, worried that he had gotten the wrong impression from Baltic's possessive hold on me. Or rather, the right impression, but without an explanation that would help him understand the complex relationship that even I wasn't sure I completely grasped.

"I want to go back to Gabriel's house, where I have my lab set up."

Baltic whirled around. "What is this? My son does *not* prefer the house of the silver wyvern over mine."

"Gabriel told Brom he could use a room in the basement to perform his experiments. He likes to mummify things."

"I'm a mummologist," Brom told Baltic.

"The silver wyvern gave you a room?" Baltic's eyes narrowed. "You are *my* son. I will give you . . ." He thought for a moment. "I will give you an entire building. There is a barn to the north—you may use that."

"Cool," Brom repeated; then his face fell. "But all my stuff is at Gabriel's house. My natron, and my dehydrator, and my dead fox, and everything else."

"I will give you new things. Better foxes, better natron."

I raised my eyebrows. "Do you even know what natron is?" I asked him.

"No," he said, blithely waving away the question. "But the natron I give to my son will be the best quality."

"If you want to dump Gareth for Baltic, I wouldn't mind," Brom whispered to me, clearly enjoying Baltic's determination to outdo what he thought of as a rival.

"Thanks. I'll keep that in mind," I told him with a little flick of my fingers to his ear.

Pavel made a little bow to me. "I am pleased to see you again, Ysolde. It has been a very long time. You have not changed at all."

Baltic said something in that language I didn't understand.

Pavel looked a bit startled, shooting me a look that I had a hard time deciphering as I answered, "It certainly has. And thank you."

Pavel gave Baltic a little nod and took off into the depths of the house.

"Brom, why don't you and Jim go outside and look around," I said.

"OK. We can look at the barn. I wonder if there's anything dead in it. . . ."

"Weird kid you got yourself there," Jim said over its shoulder as it followed Brom out the front door.

"Just see that you mind your manners," I warned it. "And don't try to escape, because you won't like how Baltic deals with pests."

"There is some business I must attend to," Baltic said, pulling out his phone.

"What sort of business?" I asked somewhat suspiciously. "Dragon business? Because if so, I want to talk to you about that."

"No, mundane business."

"You mean human-type business? I had no idea dragons did that sort of thing."

He shrugged. "Most of my fortune was claimed by others when I died. It takes some time to rebuild that, and since I will need a good deal of funds to restore Dauva, I must deal with business affairs."

"Oh. I wish I could give you some money, but I don't make very much as an apprentice, and Gareth funds us from the yearly manifestations. So I'm pretty much broke."

"I do not seek fortune from you, mate. Only your love."

I glanced down the hallway as Pavel crossed from one room to another. "Er . . . does Pavel live here with you?"

"Of course. He is my oldest and most trusted friend. He survived when the others did not." Baltic paused in checking his phone messages and slid me a glance. "Are you sure you do not lust after him?"

"Dammit! How do you know what I'm thinking? Are you a mind reader, too?"

He sucked in a huge breath, approximately a quarter of all the air in the house. "You *do* lust after him!"

"No, I do not! For heaven's sake, Baltic! I don't give a hoot about him, not in that way. I was just a bit curious about whether or not . . . oh my god! You didn't! Oh! You *did*! I can see by that expression, you did! You told him about me and my fantasy about guy-on-guy action, didn't you!"

Mollified, Baltic ceased seething at me and punched in a number on his phone. "Yes. He said you could watch the next time he has a male lover over."

"Oh! I can't believe"—I whomped him on the arm—"I *can't believe* you told him that! I am going to die of embarrassment! I will never be able to look him in the eye again! I'm never going to forgive you! How could you do that to me!"

Baltic just looked at me, waiting.

"Do you think he's going to have a guy over soon?" I couldn't help but ask.

He frowned. "I don't know. You shall have to satisfy your lustful ways upon me until he does, and even then, you may watch only, not participate. And you will not bare your breasts to Pavel or anyone else."

I gave him a look that should have shriveled his testicles. "I have no desire to have an orgy! All I said was that sometimes it was a bit interesting!"

"So you say," he muttered darkly, heading for a room I assumed was his study.

I swore under my breath at the obstinate, jealous, infuriating man, and wondered which of my male acquaintances I could hook up with Pavel.

Chapter Twelve

The day was as dark and damp as my mood, the smell of snow heavy in the air. Bright Star, my mare, moved restlessly beneath me as we waited at the foot of the hill, watching as a line of men and horses wound its way in and out of the woods, moving toward us like a massive centipede.

Baltic rode at the lead, as he always did, without a helm, his hair lank from the misty rain, straggling over his mail like inky fingers.

"What are you doing out of the keep?" he yelled when he emerged from the last of the forest that surrounded Dauva.

"I came to greet you." My gaze passed from him to count the number of dragons who followed. It was a much smaller number than had set off, no more than a quarter returning. Sorrow, these days a constant companion in my belly, gripped me painfully. "You did not stop Constantine?"

"No." It was just one word, but in it was the full measure of despair that bound Baltic so tightly. His eyes were as bleak as his expression, flat, and without any hope. His shoulders were bowed, as if he were yoked to a great weight. "He comes for you, *chérie*. He is only a day behind me, less if he did not rest at night."

I shook my head, unable to believe it. "Why is he doing this? He knows I love you. He knows I want only you. I would never remain with him even should he take me from you."

He reached me, his stallion's head hanging as low as my spirits. The horses and men looked exhausted, clearly at their limit of strength. I knew Baltic would have pushed both hard.

"Why?" Baltic gave a hoarse bark of laughter. "He believes he can sway you, turn you against me."

"He's wrong," I said, urging my mare around so that we rode into the bailey together.

"He has sworn that if he cannot have you, I shall not."

I glanced at him, startled by the pain lacing his voice.

"Yes, my love," he said, taking my hand in his. His gauntlets and bracers were stained brown with blood. "He has threatened to kill you if he cannot steal you from me, this one who professes his great love for you."

"He is a fool," I said grimly, the dull thud of hooves on the dirt the only sound.

Baltic noticed the silence. He lifted his head, glancing around. "Where is everyone?"

"I sent them away."

He looked at me for a moment, his eyes so stricken I wanted to crush him to my bosom and comfort him.

Slowly, he nodded. "Why let others suffer for my folly?"

I said nothing until I had him inside, arranging for the two remaining maids to bring water for a bath. Pavel, silent and filthy with blood and dirt, helped me remove Baltic's armor.

"I'll send one of the maids to help you," I told Pavel as he gathered up the discarded mail.

His lips twisted in a wry half smile as he bowed and closed the door quietly behind him.

"It's over, *chérie*," Baltic said, slumping into the chair before the fire. "Constantine will win. He will take Dauva, take you, and I will die."

I knelt before him, my hands on his knees, sliding up his legs to take his hands in mine. "Then I will die, too. For I will belong to no one but you."

"I would rather you lived," he said, a faint smile coming to his lips, but there was no humor in it. "I would rather we both lived."

"There has to be a way we can stop this, stop Constantine. He has all but destroyed this sept."

"There are only eighteen of us left," Baltic said in a voice stripped of emotion.

"Dauva is strong. We will survive," I said, refusing to give in to the despair that tainted the air around us.

"It is strong, but with time, Constantine will find a way in. We can hold it only so long with only a handful of men." Suddenly, he lifted his head and looked about the chamber. "Where is Kostya?"

"Er . . . about that." I rose and opened the door for the maids, who lugged in four leathers of water. I waited until they were gone before continuing. "I realize that now is not the best moment to break this news to you, but . . . well . . . I'm carrying . . . that is to say—"

"You're with child again?" Hope flared to life for a moment in his eyes. "*Chérie*, how can you think I would not be pleased with that news?"

"No, I'm not going to have a child. It's something else I'm carrying," I said, sick with the knowledge of what I had to say. I took a deep breath and said quickly, "While you were fighting Constantine, I went to Paris. There I met with Kostya and a green and a blue dragon. I told you that I was going to use the phylacteries to re-form the dragon heart, and so I did, only . . . I failed. It wouldn't allow me to re-form it, and when it broke into the shards again, instead of going into the Choate Phylactery, it . . . it went into me. Into my body."

Baltic stared at me as if he'd never seen me. "You would use the dragon heart against me?"

I marched over to him and slapped him, not hard, but shocking him enough that he leaped to his feet. "That is for even thinking that I would do such a thing."

Fury roared through him in the form of his dragon fire, a fury that spilled out onto me, twining around my legs, climbing higher and higher until I was alight with a spiral blaze. I welcomed the heat from it, merging it with my own, taking it into me and burying it deep into my soul.

For a moment, I thought Baltic was going to explode with anger, but amazingly, his fire banked and his lips quirked. "Ah, my love, what would I do without you?"

"Be wholly and utterly miserable," I said, pleased to see the life come back into his eyes. "And probably rut with every woman with two legs."

His hands slid around my waist. "You are the only woman I know who would dare greet her wyvern with the news that she now bears a piece of the dragon heart. We shall have to give you a name, now."

"I have a name," I protested.

"Phylacteries are always given names. If you are now the phylactery for the Choate shard, then it shall have to take a different name."

"We'll worry about that another time. What I need to know is how to get it out of me."

He shrugged, watching as the maids made another trip in with more water. "That I do not know. No dragon has ever been a phylactery before."

"Wonderful." I wondered if there was some learned person I could speak with, someone familiar with the dragon shards and heart.

"You did not say where Kostya is. He came back with you, did he not?" Baltic asked as he pulled off his thin linen shirt.

I knelt again and helped him with the crossties on his leggings. "Actually, he didn't."

"He left you to travel from Paris to Dauva alone?" he asked, frowning down at me.

I gestured toward the bath and went to a chest for the soap. "I wasn't alone. My personal guard went with me."

"So I should hope." Water splashed as he got into the tub. "Where is he if he is not here?"

I took a deep breath, watching as the maids poured in the last of the hot water. When they were done and we were alone again, I dampened a sea sponge and swirled it around on the soap I made especially for Baltic. It was scented with frankincense and myrrh, his favorite. He watched me closely as I knelt next to the tub and began washing him.

"My mother would never let me wash anyone," I said, wishing to avoid the pain I knew was coming. "I see now why she did so. It's very sensual, this spreading of soap on a man's body."

Baltic, distracted by the feeling of my fingers stroking across his skin, slippery little trails following each of my fingers as I lathered up the soft hair of his chest, glanced downward. "I am filthy, and riddled with fleas and lice, *chérie*. If you continue to stroke me that way, you will end up sharing the bath, and will not thank me for allowing my vermin to visit you."

I smiled, enjoying the hard muscles that lay in smooth ropes beneath his satiny flesh. Reluctantly, admitting the truth to his statement, I soaped up the sponge again and handed it to him, rising to fetch clean clothing as he briskly washed himself.

"Now you will tell me what you have wished to avoid," he said, washing the long ebony lengths of his hair, leaning forward so I could rinse the soap off with one of the remaining leathers of water.

"Kostya has forsaken you," I said simply, grabbing a linen cloth when he leaped to his feet, wincing as soapy water streamed down into his eyes. I mopped off his face, toweling his hair, and saying quickly, "He believes what all black dragons believe—that you seek to control the weyr. He refuses to be a part of it any longer. It was he who summoned me to Paris. I told him of my plan to use the dragon heart to stop the war, and he arranged for the other septs to loan me the shards so that it could be done."

"I wondered how you had arranged that," he said in

a deceptively mild voice. I wasn't fooled—he was beyond angry, beyond furious, his fire barely contained.

"Sit back down and finish bathing. I do not wish to share my bed with your friends any more than I would a bath," I said wearily, pouring him a cup of wine.

"So he has acted at last," Baltic said, slowly sitting down, absently washing his body as I retrieved a fine comb and a paste made from white bryony and honey that would kill the head lice. "I suspected he would, although I had not thought he would involve you."

I said nothing for a few minutes, rubbing the paste into his hair, then combing it over and over again until I was satisfied.

"You do not leap to his defense?" Baltic asked as I washed the paste out of his hair.

"What is there to say that I haven't already said?" I asked, pouring the last leather of water over his head. "He believes you to be a madman, willing to throw away the lives of everyone in the sept in order that you might rule supreme over the weyr. I don't blame him for leaving you—if I were he, I would do the same."

He shot me a look that sought reassurance. I leaned forward and gently kissed him, taking his breath into my mouth as my lips caressed his. "I am not Kostya, my love. I will never leave you."

"If I can't stop Constantine, you will not be left with the choice."

"There is always a choice," I said, holding up a cloth for him. "We just need to find it."

The heat of the fire melted away, easing into a different sort of warmth. Sunlight poured over me as I sat on the stone front steps of Baltic's house. I blinked as my mind was once again returned to the present, no longer disconcerted by the ease with which I slipped in and out of the visions.

"Whatcha doing?"

I looked up from where I had been hugging my legs, my chin resting on my knees, and moved the pad of paper upon which I'd been making a list before I'd slipped into the vision.

Jim plopped its big butt down next to me.

"Making a to-do list. I thought you were out with Brom."

The demon made a face. "He found a dead mouse and is looking it over to see if it's too far gone to mummify or not. Kid's a little weird, Soldy—you have to admit it."

"'Eccentric' is, I believe, the term you meant to use," I said with a gimlet glance. "He is very intelligent. He has interests beyond those of lesser children."

"Whatever. What's on your list?" It peered at the tablet. "'Call Aisling.' You better put on a pair of asbestos earplugs, 'cause she's going to be Miss Pottymouth of 2010 when she hears what you did to me."

"She seems like a reasonable person," I said with complacence I did not feel. "I'm sure I will be able to explain."

Jim snorted. "That's not a word that's often applied to her, but you're just going to have to find that out for yourself. What's next on the list? 'Call May and apologize for disappearance.' I like May. She feeds me."

"That is an excellent pointed look, but it is wasted on me. I'm sure you already had breakfast, and it's not lunchtime yet."

"You think this fabulous form stays looking this way without any help? Nuh-uh! I gotta give it all sorts of vitamins and minerals and fresh, lightly grilled cuts of beef."

"I'm sure you'll survive until lunch."

"I wouldn't count on it. Number three . . . oooh. That's going to be a doozy."

"Yes, it is."

Jim's face screwed up as it thought. "If I was you, I'd try and find a neutral place to meet the wyverns. Because if you just march into a *sárkány* with Baltic, they'll grab you both."

I gave the demon a long look. "Why are you being helpful?"

Its eyes opened wide. "Me? Helpful? Not on your shiny pink ass. I'm a demon, remember?"

"Yes, but you're being helpful. That is totally against the norm so far as demons go."

"Yeah, well." It paused to suck a tooth. "I'm more than just a normal demon. I'm like Demon Plus with super whitening power. How're you going to get Baltic to agree to meet with the other wyverns?"

"What makes you think he wouldn't?" I asked, quelling a feeling of worry about that very subject.

It rolled its eyes at me. "He's the dread wyvern Baltic! The big kahuna during the Endless War. He's probably killed more dragons than everyone else put together."

"Oh, he has not!" I said, shifting uneasily.

"You kidding? Mr. 'We use his name to scare little dragons into being good' Baltic? He's like Genghis Khan and Vlad the Impaler and Stalin all rolled into one scaly package."

"Baltic is not scaly! Almost never!"

It cocked a furry eyebrow at me. "Face it, Soldums—you don't get the kind of reputation Baltic has by working well with others, and that's what number three on your list is asking him to do."

I looked down at my list, sighing to myself as I admitted the truth. "He used to be scary. Now he's different."

"A kinder, gentler maniac is still a maniac, chicky. Tell you what—you send me back to Ash, and I'll tell her and Drake that Baltic isn't the hyperderanged, mass-murdering psycho bastard they think he is, OK?"

"No," I said firmly, putting a little tick mark next to item number three. "We're not going to tell them that. We're going to prove it, and the only way we can do that is to get everyone together, the wyverns and Baltic and me, so we can work things out in a civilized manner."

The demon eyed me curiously as I stood up, filled with determination. "You think you got a way to make all that happen?"

"I think I have a way to make Baltic understand that he will have to speak with the wyverns, yes. You forget there's a death sentence hanging over my head. He may be adorably arrogant, but I doubt very much if he will allow the weyr to kill me. I'll simply point out that if he wants that sentence lifted, he's going to have to go with me to speak to the wyverns."

"Uh-huh. That's just part of it, though, the Baltic side. How are you going to get the wyverns to talk to him?"

"That's the easiest part of all," I said, patting it on its head.

"Yeah? What do you have up your sleeve? A magic mongoose or something?"

"Nope." I paused at the door and tossed the demon a smile. "I have you."

I closed the door gently on the sound of its sputtering.

The phone calls, as I suspected, weren't the most pleasant ones of my life.

"Ysolde!" Aisling gasped when I got through to her. "Are you all right? We just got home. May's here, and she said you've been kidnapped. Did you get away from Baltic? Has he hurt you? If he has, you just let me know. I'm a professional—I'll take care of him. I'll just summon Jim from Paris, and we'll—"

"Er . . . I appreciate that offer, but it's not necessary," I interrupted. "About Jim . . . Aisling, Jim is with me."

"It's what? Why is it with you? Oh my god! Baltic kidnapped Jim when he grabbed you, didn't he? That bastard! That fire-breathing bastard! He had just better watch out the next time I see him, because I will do all sorts of evil things to him. He won't ever have children, for a start. And I think I know of someone who can curse him—"

"I would really appreciate if you didn't do any of that," I said, laughing. I could feel her surprise at the laughter, which, I admit, died quickly as I confessed, "Baltic didn't kidnap Jim—I did."

The silence that followed the statement was broken only by the noise of another receiver being picked up. "Ysolde? It's May. You're all right? Are you hurt in any way?"

"She said she took Jim," Aisling said, breathing somewhat heavily into the phone.

"She did? I thought it went to Paris."

"It was supposed to."

"Then why did Ysolde kidnap it?"

I sighed. "Because it saw that Baltic was with me. Look, this is going to be impossible to explain over the phone. I just didn't want you thinking that Jim was in any danger. It's here with us—"

"With you and Baltic? What the hell?" Aisling said, her voice rising.

"Oh, knock it off," I said irritably. Although I knew I had committed the wrong, I had expected that they would understand why I had done it.

"Did she just tell you to knock it off?" May asked Aisling.

"Yes, she did," Aisling answered, sounding rather bewildered.

"I'm sorry for my rudeness, but honestly! I thought if anyone would understand what's been happening, two wyverns' mates would," I said firmly. "Surely you two understand the strength of the bonds that tie you to your particular dragon. The same applies to me, no matter if I am in human form or not."

"But—" Aisling started to protest.

"No, there are no buts. You're the ones who were so bent on insisting that I'm Baltic's mate! For the love of all that's holy, you were ready to condemn me to death because of that!" My own voice was rising now. I made an effort to stem my growing anger.

"I never wanted you to die," May said quietly.

"Well, me either! I may be a demon lord, but I'm not a *bad* demon lord," Aisling said quickly.

"You accepted Baltic as your mate?" May asked.

I rubbed my forehead. Another headache was blossoming. "Yes, I did. And because of that, I want to call a *sárkány*."

"Um . . . all right," Aisling said. "I guess since you're a member of the silver sept, you can do that."

I didn't correct the incorrect assumption. "I want to discuss with the weyr these deaths of the blue dragons. Baltic and I will attend the *sárkány* together."

An intake of breath greeted that statement, but it was impossible to tell which woman made it.

"Since I know the weyr believes Baltic to be guilty of those deaths, and I believe he's innocent, we must have the opportunity to discuss the situation with everyone. For that reason, Jim will remain in my custody until it's over."

"You do realize that all I have to do is summon it, right?" Aisling asked.

"Oh, yes, I know you could summon it in a heartbeat." I crossed my fingers. "But you won't."

"I won't? Why not?"

"Because you are a woman of honor," I said firmly, praying my assessment of her character was sound. "In addition, you realize that Baltic needs to meet with the wyverns, and you know that they won't mind their manners unless they have a compelling reason to do so, and you, as a fellow wyvern's mate, understand the importance of making them act reasonably. For that reason, you'll allow Jim to be a hostage for the wyverns' good behavior."

"I'll do all that?" she asked, but I heard amusement in her voice, and I knew I had her support.

"You will. Jim will stay in my protection until Baltic has met with the weyr and been given safe passage out. I will not allow anyone to railroad him."

"Railroad him?" Aisling's voice lost the amusement.

May spoke softly, with no real inflection to her voice. "You have to understand that we have experience with Baltic, and although I realize you are his mate, and thus you want to protect him, he is not innocent of the blue dragons' deaths. Gabriel was there. He saw the bodies. He questioned the two survivors."

"I have always heard that dragons valued their honor, which is why I will ask the wyverns to agree to allow us safe passage to and from the *sárkány*. Jim will be returned to you safe and sound once we are away."

Aisling was silent for a minute. "All right. I will trust you. But so help me, if Jim is harmed in any way—"

"It won't be. I just want the same guarantee for Baltic."

Aisling snorted.

I gave her my cell phone number and told her to call me when a time for the *sárkány* had been set.

"Ysolde . . ." May's voice stopped me as I was about to hang up.

"Yes?" I asked, somewhat wearily. I didn't like having to be the bad guy, but someone had to end the conflict between Baltic and the weyr, and instinctively I knew he would not take any steps to do so on his own.

"Baltic . . . forgive me for asking, but you don't think he's using some sort of a thrall on you? We haven't known you long, but you don't seem like the sort of person who would tolerate, much less protect, a man who murders in cold blood."

I smiled sadly at my feet. "No, he hasn't enthralled me. That would involve sex, and . . . well . . . we haven't."

"Baltic didn't jump you the second he could?" Aisling asked, clearly agog at the notion.

"No. He might have wanted to—all right, he *did* want to—but I'm married. He understands that until I can talk with my husband and inform him that I wish to have a divorce, I don't feel it's morally right to do all the things we'd like to do."

Silence greeted that pronouncement. I was about to hang up again when May said, "That's very interesting."

"I'm glad my lack of a sex life is fascinating to you," I said dryly.

"I'm sorry, that sounded rude, didn't it? It wasn't intended that way. Ysolde . . . you said you had memories of the past. You must remember that dragons are very dominant when it comes to claiming their mates physically. That goes double for wyverns," May said.

"Oh, yes," Aisling added with a little chuckle.

"Yes, but this is different. That was in the past. This is now, today, in the present," I explained.

"Just the fact that you accepted him as a mate and he hasn't . . . well! I think that says something," Aisling added. "I think that says a lot of something."

"Yes, it says he has restraint. Call me when you have the time and day for the *sárkány*," I said, and hung up the phone, relieved it was over. "I just hope the rest of my plans go so well."

Chapter Thirteen

Idly, I rubbed my cell phone and wondered if I'd put the cart before the horse. Baltic hadn't denied that he had killed those blue dragons, and yet I had seen a moment of hurt in his eyes before he answered with a typical dragon nonanswer. "I couldn't love someone who was a murderer," I said aloud to the empty room. "I couldn't."

"What couldn't you do?" Baltic asked from the doorway, causing me to jump.

"I'll tell you if you answer two questions for me."

His eyebrows rose as he strolled across the room to me, all coiled power and sexy hips. "Just two?"

"Yes. The first is whether you had any involvement with the deaths of the blue dragons."

He paused for a second, giving me an unreadable look. "You have already asked me that question, and I have answered it."

"No, you gave me a nonanswer."

"What purpose would I have to kill blue dragons?"

I ground my teeth. "You know, this dragon thing of not answering a question outright is driving me nuts."

"It shouldn't. You are prone to the same trait."

"I am not! I'm human! I don't do that! Now please, just answer the question—did you have anything to do with those deaths?"

"Yes."

My stomach dropped like a lead weight. I was so sure he would deny it. "You did? You killed those dragons?"

"No."

He stood near to me, not touching, but close enough that I could feel his dragon fire come to life. "You just said you did!" I all but wailed.

"No, I said I had something to do with it. I did not kill them, but I knew that their deaths were possible."

"I don't understand." I wanted to run screaming from the room and at the same time I wanted to wrap myself around him, reassuring myself that he wasn't the monster everyone thought he was. "Who killed them?"

He said nothing.

I put my hand on his chest, over his heart. "Baltic, this is important. The weyr thinks you are responsible for the deaths of all those blue dragons. In fact . . . well, we'll talk about that later. But right now, I really need to know—who did kill them?"

"I had forgotten how persistent you can be when you desire something," he said with a sigh, placing his hand over mine. "I will tell you, but only because you are my mate and I trust you. Fiat Blu killed the dragons."

"Fiat Blu? He's part of that sept?"

"Yes. His sept was taken from him by his uncle."

"Why would Fiat kill his own people? And why would you know about it?"

His arms snaked around my waist, pulling me into a gentle embrace. I let my fingers wander up the thick muscles of his arms, enjoying the solid feel of him, the tingle that seemed to come to life in the air around us whenever we touched. It was a sense of anticipation that left my body extremely aware of the differences between us.

"I have no quarrel with the blue dragons or Fiat. A few decades back, when I returned to life, he gave me shelter. Later, when he lost his sept to his uncle Bastian, he sought my aid in recovering control, but he disappeared a month ago. I do not know where he has gone to ground."

"You didn't try to stop him from killing innocent dragons?"

A flicker of pain crossed his face. "I did not think he would carry out his threat. He is unbalanced, mate, but I did not believe he would massacre members of his own sept. I was mistaken."

"Those poor dragons." I spent a moment sending up a silent prayer that they found a better life before something Baltic had said finally nudged my awareness. "Wait a second—a few *decades* back?"

"Why are you making that horrified face?" He frowned, puzzled.

"You said a few decades ago, when you were reborn."

He made an annoyed gesture. "I died after you were killed, Ysolde. I've told you that."

"But you were reborn right away, weren't you?"

"No. Life was not returned to me until almost forty years ago."

I stared at him in confusion. "But when was I reborn?"

"I don't know."

"Dr. Kostich said my husband wasn't mortal. If he's not, and I was reborn right after I died . . . oh my god!"

"What?" Baltic asked as I reeled back from him.

I pointed a finger at him. "You're younger than me!"

The look he gave me was almost comical. "What does age matter?"

"Oh, it matters if you're three hundred years old and the man you're dating is . . . what? Thirty-five? Thirty-six?"

"Thirty-nine."

"Great! On top of everything else, I'm a cradle robber."

"We are immortal. In our past lives, I was six hundred years older than you. Therefore, I'm still three hundred years older."

"It doesn't work that way," I said, disgruntled.

"You are making something of nothing," he said, trying to pull me back into his embrace.

I held him at arm's length. "Tell me this, then; why were we brought back?"

He said again, "I don't know."

"How were we resurrected?"

"Do I look like an encyclopedia of the resurrected? I tell you I do not know!"

"Who is responsible for bringing me back?"

He glared at me. "You are beginning to annoy me, woman."

"They're important questions! I would like some answers!"

"I do not know the answers!" After a moment's silence, he slid me an odd look. "This man who married you—does he know about your past?"

"I thought so," I said slowly. "He certainly has always known about the fugues. . . ."

"Then we will gain that information from him before we sever him from you," Baltic said with decisiveness.

"How is it *you* were reborn?" I asked, still wondering how long I'd been alive.

"Thala arranged it." He glanced away, something about his expression immediately catching my interest and setting my Baltic radar pinging.

"Who is Thala?"

His lips pursed slightly as he gazed out of the window. "A necromancer, of course."

Necromancers, I remembered from some long distant store of knowledge, had the power to raise the dead as liches. "Glory of god! You're a lich?"

"No, of course not. I am a dragon. You've seen that for yourself," he said, still not meeting my eye.

The radar cranked up a notch. "Necromancers only raise liches."

"When they raise humans, yes. But a dragon is different."

"Oh." That seemed to make a tiny bit of sense, and as I had little knowledge of the art of raising the dead, I didn't dispute the statement. "Why would she raise you? Did you know her before you died?"

He tried to keep his head turned, ostensibly scanning the fields outside the house, but I moved around to block his view. His face was filled with something that looked like chagrin. "Yes, I knew her. Her mother was Antonia von Endres."

"Ah, the daughter of your mage friend? I see." A horrible thought struck me. "She's not *your* daughter, is she? This Thala person?"

He looked appalled. "Christos, I hope not. Not after we ... er ..."

My jaw sagged a little. "You slept with her, too?"

"No. Perhaps. Just five or six times," he said, every word making me see red. He waved the thought away. "No, I could not be her father. Thala once mentioned that her father was a red dragon."

"Where is this girlfriend of yours? Does she live here, too? Are you hiding her from me? If you think I'm going to share you, you're madder than everyone says you are! I—"

"Your jealousy pleases me, *chérie*," he said, smiling one of those arrogant, smug male smiles that men are prone to when they think women are gaga over them.

"Yeah? Then you're going to love this," I answered, making a fist and aiming it for his gut.

He caught my hand with a laugh. "You are making yourself angry over nothing. Thala lives here, yes, but she is not my lover. She was briefly, but as with her mother, that was before you were born."

"Where is she now?" I asked, mollified enough to allow him to uncurl my fingers and kiss the tip of each one.

"Your silver dragon friends have her."

My eyebrows shot up as he gently bit the pad on one of my fingers, heat flaring to life deep in hidden parts of me. "They do?"

"They captured her two months ago. I assume she is still alive, although I have not been able to locate where she is being held." His gaze turned thoughtful as he released my hand. "You are in an ideal situation to do that."

I tamped down on the spike of jealousy that rose at the suggestion. "Possibly. But—"

He stopped me with a raised hand as he turned toward the window. "Who is that? Who has made it past my security?"

The crunch of gravel being crushed beneath a car's tires reached my ear.

"I have not authorized anyone to visit us," he announced, and bolted for the front door.

I ran after him, worried that Jim had somehow summoned the police or some other form of help.

It wasn't the police who emerged from the small rental car.

"Who the hell are you?" Baltic roared as he stormed down the stairs. A woman had emerged from the car, a slight woman with brown hair and pale green eyes. She flinched as Baltic leaped down the last three stairs and pinned her against the car. "You? How did you get in here?"

"Eek!" she cried, trying to squirm away. "Tully, help me!"

"Tully?" Baltic spun around and glared at me. "You know this woman?"

"Yes. She's my sister-in-law, Ruth. Which means that must be my husband."

"Husband!" he said, his eyes lighting with unholy pleasure.

Gareth slowly emerged from the car, his mouth hanging open as he stared at Baltic. Gareth in his best moments wasn't a terribly attractive man—he stood about my height, had no hair on the top of his head, and possessed a somewhat weak chin and narrow eyes that made me think of a particularly obstinate ferret.

"Holy Mary, mother of god," Gareth said now as Baltic rounded the car, clearly about to grab him. "You said

silver dragons! You said you were with the silver dragons! You didn't say it was Baltic!"

Baltic paused at his name on Gareth's lips, squinting
at him in the bright sunlight. A flicker of recognition
glinted momentarily in Baltic's eyes, causing me to stare
at him in stunned surprise. "How do you know who he
is?" I asked, gesturing toward Gareth.

Gareth backed up, his hands in the air as if to surren-
der or protect himself as he stared at Baltic. "Good god,
she really did it. You're alive again! Holy Mary!"

"You know my husband?" I asked Baltic, running
past Ruth. She grabbed at my arm as I passed her, but I
shook her off.

"Husband? He is not your husband!" Baltic snorted.

"Yes, he is. He's Brom's father."

"I am Brom's father! You yourself witnessed the oath
between us!"

"I don't understand any of this," I said, rubbing my
forehead again. "How do you know Gareth and Ruth?
And how did you two know where to find us?"

"Attack him!" Ruth shrieked to Gareth, almost hopping with excitement. "Kill him, you fool! He'll ruin everything we've worked so hard for!"

"I can't kill a dragon," Gareth said, bolting as Baltic started toward him again. Gareth grabbed my arms
and held me like a shield before him. "I didn't know
she could do it! She's tried for all those centuries, and I
didn't think she would ever do it! Holy Mary!"

"Will you stop saying that and tell me what's going
on?" I snapped, trying to get free of his grip.

"Release my mate," Baltic said in a low growl that
made the hairs on the back of my neck stand on end.
His eyes were burning with black fire, and I could sense,

even from the few yards that separated us, that he was about to pounce.

"You can have her!" Gareth shrieked, and flung me at Baltic, making a dash for the car.

"Hey—oof. Ow!" I rubbed my nose where it connected with Baltic's chin. "What on earth is going on?"

"He will tell you," Baltic snarled, lunging for Gareth.

"No! There's nothing to tell! I swear to you! Gark!"

Before I could so much as blink, Baltic was on the other side of the car, one hand clamped around Gareth's throat as he held him a good two feet off the ground. "How did you find us?"

"Man ... hired ... save Tully ..."

"Savian Bartholomew," I growled, my fingers curling into fists. At a look from Baltic I explained, "He's a thief taker and some sort of übertracker. Gareth sent him to rescue me from the silver dragons. No doubt Gareth hired him again to find me."

Baltic snarled something obscene as his fingers tightened around Gareth's throat. "You took my mate!"

"Stop that! You're hurting him!" Ruth shoved me aside with a force that sent me reeling into Brom and Jim, who had raced outside at the sound of raised voices.

"Hoo. Maybe I'm not sorry you demon-napped me," Jim said, watching with wide eyes as Ruth leaped on Baltic's back.

"Hey!" I shouted. "Get off of him!"

"You got a video camera?" Jim asked Brom.

"No. Sullivan won't let me get one."

"Shame. I bet we could make enough money to choke a mummy with a video of your mom and that lady going at it."

"No one is going at anything—" I started to say, but

then Ruth started beating Baltic about the head, and fury rose within me. I threw myself over the hood of the car, grabbing Ruth around her waist and yanking her off Baltic.

She snarled something that had Brom looking shocked before lashing out at me with her legs, taking me down in a sort of scissor move.

"Tell her!" Baltic growled, shaking Gareth like he was a rag doll. "Tell her the truth!"

"There's nothing to tell," Gareth gasped, his face bright red as he struggled to get air into his windpipe.

Ruth punched me in the eye, snapping my head backwards, causing me to see little white stars for a moment. "Let go of him!" she yelled again, and abandoning me, threw herself onto Baltic's arm.

"Oh man," Jim said, strolling over to peer down at where I lay dazed. "That's going to leave a shiner. Hey, I can see down your top. That's a sun symbol on your boob, huh?"

Brom joined him. "Looks like it. Is that a tattoo?"

The twinkly white stars started to fade and I became aware of the fact that Jim had its nose about half an inch away from my left breast.

"Naw, it's a dragon mark. Pretty. Kind of Celtic looking with all those swirly bits on the sun's rays."

"Ack!" I yelled, shoving the demon back.

"Hello! I am not a piece of furniture," it said as I used it to get to my feet. "You grab my coat like that, you're going to rumple my fur! Aw, man! You did rumple it! Now I'm going to need brushing."

"Get off him, get off him!" Ruth was chanting as she threw all her weight into Baltic's arm in an attempt to break his grip on Gareth.

Baltic shot a look at her and set her hair on fire.

"Eeek!" She ran screaming away, slapping at her head.

"Fires of Abaddon! What I wouldn't give for a camcorder! That scene alone would have made us the hit of YouTube!" Jim said, watching Ruth run in a circle, beating her head.

"Baltic, stop it!" I said, limping over to him, my left eye starting to swell. "I know you don't like Gareth—at this point, I don't like him, either—but that's no reason to kill him. He's got to stay alive so I can divorce him. A widowhood just wouldn't be nearly as satisfying."

"You can't divorce him because you're not married to him," Baltic snarled, giving Gareth another shake before releasing the hold on his neck.

Gareth crumpled to the ground, one hand clutching his neck, gasping for air.

"Why do you keep saying that?" I asked, gingerly touching my eye. I could barely see out of it.

Baltic strode over to Ruth, grabbing her by the back of her collar and frog-marching her over to me. "Tell her," he demanded, giving Ruth a shove forward.

Ruth and I had never been the best of friends; indeed, she barely tolerated Brom's and my presence, but the look she shot me now was pure loathing. "He's not your husband. He's mine."

My mouth dropped open.

"Hoochiwawa," Jim said, whistling. "I didn't see that coming."

"Gareth's married to Ruth?" Brom asked.

"You're married to him? You're not his sister?" I touched my head, wondering if I'd hit it harder than I imagined when Ruth knocked me to the ground. "Are you sure? Gareth just told me a few days ago we'd been married for ten years."

She gave a choked little laugh as she squatted next to Gareth, who lay still struggling to breathe. "After five hundred years, I think I would know my own husband."

"Five hundred . . . oh my god. Dr. Kostich was right. He is immortal. But . . . why did he marry me, too?"

"He had to, you stupid twit! He had no other choice but to marry you when you suddenly decided you wanted to marry a mortal."

Beyond me, Baltic growled.

I kept my eyes fixed on Ruth. "I wanted to marry someone so Gareth married me instead? It was the gold, wasn't it? That's why he did it."

"Of course it was," she snarled. "We couldn't let anyone else have it, could we? And then you wouldn't stop talking about having a child, and my poor darling had to play stud to your mare. But he hated every minute of it! He told me so repeatedly!"

I digested this, my emotions tangled with anger and fury and hurt and quite a bit of confusion. "But . . . how did you know that Gareth was married to Ruth?" I asked Baltic.

"Ruth is the sister to the one who resurrected me," he answered, glaring at her as he moved over to stand next to me.

"If you're really married to him, then—" I glanced at Brom, and for the second time in a few minutes, rage whipped through me.

"Ouch. You know, even immortals can suffer from brain damage," Jim said, leaning over my shoulder as I whomped Gareth's head repeatedly into the side of the car.

"How dare you use my body! How dare you pretend you were my husband! How dare you do whatever it is you did to me just so I would make gold for you! It really was you who wiped my memory, wasn't it? Just so I didn't know what you and Ruth were doing to me! By the rood, I'll hang your guts from the highest tower!"

Gareth struggled feebly, but he was no match for me. Ruth would have attacked, but Baltic grabbed her by the arm and kept her back while I took out a little of what was evidently centuries of abuse on the man who had deceived me so cruelly.

"How dare you treat Brom the way you did!"

"Uh, Sullivan? I think he's passed out," Brom pointed out.

I released my hold on Gareth, suddenly horrified at what I'd done. "Oh my god! I tried to kill my husband in front of my own child!"

"Ex-husband, I think," Jim said.

"Non-husband," Baltic corrected, releasing Ruth as I leaped to my feet and clutched Brom to my chest. "'Usurper' is a better term."

Ruth cradled Gareth's head as I hugged Brom tightly. "Honey, I know you must be frightened and confused by what I just did to your father—"

"Actually, I was wondering if I could kick him."

"—and I have no excuse for it, none at all, but you know I'm not a violent person, and you must understand that I just had a very bad shock, and I lost my temper. Please, tell me you understand!"

"I understand," Jim said, lifting its leg. "You wanted to beat the crap out of him. I think pretty much anyone would after he played nook-nook with you all that time when he was really married to Scrunchy Face, here."

"Grah!" Ruth snarled, lunging at Jim as it peed on Gareth's foot.

The demon bared its teeth, and Ruth collapsed back onto Gareth, patting his cheeks and sniffling to herself.

"Brom?" I asked, releasing his head. He reeled backwards for a moment, his eyes huge. "Are you all right?"

"I couldn't breathe," he said, giving my boobs a wary glance.

"I'm sorry. It's just that I'm so very, very worried that you misinterpreted the little argument your father and I had."

"Little argument?" Jim snickered. "If you call beating someone to a pulp on the side of a car a little argument, then I don't want to see you when you really get pissed."

"It's OK, Sullivan," Brom said, patting my arm in a supportive manner. "I don't blame you for trying to kill Gareth. If you get mad at him again, and really do bash his brains in, can I mummify him?"

"Just tell me this, Gareth," I said, glaring down at where the man I had thought of as my husband was trying to pull himself up. "Did you ever really want Brom and me?"

He touched his swollen bottom lip, grimacing at the sight of blood on his fingers. "I wasn't going to let you get away from me, not the goose who laid the golden eggs every year."

My anger turned cold and settled in the pit of my gut. "So rather than let me have a life of my own, you bound me to you to ensure you could use me each year." I glanced at Brom, wanting to yell at Gareth for bringing into the world a child he didn't want and didn't care about, but Brom had had enough shocks for the day. "As of this moment, you are no longer a part of our lives. I don't want to see you again, and I will take legal action if you attempt to see Brom."

Gareth sneered as best he could with a battered face. "I don't give a damn about—"

Baltic moved faster than I could follow, grabbing both Ruth and Gareth and flinging them into the car. "He will not bother either of you again. You are both mine now."

"And thank the stars for that," I said, giving Baltic a grateful look that had him doing a double take.

"Whoa. I know what that's going to mean," Jim said, nudging Brom on the hip. "I think you're going to want to look away. You're too young to see what Baltic's about to do."

"You haven't heard the last of us!" Ruth swore as she started up the car. "We will not be treated this way! You may think you can hide behind the dragon, Tully, but you are beholden to us! You are ours, not his!"

"Right, that's it!" I yelled, suddenly furious again. I started toward the car, pushing up my sleeves. "You want a piece of me? You can have a piece of me!"

"Didn't your mom say she wasn't violent?" Jim asked Brom.

"Yeah."

"You can have a piece of me *right now*!" I yelled, jumping toward the car door. Just as I grabbed it, Ruth, evidently thinking twice about taunting me, jammed her foot on the gas. Baltic wrapped an arm around me and lifted me off the ground, leaving me waving my fists at the car as it spun down the drive, spewing bits of gravel behind it.

"You know," Jim said, looking thoughtfully at me as

Baltic set me down, "I used to think Ash was perfect for the role of demon lord—you should see the way she pinches me, and there's no excuse for her starving my fabulous form on those diets she keeps letting the vet talk her into—but I'm starting to think that you've got her on the 'beat the bejesus out of immortals' scale."

"One more crack out of you, demon, and you're going to need a whole lot more than a brushing," I told it, giving it one of my annoyed mother looks.

"That's exactly what I'm talking about," Jim said to Brom.

"Yeah," Brom said, agreeing.

"Well," I said, all wound up after the scene with Gareth and Ruth, "Gareth had it coming to him. Using me like he did . . . the rat!"

"I would have killed him for daring to touch what was mine, but for one thing," Baltic said.

"Brom?" I asked, figuring he would not want to kill Gareth in front of a child any more than I did.

"No." His gaze dropped to mine, and I flushed at the sight of the naked desire burning in its depths. "Now you are truly mine."

I didn't even have time to digest that before he bent down, slung me over his shoulder, and walked into the house.

"Baltic!" I shrieked, Jim and Brom trailing after us. "Put me down this instant! What did I say about treating me like I was a sack of potatoes?"

Baltic paused inside the hall, and I pinched his back, assuming he had come to his senses.

"Hey, Balters, just a little hint," Jim said, giving us a knowing look. "Aisling says she hates it when Drake gets all aggressive with her, but she sure grins like a fool afterward, so you might just want to take all that screeching with a grain of salt."

"I am not screeching!" I said, outraged, glaring at the demon. "You are going to be so sorry—Baltic! I said set me down!"

"There you are. Take care of my son and the demon," Baltic ordered Pavel, who emerged from the study.

"Dammit, I demand that you release me. I am not Aisling! I do not like arrogance!"

"What's Baltic doing with Sullivan?" I heard Brom ask as Baltic leaped up the stairs, apparently not feeling my weight slung over his shoulder at all. I spent a moment admiring that fact before I slid my hands down his back and only just refrained from pinching his butt.

"You don't wanna know. I mean, you will in about ten years, but for now, it's just going to mess with your head. You gotta trust me on this. Hey, who do I have to crotch-snuffle to get lunch around here? I'm starving, and my coat goes to Abaddon in a handbasket if I don't get five proper meals a day. You got any fresh horse-meat, Pavel?"

Chapter Fourteen

"I want to give you something," Baltic said as he closed the door to his bedroom.

"I just bet you do. I want to give you something, too— a piece of my mind. What on earth do you think you're doing, carrying me off like you're some sort of a primitive caveman? What will Brom think?"

"My son will understand that I wish to spend time alone with you, where I may worship every inch of your soft, delicious body, and where you will pleasure me endlessly until I am a shattered wreck of a dragon."

I thought about that for a moment. Brom was fine with Pavel there. Jim would be watched, and Gareth, that bastard bigamist, was no longer a factor in my life. Was there any impediment to me flinging myself on Baltic and giving in to all those desires that had built up over centuries?

No, there was not! "All right," I squealed as I suited action to thought and flung myself on him.

He wasn't expecting that, because the weight of my body suddenly hitting him sent him staggering backwards a few steps. "*Chérie*, you must wait. I have something for you."

"Oh, yes, you certainly do," I said, nuzzling his neck as I slid my hand down his chest, and further below to stroke the length of him through his pants. He groaned, his eyes closed for a moment as I felt him growing in thickness and length.

Suddenly, he pried me off him. "Ysolde, you must wait."

"You are kidding me!" I said, glaring at him with irate intent as he turned his back on me and strode over to a tall bureau. "You were begging me to do this yesterday, and now you don't want me?"

"I never beg," he scoffed, searching through a drawer of the bureau. "I am a wyvern, and your mate. I do not need to beg."

"You want to bet?" I growled, my arms crossed and my eyes narrowed as I watched him. I knew he wasn't indifferent to me—a simple glance at his fly negated that idea. "You were all over me yesterday. Why are you spurning me now?"

"Wyverns don't spurn, either," he said, his voice somewhat muffled as he squatted, his head in a deep drawer at the bottom of the bureau.

"Well, you're sure doing something, and it is not celebrating the fact that Gareth is a lying bigamist, as you should be doing. Instead, you're poking your head in some sort of a desk. What is it you're doing there, Baltic? Going to write a few letters? Pay some bills? Cut up pretty pictures and make a collage? What's that?"

He stood before me, a small wooden box in his hand.

Engraved on it, in gold, were two stylized medieval-ish dragons, their necks crossed. He put the box into my hands. "It is a gift for you."

I turned it over, examining it, my fingers sliding over the smooth, highly polished wood. "What is it?"

"Open it."

I traced the long lines of one of the dragons on the top, and looked up at Baltic. "If it contains a wedding ring, you can just take it back. I've had enough of marriage, thank you."

He made an impatient gesture. "Marriage is for mortals. You are my mate. That is for all time."

"Till death do us part," I said softly, then smiled. "And beyond."

"Open it," he repeated.

I glanced at the big bed behind me. The room was decorated in shades of cream and a cool blue—attractive, but completely not his style. "Why don't I open it later, after I've given you all that pleasure you think you're due?"

"I know I am due it," he said with maddening arrogance, then nudged my hands. "Open your present."

"I like to anticipate gifts. Once you open them, the anticipation is gone."

"Open it!" he said, a little line of frown starting to form between his brows.

"Let's have oral sex!" I said brightly, moving backwards toward the bed, patting it with a seductive glance toward him. "You like that! I remember that you do! You take off all your clothes and lie down here, and I'll give you a tongue bath that you won't ever forget."

"For the love of the saints, woman, open the damned box!"

"And you say you never spurn! You just spurned my offer of a blow job, something I thought no living man could do."

He started toward me, a look in his eye that said he'd reached the end of his pretty nonexistent patience.

"Fine!" I said quickly, crawling onto the middle of the bed while I clutched the box. "But I just want you to remember that you're the one who didn't want oral sex. Stop giving me that look! I'm opening it. See? The lid is . . . ahhh."

It wasn't really a word I spoke; it was more an exhalation of emotion. The box held a small object, somewhere between an oval and a circle, made of metal, but now dulled with age and time.

Recognition prickled along my skin as I gazed at it, waves of electricity seeming to ripple down my arms and legs. I knew this object. I knew it well, and yet it was both as familiar to me as the beat of my own heart, and foreign, something I had never seen before.

"Love token." I spoke the words without even being aware of it. "It's my love token. You made it for me. But how . . . ?"

"It was at Dauva, in my lair. You placed it there, along with all the valuables in the castle, before Constantine attacked. Kostya raided most of the lair, but he left that."

So faint I could barely make it out, a roughly drawn tree was engraved into the silver token, with three upper leafy branches, and two lower ones bearing hearts.

I smiled, a faint memory returning to me. "It's made of silver so it would not distract you when I wore it."

He watched me closely. "You remember it, then?"

"No. Yes. Both." I reached out to touch the token,

wanting to feel it, to weigh its age in my hand, but the second my finger touched the metal surface, the world began to spin.

I cried out, feeling as if I would fall, but strong arms caught me, warm and familiar, his touch stirring the embers of desire that were always within me. The room darkened, the colors shifting from light to dark, large amber pools lit by tall standing candelabras, the light of the candles flickering and shimmering along the shadows of the room.

Figures shimmered, too, the figure of a man and a woman.

"A love token?" the woman said, smiling at the man. "For me?"

"I made it for you when I sailed from Riga to France."

"It's a tree," she said, and her voice resonated within me, my lips parting to speak the next words with her. "A tree with hearts?"

"A tree because I knew it would please you. Three branches for you, me, and the sept," Baltic then and now said, one voice slightly echoing the other.

I was pulled toward the figure of my other self as if I were made of nothing but light and shadow, hesitating a moment as I glanced back at Baltic. He nodded and I let myself merge with the memory of my former self. Baltic's face changed as he, too, allowed himself to sink into his former being.

"And two hearts," Ysolde and I said at the same time as we smiled up at him.

"I give you this token as a pledge of my heart," he said, and tears pricked in my eyes at the love shining in his.

Ysolde and I kissed him, clutching the token to our chest. "It's the most wonderful thing I've ever received. I can't believe you made it for me."

"You have sworn to be my mate, and for me there is no greater bond, but you were raised with mortals. I thought you would like it."

I was so touched, both at the time, and again now, that he would go to such lengths to please me. "It couldn't have been easy to make it," I told my Baltic as the other Ysolde cooed happily at the token before offering him her mouth again.

The two Baltics shimmered, the image of one overlaying the other.

"It wasn't. I'm no artist. I almost severed my fingers a couple of times engraving the image in it."

"Make love to me," I pleaded as the other Baltic scooped up my former self and carried her to the gigantic canopied bed.

Baltic glanced at the memories of us when I moved against him, sliding my hands around to his back, stroking the muscles there, and wiggling my hips in brazen invitation. "Here? With them?"

"They're us. We're in your bedroom. Please, Baltic. I've waited so long for you, and now I can have you. You wanted to claim me yesterday—well, now I'm all yours."

"First you are aroused by the thought of males loving males; then you wished to bare your breasts to everyone with a pair of eyes in his head; and now you want to engage in mating with other people?" He bent and picked me up, carrying me to the bed with an expression that mingled irritation with desire. "We will have a long discussion about these fantasies of yours, *chérie*. I am willing to oblige you this once, but I warn you—you are my mate, and I have no intention of sharing you."

He laid me down on the bed next to the other Ysolde, who was now clad in what I recognized as a thin chemise, the black-haired Baltic kneeling between her legs, slowly pushing the chemise higher and higher.

"Whoa," I said, unable to take my eyes from them, my own emotions as conflicted as Baltic's. "This is . . . wow. On the one hand, it feels like we're watching two people about to make love. But it's us. So how can it feel so very . . . oooh. . . . kinky?"

Baltic, who had been removing his clothing, glanced over at the ghostly pair before returning his attention to me. He stood next to me, his hands on his hips, his penis fully aroused and saluting me. "As I said, we will have a discussion about this at a later time."

I looked at his groin, making a mental measurement before sliding a quick look over at the other version of him.

"What are you doing?" he asked, accusation heavy in his voice as he climbed onto the bed.

"Nothing!" I said, quickly looking back at him.

His black eyes narrowed on me as he, too, knelt between my legs. "You were comparing me to him, weren't you?"

"Of course I wasn't! What gave you that idea?"

"I saw you looking at my rod. You looked at it, and then looked at his. You were making comparisons!"

"He is you," I said, pointing at the other Baltic.

"The fact remains that you were judging my rod against his."

"I was not!" He stared at me. I stared back at him.

After about five seconds, I added, "Besides, it doesn't matter. You're bigger now."

"Aha! I knew it!"

"Look, you're making a big fuss over nothing," I said, gesturing toward the other couple. I glanced at them as I spoke, but the words dried up on my lips, and my eyes bugged out when Ysolde, lying next to me, groaned and clutched the sheets, her head thrashing from side to side as Baltic pleasured her with his mouth and hands. My mouth hung open as I blinked at the sight. It was so wrong to watch such an intimate moment between two people—but those two people were us. That was me having an orgasm that caused me to arch up off the bed, calling Baltic's name. "By the rood," I managed to get out as I watched.

Baltic smiled smugly. "You always were fast to please."

"By the rood!" I repeated as the other version of him crawled up her body, licking her with both his tongue and dragon fire. She growled, twining her legs around him as he eased himself into her warmth, her hands clutching his butt and pulling him tighter.

"Ysolde," Baltic said.

"*By the rood!*" I yelled as Ysolde arched again, her hips jerking upward. Her Baltic murmured something in her ear, pulling out just long enough to move his arms under her legs so that they rested on his shoulders, angling her pelvis for maximum penetration. "Can you do that to me, please? Like right now?"

He sat on his heels, frowning. "I do not like the fact that the sight of others making love excites you so much, *chérie*. You should be focused on me only."

"I am focused on you. Holy—is he doing what I think he's doing?"

"You wished to have a child," Baltic said, not paying the least bit of attention as his other self crammed a couple of pillows beneath Ysolde's behind, on his knees as he thrust into her with hard, fast movements. "I was simply trying to help you conceive."

I blinked, unable to look away until Baltic bit my ankle. "Mate, I am the one you should be staring at with that look of lust and desire and besotted fascination!"

"Jealous?" I asked him, trying to look at both Baltics at once. It wasn't easy.

"That would be foolish—" Even he stopped to look as the other version of us, with cries that were unmistakable for anything but those of completion, fell off the side of the bed.

"I knocked myself out for a few minutes by hitting my head on the floor," Baltic commented as I peered over at them.

Sure enough, Ysolde was on the floor, making soft little happy noises, stroking the sweaty back of the man who was still evidently embedded in her, her legs rubbing up and down on his. He didn't move.

"I hope you weren't hurt seriously."

"I wasn't. Now if your voyeuristic desires have been satisfied, will you please attend to me?"

"Sorry," I said, scooting back to my spot. Baltic looked peeved now. "But if you could do just what the other Baltic did, minus the falling on the floor and cracking your head, that would be really, *really* fine with me."

"It is right that you wish to give me a child since you gave one to the usurper," he said, approval softening his frown. "But first, I must claim you properly as my mate. Afterward, we will make a child."

I opened my mouth to tell him that one son was enough for me, but I remembered the pain in his face when he had spoken to my past self of the child we'd lost. "We'll talk later about adding to the family, all right? At this moment, I really would like you to do something other than frown at me."

He dipped his head and bathed me in fire.

I screamed and almost came off the bed, my breath caught in my throat as he started pulling off my clothing. As it did before, the fire seemed to dance on my skin, pulsating as it moved up my legs to my stomach.

Baltic pulled off my jeans, sandals, and underwear with a sweep of his hands. I writhed on the bed as the fire swept upward. The corset top seemed to melt off me as Baltic snapped the laces one by one until all that stood between me and his fire was my bra.

"You, too, are bigger," he said just as his head bent over the valley of my breasts, the bra coming off easily. His breath steamed my flesh, making me yearn for the inferno I knew he could build within me.

"I am not!" I looked down at my breasts. "You really think so?"

"I know it. You were plentiful before. Now you are"— he cupped one breast in his hand, his thumb gently rubbing across my nipple—"very abundant."

"Fire," I begged, squirming against him as his tongue flicked out over my now-aching breast.

"You must learn to use your own fire," he chastised, taking my breast into his mouth. I moaned and grabbed great handfuls of the sheets just as the past Ysolde had done, my breasts thrusting upward.

"Fire!" I ordered, and writhed happily when he chuckled and said, "So demanding. That, too, has not changed," before allowing his dragon fire to pour out of him and wrap itself around me. It burned, but it did not harm me. It warmed, but it was nothing compared to the inferno blazing within. It teased my flesh, but only Baltic's touches, soft caresses with his mouth and fingers, made me feel like I was one continuous erogenous zone.

"Embrace the fire, *chérie*," he mumbled into my breastbone as he slid lower, kissing and burning a path down to my stomach. "Claim it as your own. Use it. Shape it. Make it be what you want it to be."

I wanted to. Oh, how I wanted to, but I couldn't focus my thoughts on anything but the magic of him as he slid even lower, nipping at my hips with sharp teeth, soothed by long, slow strokes of his tongue.

"Accept the fire, my love."

"I . . . I can't," I said as he nudged my knees apart.

"You can. You are my mate. You are a light dragon. Accept it." Heat poured over me as he sent his dragon fire up my body again, the flames licking along my skin before sinking deep into me. His hands swept up my thighs, pushing them wider, his mouth hot on the sensitive inner flesh as he kissed a fiery path to my very core.

"I don't think it's possible," I said, a fever of need and want and desire all mingled together, causing a pressure within me to push higher and higher.

"It is. You must try, Ysolde. Give the fire back to me." I moaned again at the feeling of his mouth as he breathed fire on the most sensitive of flesh, gasping when he sank a finger into me. "Use it, mate. Use the fire."

A long, low cry tore from my throat as the pressure continued to build, fueled by both his fire and the passion he was triggering with every flick of his tongue.

"Now!" he demanded, and my body trembled on the brink of something so profound, I couldn't begin to understand it. The pressure inside me gave with a rush as the fire that I had absorbed roared to life, pouring out of me to consume him.

He made a noise deep in his chest, part growl, part mating sound that my heart recognized and answered. My body wasn't just alight—I *was* the flame. Baltic suddenly reached underneath me, flipping me over onto my stomach, the arm beneath my belly pulling me upward as he covered my back.

"Mate," he growled, his body hard and aggressive on mine. I arched again, unable to keep from moaning with sheer, utter ecstasy as he thrust into my body, his penis a brand that only drove the pressure inside me to the point where I knew I was going to explode.

The feeling of him within me, of my muscles trembling around him, was enough to push me over the edge. I spiraled into an orgasm unlike anything I thought possible, my soul merging with his as he joined me in a moment of absolute rapture.

My legs gave out and I collapsed onto the bed as he roared one word, his hands beside my hips as he continued to pound into me with short, fast thrusts until at last he, too, collapsed.

I tried to make sense of what had happened, but my brain gave a little whimper and told me I was on my own. I lay shaking with the sense of power that our joining had brought, Baltic's heavy body pressing me into the soft mattress.

"Did we die again?" I asked when I recovered enough ability to move my mouth.

A soft, rusty chuckle sounded in my ear. "No, but it was a close thing."

"Dear god," I said as, pulling me with him, he rolled onto his back. "Was it always like that? Because I'm serious, Baltic—I don't know if my heart can stand that every night. I'll have to take up an aerobics class, and I hate that sort of thing."

"It has always been and will always be thus between us," he said, moving my limp body so I lay draped over his chest, one of my legs caught between his. "You will learn to adjust to the more strenuous dragon matings, just as you learned to harness your fire."

"That wasn't my fire. It was yours. I just used it," I said, too drained to do more than smooth my hand over his still-heaving chest.

"It was both."

Next to us, a body hit the bed.

I glanced over, smiling as the past Ysolde dabbed tenderly at a spot of blood on her Baltic's forehead. He tolerated that for a moment, then pulled her over him, catching one of her breasts in his mouth. "Goodness. You appear to have had a lot of stamina then."

He didn't even look, just smiled, his eyelashes thick sable crescents as he lay with his eyes closed. "Give me five minutes, and I will show you that I have improved in that way, as well."

"You might have improved, but I think another round would be the end of me," I commented, unable to keep from watching when Ysolde impaled herself on the past Baltic. "You know, it's really too bad we can't interact with them."

He cracked open one eye and looked at me. "Why?"

I gestured to where his previous self bucked, Ysolde riding him as if he were an unbroken stallion, and pursed my lips a little. "Well, if we could, you and the other Baltic could . . . you know . . ."

The look he shot me was so outraged I giggled. He slapped my behind, then rubbed away the sting before closing his eyes. "Many people have told me to go fuck myself, but I never expected my mate to actually suggest that I do it."

I giggled even more, kissing the pulse in his neck, my body and heart and soul happier than they had ever been.

Chapter Fifteen

My suggestion was, I thought, extremely acceptable. "How about Strand Palace Hotel? It has conference capabilities, and their big business suite is available tomorrow."

"Are you kidding? After what happened the last time Baltic came to a *sárkány* in a hotel?" Aisling's voice was filled with scorn. "I don't think so!"

"Why, what happened?"

"He tried to shoot everyone present!"

"Oh, that. One moment, please." I covered the mouthpiece of the phone and turned to where Baltic stood glaring at me. "Did you really go to a *sárkány* recently and shoot the participants?"

"Yes." The answer was given in a grumpy tone, which, given the look on his face, was no surprise.

I took a deep breath. "You do realize how difficult it is to get the wyverns to agree to meet you on neutral ground so we can talk about things, don't you?"

"What the weyr does or thinks is none of our concern. We are outside of them. They do not matter to us."

"They matter to me," I said.

He continued to glare. "Not as much as I matter to you."

"Of course not, and stop being so insecure. I've loved you for over four hundred years. I think you can relax."

"The other you loved me. This you . . ." He raked me up and down with a wary gaze. "This you is different. You have unnatural desires. My old Ysolde would never have left me to try to position herself between two lovers."

"I didn't try anything of the sort! I just moved off you and happened to roll exactly where the old version of us was going at it. Again. For a third time in the space of an hour." I narrowed my eyes at him. "You only managed once."

His eyes blazed black fire at me. "I told you to give me five minutes and I would recover enough to pleasure you again! You are the one who stopped me. You did not wish for me to start again!"

"Regardless, I did not deliberately roll under the other you and get my jollies from him pounding away. Although I really liked the looks of that little swirl thing he was doing. Do you think we could—" A faint voice in my ear reminded me that I was on the phone. Evidently, my hand had slipped off the mouthpiece.

"—arguing with him. No, not about meeting us, about sex, I think. Evidently he only did things once and she wanted three times. And it sounds like there may have been another couple involved."

"Um," I said, giving Baltic a glare of my own. "I'm

sorry you had to overhear that, Aisling. Baltic drives me a little batty sometimes."

"Only sometimes?" she asked; at the same time he snorted and said, "It is your bizarre fantasies that make me insane."

"My fantasies are not the least bit bizarre!" I said loudly.

"No, of course not," Aisling said, laughter in her voice. "Although I have to say, you're the last person I had pegged for a swinger."

I took another deep, deep breath, and managed to hold on to my temper. "All right, a hotel is out."

"Yes. Our house is big enough if we open up the downstairs to make one big room."

I glanced at where Baltic was now pacing beside me, his hands behind his back. He glared at the floor as if it personally offended him.

"I think we're going to have some objections to the neutrality of that location. How about Hyde Park? That's large."

"Too public," Aisling said. "And too many portals there. If the dragons start fighting, things can happen, and I'm not back to full Guardian duties yet. What we need is something private, yet roomy."

"How about Baltic's house, the one with the garden?" I asked, my spirits lifting just thinking about it.

He raised his eyebrows at the suggestion, looking strangely thoughtful.

"Let me check." Muffled voices followed that, too muffled for me to make out. "An objection has been raised for that location, as well. It's been pointed out that you could escape to the beyond there."

I sighed. "Tell May hello."

"She says hello," Aisling duly repeated. "May wants to know if they should bring Brom's and your things, or if you'll be picking them up?"

"If it's not too much trouble, that would be lovely. I guess that leaves us with only one solution."

"What's that?"

I kept my eyes on Baltic as I spoke. "You'll just have to come here. Baltic's house isn't huge, but there are ample grounds, and I think everyone would feel better if we held the *sárkány* out in the open."

"No!" Baltic bellowed, whirling around to face me. "You would bring my enemies here?"

"They wouldn't be your enemies if you stopped shooting at them!" I pointed out.

"And blowing up their houses," Aisling said. "And trying to steal their mates."

"Yes, and blowing up their houses, and . . . what was that?"

"Stealing their mates. Didn't May tell you? May, didn't you tell her that Baltic was trying to steal you with the shard?"

"Gargh!" I yelled, and for the first time, I felt Baltic's fire raging within me of its own accord.

"Oops. I take that as a no," Aisling said softly. "Oh dear. I think I set Ysolde off—"

"You tried to take May?" I yelled, clutching the phone so tightly, my knuckles were white. The pressure built within me, and I spat out a fireball the size of a grapefruit that slammed against his chest, rocking him backwards. "You tried to claim another mate?"

Baltic looked stunned for a moment, then worried. He absorbed the fire, his hands spread in placation. "*Chérie*, it wasn't like that at all—"

"Don't you *chérie* me, you scaly-skinned monster! You wanted May! You never really wanted me, did you? I was dead, so you looked around for the first piece of dragon ass you could find, and you tried to take her!"

"I wanted the shard, yes. I wanted it so that the dragon heart could be re-formed. I never really wanted the silver mate—"

"Then why did you try to take her?" I spat out another fireball, this one a little larger. He caught it before it could slam into him, extinguishing it as he slowly came forward, hesitantly, as if I were a dangerous animal.

I narrowed my eyes and wished I could switch into dragon form.

"My intention was to remove her from the silver wyvern, not to claim her for my own mate. He should never have had a mate in the first place."

"Oh, really? Why not?"

He looked disconcerted and waved away the question. "That is a matter for another discussion."

"I don't think so!" I held the phone back up to my ear. "Aisling, are you still there?"

"Er . . . yes. Ysolde, I'm sorry, I had no idea that you didn't know about—"

"Why shouldn't Gabriel have a mate?" I asked, ruthlessly interrupting her.

"Ysolde, you will not question others when I am here to answer anything you wish to know," Baltic said arrogantly, but I shot a bigger fireball at him, one that knocked him back a couple of feet, onto the couch. He dropped the arrogance and went straight for seduction. "My love, you distress yourself unduly over a minor incident."

"He cursed them to never have a mate born to them," Aisling said succinctly.

"Please hold. A curse, Baltic?" I asked, wrapping my fingers across the mouthpiece again.

"You were dead! Constantine killed you! That damned Kostya was trying to hack off my head! I had to curse someone, and Constantine ripped my life from me by killing you. Of course I cursed them!"

A memory of the pain he suffered when I was killed shimmered in his eyes and effectively squashed my ire. "You're going to have to lift the curse, you know."

His expression darkened. "I do not *have* to do anything, mate."

"You cursed the silver dragons because their wyvern killed me. But I'm not dead any longer."

"You are also not the same Ysolde you were."

"I do not have strange sexual kinks!" I yelled, slamming the phone down on the table. I poked him in the chest because I knew it would irritate him. "Things just conspire to make it look that way! By the rood, Baltic! Just because a little guy-on-guy action isn't objectionable to me, you think every little peccadillo is some majorly perverted desire on my part! Oh, hell." I looked down at the phone, picking it up carefully. "You heard that, didn't you, Aisling?"

A muffled laugh followed. "I'm afraid we all did, thanks to the invention of the speakerphone."

"Oh, god." I closed my eyes for a moment, overcome with embarrassment. "I will give you directions to the house."

"You will not tell them where we live!" Baltic ranted behind me.

"I trust you will continue to honor the agreement regarding Jim. Once the *sárkány* is over, I will turn it over to you."

"Your turn to hold," Aisling said, but she had an actual hold on her phone. A slight humming noise filled the earpiece.

"Mate! I forbid you to do this!" Baltic said, grabbing my arm.

I set the phone down, turning to face him, sliding my hands into his hair, gently removing the leather thong. "I love you, Baltic."

"I will not allow—er . . ." His tense jaw relaxed as I nibbled along it, gently biting his lower lip. His hands, which had been gripping my arms, moved around to cup my behind, pulling me tight against him.

"I love you more than anything in the world, but I would like us to live in peace with the weyr. Please do this for me. For us." I sucked his lower lip into my mouth and tried to summon his fire, but it seemed to be banked. "Fire?"

It roared through me as he claimed my mouth properly, his tongue being every bit as demanding as he was. Just as I was seriously contemplating wrestling him to the floor and indulging in a few acts I'd seen my past self perform, the door opened.

"Fires of Abaddon, they're still at it? Brom, my man, you don't want to see this."

"Don't want to see what? Oh. Sullivan is kissing Baltic."

"Father," Baltic said, breaking off the kiss to inform Brom.

"Huh?" my son asked, eyeing me as if I were one of his experiments. "How come your hands are on her butt?"

"I like her butt," Baltic said, giving the object in question a little squeeze. I bit his chin. "You will refer to me as 'Father' henceforth."

"But your name is Baltic," Brom pointed out.

"Hey, is that Aisling I hear squawking on the phone?" Jim asked as it wandered over to where I'd set down the receiver. "Ash, babe, you there?"

"Oh, damn, I forgot her again." I turned in Baltic's arms, but he didn't release me.

"It is not fitting that you refer to your parents by their names. It does not show respect. You will therefore refer to me as 'Father.' I will leave it to your mother to decide if she wishes to tolerate you referring to her by her surname."

"No, it's cool," Jim said, plopping down next to the table, its head lying next to the phone so it could talk and hear. "Pavel made sage-roasted game hens for lunch, and I had a whole one to myself. He needs to give the recipe to Suzanne because it was seriously yummy. And Ysolde said she was going to brush me later. No, they stopped kissing, although Baltic's hands are almost on her boobs. Right in front of the kid, too."

Baltic's hands, which had indeed been moving up from my stomach, froze.

"I don't like 'Father,'" Brom said, his brown eyes serious as they considered Baltic.

"Papa?" I suggested, placing my hands over Baltic's and leaning back into his chest. Despite the worry of the upcoming *sárkány*, I felt aglow with happiness. That Baltic cared so much about how Brom referred to him was a good sign. Brom would have a real father at last, one who cared about him.

"Yeah, yeah, but you're overreacting, Aisling. I'm fine—no one's hurting me. Ysolde keeps giving me scary mom looks, but I don't think she can help it. Besides, it's wild seeing Baltic being all lovey-dovey with her. How the mighty can fall."

Brom wrinkled his nose. "I'm nine, Sullivan, not two. How about 'Dad'? The others at the mage school call their fathers Dad. Most of them. There's that weird kid who calls everyone Carrot, but no one pays much attention to him."

Baltic's fingers twined through mine. "You sent my son to a mage school?"

"Dr. Kostich thought he might have some talents in that direction, so I enrolled him in it. Unfortunately, he seems to have inherited my lack of abilities when it comes to things arcane."

"Ixnay on the ecretsay ummonsay," Jim said, casting a worried glance my way. "Oh, great, now she's giving me another of those looks, the kind that says I'm going to be sent to my room without supper."

"You will if you don't give me the phone," I told it.

"Gotta go. Pavel said he's doing goulash for dinner, and he promises it'll be almost orgasmic."

"What's—" Brom started to ask.

"Out!" I told the demon, taking the phone from it. "Brom, Baltic will be happy with 'Dad.' You go practice saying it somewhere else, please. And Jim, so help me god—"

"I know, you'll skin me alive or some other heinous act if I explain to Brom what 'orgasmic' means. I didn't actually mean to say that in front of him. Sometimes I forget he's only a kid."

"That's all right," Brom said, patting Jim on the head as the two of them exited the room. "Sometimes I forget you're a demon. You want to play catch?"

"Naw. Let's go play on Pavel's Xbox. He's got a road-racing game I love."

"Aisling?"

"Still here. And you have my permission to yell at Jim. I can't believe it'd say something so inappropriate in front of a child. Honest to Pete! It knows better than that! Drake, stop trying to take the phone away from me! I'm not done."

"I take it we're off speakerphone?"

"Yes, I thought after that last argument, it would be better. Drake wishes to speak with Baltic, but I did want to remind you that should anything happen to Jim, I will rain down destruction as you've never seen it. Not that I think you'd do anything to it, because you seem very maternal, and we moms have a sense about those things, but I feel obligated as its demon lord to say that. Fine! You can have the phone. Sheesh, pushy dragons . . ."

"Oh, Aisling?" I said, smiling to myself.

"Yes?"

"The next time you have Drake alone, ask him about a small inn in Paris called the Hangman's Balls. Mention the year 1699."

"All right," she said slowly. "I will. Here's Drake."

"A moment, please," I told Drake when he asked for Baltic. I held the phone to my chest. "You will be polite."

"I am a wyvern," he said airily.

"You will not say rude things to Drake no matter what he says to you."

"You may leave. I will speak with the green wyvern by myself."

"We are trying to establish a relationship with these people. Please remember that."

He tried to take the phone. I hung on to it. "You may leave now, Ysolde."

"Not until you promise to be good."

"I'm always good. Give me the phone."

"Just remember what I've said, that's all."

"I am not a child who needs to be schooled in matters of weyr etiquette," he answered, trying to pry my fingers off the receiver.

"You're also notoriously short-tempered, don't give a damn what anyone else thinks, and have a chip on your shoulder approximately the size of Rhode Island."

"Mate," he said, a warning light in his eyes.

"Yes?"

"Do your many and varied sexual kinks run to spankings?"

"I don't have sexual kinks, and no—you wouldn't!" I gasped as he tried to pull me over to the chair. "All right, I'll leave, but if you mess things up after I've worked so hard to straighten them out, I will make your life a living hell—just see if I don't!"

As I closed the door I heard him say, "What? Yes, it worked. I recommend using the threat of it as a method of controlling an unruly mate—"

Chapter Sixteen

"By the rood, they can't be early, can they?" I paused on my way through the French doors in the sitting room to peer out of the glass next to the front door. A car was pulling to a stop. "I'm not ready! We don't have all the beverages out to the field yet, let alone the canapés!"

"I can help you with the canapés," Jim said, licking its lips as it emerged from the kitchen hauling a large basket. "Oooh, visitors?"

"If your demon lord came early just to catch us by surprise—oh, no!"

"Who is it?" Jim asked, peering around me. Its eyebrows rose. "Heh. This ought to be fun."

"What is Savian doing, telling everyone in the Otherworld where I am?" I muttered as I set down the tray of cut glass crystal goblets and opened the door. "Good afternoon, Dr. Kostich."

"Tully," he said, inclining his head toward me. "I trust

you will excuse my unannounced arrival. I have matters of great import to discuss with you."

"Actually, I'm a bit busy today. Could you come back another time? Say, next year?"

The look he gave me said much, and none of it was in my favor. He strolled past me into the house, casually tossing over his shoulder, "I assume you have the von Endres blade by now. I have come to collect it."

"Oh, lord," I swore, looking heavenward for a moment. "Why me?"

"What's going on . . . oh man. Greetings, your eminence," Jim said, almost groveling toward Dr. Kostich. I didn't wonder that the demon, normally the most flip of beings, had adopted a respectful air. Clearly it had come into contact with Dr. Kostich before.

I turned slowly back to the foyer, trying to think of a diplomatic way to explain to the head of the Otherworld that I would not be stealing Baltic's sword.

"What are you doing here?" Kostich asked, staring at Jim where it sat in the center of the narrow hall.

Jim dipped its head again in a doggy bow. "Ysolde's making me be a pack mule. I didn't know you were going to be here, though. Not that there's anything wrong with you being here," it added quickly as it backed up a few steps.

"I dislike demons," Dr. Kostich told it, his eyes narrowing and his fingers twitching as if he might cast a spell.

"Ysolde!" Jim almost yelped, hurrying over to press into my leg. "You promised Ash to keep me safe! Don't let him do anything to me."

"You're a demon," I told it, patting it on its head

nonetheless. "He can't harm a demon. No one can but a demon lord. Not permanently, anyway."

"Wanna bet?" Jim peeked out around my leg at my former employer.

My eyebrows rose. "You can harm a demon? Not just its form, but the demon itself?"

Dr. Kostich just smiled.

"Don't worry, I won't let anyone harm you," I said meaningfully. "Jim is my guest, Dr. Kostich."

The demon moved out a few steps. "Hostage is more like it. Ysolde demon-napped me. Not that I mind, because she's cool and all."

"I can't imagine why she would want to do that—" The words dried up on his lips as Baltic emerged from a back room. He paused at the sight of Kostich. The two men stared at each other.

"Uh-oh," Jim said, backing up again.

"You!" Kostich said, pointing dramatically at Baltic. "It is you!"

Baltic shot me an irritated glance.

"I didn't tell him where we were," I answered the look. "Savian did."

"Now you will pay for your crimes against the L'audela!" Dr. Kostich announced, and began to cast what I knew was a morphing spell.

"I really should have killed you when I had the chance," Baltic snarled, holding out his hand. The light blade materialized in a burst of blue-white light.

"No!" I yelled, running to stand between them. "I will not have this! Not now! Not today! Not when I haven't made the lemon sorbet yet!"

Baltic, in the act of raising the sword over his head,

presumably to strike down Dr. Kostich, paused and frowned at me. "Lemon sorbet?"

"For after the *sárkány*. I thought a little lemon sorbet and some ladyfingers would be refreshing."

He lowered the sword, his lips tight as he turned to face me. "This is not a party, Ysolde!"

"Lemon sorbet does not constitute a party," I pointed out.

"Regardless, I will not feed my enemies!"

"Might I interject a note of seriousness into this bizarre conversation—" Dr. Kostich started to say.

"Don't think it will do any good," Jim answered as I pushed my way past Dr. Kostich to face Baltic.

"They are our guests, and I will be damned if I have it said that people came to my house and I did not offer them common hospitality."

"Sorbet is not common hospitality," he argued. "It's dessert."

"I thought people would like something to cleanse their palates after the canapés!" I said, slapping my hands on my thighs. "Pardon me for being civilized."

"Canapés? Now you have canapés?" His face was beginning to flush, always a sign his temper was slipping. "What next, champagne?"

Pavel emerged from the door leading to the basement, a cardboard box in his hands bearing the name of a famous brand of champagne. Baltic looked at him in disbelief before turning a scowl on me. "That's my vintage Bollinger's!"

"It won't hurt you to share."

"With people who want me dead!" he yelled.

"I completely understand their feelings," Dr. Kostich said. "About the von Endres sword—"

"That's it," Baltic said, raising the sword again. "I'm killing him; then I will deal with you, mate."

Dr. Kostich took a step back, his hands going through the intricate twists and turns of a morphing spell.

"You will not hurt him! I will never forgive you if you hurt him!" I told Baltic.

He glared at me, his eyes sparking onyx, his jaw tight with tension. "You are pushing me too far, woman!"

"I just want everyone to get along!" I yelled, so frustrated I could . . . well, yell. "Why can't people stop trying to kill each other and steal things from each other and so help me god, Dr. Kostich, if you complete that morph spell, I'll slap you with one myself!"

My former employer lifted his nose, his fingers dancing in the air as they drew near to completing a particularly detailed morph spell that would turn Baltic into some other form. "You are under an interdict. Your magic does not work."

"Wanna bet?" I snarled, and pulled hard on the dragon fire within me, letting my own fingers do a little spell casting.

A banana materialized out of the air and fell to his feet.

He stopped his morph spell. Everyone stared at the banana.

"Um. That was supposed to be a slavering tiger," I said, prodding the fruit with the toe of my shoe. "I guess the interdict is making my magic wonky."

"Understatement time," Jim said, sniffing it. "You want me to pretend I'm a tiger and stab the archimage with it?"

We all ignored Jim.

"You should not be able to even cast a spell," Kostich said, giving me a long look. "It is not possible that you can do so with the interdict placed upon you."

"My mate is not a normal woman," Baltic said, hauling me into his side with his free arm. With the other, he waved the sword at Kostich. "She is a light dragon. She is beyond your understanding."

"You!" Kostich snapped again, glaring at Baltic as he gathered up arcane energy into a bluish white ball.

"Here we go again," Jim said, taking the banana to the bottom step of the staircase. "At least I have snacks for this show."

"Don't you dare!" I told Kostich just as he released the arcane ball. Baltic parried it with a flash of his light blade.

"Very Wonder Woman," Jim said, its mouth full. "How are you with bullets?"

"Oh!" I yelled, glaring at the mage, rolling up my sleeves. Baltic hauled me back as I was about to pounce on my former employer. "Let go of me, Baltic! No one throws arcane magic at my man!"

"Dragon," Jim corrected.

"Move out of the way," Kostich warned, pulling on his power to form another arcane ball. "I shall smite the dragon where he stands!"

I twisted in Baltic's grip, shoving him hard to the side. Kostich's ball of power shot past us and hit a vase standing on a pedestal, exploding both into a bazillion tiny pieces.

"Steeeerike!" Jim said, tossing the now empty banana peel onto the floor in front of Kostich.

"What the hell are you doing?" Baltic asked as I continued to shove him toward the drawing room. "Leave me be, mate! I must attend to that deranged mage once and for all."

"I am not deranged!" Dr. Kostich bellowed, turning as he pulled together yet more power, forming it between his hands into a sphere that glowed blue. "Now stand still, damn you, so I can smite you!"

"Oh, no, he's not deranged," Jim said, cocking an ironic eyebrow.

"Stop it!" I shouted as Baltic yanked me sideways, out of the path of the ball of power. It went through the window, shattering the glass along the way.

"You are so going to pay for that window!" I said, storming toward Kostich.

"Mate, will you get out of the way so I can kill the mage?" Baltic snarled, his blade flashing from side to side as Dr. Kostich, muttering imprecations under his breath, quickly threw tiny little sparks of light at him one right after another.

"No one is killing anyone—you bastard!" I gasped as Dr. Kostich, whirling around when the wind caused the door to close loudly, sent a blast of arcane power into the tray of leaded crystal goblets. "Those were for the après-*sárkány* lemon sorbet! Right! That's it! No more Miss Nice Whatever-the-hell-I-am!"

"Dragon," Dr. Kostich said at the same moment Baltic said, "Mate," and Jim added, in not nearly a quiet enough voice, "Crazy lady?"

I snatched up a small Chippendale chair with a cream and pale blue striped seat, and lunged toward the mage with it held out before me, as if I were a lion tamer and he were a particularly obstreperous lion. "Back! Back, I say! You can't have the sword! You can't have Baltic;

he's mine! Go away, and don't bother us again! Er . . . do I get paid for the last two weeks even though you put the interdiction on me? Because I haven't seen my paycheck deposited yet, and I promised Brom he could pick out a large dehydrator for his birthday, and that's only a couple of weeks away."

A burst of whitish blue light flared in front of me, the chair I held disintegrating as the arcane power blasted it to smithereens. I stared in surprise first at my hand, which held one surviving leg of the chair, then up to Dr. Kostich. "You aimed that at me!" I said, aghast.

A low growl of anger came from Baltic, and suddenly, the room was full of a white dragon, fire erupting around him as he slammed into Dr. Kostich, the two of them tumbling to the highly polished marble floor in a confusion of dragon limbs, tail, and flailing mage legs.

"No one touches my mate," Baltic snarled, pinning Kostich to the ground, puffing a few wisps of smoke a scant inch from Kostich's face.

"Oooh. He's drooling on him. That's just completely gross," Jim said, watching from the safety of the stairs.

"Those who live in glass houses," I told the demon before marching over to Kostich's head and poking at him with the chair leg. "And you owe us for this chair, too! It was an antique!"

Kostich squawked something, his face beet red, his body writhing as he desperately tried to get air into his squashed lungs.

No one heard the front door open until the voice spoke.

"Are we early? Oh. Er. Hello, Dr. Kostich."

"Heya, Ash," Jim said, hopping down the stairs to

greet its demon lord. "Lemon sorbet's not ready yet. Why don't you come back in an hour?"

"Uh . . ." I blinked at the people crowding the doorway. Aisling, Drake, and his two redheaded bodyguards were crammed into the door, all with the same identical expressions of surprise. "Hi."

"Hi," Aisling said, looking at where Baltic was flattening Dr. Kostich. "Hello, Baltic. I don't think we've formally met."

"Do you know who I am?" Dr. Kostich spat out, somewhat breathily, to be sure. "I lead the Committee!"

I straightened up and smiled at the dragons as Aisling stepped carefully over the broken crystal goblets, Drake right behind her. "You are a little bit early, but that's all right, although as Jim says, the sorbet isn't ready yet. Oh, hell! Jim!"

"I can have you all banished to the Akasha! I'm just that powerful!" Dr. Kostich wheezed.

I ignored him and turned to glare at the demon.

"What? Who? Me? I wasn't smelling his butt!" Jim said quickly, backing away from where Baltic lay crushing Dr. Kostich.

"You're all going to be charged for these grievous crimes against my august person!"

Baltic swung his neck around to send a little circle of fire at the demon. I caught the fire as it passed me and tossed it back to him with a frown.

"You're supposed to be elsewhere, so that Aisling has to make Drake do what she says!" I told the demon. "You can't be a hostage for their good behavior if you're right here!"

"That's not my fault," Jim said, sitting on Kostich's foot.

"Including the demon, who has just broken my foot! Get off, you soulless beast of Abaddon!"

"Aisling is the one who came early," Jim added.

I frowned at the woman as she stopped in front of Baltic and Dr. Kostich. "You did this deliberately, didn't you? You came here early just so you would catch me in the middle of my preparations, just so you could make me look bad. That's really not at all nice, and after I went to the trouble of making a cheesecake!"

"What sort of preparations?" Drake asked, pulling Aisling back a couple of paces when Dr. Kostich freed one hand and tried to grab her. "Were you setting traps for us? Arranging for an ambush? Another bomb?"

"Lemon sorbet and canapés," Jim said, drooling on the mage's leg. "Ysolde let me taste-test the smoked salmon rolls, too. Speaking of which, I'd better get back to the kitchen. Brom is in there with Pavel, helping him with the cucumber-crab munchies, and the kid has a hollow leg. I bet he's getting to lick out the dish."

"I insist that you free me!" Dr. Kostich demanded. "I will not be able to eat canapés if my ribs are crushed into my lungs!"

"You're *catering* the *sárkány*?" Aisling asked, looking almost as if she didn't believe it.

"There, you see? Even the green mate agrees it's ridiculous to serve food at such a time," Baltic told me with infuriating self-righteousness.

"I am not catering anything," I said with a frown at both of them. "I'm just making a few little nibblies to enjoy while we're discussing this issue of whether or not they're going to execute me."

"What?" Baltic asked, his head whipping around to me.

"I'll tell you about it later," I said, nodding toward the others.

"You'll tell me about it now!" he ordered, tapping his claws in an annoyed fashion.

"Argh!" Dr. Kostich yelled.

Baltic shifted his forefoot so his claws weren't directly on Kostich's face. "What do you mean, whether or not they will execute you? What reason does the weyr have for wishing you dead?"

"That's it! I have reached the end of my patience. I will destroy you myself if no one is going to save me from this fat dragon!"

"He is not fat," I snapped, and thought seriously about kicking the archimage. "All dragons look like that!"

"You wouldn't say that if you were lying here in my place," Kostich grumbled.

Jim opened its mouth to say something, but stopped when both Aisling and I glared at it.

"Er . . . why *is* Baltic lying on Dr. Kostich?" Aisling asked.

"Well, you know, I've heard a rumor that Ysolde kind of likes a little mano a mano action—" Jim started to say. I threw the chair leg at it, followed by a small ball of arcane magic. Midway to the demon, it turned into another banana. "Ooh, more snacks. Thanks."

"Mate, you will answer me!"

"I can't see. Everything is going black. If you kill me, I swear I will haunt you all!"

"Did you just conjure a banana at Jim?" Aisling asked, taking a step to the side to watch Jim eat the banana.

"Yes." I sighed, gesturing toward my former employer. "He put an interdict on me. None of my magic works right."

"You shouldn't have magic, period, and you won't by the time I'm through with you and this obese behemoth—"

"Oh, for heaven's sake," I said, tugging on Baltic's tail. "Let him up. If we're going to have explanations, we'd do better having them in a civilized manner."

"With lemon sorbet and bacon-wrapped mushroom caps," Jim agreed.

Baltic glared down at Kostich, who was moving feebly beneath him, but shifted back into human form, dusting himself off as he got to his feet.

The two green dragon bodyguards helped Dr. Kostich up, half carrying him over to a chair where he collapsed, breathing heavily and spreading fulminating glares amongst everyone present.

Silence fell. Baltic and Drake stared at each other for a few seconds.

"Baltic," Drake said at last when Aisling nudged him with her elbow.

"Drake Vireo," Baltic said, acknowledging the greeting.

They stared some more, not outright growling at each other, but I could tell their hackles were up.

"Drake," Aisling said, the word full of unspoken meaning as she nodded toward us.

He sighed. I tried not to giggle at the martyred look on his face. "You look well, Ysolde. As does your mate."

"Thank you," I said, glancing at Baltic. He stared moodily at Drake. I pinched his arm. He continued to stare. I dug my nails into his wrist until he snapped, "For god's sake, woman! I am the dread wyvern Baltic! I do not make polite conversation!"

"You do now. Go ahead. It won't hurt you."

He took Drake's martyred look to a whole new level of pain. "My mate has decreed that you are welcome in our home."

"You can do better than that," I said, pinning him back with one of my most effective mom looks.

"One day, mate, you will push me too far!" he informed me with narrowed eyes and flared nostrils.

I kissed the tip of his nose. He just looked even more outraged.

"Go on. You can do this."

A small wisp of smoke escaped one nostril. I smiled at it; his answering scowl promised retribution at the earliest opportunity. But in the end, he managed to say to Drake, "Your appearance is much as I remember it from the last time I saw you."

"Now that didn't hur—"

"The last time you tried to kill me, that is," Baltic interrupted. "When you ran me through with a long sword, and tried to decapitate me with a battle-ax. I believe you also shot a few crossbow bolts into my legs in an attempt to break the bones."

Silence filled the hall again. Drake studiously picked a piece of nonexistent lint off his sleeve.

"And if I'm not mistaken, you had a dagger or two that you used on my spleen."

Aisling stared at her husband, who was now blithely examining a painting on the wall.

"Not to mention the grappling hook that you creatively used by sinking it deep into my—"

"That's your idea of a welcome, is it?" I asked, stopping Baltic before he could make me sick to my stomach.

He shrugged. "I didn't mention the two morning stars he used to try to bash out my brains. I could have, but I knew you would prefer to keep things on a social level."

"I think that's one for our team," Jim said, nodding its approval.

Aisling transferred her gaze to it. "Hello! You're *my* demon! You're on our team, not theirs!"

"Soldie kidnapped me. That means I'm on her team until she lets me go. Right, guys?"

"Why do I suspect that the only reason you want to be on my team is because I have a kitchen full of canapés?" I asked it.

"A demon has to have priorities."

"Jim, heel," Aisling said wearily.

"Oh, fine!" I stopped the demon as it was about to obey. "Just go right ahead and ruin all of my plans! You aren't supposed to be here yet. Jim is supposed to be hidden away! I try to have a nice *sárkány*, but no, everyone has to ruin it."

"Hello," May said, popping up behind the two red-haired bodyguards who had taken up positions behind Drake. She slipped between them, looking around with interest. "Are we late?"

Chapter Seventeen

"Why does Dr. Kostich have his shirt off?"

"I'm checking for broken ribs," the mage answered May, looking up. "Is the healer here? I will need witnesses to the assault charges I will be laying against these dragons."

"Yes, he's here. Gabriel?"

The two guards moved aside to allow Gabriel's entrance.

"Good afternoon, Ysolde." His eyes flickered to Baltic, narrowing on him.

The air positively bristled with electricity. I scooted in front of Baltic, so my back was against his chest. "No fighting. I'm tired of fighting. People who fight will not get any lemon sorbet. If you insist on ignoring me, I will turn you into a banana. Got that?"

"Oh, man!" Jim complained behind us. "Way to ruin a good *sárkány*."

Gabriel looked startled. "A banana?"

"Her magic is off. Dr. Kostich did something to her," Aisling told him.

"Interdict," Dr. Kostich snapped, still feeling his ribs. "The fat dragon and she will pay for this."

"He is not fat!" I yelled. "He's just big-boned! Look!" I yanked the tail of Baltic's shirt out of his pants, pulling it up to expose his belly. "See? Classic six-pack!"

"Ooooh, very nice," Aisling said, admiring Baltic's lovely ripple of muscles.

He rolled his eyes and tucked his shirt back into his pants.

Drake set fire to Aisling's feet.

"I was just looking," she told him. "I'm allowed to look."

Drake's eyes were shiny emeralds. Pissed-off shiny emeralds. "No, you're not."

"Look, you're in enough trouble already, Mr. Having Foursome Orgies in Medieval France."

"It's all that lemon sorbet you're feeding him, no doubt," Dr. Kostich said to me, pulling up his pant leg to look at his shin. "Very fattening. Well, you won't have any of that while you're suffering for eternity in the Akasha, so you might as well enjoy it one last time."

"Lemon sorbet? I love lemon sorbet," a light, airy voice said, followed by the arrival of May's twin, Cyrene. "Where's the sorbet?"

Kostya was on her heels, a fact Baltic didn't realize until the black wyvern entered the house.

"Traitor!" Baltic suddenly roared, shoving me aside, shifting into dragon form again. I tripped over Jim and fell onto the bottom stair, my head hitting the chair leg where it lay.

"Baltic!" Kostya screamed in reply, and he too

changed. Everyone scooted to the sides of the hall as the black and white dragons tumbled around, their claws slashing, dragon fire blasting everything.

"I have had enough!" I yelled at the top of my voice, and snatching up the chair leg, started beating the two dragons with it. "You boys are not going to fight in my house!"

"Uh-oh. Someone's in trouble with Mom," Jim said. "You better watch out, Balters, or she'll bananate you."

"Mate!" Baltic protested as I whomped him on the butt with the chair leg.

Kostya snarled and lunged at Baltic, but I smacked him under the chops with the chair leg, causing him to stop and shake his head, a shocked look on his dragon face.

"You change back, both of you, or else it's banana time!" I said, shaking the chair leg at them.

"This is intolerable," Baltic said, shifting back as he stalked toward me, his hands on his hips. "You will not treat me in this manner! I am a wyvern!"

"Of what sept?" Kostya asked, wiping a thin trickle of blood from his nose as he, too, shifted into human form.

"We'll get to that at the *sárkány*," I said, absorbing the fire that Baltic snorted on me. "Calm down, please, Baltic. I know you feel that Kostya betrayed you, but ... but ... oh, no, not again ..."

The world spun. I reached out blindly, desperate to find Baltic, his hand catching mine just as I swirled into nothing.

Nothing but white. It was all around me, biting cold and deep into my blood, roaring in my ears. The roaring resolved itself into the sound of the wind, an endless shriek that whirled around and through me.

The white ebbed and flowed in time with the wind, and I realized that I was standing in the middle of a blizzard.

"Snow," a voice said behind me.

I turned. Baltic still held my hand, looking around us with interest.

"What are you doing here? This is a vision. You're not supposed to be in my visions."

"I participated in the last one you had," he pointed out.

"That wasn't really a vision. It was just more a reliving of a moment in time, triggered by the love token." I touched the chain I wore around my neck, the token lying between my breasts, my fingers trailing down the front of the fur-lined cloak that was clasped about my neck. "This is different. This is the same sort of vision or dream that I've had before."

"Perhaps the shaman is right, and your dragon self is urging you to wake up," he suggested, turning around. "Dauva. We're on the hill outside of Dauva."

"I don't think it's quite that simple."

"Ysolde!"

I whirled when my name was carried on the wind.

"Constantine!" Baltic snarled, reaching for the sword that he no longer carried.

A dark shape emerged from the whirling snow, his hair white with it as he stretched his hands out to me. "My love, you should not be out here. If one of my men had seen you cross before I did—"

"You will die for that!" Baltic shouted, leaping forward to grab Constantine, but nothing met his grasping hands, his momentum sending him straight through Constantine to a deep snowdrift some feet behind.

"I had to come," I heard myself say, evidently locked into the past enough to repeat what I'd said so many centuries before.

"Mate!" Baltic gasped, getting to his feet. The pain in his face was almost more than I could bear. I reached out for him, but it was Constantine who took my hand.

"My love, I knew you would come to me one day."

"No!" Baltic snarled.

"No," I repeated, pulling my hand from Constantine's grip, and shaking my head, the hood of my cloak sliding back, leaving me exposed. "My heart belongs to Baltic, and it always will."

Baltic stood up to his knees in the snow, his dark eyes watchful and wary.

"I came here not to give myself to you, but to plead with you to leave. Leave now, before anyone else dies. This battle between you and Baltic is for nothing, a senseless slaughter, and I will not have the blood of any more innocent dragons staining my soul."

"You are my mate." Despite the roar of the wind, Constantine's voice was low and rough. "He took you from me. It is my right to reclaim you."

"She is mine!" Baltic growled.

"You know that Baltic holds my heart—I've told you that often enough. You must believe me when I say nothing will change that. Please respect my decision, and leave us in peace."

I started to turn back toward Dauva, but he stopped me, gripping my arm. "I can't let you go, my love."

"Do not!" I snarled, whirling around and slapping his hand off me, fury causing my dragon fire to spill over and form a ring around him. "Do not use that word! You do not love me, Constantine! You cannot love someone whom you systematically destroy!"

He reeled back a step. Baltic tried to shove him, but there was nothing there for him to touch. Instead he fought his way through the snow to where I stood. "I always knew he was mad. Look at his eyes, mate. Look at his face."

I had to admit, Constantine's eyes glinted with a strange light, even in the middle of a snowstorm.

"He has turned you from me," Constantine said sadly, bowing his head. "I must do what I must do, Ysolde. I have sworn to protect you, and I will do that the only way I know how."

"Protect her?" Baltic yelled at the figure of Constantine. "It's me you want to destroy—you always have, ever since I challenged you for the right to be heir."

"I am tired of protesting against your folly," I said, suddenly exhausted from the weight of all those dragons who had died, and would die, for no real purpose. Baltic's words sank in and I glanced at him. "You challenged Constantine?"

"That is the true reason this war has continued. He was named by Alexei as his heir, but I knew he held only his own interests close to his heart, not those of the sept. I challenged him for the right to be heir, and won. He never forgave me for that, and soon after I was named wyvern, he rallied a handful of dragons, lying to them, bribing them, convincing them that they could never be happy under my rule."

It made sense. It made all too much sense. Constantine was a man of great pride; all wyverns were. And for him to lose both the sept and me to Baltic . . . I wasn't surprised it would generate a deep, seething hatred that would spread to everything Constantine perceived as belonging to Baltic.

"There is no hope if you remain with him," Constantine told me, passing a hand over his face as if he, too, was weary.

"Only because you are too foolish to see it," I answered. "I must return before Baltic notices I am gone."

"At this moment I'm probably in the caves, fending off Kostya's attempt to sneak into the castle through the lower passages," Baltic said, then whirled around to face Constantine, swearing in Zilant as he did so. "This is when he killed you! Flee, mate! I will keep him from striking you down."

I turned on my heel and started down the steep incline toward the exit of the bolt-hole I'd used to escape the keep unnoticed. I wanted to stop, to grab Baltic and make him leave with me, but my body had to follow its actions of the past. "You can't," I called to him as I slid down a small slope toward a clutch of trees that loomed up grey in the whipping snow. "You can't touch him, remember?"

He swore long and profanely, starting after me.

A sudden blast of icy wind sent me sprawling forward. Behind me, Constantine called out my name. "Ysolde!"

I looked over my shoulder, but could see nothing, no sign of Constantine or Baltic.

"Mate! Where are you?" Baltic cried, his voice faint as most of it was whipped away on the wind. "I can't see you. Run from him! Don't let him find you!"

"I can't," I answered, getting to my feet. As I did so,

the wind lifted my cloak and swirled it around me, blinding me as a sudden blow struck my back.

I screamed, struggling both with the snow I'd fallen into and with the cloak, heavy and wet, effectively capturing my legs. I fell back into the snow and the whiteness consumed me, leaching into my being until I was as pure as it was, suddenly adrift.

The white swirled around with a beauty that brought tears to my eyes . . . until I noticed the red in it.

"What . . ." I gasped as I rose higher, and I realized I was looking at myself, at the past Ysolde lying facedown, a fan of crimson staining the snow and the cloak. "Baltic! Oh my god, Baltic!"

"I'm here." He stumbled into view, stopping when he saw the figure holding a long, curved sword.

"Noooo!" Baltic howled, falling to his knees, his head thrown back in agony.

Constantine stood at my feet, looking at my body with eyes that were flat and devoid of all expression.

A drop of blood sluggishly gathered at the tip of the sword he held, trembling with the force of the wind, finally releasing to fall with infinite slowness onto the field of white.

My eyes blurred. I turned my face out of the stinging wind and noticed a trail of crimson spots that led away from my dead form, away from Constantine, but before I could say anything, the sound of Baltic's cry echoed in my ears. The whiteness darkened, thickening and reforming itself into a dark, dank, confined space.

Baltic was on his knees, his head thrown back, in the same position of anguish, but now it was he who held a sword in his hands.

The last few notes of the echo faded away, and I realized I was in one of the caves beneath Dauva.

Baltic slowly turned his head and looked beyond me. "It is over."

"It should have been over a century ago," a voice said, the shadow behind me resolving into Kostya. "But you would not listen to me. No more black dragons will die for you, Baltic. You are the only one who will die, and with your death, the sept will be free." Kostya raised his sword high. "You need not fear for the fate of Ysolde. I will see that she is taken care of."

Baltic merely laughed, the sound of it horrible, filled with hopelessness and anguish that had no end and no beginning. He bowed his head, letting his sword fall to the stony ground with a dull clatter. "At least I will be with her again."

I screamed and leaped forward to stop Kostya, tears streaming down my face, but I was just as unsubstantial as Baltic had been at the scene of my death. I heard the sword cut through the air, but could not watch the sight of Kostya killing my love. I spun around, a spray of blood hitting my cheek, mingling with my tears as I collapsed, sobbing as if my heart had been destroyed.

"My love, do not do this. It is over. I am here. You must return to me now. Ysolde, heed me!"

I opened my eyes, finding myself on the floor, cradled against Baltic's chest, my face and his shirt wet.

"I'll kill him," I said, my throat aching and my voice hoarse.

"Is she all right?" May asked. "Did she hit her head when she fell? Gabriel, maybe you should look at her."

"Now you know how I feel," Baltic said, the faintest hint of a smile on his lips.

I pushed myself away from him, the memory stark in my mind as I got to my feet.

"You," I said, my voice low and ugly as I started toward Kostya. "He was unarmed when you killed him!"

Kostya's eyebrows rose, and he had the nerve to look shocked as I grabbed my chair leg and raised it over my head.

"No, mate." Baltic caught me as I ran toward Kostya, intent on destroying him.

"You dropped your sword! You weren't even holding it when he killed you!" I yelled, fighting Baltic to get to Kostya.

"Eh . . ." Kostya looked startled for a moment, then frowned. "What are you talking about?"

"I was dead by then," Baltic said, wrapping both his arms around me and pulling me tight against his body. "Ysolde, I was dead. Constantine had killed you. I could not exist without you. It didn't matter that Kostya struck the blow—I could not have survived without you."

"It seems I have arrived at a most interesting moment," a light Italian voice said.

I spat out a word I would never have said in front of Brom, dropped the chair leg, and turned in Baltic's arms to hold him tight.

"Apparently, Ysolde just had another . . . er . . . dream, for lack of a better word," Aisling said slowly. "And I think Baltic went with her."

"Ah," Bastian said, obviously confused.

"Constantine did not kill Ysolde," Gabriel said, looking angrier than I'd ever seen him.

"We saw him," Baltic said as I sniffled one last sniffle into his shirt, turning to face the others who stood in a semicircle around us.

"You've taken Jim?" I asked Aisling, noticing that the demon wasn't present, although my spirits were too dulled to care much.

"No." She gave me an odd look. "We had an agreement, and we're standing by it. Jim will remain with you until the *sárkány* is over. Right now it's in the kitchen, no doubt trying to mooch food away from your son."

"You saw him?" Drake asked us, frowning slightly. "You saw Constantine kill Ysolde?"

I hesitated for a moment, remembering the trail of blood that led away from my body.

"Yes," Baltic said, his arms tight around me. "We saw him standing over her lifeless body, a sword in his hand that dripped with blood. There was no one else there, just him."

I said nothing. The situation was too charged to discuss the trail of blood at that moment. The dragons were all on edge enough; I would have to speak later with Baltic, when we could discuss what it meant.

"No," Gabriel said, shaking his head as he looked at his mate. "I can't believe that. It doesn't make sense. Constantine wouldn't do that."

Baltic growled something very rude. "Did you know him?"

"No." Gabriel's fingers flexed. "But my father served as his guard. He would not have done so had Constantine been without honor."

"Well, I *did* know him. There was no one else with Ysolde's body. I myself witnessed him telling her that he would do what he had to do. Is that not so, mate?"

I nodded. "He was furious with Baltic, and wanted nothing more than to destroy him. He said he felt affection for me, but . . ."

I stopped speaking, unwilling to speculate in front of the other dragons.

"Do not distress yourself again, mate," Baltic murmured in my ear, his arms tightening around me.

"That doesn't make sense," Gabriel said, shaking his head, his hand seeking May's hand as if for comfort.

"Believe it, or don't believe it—I don't really care. In fact, at this moment, I'm inclined to go along with Baltic's assertion that we don't need anything to do with any of you, or with the weyr." I clutched the love token I'd hung on a silver chain, sick of the constant struggle that seemed to fill my life now.

"Well, I have no idea what to say to that," Aisling said, glancing at Drake. "I have to admit, though, that I'm starting to think that maybe talking with Baltic is a good thing."

Bastian strolled over to us, and before either Baltic or I could react, punched Baltic smack-dab in the nose. "They tell me you're Baltic even though you do not look like him. I am glad. You will suffer for a very long time before you die for the deaths of my dragons."

I held Baltic back when he would have jumped on Bastian. "Please, don't," I begged him. "He'll just hit you back, and then I'll end up turning him into a banana, which means I'll have to ask Dr. Kostich for help, and he'll just call you fat again, and that'll lead to me wanting to punch out his lights, and we'll all end up brawling until there's nothing left but you, me, and a bunch of bananas. And some melted lemon sorbet."

Baltic looked like he was going to go ahead and deck Bastian anyway, but when I touched his cheek and said, "Please?" he refrained.

"Febales!" he grumbled, his expression as black as his

eyes. "I hope you like the looks of be with a crooked dose, because he just broke it."

"Oh!" I said, examining his face. His nose was swelling rapidly and had a decided list to the right. "Oh, dear. I don't know how to set a nose. Gabriel, do you?"

Gabriel stood silent, his lips in a mutinous line.

"I'm sure he does," May said, prodding her mate in the side. "Go on."

"No," Gabriel said, staring daggers at Baltic.

Bastian and Kostya nodded their agreement with Gabriel's obstinate stand.

"Oh, for the love of all the saints!" I said, pushed almost past my point of patience. "It's just a nose!"

"I'b fide," Baltic said nasally.

"You're not fine. You need that set properly. Gabriel, please do this. If you insist on being stubborn, you can do it for my benefit, not for Baltic's."

"Do you have any idea how many times he's tried to kill me, kill my mate, or steal her in the last few months?" Gabriel said, pointing at Baltic. "I'm not going to set his damned nose."

"I nebber tried to kill your bate," Baltic said with as much dignity as one could have with a nose approaching the approximate size, shape, and color of a ripe apple. "Steal her, yes. But not kill her."

"I won't do it!" Gabriel said, but at a look from May, he marched forward, muttering things under his breath that I felt were better to pretend I didn't hear, grabbed Baltic's nose between his thumb and forefinger, and gave it a quick jerk. A horrible snapping sound made everyone present cringe. Everyone but Baltic, who swore profanely as he felt his poor, abused nose.

"There. It's set. Can we get on to the part of the day where we sentence Baltic to death?"

A banana clipped him alongside his head. He shot a startled look at me.

I, wearing an innocent expression, tended to the tiny bit of blood that seeped out of Baltic's nostril, and said, "Why don't all of you go out to the north pasture, where a tent and tables and chairs have been set up for the *sárkány*. Baltic and I will check on the canapés, although at this point, I don't really give a damn about them either, but my mother raised me to show guests common courtesy even if it killed me. Which it did, but that's neither here nor there."

Chapter Eighteen

"Did I see artichoke hearts? I love those." Cyrene peered anxiously down the table. "With garlic and parmesan? Does anyone see them?"

We were in the north pasture, a large open field mottled with wild grass and bare earth. I would have preferred a more civilized setting, but the only way I could get Baltic to agree to have the *sárkány* at his house was allowing it to be held in an open field, where no one could hide in ambush. I didn't think the wyverns would do something like that, but agreed with him that it would be best not to take foolish chances.

The ladies were seated around a couple of tables pushed together. The wyverns were together in a small clutch, obviously discussing something about the *sárkány*. Baltic stood alone, watching everyone with a glower that would have leveled a T. rex.

Pavel and I had spent the day in the kitchen, making a few snacks that I intended on serving after the *sárkány* itself, but it appeared that all the discussion about the lemon sorbet had set appetites on edge.

"Here's a plate for you and Jim," I told Brom as I handed him a tray with two plates piled high with hors d'oeuvres and canapés. "You may eat it in the kitchen, and afterward, Pavel said you could play with his video game machine."

"I don't see why we can't stay out here and watch Kostya have a couple of hissy fits," Jim complained, nosing the tray to see what was on it. "Hey, we don't get any of the famous sorbet? My mouth is all set for it!"

"I left some for you in the freezer, and I prefer that you and Brom stay out from underfoot during the meeting. Speaking of which, don't pester the dragons, either. All the guards are remaining in the house, and none of them looked very happy."

"Yeah, yeah, I can handle a couple of bodyguards."

"Don't handle them—leave them alone. We had enough of an argument to get them to leave the wyverns out here alone."

"She just wants us out of the way in case Kostya comes unglued on Baltic again," Jim told Brom as they started toward the house. Brom stopped and turned back, a suddenly worried look on his face.

I muttered something rude under my breath about Jim's big mouth, hurrying over to Brom. "Sweetheart, nothing is going to happen. It's just a meeting."

"Oops," Jim said, looking contrite. "Uh . . . yeah, B-man. I didn't mean that Kostya was going to hurt Baltic or anything. Besides, if he tried, your mom would turn him into fruit."

"That's right," I said, giving Brom a quick hug. "No one is going to get hurt."

He continued to look worried. "Can I talk to Baltic for a minute? I mean Dad?"

"All right," I said slowly, wondering if Jim had been saying anything to him about the fact that the weyr wanted Baltic executed. I glanced over at the man in question, who was standing with his arms crossed, watching everyone with grim suspicion. At my nod toward Brom, he strode over. "Brom wishes to speak with you."

He raised his eyebrows and looked expectantly at Brom, who squirmed slightly and said apologetically, "Can I talk to him alone, Sullivan?"

"Er ... certainly." I moved off to check that the sorbet was still packed tightly in ice and not melting under the warm summer sun, before standing behind my chair.

"Oooh! Is that pesto?" Cyrene made happy little noises. "This is so good, Ysolde. You have to cater all the *sárkánies*!"

"Thank you, but I think I'll pass on that offer."

After a few minutes, Baltic returned, his expression unchanged. I watched Jim and Brom return to the house before turning to him. "What was that all about?"

"He was worried about you."

"About me? Hell! Jim must have told him about the execution order."

"No. He was worried that if the weyr did something to me, you would be left helpless. I told him that he had nothing to worry about."

"Because I'm not weak or feeble or without the ability to take care of myself," I said, nodding my approval of the way he dealt with Brom's concern.

"Because the weyr has no control over me," he corrected.

A horrible feeling came to life in my gut. Before I could warn him of it, the wyverns marched over to the table, Kostya taking up a spot at the head. "The wyverns are all present. The *sárkány* can commence."

"Would you pass the crème fraiche cherry apricot scones?" Aisling asked May, who sat diagonally across the table from her.

I moved to stand next to Baltic, slipping my hand in his to both offer and receive comfort. His fingers curled around mine, making the fire in me stir just a little.

"This *sárkány* is called to order to address the issue of the deaths of the sixty-eight blue dragons in France."

"This olive tapenade is fabulous," May said, moaning with delight as she popped a tapenade pinwheel into her mouth. "Almost orgasmic with the touch of cognac."

"Present are the wyverns of all five septs, with the exception of Chuan Ren, who has sent her son Jian to act in her stead."

Jian acknowledged the comment, taking a bite of a pesto, basil, and tomato freschetta.

"Who has the arancini?" Aisling asked, looking around.

"Lemon thyme, or mozzarella and basil?" Cyrene asked, holding up two plates.

"Oooh. Lemon thyme, please. Sweetie, would you like more arancini?"

"This is like a bizarre love child of Martha Stewart and the Nuremburg trials," I whispered to Baltic, noting that a couple of glasses were empty. I slid my hand from his and fetched a covered pitcher.

"Baltic, former wyvern of the black dragons, you have been charged by the weyr with the deaths two months ago. How do you plead?"

"I do not plead anything," he said loudly, his voice once again normal due to the ice pack I'd made him hold on his nose. "I do not need to answer the charges. They are ridiculous, and without proof."

"More iced tea, anyone?" I asked, holding up the pitcher. No one said anything, although Kostya looked like he was about to explode. "No? Champagne, then?"

"Christos!" Kostya swore, slamming his hands down on the table as everyone held up their glasses for a refill. "This is a *sárkány*, not a brunch! Can we get on with the meeting?"

"There's no need to be quite so testy," I said as I poured champagne, making sure to splash his over the side. "I don't see why we can't do this in a civilized manner."

"Civilized coming from a dragon . . . that's certainly an oxymoron," a voice said behind me.

"I thought you were going to get rid of him?" Baltic asked as Dr. Kostich strolled up.

Kostya sank into his chair, banging his head gently on the table a couple of times.

I narrowed my eyes at my former employer. "I did. I called him a taxi and saw him get into it."

"I decided it would be wiser for me to remain here, where I can keep an eye on you and the hefty wyvern until the watch comes to detain you both," he said, looking over the buffet table. "Does that herbed goat cheese have garlic in it? I'm allergic to garlic."

"I give up," Kostya told Cyrene. "I can't fight herbed goat cheese and champagne."

"It's very good herbed goat cheese," she said, offering him a bite.

"Mate!" Baltic said, his hands on his hips, clearly expecting me to do something.

"What do you want me to do?" I asked. "He's an archimage!"

"A fact neither of you seems to give its due respect," Dr. Kostich said, somewhat garbled since he'd just stuffed a mini cherry scone into his mouth.

"He's placed an interdict on me. You've seen how it makes my magic go awry—I couldn't make him vanish, even if I had that sort of power."

"You never were much of an apprentice, although I will admit you tried," he said, taking a loaded plate to a free chair at the table.

"Not to mention the fact that he's the head of the L'au-dela," I finished.

"Is he supposed to sit with us? I thought this was just for wyverns and their mates," Cyrene asked Kostya, frowning at the archimage.

Dr. Kostich ignored her. "Hence the fact that the watch is, at this very moment, speeding its way here to arrest you."

"What does it matter?" Kostya answered, his features set in a pout. "No one is listening to me. No one cares about anything but their bellies. No one wants to see justice done. I'm the only one here who is actually concerned about making Baltic pay for his heinous crimes—are those crab and papaya rice rolls any good?"

"Your watch cannot touch us," Baltic told Kostich, who frowned at him, but was unable to speak due to another mini scone he was eating. "Dragons are not governed by the L'au-dela. He has no authority over us, mate, so you need not fear that his threats are anything more than idle."

"I assure you they're quite real," Kostich answered, bits of crumbs flying as he spoke around the mouthful of scone.

"Voulez-vous cesser de ma cracher dessus pendant que vous parlez?" Aisling murmured.

Dr. Kostich, sitting across from her, stared.

"Sorry. I've been dying to find a chance to say that," she said, brushing the crumbs from in front of her plate. "Rene will be so proud."

"That's right," I said slowly, thinking about what Baltic said. "Dragons aren't part of the L'au-dela."

"Dragons aren't, no," Dr. Kostich said, taking the glass I'd set down for Baltic, sipping the champagne with a thoughtful look. "Quite a decent vintage. My compliments. As I was saying, your chubby mate is right—I have no authority over dragons. However, I do over humans, and you, my ex-apprentice, are close enough to human to count as one. It is true that I would have a hard time punishing him, but you are a very different matter, and since I can't have the one who perpetrated the crimes against me, I will take the next best thing: you."

"Just once I'd like to be charged with something that I've done," I said. "What do you think you're going to do to me?"

"I've already told you—banishment to the Akasha."

A horrible feeling gripped me in cold, clammy hands. Banishment to the Akasha was no laughing matter—the place the mortal world thought of as limbo was not one which many beings ever escaped. "You can't do that," I protested.

"I can, and I will."

"Baltic?" I asked, turning to him, suddenly worried. "What will happen to Brom and you? I don't want to go to the Akasha."

"You won't, *chérie*. I would never allow it. This mage is blowing hot air, nothing more."

Dr. Kostich glanced at his wrist. "The question will become moot in less than an hour when the watch arrives to take Tully away."

"Touch her, and you will die," Baltic said simply.

Kostich pointed a fork at him. "It's that sort of attitude that has kept the dragons and the L'au-dela at loggerheads for centuries. Even your ambassador was arrogant and impossible to deal with."

"Ambassador?" Aisling asked Drake. "We have an ambassador with the L'au-dela?"

"Fiat," he answered, his eyes bright as he watched us.

"That was the former ambassador. We received notice he was excommunicated, or whatever it is you dragons do, and removed from the post. We are awaiting the appointment of a new ambassador, to whom I will certainly lodge detailed complaints about my treatment at the hands of that behemoth."

"Archimage or no archimage," I said through gritted teeth, "knock off the references to Baltic being large. It's only his dragon form that's big."

"You know," May said slowly, looking distracted, "something has just occurred to me. Ambassadors have diplomatic immunity, don't they?"

Lightbulbs seemed to go off in many heads at that moment. I looked thoughtfully at May.

"Yees," Aisling drawled. "What a good idea. The weyr

needs an ambassador, and Ysolde needs protection from Dr. Kostich."

The latter glared over the table at her as he helped himself to more champagne.

"If Ysolde was ambassador, he couldn't touch her, and voila! Two problems solved at once. What a perfect solution."

"No, it isn't," Kostya said, in the process of consuming a mound of food piled high on his plate.

"Oh, stop being so obstinate," Aisling told him. "We know you don't like Baltic, but Ysolde hasn't done anything wrong. There's no reason she couldn't be the ambassador for the weyr. She certainly will do a better job of it than Fiat."

"She's not a member of the weyr," Kostya pointed out.

"I'm not?" I asked, feeling somewhat adrift, both conversationally and emotionally. "I thought I was a silver dragon."

"You were silver, then black, but now you are neither, and as such, you are not a member of the weyr," Drake agreed with his brother.

"There's an easy solution to that," May said.

Everyone turned to look at her.

"Baltic's sept will have to join the weyr."

Kostya snorted. "That would never happen. The weyr would not tolerate the blight dragons."

"Light," Baltic snarled, starting toward him. "We are *light* dragons. You are the blight."

Kostya leaped up, his hands fisted.

"Oh, lord, there they go again," Aisling commented to the table. "And I thought it was bad with Kostya and Gabriel. You'd better get your bananas ready, Ysolde."

"No," I said.

"No?" May asked, watching as Baltic and Kostya both turned surprised gazes upon me.

"No. If they are so hell-bent on fighting, they can fight."

Kostya smiled. Baltic shifted into dragon form.

"Definitely overweight," Kostich said, eating a bacon-wrapped scallop.

"But in human form," I told the two dragons. "And with no weapons. Just fists."

A little puff of smoke escaped Baltic, but after a moment's thought, he shifted back to human form, eyeing Kostya. "Fisticuffs, eh? It's been several centuries since I've had that pleasure."

Kostya tossed off his jacket and rolled up his sleeves. "The pleasure is going to be all mine, Baltic."

"Over there, not here," I said, pointing to the other side of the pasture that was mostly dirt. "I don't want any more of this crystal broken. You can have five minutes to beat the living daylights out of each other, and after that, you have to behave in a polite, decent manner. Do you both agree to the terms?"

Kostya's gaze was shifty. "Define decent."

"No more leaping up at every little thing you perceive as an insult. I'm tired of you two being at each other's throats, and I imagine everyone else is tired of it, too."

The women nodded. The men avoided meeting my eyes.

"You wouldn't mind if their sept was in the weyr, would you?" Aisling asked Drake as Baltic and Kostya moved off about sixty feet, Bastian and Jian going with them, whether to referee or to cheer Kostya on, I had no idea.

"It's not quite that simple," Drake said. "There are rules to admitting a sept. I'm not even sure that Baltic actually has one."

"But if he did, they could join, and then Ysolde could be ambassador, and Dr. Kostich could—" Aisling bit off what she was going to say as the mage looked at her.

Baltic, with a yell, flung himself at Kostya, who answered by twisting to the side and landing a nasty kick on Baltic's thigh.

"Could what?" Kostich asked, his pale eyes intense.

"Leave us alone?" she asked sweetly.

Dust rose from the field where the two men were now circling each other, periodically lashing out with arms and legs.

Kostich made a derisive noise. "I have never sought anything from dragons other than the sword that rightfully belongs amongst mages, a fact you should well know, Guardian."

"There is no place in the weyr for a sept that slaughters members of another in times of peace," Gabriel said, watching interestedly as Kostya head butted Baltic, who roared in outrage. The two men went down in a cloud of dust.

"Baltic didn't kill those blue dragons."

"So you say." Gabriel's silver gaze switched to me. "But we have only your word to that effect. It is hardly enough for the weyr to dismiss the charges."

"If you are going to go through that argument again, I shall go watch the combatants. I believe a little spell increasing the black dragon's speed is in order. . . ." Dr. Kostich rose from the table, tossed down his napkin, and strolled off toward the fight.

My chin went up as I addressed Gabriel. "I see now why Baltic has been so resistant to meeting with you. Your mind is already made up."

Silence fell . . . silence tinged with the grunts and muffled cries from the two men who were once again on their feet, dirty, sweaty, and dabbed with blotches of crimson.

"He had to have done it. He was working with Fiat," Gabriel said, sounding as if he was trying to convince himself.

"So were you, from what Jim told me," I countered, my ire starting to rise.

Gabriel looked startled. "I am not conspiring with Fiat!"

"Not now, but you have. Or did Jim lie when it told me that you helped Fiat poison Aisling and take her as his mate?"

The silence fell again.

"You bloody bastard! I just had that set!" Baltic yelled in an outraged voice, grabbing Kostya by the throat and flinging him a few yards. "That's it! If I'm going to have a crooked nose, you're going to have one as well!"

Both men disappeared again into the gently swirling cloud of dust.

"Oh, dear, I hope not. I like Kostie's nose the way it is," Cyrene said, not even looking at the two combatants.

"Well?" I asked Gabriel, who appeared very uncomfortable.

"She's got a point, you know," Aisling said. "You were working with Fiat then."

"I was trying to stop him from doing worse than he did!"

"My point is merely that it's possible that Baltic could have helped Fiat obtain one goal, but wasn't wholly in accord with his plans. Which is what he did."

"It comes down to proof," Drake said slowly. "You have none that he is innocent of the crimes, and we have witnesses that say he was with Fiat in France during the time of the killings."

I looked at them all sitting around the table, so frustrated with everything that I could scream. How could they not see that Baltic was innocent? How could they believe he could ruthlessly kill so many dragons? "Let me ask you this, Drake: have you ever known Baltic to kill dragons in cold blood?"

"He has killed many dragons, of all septs," Drake said, avoiding the question.

"This is a waste of time," I said, disgusted. I knew then that we would never get the wyverns to understand that Baltic was innocent.

"I am afraid continued arguments would be fruitless, yes," Drake said.

I looked down at my hands for a few moments, my fingers clasped so tightly together that they were white. "Baltic will not allow himself to be martyred, nor will I."

"You leave us no options," Gabriel warned.

"You must understand that if Baltic refuses to answer for the charges laid against him, there will exist between us a state of war," Drake said.

"No," Aisling said, her face pinched. "Not another war?"

War. The word reverberated in my heart, tearing off little pieces of it. War again. With war came death and destruction, and suffering that would know no end.

"Not again," I whispered.

"What war?" Cyrene asked, looking confused.

I wanted to explode into a million pieces and drift away on the wind. I wanted to go to sleep and not wake up. I wanted to hide in Baltic's lovely house that made my soul sing, and never leave it.

I wanted Baltic.

"The war between Baltic's sept and the weyr," May said sadly.

"They've declared war?"

"You've declared it on us," I answered.

"You do not have to tread this path," Drake said, his eyes dark.

"You won't allow us to do otherwise."

"A war is not to be undertaken lightly," he said, taking Aisling's hand. "It affects everyone in the sept. Those who are at war are considered viable targets for attack."

A cold chill swept over me, piercing me with fear greater than any I had ever known. "Brom," I whispered, a horrible vision in my head of him being used as a hostage. Or worse.

"We do not attack children," Drake said stiffly, ire flashing in his eyes. "Mates, however, are a different matter."

"Nothing has changed," I said softly, despair filling me at the knowledge of what lay ahead. "There was a war then, just as there will be now. There was death and pride and the refusal to admit a lost cause then, and it's all being repeated. I know how it will end, and I will not allow that, not again."

"There has to be something we can do," Aisling said to Drake.

He shook his head.

I looked up, tears bright in my eyes as I stepped first on the chair, then onto the center of the table. "I won't have it!" I shouted, opening my arms up wide. "If you won't end this now, then I will!"

"What's she doing?" Cyrene asked as Drake leaped to his feet, grabbing Aisling and pulling her back away from the table.

I closed my eyes, allowing Baltic's fire to swell within me, growing in intensity, building the familiar sensation of pressure as I summoned the words that would send them all far away from me.

"Kostya?" Cyrene said worriedly as she started to back away from the table.

"Run, little bird," Gabriel told May as he hauled her to her feet, giving her a shove toward the house.

"What's going on?" Aisling asked as Drake, having difficulty in making her follow him, bent down and scooped her up. "Drake! What do you think you're doing?"

The air around me rippled, gathering in a circle with me at its center, the power swelling inside me as I shaped it, visualizing the only possibility left to me. "Taken with sorrow," I cried, allowing the fire to consume every iota of my being as I used it to cast my spell.

"I thought she was under an interdict?" May asked Gabriel as he told her again to run.

"Kostya?" Cyrene asked again, her voice more strident. *"Kostya!"*

"All I cast from me," I said, my voice ringing like the purest bell. It must have reached Baltic, because suddenly he stopped pummeling Kostya and turned to face me.

Kostya tackled him, but Baltic simply flung him to the side as he started toward me, Dr. Kostich on his heels.

"Is she casting a spell? It sounds like a spell," Aisling said.

"Devoured with rage," I bellowed, the fire beginning to flicker along my skin as I raised my face to the sky, my heart sick with knowledge that nothing would ever be right.

Dr. Kostich ran toward me, flinging away his glass. "Stop her! That's a banishing spell! You must stop her!"

"A banishing spell? Mages can't send people to the Akasha," Cyrene called to him. "Can they?"

"No, but she can remove us from this location. Just stop her!" he shouted.

"But her spells don't work," Cyrene said, turning back toward me.

Baltic sprinted past Dr. Kostich, reaching me just as I released his fire, channeled into the vision of what I wanted most. "Banished so you will be!"

For a moment, nothing happened. It was as if the world held its breath to see what effect the interdict would have on the spell. Baltic skidded to a stop next to me, his eyes shaded like dark pools of water glinting in the sunlight, and then suddenly, the air shimmered again, thickening, twisting, morphing itself into the shape of a dragon.

"The First Dragon," I heard May gasp.

Heat shimmered on my skin like electricity, crawling up and down my arms and back as the dragon looked first to May, then to me, his eyes filled with infinity. Like Baltic, he was white, but more than white—all colors seemed to dance in harmony, illuminating the dragon, a soft glow wrapped around him that shifted and moved.

Baltic leaped up to stand behind me, his body warm

and strong and so infinitely precious, tears burned behind my eyes. The First Dragon looked at him and smiled, shifting into a human form, that of a man . . . and yet, it wasn't a man. Not even his human form could hide the fact that he was a dragon.

Around us, the other dragons stood frozen, staring at him, their expressions ranging from stunned disbelief to outright awe. I knew just how they felt.

"Why did you call me, Baltic?" the First Dragon asked, his voice as strong as the wind, but softer than the lightest down.

"It was my mate who summoned you, not me," he answered, his arms sliding around me protectively.

"I . . . I didn't know I was going to do that. I meant to do something else." I was so shocked by what I had done that it was almost impossible to speak.

The First Dragon's eyes, those uncanny, all-knowing eyes, turned from Baltic to me. I felt the impact of his gaze right down to the tips of my toes. He reached toward me, touching my forehead.

"Remember." The word seemed to echo in and around me, a haze coming up over me that was like nothing I'd experienced before in either a fugue or the visions that I'd had of the past.

The haze turned white, whipping around me with an icy bite. Once again I stood on a snowy hillside, a blizzard raging around me.

But this time, the others were present as well. It was as if the First Dragon had simply lifted up everyone standing in the field and placed us in a different time and place. We stood in a circle around two forms, one fallen, scarlet still staining the snow at the First Dragon's feet.

"A life has been given for yours, daughter," the First Dragon said.

My dead form shifted, then slowly stood up, whole again, my eyes vacant and unseeing. "Who gave it?" the other Ysolde asked.

"It was given willingly."

"Baltic? Did he—"

"Much is expected of you." The First Dragon's words were whipped away on the wind as soon as he spoke them, and yet they resonated within me. "Do not fail me again."

As the last word faded on the howl of snow and ice and wind, the First Dragon touched the risen Ysolde's forehead in the same spot he'd touched mine, and she collapsed onto the ground—but she wasn't dead. She hunched over, sobbing, buffeted by the snow before finally getting back to her feet, staggering down the hill and into the white oblivion.

Chapter Nineteen

"Fascinating. Absolutely fascinating. That almost makes up for the fat dragon sitting on me."

I shook my head, more to clear my vision than to disagree. The white mist in front of my eyes slowly evaporated, the vague figures resolving themselves into familiar people.

"That was an interesting experience," Aisling said somewhat bemusedly as she leaned into Drake. "Is that what all your visions are like, Ysolde?"

"No." I turned to Baltic, needing to feel his fire, needing his love. I clutched his silk shirt, shaking it in a demand for reassurance. "Do not fail me *again*? I failed the First Dragon before? When? What did I do? I don't even know him! How could I fail him, if I don't even know him? Is that why I was killed? Because I failed him somehow? Why didn't anyone tell me I was supposed to do something for him? Glory of god, man, why aren't you answering me?"

He gently pried my hands off his shirt, his thumbs stroking over my fingers, squinting at me with an odd look on his face as he did so. "I will answer you if you stop talking long enough to let me do so. What is on your forehead?"

"Who cares about my forehead!" I wailed, feeling as if the earth had suddenly dropped out from under me. "The First Dragon is pissed at me! I failed him! Dear god, Baltic, he expects much of me. What much? What am I going to do?"

"It's the sept emblem," he said, still staring at my forehead, suddenly looking very pleased. "It is a sun. The First Dragon has marked you."

"Is that good?" Aisling asked Drake.

"Yes," May said before he could answer, smiling a secretive sort of smile. "To hold his regard is an honor."

"Which is interesting, considering that he knew your name," Drake said to Baltic, looking extremely thoughtful.

I was still having problems with the idea that I'd somehow failed the First Dragon in the past. "What did he mean, much was expected of me? What sort of things are expected?"

"I don't know," Cyrene said, looking confused. "Should I know?"

"Yes, how is it the First Dragon knows your name?" Kostya asked Baltic, one eye swollen shut, his nose bleeding, and his lower lip cut.

Baltic evidently fared better than Kostya had—there was a red lump on his jaw, and a jagged-looking cut over one eye, but his nose didn't appear to be broken again despite his growls during the fight. He didn't respond to Kostya, instead watching me, looking very much like a cat who'd gotten into a bowl of cream.

"This changes things," May told Gabriel.

He frowned. "How so?"

"She can summon the First Dragon. Don't you see? She's tied to him. And so, assumedly since the First Dragon recognized him, is Baltic. You can't war with a sept that has ties to the First Dragon."

"Absolutely not," Aisling agreed. "I don't know as much about him as May does, since she dealt with him when she re-formed the dragon heart, but what I've heard makes me think that summoning him is almost an impossible act."

"We've just witnessed such an act, so it cannot be impossible," Dr. Kostich commented from where he was sitting, drinking Baltic's expensive champagne.

"No, but Aisling's right—I talked to Kaawa after I re-formed the heart, and she told me that the only way to summon the First Dragon was to re-form it—and that has only happened a couple of times. Ysolde did it three hundred years ago. I did it two months ago." May's gaze shifted to Baltic. "Kaawa didn't mention other times it has been re-formed."

"The dragon heart has only been re-formed four times," Baltic said, his gaze on my forehead again. I *tsk*ed to myself and rubbed it, not feeling anything different. "Attempts have been made several times, but it is not an act that is easily accomplished."

"There, you see?" Aisling said, prodding her husband. "You have to cancel the war now."

Slowly, he shook his head. "This changes nothing."

"Agreed. Baltic refuses to acknowledge the weyr's decision; therefore, he is at war with us," Kostya said, his eyes as black as deep night.

"Gabriel?" Drake asked.

Gabriel and May had been exchanging a glance filled with meaning. "Agreed," Gabriel said slowly, turning to me. "I'm sorry, Ysolde."

"Not as sorry as I am," I said, my throat tightening with tears.

"Bastian? Jian?" Drake asked the two silent wyverns.

"All I seek is retribution for the deaths of my sept members," Bastian said reluctantly. His gaze examined Baltic for a moment, the hostility which had been banked in his eyes slowly fading as he shook his head. "I don't know what to believe anymore. It seems inconceivable that the First Dragon would tolerate someone who would murder his descendants, and yet, the evidence is there—Baltic was with Fiat."

I slid a look up at Baltic. "You're tired of denying it, too, huh?"

"Extremely so."

"I will agree with the other wyverns," Bastian finally said, looking at Jian.

"Chuan Ren welcomes the opportunity to war," he said.

"And you?" I couldn't help but ask.

He inclined his head slightly, his expression unreadable. "I am my mother's son."

"Typical dragon answer," Aisling said, snorting to herself.

"Then we are in concurrence," Drake said.

Gabriel's face was somber as he said, "Ysolde de Bouchier, born into the silver dragons, it is with deep regret and no little amount of sorrow that I pronounce you ouroboros."

Something inside me gave at his words, some intangible little connection to him and May and the other silver dragons. It was as if tiny little silken cords were suddenly severed.

"Ysolde de Bouchier," Kostya's deep voice said. I looked at him, tears filling my eyes. "Once mated to a black dragon, I pronounce you ouroboros."

I reeled backwards into Baltic. He righted me, his face dark with anger as he glared at the wyverns.

"You are henceforth named ouroboros and outside of the weyr," Drake said, his face impassive, but his eyes glittering with emotion. "From this moment, a state of war exists between us. Should you seek mediation with regards to this, you may request a parlay with any wyvern recognized by the weyr. Safe conduct will be granted to and from the parlay."

I bit back a sob. Everything was going wrong again. "I don't want any more deaths," I told Baltic, clinging to him shamelessly.

"There won't be," he said, looking over my head at the other wyverns. "So long as they leave us alone."

Gabriel looked like he was going to say something, but just shook his head instead, and with his arm around May, walked away.

"Ysolde—" Aisling reached out to touch me, but Drake took her hand, pulling her after him as they, too, left. "Please send Jim back tonight. I imagine you're getting pretty tired of it by now."

Bastian and Jian, with an exchange of looks, murmured something and followed them.

"Ah. Looks like the watch has arrived at last," Dr. Kostich said, glancing toward the drive. A black van was parked behind the wyverns' cars. He slid a glance toward us, hesitating for a few moments. "I believe in light of the day's experience, I would be willing to drop the charges of assault against me on the condition that you give into my keeping the light sword of Antonia von Endres."

"You are mad," Baltic said.

"On the contrary, I'm quite sane. I am also very serious that Tully will pay for your abuse of me on the occasion of your attack on the silver wyvern's house, as well as today." He lifted his hand, and a couple of men emerged from the van, jogging across the field toward us.

I clutched Baltic's hand, panic swamping me. "You are not taking me to the Akasha!"

"No, he is not," Baltic said calmly.

"It's your decision," Kostich said, looking only mildly interested in the whole affair. "The sword or your mate. Or do you intend to be in a state of war with the L'audela, as well as the weyr?"

"So help me god, if I didn't have this interdict on me, I would turn you into a fruit salad," I told him.

His eyebrows rose. "I never knew you had such a temper. I would never have engaged you had I known. It will matter little to you in the Akasha, however. Bryce, Dermott, please take Tully Sullivan into custody. We will return to Suffrage House in Paris where a formal trial will be held tomorrow—"

Baltic snarled an invective, jerking his hand out to the side, the motes of air gathering around it until a long, shining blue-white sword formed. "The day will come, mage, when I will claim this sword again."

"Indeed?" Dr. Kostich caught the sword as Baltic hurled it at him. "You may try, dragon, you may try. I will accept this in lieu of punishment for your mate. Tully . . ." His mouth tightened as he looked at me.

I lifted my chin and gave him a look that let him see Baltic's dragon fire raging inside me.

"The sorbet was excellent. My compliments."

He strode off with two puzzled-looking members of the watch, his hand rising to deflect the arcane ball– turned-banana that I hurled after him.

"Damn him. Damn him!" I railed, turning to Baltic. "Why did you give that to him? I know you loved that sword."

"If I told you that you mattered more to me than anything, even something so unique as the light blade, would you do unnatural things to me?" he asked, his fire simmering in both of us.

"I've told you I don't do unnatural things! Why you insist on thinking my simple little common everyday sexual fantasies are bizarre and depraved is beyond me."

He just waited, his eyebrows raised in silent question.

"What sort of unnatural? You mean something like tying you down and coating your entire body with chocolate so I can lick—"

A noise behind me reminded me we weren't quite alone. I spun around, my cheeks heating as Kostya gave me a very odd look.

"Tying him down, hmm?" Cyrene said thoughtfully. "Milk or dark chocolate?"

"Milk. Belgian. Or Swiss," I answered.

"Melted, of course?"

"You can do so ahead of time, but I think it would be more fun to melt it right on him with dragon fire."

"Hmm," she repeated, looking at Kostya.

He cleared his throat, trying to scowl but seemingly

not able to with Cyrene's speculative gaze on him. "If I see you again, Baltic—"

"You will try to kill me," he answered wearily, sliding an arm around my waist. "Yes, I know—again."

Kostya was silent for a moment, some of the antagonism leaving his face. "I am glad you are not dead after all, Ysolde."

"Thank you. It's nice to be alive," I said with no little irony.

He bowed to me, then glanced at Baltic. "I would have taken care of her."

Baltic waited for the count of five before answering. "I know. I never distrusted you with regards to my mate."

"You never had cause to," I said, frowning a little at Kostya. "Not since that time when you showed up to claim me, and Kostya ran from me because he was afraid I would accept him, instead."

A little smile flickered at Kostya's lips at the memory, and for a moment, I was transported back to happier times.

"Oh, really? I'm going to want to hear about this," Cyrene said, tugging on his arm. "Come on, let's go home. I want to swim in the pond."

"The pond," I said, thinking of that beautiful home, with the even more beautiful grounds.

"That house was built for Ysolde," Baltic called after Kostya. "She will have it again."

"You can try, dragon," Kostya said in mimicry of Dr. Kostich. "You can try."

We stood together alone in the field, the afternoon sun beating down on us, the smell of the warm earth sinking deep into my soul, where Baltic's fire resided.

I let my gaze roam over his face, over the high, Slavic cheekbones, along his widow's peak, to the eyes that shone like polished ebony. "Everything is wrong, Baltic."

"Not everything."

"We're at war with the weyr."

He shrugged. "We don't need them."

"We do. They are our kind. More importantly, I want to be a part of the weyr. I want there to be peace between us."

He took my hands, his mouth hot on my fingers as he kissed them. "I don't know that I will be able to give you that."

"We'll work on it together, OK?"

He said nothing.

"Then there's the First Dragon. How do you know him?"

He dropped my hands and wrapped an arm around me, gently urging me toward the house. "If I tell you all my secrets now, what will you have to worm out of me with your inventive sexual persuasions?"

"Typical dragon answer. I can't tell you how annoying that is."

"I am not typical. I am the dread wyvern Baltic."

"You are the annoying wyvern Baltic, that's what you are. What are we going to do about this thing that the First Dragon expects of me? How can I do whatever it is when I haven't the slightest idea what he was talking about? And how did I fail him in the past?"

"Questions, questions, you were always full of questions," he sighed, pulling me tighter against his body until his heat became mine.

"What about your sword? That's not right that you should just hand it over to Dr. Kostich."

"There is a difference in surrendering something temporarily, and relinquishing the same," he said cryptically.

I glanced up at him, squinting against the low sun. "If you're going to steal it back from him, I want to help. I can't believe I slaved for that man for all those years. Talk about ungrateful. Do you think Kostya would let us buy that house? This one is nice enough and all, but that house is just so us. And while I'm thinking of it, who was it who gave his life for me? It wasn't you, was it? You were already dead. So who did that? I wonder also if I need to get a divorce from Gareth. Were we even really married, or did he just say we were?"

Baltic sighed again. "You wear me out with all these questions, mate. Can you not think, instead, of all the ways in which I will use chocolate upon your body?"

"Stop distracting me. I'm angsting, and I can't do it if—wait, on *my* body? Oooh. Now that is kind of kinky...."

Read on for an excerpt from
Katie MacAlister's next Dark Ones Novel

In the Company of Vampires

Coming from Signet in November 2010

I sighed and smiled at Kurt. "The Vikings have been sent to help me with a little situation. They won't cause any problem with the customers. Right, gentlemen?"

"We have sworn to not slay anyone you do not authorize us to slay," Eirik said with a frown. "Although I dislike you binding us to such an oath, virgin goddess. It makes us feel helpless."

"You guys are anything but helpless, and you know it. Is Imogen up yet, do you know?"

Kurt blinked. "I don't know. I haven't seen her this morning. Did he say *virgin* goddess?"

"No, he didn't," I said loudly, narrowing my eyes at each and every one of the Vikings. They grinned at me, the rats. "She knows I was coming, so I'll just go say hi and get my Vikingahärta from her." And get the meeting with Ben out of the way.

Inner Fran could not help but wonder if he missed me.

I hurried toward the gold-and-white trailer decorated with scarlet hands and runes, which was Imogen's home when she was traveling with the GothFaire, ignoring both Inner Fran and my suddenly rapidly beating heart.

Kurt called something after us, but I was suddenly frantic to see Ben. Imogen! Not Ben, but Imogen! I didn't want to see Ben at all. In fact, I'd pay good money to have someone haul him away so I wouldn't accidentally run into him.

Inner Fran told me it was the purest folly to lie to oneself. I gritted my teeth and told her to go do something rude to herself. As we walked to Imogen's trailer, I stopped and turned to the Vikings. "Uh . . . guys, would you give me a few minutes alone with Be . . . er . . . Imogen?"

Eirik looked suspicious. "If you command it, virgin goddess. What should we do while we are waiting for you?"

"It would be really helpful if you could scout around the area and see if there are any signs Loki was here."

His suspicion turned darker. "We are not scouts! Vikings do not scout! We are above such things!"

"Well . . . what do you do?" I asked.

"We pillage," he answered quickly. "We plunder."

"We kill," added Finnvid. "A lot."

"Don't forget drinking. We drink a lot, as well."

The other two nodded

"It's too early to drink, I don't want anyone killed, there will be no pillaging, and since I know one or the other of you is bound to add this to your list, no oiling of breasts, either. At least not out in public. What you do in private is thankfully your own business." I filled my expression with as much pathos as I could pack into it. "But if you don't want to look around for signs of Loki, and where he might have gone, I'll have to find someone else to do it."

Eirik's nostrils flared. "We were assigned by the goddess Freya to aid you! You will have no others. If you desire us to scout . . ." He shuddered. "Then we will lower ourselves to scouting."

"Think of it as being Viking ninjas." I leaned in and lower my voice to a conspiratorial level. "Stealthy and covert."

"Stealthy," Finnvid said thoughtfully.

"Covert?" Eirik glanced at the others. "Have we ever been covert?"

Isleif shook his head. "No, but I watched a movie about ninjas. They were most deadly and feared by all. Just like us. We will be ninjas, virgin goddess. *Viking* ninjas."

"The best kind," Eirik agreed.

"Sounds good. You go be stealthy, covert Viking ninjas"—really, I deserve an award for being able to say that without so much as one titter or a twitch of my lips—"and I'll meet you guys back here in a couple of hours, OK? You remember which trailer is my mom's?"

They nodded.

"We must go shopping again," Isleif commented as they headed off. "The ninjas in the movie had special armor. We will need the same."

"Aye." Eirik's voice drifted back to me. "We will find the local ninja store, and use the weasel gold to buy everything they have. . . ."

"Heaven help the local shops," I murmured before taking a deep breath and tapping at the door. I waited a moment, but heard nothing, opening it just a smidgen, enough to poke my head in to see if Imogen was up. The long living area was devoid of anyone. Perhaps she and her Gunter were out getting morning coffee and breakfast.

"Best thing is to just wait for her," I said, ignoring the fact that my stomach did a few excited back flips as I entered the trailer. "Ben is not here, stomach, and Imogen has a boyfriend. Stop being so excited. Ben won't be up and about until it's dark."

Unless, of course, Imogen's boyfriend wasn't staying with her. Which meant . . . I glanced down the narrow passage to the door that marked Imogen's bedroom. It was quiet, very quiet—the sound of quiet that comes when no one else is around. Perhaps, I decided, I should just double-check to make sure no one was in Imogen's bedroom. Just a quick peek to ease my mind and calm my unduly excited stomach.

I opened the door the bare minimum amount needed to slid through so no sunlight could sneak in and harm any vampires who might be sleeping therein.

The room was dark and warm. A muffled grunt came from the bed.

"Ben?" My heart beat wildly, and my stomach did flip-flops. It *was* him! He was right there in front of me. I should leave. I should run away as fast as I could. I should put him from my mind and heart.

I groped my way along the bed to sit on one end of it, pulling off both sets of gloves before reaching out to find him. My hand touched bare flesh.

A light clicked on at the exact moment that I realized the man wasn't Ben. I snatched back my hand as two surprised hazel eyes met mine. *"Was ist es?"*

"Er . . . hi. You're not Ben."

The man pulled the blanket up over his naked chest. "Who?"

"Ben. Benedikt. Are you Gunter, by any chance?" I asked, hastily getting off the bed and backing toward the door, my face redder than a baboon's butt.

"*Ja.* You are Imogen friend?"

"Yes, I'm Fran. I'm sorry to disturb you. I thought you would be out with Imogen. And then I thought you were Ben, but clearly you're not. Where is she?"

"He?"

"No, she, not he. You know, the word 'she.' She is female; he is male."

He blinked at me. "In trailer," he said, waving a hand toward the window. "Tattoo trailer."

"Oh. OK. Thanks. Sorry again about waking you up. Nice meeting you." I slipped out of the room, closing the door behind me, leaning against it for a moment while I covered my burning cheeks with my hands. "Just when I think you can't be a bigger idiot, you top yourself. Nice job, Fran."

I all but ran down the line of trailers until I reached one with familiar artwork. I'd never had much to do with Gavon, who did tattoos and custom piercings at the Faire, mostly because he struck me as somewhat creepy, but I had a faint memory of Imogen being friends with him.

I knocked on the door, mentally writing an apology to Imogen for barging in on her boyfriend when the door opened. A woman stood in the doorway. I stared at her bare legs, stared at her thigh-length silk robe, stared at a pretty face topped with a cloud of soft, curly brown hair. This was not Imogen.

"Yes?"

I gawked at her for a minute. I'd always thought Gavon was gay. . . . Maybe I'd been wrong, and this was his girlfriend? "Is Imogen here?"

"Imogen? No. Her brother is." She continued to stand there, looking me over with narrowed blue eyes. I suddenly felt every inch my six-foot, built-like-a-linebacker self, not to mention the wrinkled T-shirt and pair of jeans I wore.

"Ben's . . . here?" My stomach turned a complete somersault. I groaned to myself. Somehow in the conversation with Gunter, we crossed our lines regarding pronouns. "Right here?"

"Yes. You wish to see him?"

No. I absolutely did not want to see him. I had not gone through the hell of the last year for nothing. I had made a decision, and I was going to stand by it.

"Yes, please," I heard someone say, and realized with horror that it was me.

"He was sleeping when I left him," she said in a voice with a faintly French accent. "Why do you want to see him?"

My heart shattered. Just like that, it was whole one moment, then in a billion pieces the next. Poof! Dust. Not that it had any right to shatter, but you try reasoning with a heart. It's impossible. "You're not Gavon's girlfriend, are you?"

"Gavon? No. I took over his business. I am Naomi, the tattoo artist. I am Benedikt's girlfriend. And you are . . . ?"

"Fran Ghetti." Pain seared my soul with such intensity, I had to clutch the side of the trailer to keep from keeling over at her feet.

"Ah, the *former* girlfriend." Her look scalded me up and down with enough acid to peel off at least three layers of skin.

I made an effort to get hold of myself, and my sanity. "If he's sleeping, I won't disturb him."

"Benedikt is mine, now. Did he not tell you? Poor little American. Did you believe that he still wants you? Desires you? He does not even think about you. He thinks only of me."

Her voice turned suddenly syrupy and sickeningly sweet. It was just what I needed, because her words pulled me out of a massive well of self-pity, and into the land made up of me turning her into a wart-encrusted cockroach. "There's nothing *little* about me, chicky. Now, if you don't mind, I'd like to talk to Ben."

She made an annoyed sound, but stood aside. I climbed the steps and edged past her, hardly able to catch my breath, so fast was my heart beating. I couldn't believe it, couldn't believe the proof that was before me. Ben had moved on. He had really moved on. While I'd been spending miserable nights telling myself that I'd gotten just what I wanted, Ben, the bastard, had just blithely gone on with his life.

I glanced over my shoulder at Naomi. She smiled a slow "I've slept with Ben because he's so over you" smile. "He's in my bed. He was so exhausted after our night together. He went right to sleep."

I turned back toward the door. With every step, the pain in my heart morphed into anger—a fury so hot, I thought I would spontaneously combust by the time I flung open the door.

"Nrrf?" a voice said from the bed, then yelped as sunlight streamed in around me. "What the hell are you doing, Naomi?"

The man who rolled over onto his back and sat up, his

short hair mussed, his eyes confused and sleepy, brought me to a halt.

"I just came to tell you that I was here, and I never want to see you again. Not that I had planned on doing that, because I thought Gunter was saying Imogen was in this trailer, not you, but as long as we're both here, it's as good a time as any to get a few things off my chest. So I will. I never want to see you again, you two-timing, cheating rat bastard."

His eyes widened as they focused on me. "Francesca?"

I stared at him for a moment, pain and anger roiling around inside me. "I'm so glad to know I was right about freeing us both. I'm delighted to see that it took you absolutely no time to find a replacement for me. I'm nigh on ecstatic that I meant so little to you that you couldn't wait to screw the first girl you could find!" I ripped off the ring I still wore on my middle finger and threw it at his head. "I'm so happy, I could bloody well burst into a Broadway show tune!"

"Francesca—"

"I told her, but she wouldn't listen to me," Naomi said from the doorway. "Now do you see, little American? He is mine, not yours. Aren't you?"

I saw red as she leaned forward and pressed her lips against his mouth. Ben's eyes were the color of honey oak, and filled with an expression I couldn't read.

"Is that true, Ben?" My voice came out croaked and hoarse.

His lips tightened. "Yes. I'm sorry. I was going to tell you. I just . . . I didn't expect you to come to Europe for another year."

Naomi nibbled on his ear, cooing softly into it. I

stared at him for a few seconds, not believing what I was seeing, not understanding the words he spoke. I had left him, I had told him I didn't want to be his Beloved, and yet somehow, I had remained true to his memory. I hadn't dated, hadn't been interested in other men. I hadn't even *seen* other men. I had left him, and he had done just what I had wanted him to do—he had got on with his life.

While I remained in limbo, bound to a man who now didn't want me.

Anguish overrode my anger and I choked on the bile triggered by my own hypocrisy. I spun around and ran blindly from the room, the mocking laughter of Naomi following after me.

New York Times bestselling author
KATIE MACALISTER

Steamed
A Steampunk Romance

When one of Jack Fletcher's nanoelectro-mechanical system experiments is jostled in his lab, the resulting explosion sends him into the world of his favorite novel— a seemingly Victorian-era world of steampower, aether guns, corsets, and goggles. A world where the lovely and intrepid Octavia Pye captains her airship straight into his heart...

For videos, podcasts, excerpts, and more, visit
katiemacalister.com

S0045